W9-AUT-546

AMAZON LORE AND LEGEND . . .

From the tale of the Lady Bruna Leynier,
who defended the rule of the Alton
Domain with her own mighty blade . . .
to a desperate rescue of women
enslaved by Dry-Town bandits . . . to a
Renunciate's taming of a blood-thirsty
banshee . . . to an Amazon struggling to
master the technology of Terrans . . . to
the founding of a distant Guild House
. . . to an Amazonian mission to the
stars . . . here are eighteen stories about
incredible women meeting the
challenge of a world ruled by men,
women proud to bear the name of—

FREE AMAZONS
OF DARKOVER

These Darkover novels and anthologies
by MARION ZIMMER BRADLEY
are available in DAW editions:

DARKOVER LANDFALL
THE SPELL SWORD
THE HERITAGE OF HASTUR
THE SHATTERED CHAIN
THE FORBIDDEN TOWER
STORMQUEEN!
TWO TO CONQUER
SHARRA'S EXILE
HAWKMISTRESS!
THENDARA HOUSE
CITY OF SORCERY

and with the Friends of Darkover:
THE KEEPER'S PRICE
SWORD OF CHAOS

FREE AMAZONS OF DARKOVER

An Anthology

by

MARION ZIMMER BRADLEY

and the

FRIENDS OF DARKOVER

Edited by
Marion Zimmer Bradley

DAW BOOKS, INC.
DONALD A. WOLLHEIM, PUBLISHER

1633 Broadway, New York, NY 10019

Copyright © 1985 by Marion Zimmer Bradley

All Rights Reserved.

Cover art by Richard Hescox.

DAW Collectors Number 657.

First Printing, December 1985

1 2 3 4 5 6 7 8 9

PRINTED IN U.S.A.

Contents

Introduction: About Amazons

I had no notion, when first I created (out of a dream) the Free Amazons of Darkover, that they were to become the most attractive and controversial of my creations, drawing more fan mail than all other subjects put together. Not only are there now several Amazon Newsletters among female fans, there are at least a dozen women I know of (not counting those I don't) who have legally changed their names to the Free Amazon style; as well as a number of Guild Houses in various cities where women try to live by some version of the Amazon, or Renunciates Oath.

The Free Amazons have undergone considerable changes since that dream (in 1962 or thereabout) created a Free Amazon, Kyla, as a mountain guide in *The Planet Savers*, Ace Books, 1962. I myself hardly recognize, in Kyla n'ha Raineach, the character who was to start everything.

In the introduction to the Gregg edition of the Darkover Books, I commented as follows:

"I have been asked many times how a society as traditional and patriarchal as Darkover managed to evolve a society of Free Amazons. The answer is that it didn't. At the time when I wrote *Planet Savers*, then known by the title of *Project Jason*, I had no notion of creating a society of Darkover; I simply needed to give the book's protagonist a reasonable background, and a problem. A basic outline for any good work of fiction is that the main character must have the opportunity for growth and change. I needed to give Jay/Jason a problem. Could Jason accept a woman as leader of an expedition? And if *he* could, could his submerged alternate personality, Jay Allison, mysogynist and probably homosexual as well, manage to accept her and cooperate with her? Kyla walked out of my subconcious mind as a problem for Jason; a challenge to his leadership, no more.

(This problem is not limited to pre-liberation days of 1960 or thereabout. In her excellent book about a Himalayan all-woman climbing expedition, *Annapurna: A Woman's Place*, which was to serve as background for a later Free Amazon novel, *City of Sorcery*, Arlene Blum comments on the male chauvinist makeup of mountain-climbing expeditions. For those who think I exaggerate, I suggest reading Blum's book; one would-be climber was told—in 1977!—that she could not be included on such an expedition unless she felt willing to sleep with all the male members, while on one Everest expedition woman applicants were told that they could come as cooks and camp-keepers but were not to be allowed above Base Camp. The folly of this attitude was demonstrated when the first Japanese Everest expedition put a five-foot woman atop the world, and later when four members of Arlene Blum's Annapurna expedition climbed that eight-thousand meter mountain, although two of them never returned.)

The first of Darkover's many Free Amazons was described as follows, by the story's narrator, Jason.

"And I almost backed out when I saw the guide. For the guide was a woman.

"She was small for a Darkovan, and narrowly built, the sort of body that could have been called boyish or coltish, but certainly not, at first glance, feminine. Close-cut curls, blue-black and wispy, cast the faintest of shadows over a sunburnt squarish face, and her eyes were so thickly rimmed with heavy dark lashes that I could not guess their color. Her mouth was wide, and her chin round. She held out her hand and said rather sullenly 'Kyla Raineach, Free Amazon, licensed mountain guide.'

". . . the Guild of Free Amazons entered virtually every field, but that of mountain guide seemed somewhat bizarre even for an Amazon. She seemed wiry and agile enough, her body under the heavy blanket-like clothing as lean of hip and flat of breast as my own."

Kyla successfully leads Jason's party, and perhaps predictably (at least to one critic of the novel) falls in love with him. I had never intended to bring back the Guild of Free Amazons, but perhaps the invention meant more to me than I thought at the time, for in the sixth of the Darkover novels, *World Wreckers*, which I actually intended as the last of that series, (my own moral equivalent of throwing Sherlock Holmes over the Reichenback Falls) two Free Amazons appeared in the novel. They were described as a freemate couple (probably, though not explicitly, lesbians, to balance the sexual-identity crises of the male characters).

At that time I had been attempting to portray accurately an alien society's sexuality; and felt compelled in honesty to confront this problem because studies have shown that no society has been able to eliminate homosexuality. Even the most shocking penalties, including death in the Middle Ages, have never eliminated it; in permissive societies, it is all but universal. (I define *permissiveness* as refusal to brainwash kids into the hangups of their parents.) Even in Red China, I daresay it appears there too . . . though the Communist Chinese claim there is not a single homosexual in all of their country.)

"Both were members of the Guild of Free Amazons and wore the typical Free Amazon dress; low boots of undyed leather, fur-lined riding trousers, a fur smock brief enough for riding, and heavily embroidered leather jackets and hoods. One had pale red, braided hair, coiled low on her neck and tucked into her hood; the other, close-cropped dark curls. They both had the somewhat hard, boyish look which women wear when they choose, against all the sanctions of a patriarchal society, to do a man's work and take a man's freedom.''

I have been asked where these descriptions came from. As nearly as I can remember, my role model for most of the Free Amazons was a farm woman who lived near my family home; with her father aging and bedridden, and her husband in the army, she ran two farms as efficiently—or more so— than any man I have ever known. She was certainly the first woman I ever knew who wore trousers all the time—in 1945 a very different thing than in the 1980s, when blue jeans have become the universal dress of both sexes. The men in my family, and many women in the farm community where I lived, did not approve of her; I thought she was wonderful, though she did not like children and I doubt I spoke to her a dozen times except when I went at my father's request to get a fire permit—she was the county fire marshal, as well. I myself rarely wore even tailored women's slacks until the sixties, when I discovered with delight the comfort and freedom of wearing pants . . . I still cannot imagine why anyone would wear skirts unless she had to, although, paradoxically, one of my brothers feels that way about trousers, and by preference wears a kilt! Tastes differ, and as a character in another book of ours is fond of saying, ''I rejoice in the diversity of creation.''

The Darkover series did *not* end with *World Wreckers*. When Don Wollheim founded DAW Books and invited me to submit a novel for him, he suggested another Darkover book, saying it was a ''known series'' and the distributors liked them. I wrote *Darkover Landfall*, attacking the problems of survivalism, and not till *Shattered Chain* (1976) did I bring in Free Amazons as major characters in any book. Kindra n'a Mhari, Free Amazon, Renunciate, was intended to be the major character in this book; however, Lady Rohana walked out of my subconscious to play the leading part.

Feminist writers did not like *Chain*. At least one writer called me "unequal to the challenge of dealing with an all-female society." Since there hasn't been, and I don't think there will ever be one (and if there were it would self-destruct in one generation), I personally feel it's a cop-out to create a society where all the Y chromosomes have all conveniently disappeared or died out. (Although I received a manuscript from a woman who propounded, I believe seriously, a theory that at present the technology exists for women to have parthenogenetic daughters, and that said technology is being suppressed by men who wish to conceal it, lest women cease to need men even for reproduction.) I can't imagine why a one-sex world would attract anyone; sheer paranoia. Personally, I think two sexes are an *excellent* idea. A world where everybody's alike would be worse even than the society run by Big Brother.

A few years later, I gave Kindra a story of her own, creating the background of Camilla n'ha Kyria, the *emmasca* who was a well-liked character in *Chain*. *To Keep the Oath* (1979) dealt with the restrictions of Free Amazon recruitment in the society of Darkover—a restrictive society can remain so much longer if honorable escapes are allowed, and I regarded the Amazons as one such honorable alternative.

After *Shattered Chain*, many Darkover fans regarded the Amazons as the most interesting part of the series. The Friends of Darkover began to receive more letters and amateur stories about the Amazons than about any other subject whatever. Some women even took, and attempted to live by, a version of the Oath, or even changed their names legally to

Amazon names. A group of SCA people (Society for Creative Anachronism, a group dedicated to reviving medievalism) actually sought permission to organize their group as a Guild House rather than a kingdom, and a few women's communes organized themselves as Guild Houses. This persists to this day; it is a rare s-f convention where some would-be Amazon fails to ask me to accept her Amazon Oath. I usually question the women seriously to see if they are aware of the number of restrictions and renunciations involved in this and if they seem to be serious, I accept their oath. It is a fantasy, I suspect, at least no more harmful than the "adoption" of Cabbage Patch dolls.

There were many readers who wanted to know more about the everyday life within an Amazon Guild House, and thus, almost by popular demand, arose *Thendara House*, continuing the stories of Magdalen Lorne and of Jaelle, who swapped places in the Empire. In so doing, of course, both outgrew the limits of their former selves.

After *Thendara House*, in examining the Amazon Oath, one of my Amazon foster-daughters went so far as to create a version of the Oath by which a woman could live in an advanced technological society. The existence of this version of the Oath (printed at the end of the book) actually touched off the thought of the Bridge Society which became central to the latest Free Amazon novel, *City of Sorcery*, and such characters as Vanessa ryn Erin.

Ever since *Shattered Chain* many women have wished to write Free Amazon short stories. For a time we received more stories about Free Amazons than on all other subjects put together. Two of the best-liked stories in the first volume of Darkover short stories were Linda McKendrick's "The Rescue," a humorous story attacking a serious problem: between a man who respects a woman's independence, and a woman who does not, who is nearer to the spirit of the Oath? The other, by Patricia Mathews "There is Always an Alternative," is a grim story of the desperation which might drive some women to drop out of their society.

It was Patricia Mathews, in a fan-written "Darkover" novel, which she later wrote into a world of her own, who created the Sisterhood of the Sword. I liked the idea and Pat gave me permission to use the Sisterhood, which I did in *Two to Conquer*, together with another "mainstream" of honorable alternatives for women. Even in the Middle Ages here on Terra, women choosing to opt out of their society were allowed to go into convents; and every culture without exception seems to have had shamanesses or healing sisterhoods. So I created as a counterforce the Sisterhood of Avarra and these two were, at the end of *Two to Conquer*, beginning to merge. Later in *Hawkmistress*, the main character, Romilly, enters the Sisterhood of the Sword. The Amazons continued to be the most popular facet of Darkover; when we were publishing the Darkover Newsletter and a Darkover fiction fanzine called *Starstone*, our most popular sellers were two collections called *Tales of the Free Amazons* and its companion *More Tales*. We simply could not keep these two in stock, even though these two were commercially distributed in women's bookstores locally. However, a totally unrealistic pricing policy forced us to withdraw them from publication; and when it became possible to do a third Friends of Darkover anthology, we decided to reprint the best of both editions, at the same time soliciting a few somewhat more professionally written stories for the volume.

Every couple of months I get a letter from some (usually male) fan who complains that I am losing touch with the "real" Darkover, and writing only about women's issues. These letters depress me for a few minutes until I realize that for every such letter, I receive ten or twelve from women, actually rejoicing that I have written for them, about *their* problems and *their* lives. There are so many science fiction books written exclusively for men that I'm afraid I don't have much sympathy for these male fans. I recommend to them all the writers from Anderson to Zelazny.

I can honestly look at my first Free Amazon character, Kyla, and say to her "You've come a long way, brainchild." And, guided by her, so, I think, have I.

Marion Zimmer Bradley

About Walter Breen and the Oath of the Free Amazons

When The Shattered Chain *was first published, one disillusioned ex-Darkover fan reviewed it under the title "The Shattered Dream," stating that his illusions about Darkover as a good society had been wrecked by the "radical feminism" and "man-hating" of* The Shattered Chain. *He also stated that no man could possibly accept this kind of relationship with any woman. In refutation, I present my own husband's analysis of the Oath, which he helped me devise, and which was printed in the* Darkover Concordance *(Pennyfarthing Press, 1979, now out of print).*

Walter Breen is a technical writer on the subject of rare coins, a professional numismatist, who is in the unenviable position of knowing more than I do myself about Darkover—he remembers all the things I have forgotten. We have been married since 1964, and have two children, both now in college.

MZB

THE OATH OF THE COMHI-LETZII OR "ORDER OF RENUNCIATES"

Commonly Called the "Free Amazons," with Explanatory Commentary

From this day forth (I swear):

Men dia pre'z'biuro (ritual formula)

I renounce the right to marry

As marriages were arranged by families, this represents a renunciation of all family ties and obligations, including the mutual obligations between the Amazon and her parents, implying also renunciation of heritage.

save as a freemate.

The exception implies that the Amazon asserts the retention of the right to take a bed partner or lover within the legal status of freemate, bound by mutual promises. Freemates shared property and the responsibility for raising their children.

No man may bind me *di catenas:*

This renounced the privileges, dowries, matrimonial transfer of land and other properties, or of titles, inheritances for herself or her children, and other rights conferred by this most ancient

16

form of marriage. By implication, it also renounces acceptance of authority (or the protection) of a Domain lord (even the Hastur lord), who would normally lock the *catenas* onto both parties in such a union in token of Comyn acknowledgment of the status so conferred.

and I will dwell in no man's household as a *barragana*.

From the most prestigious to the least prestigious (save prostitution) of all unions: all are renounced. The two clauses are exactly balanced in casta.

I swear that

I am prepared to defend myself by force if I am attacked by force,

Two more balanced clauses. The sense is renunciation of the protection normally expected from father or husband, and assertion that she can and must learn to survive without it.

and that I shall turn to no man for protection.

Renouncing any further claim on family even for the necessities of life. Henceforth her home was no longer her father's house but her Guild House.

From this day forth I swear:

I shall never again be known by the name of any man, be he father, guardian, lover,

Renouncing any identification with caste, clan or family of origin, as well as with family acquired by wedlock.

or husband, but
simply and solely as

(given name) *nikhya
mic* (mother's
given name).

e.g. Margali, daughter of Ysabet.
Mother-daughter tie, the ultimate biological link, is affirmed in
this limited degree.

From this day forth I
swear:

I will give myself to
no man
save in my own time
and season
and of my own free
will,
at my own desire;

What is being renounced is the
social ties of wedlock, not sex
or even love. What is asserted is
the ownership of her own body
and the right to dispose of it as
she wishes, rather than the
obligation to be at a man's
demand.

I will never earn my
bread as the object of
any man's lust.

Not only prostitution is being
renounced, nor yet only
barragana status, nor yet that of
the type of entertainers whose
income depends on showing pretty
faces and figures to men, but
also any occupation whatever in
which the Amazon would have
to appear principally or solely as a
sex object, e.g. by adhering to
Terran dress codes.

From this day forth I
swear:

I will bear no child to
any man

Renouncing the prime purpose of
all forms of marriage on
Darkover.

save for my own
pleasure and at my
own time and choice;
I will bear no child to
any man
for house or heritage,
clan or inheritance,
price or posterity;

Parallel to clauses in the previous section.

I swear that

I alone will determine
rearing and fosterage
of any child I bear,
without regard to any
man's
place, position, or
pride.

Withdrawing her progeny from any claims family or clan—even Comyn—might otherwise make. In practice, there is no limit on who could be chosen to foster an Amazon's child; daughters are normally raised in the Guild House, sons after age five (not the safest age for separation!) are sent from the Guild House to fosterage wherever the mother chooses, though this could also be done earlier.

From this day forth
(I swear)

I renounce allegiance

Renouncing any form of protection extended by those same institutions.

to any family, clan,
household, warden
or liege lord, and take
oath that

Recognizing even that the will of Hastur is not the law of the land.

I owe allegiance
only to the laws of the
land
as a free citizen must:

Asserting that she is not an
outlaw. Free citizen: normally
male status.

to the kingdom, the
crown
and the Gods

The order here is ascending: the
social system, its ruler, and the
Four Gods as successively higher
authorities over her own will.

(From this day forth
I swear)

I shall appeal to no
man as of right,
for protection, support
or succor;

Normally a woman had a legal
claim for protection on either
her family of origin or her
husband's family; this is
renounced and the proper direction
of such claim is asserted in the
next clause.

but shall owe
allegiance only
to my oath-mother,
to my sisters in the
Guild,
and to my employer
for the season
of my employment.

She who administered the Oath
to the new Amazon. Guild-sisters
means primarily those in her
Guild House, but by extension all
other Amazons. The mention of
her employer testifies to the
ancient tradition that employment freely entered into for gain
entails a contract, either written
or verbal or implicit, of mutual
obligation to protect each
other's interests.

And I further swear
that

the members of the Guild of Renunciates shall be to me, each and every one, as my mother, my sister, or my daughter, born of one blood with me,

Family-by-choice, but with the same obligations which would normally bind members of a family-by-blood each to the other.

and that no woman sealed by oath to the Guild shall appeal to me in vain.

Assumes the mutual obligations of protection which would normally exist between father and daughter or between husband and wife.

From this moment, I swear

Intensified form of ritual formula.

to obey all the laws of the Guild of Renunciates

In parallel to the previous section; rights imply duties.

and any lawful command

The key word here is *lawful*.

of my oath-mother, the Guild members, or my elected leader for the season of my employment.

Only in such circumstances as any of these would have occasions to give orders.

And if I betray any secret of the Guild, or prove false to my oath,

than I shall submit myself to the Guild-

mothers for such
discipline as they shall
choose;

and if I fail,   Fail to fulfill the preceding
                                clause, i.e. to resume Amazon
                                status.

then may every
woman's hand
turn against me;

let them slay me like   Rather than normal legal
an animal   execution. Animals were not
and consign my body   normally buried.
unburied

to corruption
and (consign) my soul

to the mercy of the   Any Darkovan would understand
Goddess.   Avarra as here invoked.

About "The Legend of Lady Bruna"

A long time before I wrote anything much about the Free Amazons, I wrote of Bruna Leynier, who, after the death of her brother with his son still unborn, took up the sword and the hereditary position of commander of the Guards for the Comyn. This story is mentioned briefly in Forbidden Tower *(1977), but notes from it appear among my Darkover files as early as 1955. The following version of the "myth" was written for* Thendara House *(1983), but was deleted from the final version of the book as irrelevant to the identity crises of Magda and Jaelle. It did appear in a small publication called* Legends of Hastur and Cassilda *as part of the massive file of legends and folk tales of Darkover. Several Darkover fans have written stories about Lady Bruna, including Joan Marie Verba's "This One Time," which appears later in this volume. It occurred to me that a legend of this sort would of course be popular among the women of the Guild House, as a prototype of the independent woman and a role model for Renunciates. Therefore I am including it here.*

MZB

THE LEGEND OF LADY BRUNA

by Marion Zimmer Bradley

. . . Janetta brought an old volume, bound in heavy, crimson-dyed leather, and laid it in Mother Lauria's lap.

"Well, daughters," the old woman said indulgently, "what would you have me read to you, then?"

"The Lady Bruna," Cloris said, "about the Lady Bruna Leynier, who took up sword and commanded the Guardsmen—"

"Yes, yes," Rafaella said. "We have a Margali in the house now, and she should hear the tale of her namesake."

Mother Lauria glanced at Magda over the top of the heavy book. She asked, "Were you given your name from this old legend, Margali?"

"I don't know," Magda said. "I have never heard the story, and I do not know if my mother knew it." Although, she reflected after she said it, Elizabeth Lorne had known virtually every tale and ballad of the Kilghard Hills and the Hellers. Mother Lauria opened the book, and began to read . . .

In the old days in the Kilghard Hills, there were three noble families in the Alton Domain; for a long time they dwelt in peace, but somehow it came to pass that blood-feud came among them. And, as is well known, when brothers quarrel, enemies step in to widen the gap, and so for many years blood-feud raged among the Lanart kin and the Leyniers of

Armida and their kin the Lindirs; and then, in the reign of King Alaric, in the days when the Hasturs were kings in Thendara, these three families met to determine what should be done, so that the Great Houses of the Alton Domain should not die out forever. Now in this time the head of the clan was Dom Kennard Leynier, and he was a young man, for his father and grandfather had died, and his great-grandsire, old Cathal Leynier, was too old to maintain headship of the clan. And so Kennard was married to Margali Lanart, and after this marriage had been made, and the couple were wedded and bedded, as the custom was in the hills, then Domenic Lindir, who was a cousin to Margali (for her mother had been of the Lindir kinfolk), came to Dom Kennard and sought the lady Bruna Leynier, Kennard's sister, in marriage.

"For then," he said, "our three houses will be bound with double ties and we shall be friends thereafter."

It seemed that this would bring peace into the Alton Domain, and so the marriage was arranged among all the menfolk; but when the day came for the marriage, then the Lady Bruna Leynier said, "This shall not be; I shall wear bracelets for no man living, and certainly for no man of Lindir kindred whose hands are red with the blood of my kinsmen." And so Domenic Lindir left the house of Leynier very angry, and the feud broke out again and raged for another year, more fiercely than ever; they fought until no adult man of Lanart or Leynier kindred was left alive but a few young boys. And in that time Kennard Leynier died, and was borne to the burial place at Hali, and at his graveside Margali revealed that she was with child by Kennard, and that his heir would be born half a year hence.

And when Kennard was laid in earth, then came Domenic Lindir again to Armida, and said to old Cathal Leynier, who had assumed Regency of the Domain for Margali, even though he was near to a hundred years old, and could not command the Guards as the Leyniers of Armida did in those days, "I will wed the Lady Bruna if she will have me now. And I will swear that her oldest son shall be Heir to Armida in the Alton Domain, and command the Guard when he comes to manhood, but in the meantime I shall command the Guards and be Regent of Alton Domain.''

The Lady Bruna did not look upon Domenic, but only upon old Cathal, and she said to him, ''I have sworn an oath that I will wear the *catenas* for no man living; and I wonder at you, Uncle, that you think to bring among our kindred a man whose hands are stained with the blood of all our kinsmen and with my brother Kennard's blood.''

Domenic Lindir said, looking on Bruna, ''Even for the Regency of Alton I would not wed with this ill-spoken brazen-tongued hoyden who presumes to speak among men; she may live and die virgin for all it matters to me.''

''That doom I will bear gladly,'' said the Lady Bruna, and she thrust her hand into the fires of Hali and swore it.

Domenic Lindir said, ''Since Kennard's sister has sworn to wed no man who could contest the Regency of Alton, then I will have Kennard's widow for my wife, and I swear that when her son is born he shall be fostered as my own; and he shall command the Guards when he is grown, and my eldest son shall be second to him always.''

''That seems to me fair dealing,'' said old Cathal, and made the bargain. But the women spoke apart, and when Margali was brought before Domenic for the wedding, she said, ''You are quick to wed when Armida is your dower gift; but I will marry no man whose hands bear the stain of my husband's lifeblood. Will you, Domenic, thrust your hand into the fires of Hali and swear to me that you had no art, nor part, nor malice, in the death of my husband and the father of the son you are so quick to foster?''

Then Domenic looked angry, and asked old Cathal, ''Will you let your house be ruled by these women? For, although it is the voice of Margali, the words are those of the Lady Bruna, and I will not be ruled by her will!''

Cathal asked him, ''Then you will not swear that you had no part in the death of my great-grandson, nor that you are guiltless of his blood?''

''I did not come here to swear forced oaths,'' said Domenic, ''but to make a fair offer which will amend this feud. I will swear no oath at any woman's bidding.''

''But you will swear it at mine,'' said Cathal Leynier, ''or you will not wed with the Lady Margali, today or any other day.''

Domenic laughed and pulled the old man's beard and said, ''Will you stop me, old man? As for you, Domna Margali, if you will not wed with me, then I shall wed you to one of my brethren; and since you have refused to let Kennard's son be mine, and command the Guards, then he shall be set aside, and my eldest son shall command the Guards in his place.''

''That shall never be,'' Cathal Leyneir said, ''for the son of Kennard is commander of the Guards, and Heir to Alton from his mother's womb.''

And Domenic Lindir laughed and pulled the old man's beard again and spat in his face and thrust the old man, weeping, to the ground, saying, ''How will you keep the Domain for him, old graybeard? Will he challenge me from his mother's womb, then, or will one of these unruly women keep it for you?'' And he laughed, and went away. And when he had gone, then Margali and Bruna came and lifted Cathal up and wiped his face and dried his tears and comforted him, saying, ''Grandsire, we will be revenged on this man.''

''And how will you do that, being two women, and one of you heavy with child? Will you have it, you two, that the rule of the Alton Domain shall pass into the hands of the Lindir kindred? I beg of you, Margali, be reconciled with Domenic and wed him, for the good of the Domain, and for the sake of Kennard's son.''

"For the sake of Kennard's son," Margali said, "I will wed no man who has spat on the gray hairs of his venerable forefather."

"There is no honor in a grave," said Cathal, "and I shall soon lie there. I only beg of you, you women, that somehow it shall be arranged that Kennard's son may not lie there beside me! And there is none to command the Guards until he comes to manhood."

"Do not say there is none to command the Guards," said Bruna, "for I will myself take sword and command them in my brother's place until Kennard's son whom Margali bears shall be come to manhood. And when that day is come, I will yield up command of the Guards to him, and he shall take his father's sword from my hands and from no other."

And Cathal Leyneir said, weeping, "Let it be so, Bruna, for you are strong and brave as any man of our clan."

And with his own hands he tied Kennard's sword at her waist.

"Now," he said, "it remains only to give Margali in marriage to some kinsman who can guard her and her son; and since she will not have Domenic Lindir, we must seek somewhere, and quickly, and we cannot delay to pick and choose, for until Margali is wedded, she is at Domenic's mercy, with no husband to protect her."

Margali looked at Bruna, who wore her husband's sword, and flung herself into Bruna's arms, weeping, and said, "Spare me this fate, my sister, you who are Regent of Alton and have the right to say yes and no to marriages within the clan!"

"Willingly," Bruna said, "but you are young, and a day will come to you, although now you are weeping for grief over Kennard's grave, when you will seek a lover again, or a husband; and then you will conspire with him to take the Domain from my hands."

"That shall never be," said Margali, "and I will swear it to you, that no man living shall part our oaths."

"Is it so? Then let it be as you will," Bruna said, and together they journeyed to Hali before anyone could prevent them, and there in the holy place, before the sacred things, they took oath together. Margali swore that she would take no man for husband save he who should acknowledge the Lady Bruna as his overlord and the Regent of his Domain. "For I know well," she said, "that no man living would take that oath. If I swear I will take no husband at all, then can my oath be set aside as the oath of a widow in grief; but if I swear I will take no husband save he who shall meet my conditions, then is that oath lawful, and I may keep it until death."

And she swore. And Bruna swore in her turn that she would take Margali under her protection on the terms of a freemate, and swore to foster Margali's son as Heir to Alton.

But when this thing came to be known, that the Lady Bruna had taken Margali in a freemate's oath, all the Hastur-kin at Thendara said, "This thing is scandalous, that two women should swear to one another as if they were wedded; shall we be ruled by women who will not be lawfully subject to their husbands? For if we allow this oath, what woman will wish to wed?" And so they took the women to the Hastur at Thendara and asked for his judgment.

The Lady Bruna said, "I am Regent of Alton, and I will so abide the lawful challenge. And as for you, Margali, do you wish to be free of your oath?"

"I will free her whether she will or no," said Domenic Lindir. "She had refused to wed with me, but I say that only a madwoman would make such an oath with another woman, and therefore a madwoman's oath can have no standing here."

"It seems to me," said Margali, "that it needs no madness to refuse such a marriage as you would have made for me.

Who but a madwoman would wed with her husband's murderer?"

At this Domenic was angry and would have struck her, but that Bruna, wearing Kennard's sword, came between them and said, "I am Regent of Alton; if you would have dealings with an Alton woman, you must deal with me."

"I do not deal with women, mad or sane," said Domenic. "If there is a man of the Alton Domain to act as Regent, I will dispute with him, but not with you."

"I am not a man," said Bruna, "but I am an Alton, and if I must prove myself a better man than my brother's murderer, I will do so." And she drew her sword, and called challenge upon Domenic in that place, and they fought, and after a little, she slew him quickly. And then she made his brothers swear to keep the peace, which they did, for they said, "This woman is as good a sword as any man." And from that day, the Lindirs have been paxmen and servants to Alton.

And so all the Hastur kin gave judgment that the Lady Bruna had won the right to command the Guards and to reign as Regent of Alton, and to foster the son of Kennard.

"But what of these women?" they asked. "For it stands not within the law that one woman should take another in marriage."

"Why not?" asked the Lady Bruna. "For what is marriage, but that I can guard her with my sword, and care for her well-being, and protect her against any other marriage which might be forced on her for political reasons or matters of family and inheritance? I cannot give her children, but she already bears the son of Kennard, and who knows but one or the other of us might some day choose to bear a child of Alton blood to the Domain? I ask her now, in the sight of Hastur and the Gods; do you wish to be free of your oath, my sister?"

"I do not," said Margali. "None but you, my sister, shall foster the child of my body, this or any other."

And then Bruna and Margali stood before the Council at Thendara and swore together that they would love after the fashion of Cassilda and Camilla for all their lives, and that neither would ever take any man for husband, and that they would foster one another's children as their own; and they thrust their hands into the fire and drew them forth unburned; and so Hastur allowed the oath to stand as lawful.

And so the Lady Bruna Leynier commanded the Guards for twenty years, and when Margali's son was grown to manhood, she yielded up the sword of Kennard to him, but she was Regent and Counselor to Alton for all her life. And when Kennard's son was five-and-twenty, Bruna died in battle against the Dry-Towners; and Margali dwelt all alone at Armida and mourned her sister lifelong, taking no husband, and she was an old woman when she died. And all these things took place in the realm of Gabriel the Second, when the Hastur kings dwelt at Elhalyn.

Mother Lauria closed the book. She asked, "How like you your namesake, Margali?"

Magda had been touched by the story; she thought of how she had struck down the bandit who had menaced Jaelle. She asked, "Is it a true tale or only a legend?"

"I do not know," said Mother Lauria, "but it is true that in the reign of Alaric, who was succeeded by his son Gabriel the Second, there was a Lady Bruna Leynier who was allowed to command the Guards after her brother died; and that she slew three men who would have challenged her for that right. And it is true that the Hastur kin allowed her to take her brother's wife under her protection until their child was grown to manhood, so that no other marriage could be forced on the woman. Whether it was as the story says with Bruna and Margali, no one can say; they have been dead so long that even their bones are dust, and what befell them in their lives is no longer a matter for any-

thing but guesswork and old tales. I like to think that they loved one another as the story tells, but that will never be known until time ends and Eternity begins, and then it will not matter.''

About Margaret Silvestri and "Cast Off Your Chains"

From the very beginning the two extremes in Darkovan society have been the Free Amazons and the Dry-Town women, literally chained as "possessions" of their husbands. While there have been several stories written on this theme—Dry-Town woman versus Amazon—this has been the most popular, and was printed in Tales of the Free Amazons.

Margaret Silvestri is a registered nurse, divorced, with a young daughter; her main involvement with science fiction has been with the Spellbinders, a local organization which puts on science fiction conventions for charity. She is also a folk musician and writes songs "when inspiration strikes, which isn't as often as I'd like."

MZB

CAST OFF YOUR CHAINS

by Margaret Silvestri

"I want to see the desert."

The request had seemed peculiar at the Guild House, but then she'd heard all these *Terranan* were peculiar. However odd the idea, the woman had the official sanction of both the Terran and Darkovan governments, and her generous monetary remuneration had stopped any further inquiries. But after the long horseback journey over the mountains and two days in the desert, the nagging questions were returning.

Gilda n'ha Camilla stole a brief look at the Terran woman. She had affected the dress of a Free Amazon to conceal her identity, but her mannerisms betrayed the disguise. Luckily, they'd met no one familiar enough with Free Amazons to penetrate the deception, since the Terrans were not well liked among the superstitious mountain folk. Gilda recalled what little she knew of her employer. Her name was Marissa Del Gado. Although she was Terran, she passed easily for Darkovan with her dark coloring. Since more spaceport personnel never bothered with the language, she had been surprised that Marissa spoke fluent *cahuenga* and some *casta*. Evidently she had some interest in the world on which she was temporarily stationed.

Marissa hadn't talked much, but now she seemed even more withdrawn, her eyes constantly searching the barren terrain until Gilda's suspicions jelled into concrete questions.

As they made camp, Gilda determined to get some answers before she rode farther.

While the Amazon guide erected the tent, Marissa unsaddled the horses, wiping them down as they drank from the small pond of brackish water. She watched Gilda in fascination as the Amazon swiftly set up camp with a minimum of lost motion. She'd had good luck when she engaged her as a guide. With the horses tended and safely tethered, she drew off some of the water for herself. It was warm and tasted of sale, but it was wet, and the only water they'd find.

Inside the tent, Marissa stripped to the waist, bathing her sweat-encrusted flesh with a moistened cloth. Although it made little difference in cleanliness, the warm wetness revived her spirits. When the Amazon entered the tent, Marissa self-consciously covered her slim breasts, but when Gilda took no notice, quickly finished, pulling on a fresh tunic. So nudity taboos differed here, too. She'd never be able to understand this culture.

"Did you want to go farther into the desert?"

The question startled Marissa and she looked up into piercing gray eyes. "Yes. . . . Why do you ask?"

"You said you wished to see the desert. We have seen two days of it now. It changes little. If that was truly your reason for this journey, I see no reason to continue."

"What makes you think I have another motive?"

"You search the horizons as if looking for something. You want to keep going when the need is over." The Amazon faced her sternly. "If I'm to continue, I must know why."

Marissa considered the situation gravely, nervously tapping the knife belted at her waist. She could not afford to lose the guide. "All right, I'll level with you. I'm looking for my sister, Teri. She was doing sociological research in a small Dry-Town village, and I lost contact. Teri always sent regular reports in her letters to me. . . . Two months ago they stopped. I haven't heard anything since and I'm worried."

"Two months is not a long time, considering the area. Caravans are irregular at best . . . and then there are bandits, raids. . . . Surely you aren't making this long trip simply on that." Gilda was still skeptical.

"No, I wasn't concerned until the dreams began. Dreams of my sister in trouble. . . . I couldn't tell what was wrong, only that she needed help. Before I came to the Guild House they got worse . . . She was dying. This probably sounds quite mad, but I know she's in trouble."

"Are you a *leronis?*"

Marissa frowned as her mind translated *leronis* as sorceress. This world was really full of superstition; now the Amazon thought her a witch. She couldn't very well explain the concept of premonitions and extrasensory perception to someone who believed in witches. "No, but she's not just my sister. . . . We're twins, and sometimes I can feel her thoughts."

The Amazon nodded, but Marissa doubted that she really understood. That didn't matter; what mattered was her mission.

"Will you continue to guide me?"

"Why should I not?"

"I lied to you. I wouldn't blame you if you went back immediately."

Now it was Gilda's turn to be astonished by the strangeness of the Terran. Would one of the Terrans truly leave another lost in the desert? Perhaps Hastur was right to limit the Empire influence on Darkover. "It would have been better had you been truthful, but I agreed to guide you. Even if I wished to break our agreement, I could not. It would bring great trouble to the Guild House were I to leave a mad *Terranan* alone in the desert."

Marissa silently accepted the epithet. She probably did seem insane to the Darkovan woman, with her talk of dreams, but as long as Gilda stayed as her guide, she could think anything she wished. Apparently the Amazon considered the discussion ended; she went on to another topic.

"From here, we will travel at night and sleep during the day's heat. In which direction do we travel?"

Marissa was not certain. "The same way. I'm not sure where . . . only that we're getting closer."

The two women traveled farther into the desert, riding by moonlight, their only landmark an intangible thread of emotion. They saw nothing but sand and spicebush and an occasional reptile. Marissa was positive from the Amazon's surreptitious glances that Gilda now truly believed her to be a madwoman.

Whether it was luck or some incomprehensible inner feeling guiding them, the fourth day brought a small village into view. Twenty or thirty houses encircled a cluster of wells, and patches of shaded green marked carefully tended gardens. As the two women rode into the square, they felt curious eyes watching them. Glancing to one side, Marissa caught sight of several children peering excitedly out of a doorway, but at her gaze they ducked shyly back. Gilda had dismounted by the well, and Marissa hurried to join her, watering the horses.

The Terran glanced around at the deserted streets. "Where is everyone?"

"We're strangers," Gilda explained. "In the Dry Towns, any stranger is suspect. They'll show themselves when they see we're harmless."

"I see you're right. . . . Here someone comes." Marissa indicated a gray-bearded man crossing the square toward them.

"Greetings to you, strangers. I am Drocar, and I offer the hospitality of our poor village."

Gilda bowed respectfully to the elderly man. "We thank you for your hospitality, and wish to repay your generosity."

"No, we could not accept it," Drocar demurred. The

Amazon politely insisted. After several minutes of apologetic haggling, the village elder accepted the coins, as Gilda had known he would. "Your generosity is appreciated. Now if you will tell how we may serve you, *domna?*"

Gilda was silent, letting Marissa speak. "We are searching for my sister, Teresa. I thought she might be here. She is small and dark-haired."

"Yes, yes . . . the Lady Teresa. She is staying at the home of Arturin. Please come." The elderly man trotted off at a pace that belied his stooped appearance.

Marissa followed quickly to a large mud-brick house off the square. Drocar spoke rapidly in an unfamiliar dialect to a plump woman. Following the two inside, Marissa had little time to observe her surroundings, but what she did see was plain, almost austere. They passed through several rooms and halls until the servant knocked gently on a door. She must have received a reply because she ushered Marissa inside, then left with Drocar.

A small white-gowned figure lay propped up on pillows, dwarfed by the huge bed that dominated the room. Long dark-brown hair tumbled over thin shoulders. Even before she saw the face, Marissa knew she'd found her sister.

"Teri . . ."

"Mari?" The voice questioned as the girl turned toward the sound in disbelief. Half-healed bruises showed gray discoloration on her cheeks and forehead. "Is it really you, Marissa? I'm not dreaming?"

"It's no dream, Teri . . . although a dream brought me here." Marissa described her journey.

Gilda had entered unobtrusively, but now Marissa noticed the Amazon's presence and beckoned her closer.

"This is my sister, Teresa. . . . Gilda was my guide. Without her, I could not have come."

The Amazon acknowledged the introduction. "We have been offered rooms here. The horses are already stabled."

Marissa nodded thoughtfully. "Now tell me what happened to you, Teri. The dreams showed me only that you were in danger."

"The village I was in was raided by Dry-Town bandits. I'm told that's a fairly common occurrence. I was captured in the raid along with several other young women. We were taken to Punjar to be slaves. I was sold to a bandit named Ulric . . . as a concubine."

Marissa bit her lip. "You were abused?"

The pale girl laughed a short bitter laugh before she replied, "I did not come by these bruises out of great love."

"I would not have allowed such filth to abuse me." The Amazon's voice was derisive.

Teresa's dark eyes locked with Gilda's. "I was given little choice in the matter."

"Had you no knife?"

"It was taken from me."

The Amazon was openly scornful now. "I would have used the blade against myself before permitting the vermin to touch me."

"Would you, Amazon? Then it is a good thing I am not you. Why should I be punished for a Dry-Town bandit's crime?" The Terran woman was adamant. "What profit would there be in my death? My loss would mean nothing to Ulric, except the minor inconvenience of buying a new slave. By waiting, I managed to escape, and now have a lifetime to plot revenge."

"Is that the Terran way?"

"I do not know. It is *my* way."

Marissa had recovered from her shock and was concerned more with Teresa's escape than a philosophical discussion. "But how did you escape?"

"Punjar is not as well guarded as many cities. By appearing cooperative I gained enough freedom to escape into the desert." Teresa paused reflectively. "The desert was more my enemy than the Dry-Towners. There was no pursuit, no need for hunters. The sun did their job. I would have perished in the desert except for these villagers. Some of their men found me in the desert and brought me here. Arturin's wife, Alana, nursed me back to health.''

"Are you well enough to travel?"

"Yes. Alana is just overcautious."

"Good. Then we shall return immediately to Thendara. I'll make the arrangements."

"No!" The abrupt order stunned Marissa into confused silence. "I'm not going back to the spaceport. I belong here."

"Here? After what's happened, you want to stay here and risk that again? Why?" Marissa demanded angrily.

"Because someone has to help those women, and I've developed a plan to help them escape."

"Escape! Those women have no desire to escape. They enjoy their prison." Gilda sneered in contempt. "I doubt they would leave if you threw the gates wide open and forced them out!"

"Maybe you're right about many of them, but there are those who were captured as I was, ripped away from family and home. They had no choice. I plan to give them that choice."

"But how? The cities are guarded."

"Many of the cities have grown lax in their luxury. It should be easy to get in and out." Teresa's eyes lit up as she unfolded her idea. "My plan is to seek out those who want their freedom . . . to help them one or two at a time . . . never enough to cause alarm . . . and spirit them quietly out of the Dry Towns."

"Like the ancient underground railroad on Terra that helped Negro slaves to escape." Marissa understood the idea, but still she frowned.

"Exactly. For now, that will be my revenge on Ulric . . . that I will give life back to the women his kind enslave."

Marissa saw deep commitment in her sister's eyes, but the idea frightened her. "But that's so dangerous. Why must you do it? If those women wanted to escape, they would. You did—and this isn't even your world! They were born to it. Why can't they escape by themselves?"

"Escape to what? The desert sun? I did so only out of ignorance!" Teresa's temper flared. "I nearly died. If they escape, they can expect only sun and sand and thirst . . . and if they are so lucky as to reach another city, what can they look forward to, but more chains and perhaps another master far worse than the last?"

Marissa faced the angry words with her own demanding question: "But why you? Why must *you* risk your life for them?"

Teresa flung her legs over the edge of the bed, lifting the voluminous linen gown so she could walk. Opening a rough-hewn trunk, she rummaged through neatly folded clothing, pulling forth a tied bundle. She unlaced the nightgown and stepped out of it. Marissa was surprised by how gaunt her twin was.

"What are you doing?"

"You asked me why. I'm going to show you why." Teresa finished pulling on her riding clothes. "It will mean a journey of two days by horseback . . . to Punjar."

"You want to enter a Dry-Town city?" Gilda asked sharply. "I will not go there."

"Then stay here, Amazon. I know the way. And I need prove nothing to you." Teresa's voice was neither hostile nor friendly, merely a blank statement of fact.

Gilda eyed the Terran woman appraisingly. "I will go with you, as far as the city outskirts. There I will wait. Amazons are not well received in the Dry Towns."

"Good. Ready the horses. The moons will provide fine

light this night. I will inform Lady Alana of our decision."
Teresa left to make the other preparations for the journey.

The horses were packed lightly; the trip to Punjar was not
long, and to travel lightly would provide an extra measure of
safety.

They saw nothing to alarm them, but as they approached
Punjar, apprehension overcame them all and they traveled in
silence. On the second night, the city loomed ahead and
Gilda chose a campsite on an outcropping of rock. She passed
out some dried meat and bread; no fire could be lit this close
to the city.

"Now that we're here, what do you plan to do?" Marissa's
tone suggested she was humoring her sister's whims.

Teresa answered softly, "Show you why I have to risk my
life. Here, put these on." She shoved a bundle of clothing
into Marissa's hands.

Shaking out the garments, Marissa was puzzled by a length
of gilden chain attached to two wide wristbands. "What is
this?"

"The symbol of a mastered woman. You would not last
long in Punjar without it. Put it on like this." Teresa demonstrated with an identical set of chains. "We will slip into the
city while still dark, then infiltrate the women at the well.
They constantly change, so two new faces will go unnoticed
in the crowd. Then I will answer your question as to why."

Gilda returned from the horses, eyeing the chains with
undisguised revulsion. "You should go now. It will be light
soon."

Teresa nodded, but gave one last order. "If we have not
returned by moonrise, return to your home . . . and God go
with you."

Punjar was a sprawling city once encircled by solid walls,
but rapid growth had forced building outside the stone walls.
It was here that the two women approached, gliding carefully
through the shadows, their chains held tightly lest the clash-

ing links betray their intrigue. Until they were safely inside the ring of houses, Teresa signaled silence; then she motioned to several large crockery jars near one house.

"Water jars . . . our pass inside the walls." Selecting one, Teresa continued on with the jar balanced expertly against her hip. Marissa swiftly mimicked her twin's actions, but it was a poor imitation.

"Teri, what if you're recognized?"

"I've taken precautions." Teri drew a filmy veil over the lower half of her face and wrapped it around her throat. "Many women go veiled."

Spotting several women, Teresa quickened her pace to join them as they passed through the city gate. The guards leered from their posts, but never stirred.

Pressing close to her sister, Teresa whispered harshly, "Observe carefully the role of women in the Dry Towns."

Marissa followed her closely through the dusty streets. The metallic tinkling of chains grew louder as more women joined the procession to the wells. Marissa's dark eyes cautiously studied them, widening in surprise at the sight of two very young girls hurrying along, chained like their elder counterparts.

"But those girls? They're only children."

"Twelve. . . . Old enough to be chained and wed," Teresa hissed.

Waiting her turn at the well, Marissa rubbed the golden bands nervously. The bracelets chafed her wrists, and Marissa felt uncomfortable wearing them, though she knew they were unlocked and could be removed at any time. Feeling hot eyes upon her, she lowered her head and spotted the cause nearby. Dirty-clothed beggars sat in the building shadows, their stares openly lustful. Marissa shivered, disgusted and sickened by the stares, her body gooseflesh as if insects crawled over her skin. Hot shame ran through her; chained like an animal and paraded through the streets for the licentious pleasure of filth and vermin. She swiftly searched the faces of the women around her, wondering how they could endure such humiliation.

"Come!" Teri's command pulled her from her thoughts, and she obediently followed, trying to balance the heavy water-filled jar. Crossing through several alleys, Teresa finally halted, setting down her burden. Marissa copied the action gratefully; her arm was numb and her hip sore from the weight.

"What now? Do we leave?"

Teri shook her head. "You have seen nothing! A caravan arrived yesterday, so there will be a crowd in the market. You can mingle with the master's chosen favorites there."

"Can't we just leave now?" Marissa begged urgently. She hated this masquerade.

"What's wrong? Doesn't the role of a Dry-Town concubine appeal to you?" Teri asked sarcastically. "You need to see more."

The marketplace was merely a cleared area between the rows of houses where traveling merchants set up their stalls and tents. Beady-eyed traders yelled loudly, hawking their wares, and in other stalls, merchants sat indolently among their goods, their sleepy-lidded appearance disguising minds of cunning hagglers. As the sisters passed among the merchants, Marissa scanned the other women visiting the stalls. They seemed well dressed, their bodies powdered and perfumed, and they laughed excitedly over the merchandise like any other women.

"Look about you at the best a Dry-Town woman can expect."

Marissa looked again. This was the best? The women glided by, their chains tinkling; they looked happy, but reminded her of a rich man's pet, perfumed and groomed, safe on its leash, to be pampered or destroyed at the master's whim.

"Tarisa . . ." The oddly accented name, spoken so close,

startled Marissa and her head jerked up to see a bronze-skinned girl with shining black hair and wide blue eyes.

Teri obviously recognized the girl; her hand clamped down on the girl's arm, signaling caution. "Elys . . . walk with us."

Aside to her sister, Teri explained, "Elys is from the village I lived in. She was captured with me."

"Tarisa . . . I had heard you escaped here . . . I am sorry it is not true."

Teresa glanced quickly to all sides, but there was no one close enough to hear. "I did escape, Elys."

The wide eyes stared in horror. "You were recaptured?"

"No. I am still free. I came back on my own today, before the sun, and I will leave at dusk."

"Leave? How? And why did you return?"

Teri had to silence the girl's excited questions for fear of attracting unwanted attention. "I wanted to help others escape. How are you, Elys?"

The girl stared at the dirt, scuffing it with one foot, gnawing her lower lip in agitation. "I was sold to the House of Kantol."

The quick gasp and pitying look on her twin's face brought questions to Marissa's mind; she raised her eyebrows in silent inquiry.

Teri's reply was quiet: "Ulric is considered a prince, compared to Kantol. He's said to have the heart of a banshee."

"Has he hurt you greatly?"

Elys seemed ashamed as she spoke in low strangled tones. "I became resigned to my fate . . . I learned cooperation, and so was given some small freedoms. It is better than the beatings."

Teri touched the girl's shoulder gently, her voice compassionate. "I understand your decision. I too . . . cooperated . . . to gain a little freedom."

"But you used your small freedom to gain your whole freedom." Elys's voice was awed as a glint of hope struck her. "You are going to escape tonight? Both of you?" The words spilled forth. "Take me with you! Please take me. I can travel fast. If you don't help me—then kill me! I can bear this no more, knowing freedom was within my grasp!"

The girl was close to hysteria, and Teresa quickly pulled her away from the mainstream of traffic, trying to calm her. "We'll take you . . . hear me? But we have to go tonight. Will you be missed?" Teri cut straight to the heart of the problem.

"I've been given a free day to see the caravan. And Kantol does not often call for me, so I should not be missed . . . at least not until late."

"By then, we'll be miles away." In her own mind, Teri qualified that statement. *If we have a lot of luck.*

Outside the city, Gilda waited and watched the sun. It was low on the horizon, now, and the twilight shadows kept her jumpy. She didn't like being this close to the Dry-Town city. Nervously, she crept to the rock edge, her eyes scanning for a sign of the *Terranan*. They'd gone on a fool's errand and would most likely die chained in a Dry-Town brothel. Moonrise would be soon, but Gilda did not like the thought of leaving the Terrans behind. It would surely cause trouble for the Guild House.

Not even a grain of sand shifting escaped the Amazon's ears this night, and though the three women had thought their flight silent, Gilda was ready for them when they slipped behind the rocks. The sight of the Amazon, weapon drawn, frightened Elys, but she swiftly adjusted to the new conditions. The Terran women were already changing into their riding clothes. Teresa tucked her chains into the pack and watched in silent amusement as Marissa yanked the bracelets from her own wrists and flung them angrily to the ground. She'd convinced Mari; half the battle was won.

"Pick up the chains. I'll need them next time I pull this

stunt." Teri's voice held no reprimand. She understood Marissa's repugnance.

During the exchange, Elys and the Amazon had stood as if planted in place, silently staring at one another. Finally Gilda moved to the horses, arranging the packs.

"The horses are ready. Who is she?" Gilda's look was critical. This journey had been carefully planned to minimize the risk, and now the *Terranan* endangered them all by picking up strays in the Dry-Town.

"Our first escapee. She'll ride the pack horse. Let's get the hell out of here." Teresa swung onto her mount, walking it slowly away from the city.

Gilda took the point, guiding them with some unerring instinct or skill, Marissa didn't know which, but she'd seen the Amazon in action often enough to respect the guide's directions as they traveled into the desert wastes. They rode in silence, anxious only to put distance between themselves and Punjar. It wasn't until some hours later that they slowed the pace. Even then, they rode cautiously, casting apprehensive looks over their shoulders, alert for any sign of pursuit.

As the sun rose bloody red over the desert sands, Gilda signaled a halt. Some spicebush nearby provided the only shade, and the Amazon indicated they'd rest there during the day's heat. The pungent smell of spice flooded the air and every breath they took. Having tended the horses, Gilda apportioned out their rations, but her eyes went again and again to Elys. Teresa hovered by the girl, patiently tinkering with the bracelets until the locks sprang, and the chains fell to the ground.

Marissa watched, silent, as the girl rubbed her wrists, then lifted her arms, marveling at their new lightness. She hated to disturb the touching moment as Elys realized her regained freedom, but a sudden thought occurred.

"Teri . . . what happens to Elys now?"

"I . . . I hadn't thought of it. This was such a sudden

decision . . . that was the one thing I hadn't figured out yet
. . . what to do with the women who escaped.'' Teresa
looked, distraught, toward Elys.

"Couldn't she go back to her family?'' Marissa asked.
That seemed the most logical solution.

"I have no family.'' Elys couldn't look up from the ground.
"And if I did, I could not return . . . not after my disgrace. I
would shame my family. Better for me to die a slave.''

"No.'' Teresa spoke firmly. She could not let Elys down
now, not after a fleeting taste of liberty. "There has to be
some place you could go, where your past would not matter
. . . where you could start life afresh.''

A pained silence followed Teri's statement, the only sound
that of the Amazon returning from checking the horses. Suddenly a small hope showed on Elys's face as she watched
Gilda sit down.

"I have been told of the Free Amazons, who walk un-
chained among men . . . who earn their own bread. Take me
with you to the Amazons!''

"You?'' Gilda looked at the girl in disbelief. "You think
to become a Renunciate? At the first difficulty, you would
break your vow by begging some man's help.''

"No!'' Elys's denial was sharp. "Have I asked a man's aid
here? Was it not these women who brought me from bondage? I have no family to run to. I have earned my bread from
childhood as a servant, and am no stranger to hard work.
Would you send me back to bondage? Then put the chains on
again yourself!'' She threw the chains at the Amazon's feet.
"Would you who value freedom so greatly deny me that
choice?''

Gilda smiled approvingly. Here indeed was the spirit of an
Amazon. "I will take you to the Guild House, but you must
receive instructions, and then, if you still desire it, take your
vows. They are not to be taken lightly, without understanding.''

The look of intense relief and gratitude brought tears to

Marissa's eyes. Teresa had been right. This was worth the risk.

"That's it! That's the answer!" Teri's exclamation startled the others, and they stared at the excited woman. "Don't you understand? We needed a place to send the women . . . a place where they can start again, where the past wouldn't matter. Would the Amazons accept them all?"

"The Amazons accept any woman willing to take the vows." Gilda thought over what the Terran was proposing.

Before Teri could speak, Elys interjected, "Many would take the vows gladly for a chance to do honest labor. Without help, they would have no other choice but to sell themselves again. If the Amazons only offer us the chance, we will work willingly." Elys beamed, her eyes sparkling with a joy she'd thought lost.

Observing the three, Marissa saw the dream grow and take solid form among them. They were so different—Terran, freed Dry-Town slave, and Amazon—yet the dream bound them together. A dream of liberty, and she'd seen it become reality. Teri would free the women from their despised slavery, and the Amazons would help them build new lives within the close family of the Guild House. It would be a long, slow process, but perhaps the years to come would bring true freedom to the women of the Dry Towns, a time when they would all cast off their chains forever.

About Sherry Kramer and "The Banshee"

Sherry Kramer is a local Darkover fan who uses an Amazon name and has published, with two friends who make up the Valle d'Oro Guild House, a Free Amazon newsletter. She lives on a ranch north of Sacramento "with an alarmingly large number of animals—there are 110 living bodies here, and only two of them human." She gives the count as "7 dogs, 3 cats, 8 goats, 2 horses, 26 chickens, 22 ducks, 2 geese, 7 goldfish, 22 tropical fish, 7 mice, 1 iguana and 1 corn snake." Whether this inspires one with envy or horror (two reactions I've heard) we still find it mildly incredible that "despite showing the dogs in obedience trials, milking and showing the goats, trail riding and caring for the needs of all the other creatures, I still manage to write once in a while." As far as we know, there are no banshees or deaf-hounds on the ranch. "The Banshee" was first published in Tales of the Free Amazons and just missed inclusion in the first volume of stories by the Friends, The Keeper's Price; in fact, I thought it had been included, and expressed my regrets to Sherry that it could not be considered for this volume for which it seemed even better suited. Sherry reminded me that it had not appeared in Keeper's Price; I checked the contents page of that *anthology, and she was right. I had evidently confused it in memory with Linda McKendrick's* The Rescue, *one of the better Free Amazon stories in the earlier volume. I'm happy to remedy that omission and present "The Banshee" here.*

MZB

THE BANSHEE

by Sherry Kramer

"If you have only watched the winter from your warm fireside, you may love her as a sweetheart but you cannot know her as a bride."

So goes the Darkovan proberb. After nearly a year on Darkover, I had no need to watch the winter. I could hear it plainly enough, screaming and moaning around the squat stone *forst*. As soon as the storm cleared, we would go down the mountain and back to Thendara. Winter was my jailer. I should have been gone weeks ago. I did not watch the winter, and I did not love it as sweetheart or otherwise. I'd had enough of winter, as I'd had enough of Darkover.

I heard the soft scrape of Darla's boots on the stone floor, and turned to watch her. "How's the weather?" I asked. "Will it break soon, do you think?" Since the Free Amazon had been my guide, I had learned to respect her weather sense.

"The snow has stopped," she said, "but it is only a pause. As long as the wind blows like that, we are due for more." She took a stoneware goblet from the table and poured a drink from the jug that Mhari had brought in a few moments earlier. "We were lucky to reach the *forst*. It's much more comfortable than a way-station would have been. And better stocked. We can wait out the winter here, if we must."

"Provided Eduin and Mhari agree."

Darla looked surprised. "Do you truly think any host

would turn his guests out in this weather? It would be no less than murder. Do you hold our mountain people so low as that?''

"No, no, of course not. Though a philosopher once said, 'guests and fish both begin to stink after three days'. . .''

"A Terran philosopher, no doubt,'' she said. "Here in the mountains, company is too rare to become unpleasant.''

"And it's too cold for fish to stink,'' I murmured, with a smile. "All the same, I have to get back to Base. The specimens. . .''

"Are quite all right. They'd keep the winter, if need be, frozen in that snowbank. But I will get you back to Thendara. Alive. As I was contracted to do. But not today, or tomorrow. Probably not this week.''

"I'm already late. We should have been back two weeks ago.''

She spread her hands. "Even Comyn Council does not command the weather.''

"Another proverb?''

"A fact.'' She took a sip from her goblet. "This is excellent. Have you tried it?''

"Some kind of wine, isn't it? No, I've not had any.''

She poured me some. "Winter wine. Fermented from brier-plums, then left in the snow to freeze. This is the part that didn't freeze.''

I took a sip. It was tart and smooth, with a faintly resinous aftertaste.

Darla settled herself comfortably near the fire. She had changed her high outdoor boots, into which the loose trousers she favoured could be tucked, for soft, fur-lined, ankle-high "house boots'' when she had come in, and left her wet boots and cape in the hall.

"You are not happy tonight, *Terranan*.'' She was one of the few Darkovans who said that word without making it sound like a curse.

"You know I'm not from Terra," I said. "I was born on Meadow."

"I know. But you are *Terranan*, for all that." She smiled. "Is there some work undone that we should do yet before you leave? Tell me, Janna . . . Janet . . . and perhaps we could still. . . ."

"No, nothing. You've been invaluable. I have enough specimens to keep the analyzers busy for a while. There's always more to do, of course. We can't more than begin to understand the ecology of Darkover yet, but we have made a beginning. A good one, I think." In its way, Darkover was more complex than Terra, because of the intermixtures of Terran and native plants and animals.

"Then what bothers you?"

"Excessive time for thought, I suppose." I poured myself more of the wine. "I was wondering where I'd be sent next."

"Why not stay on Darkover? You say there is more to be done."

"No!" It came out sharper than I had intended. To soften it, I went on, "The going is always fine. It's the staying that gets you down. An error in my personality, no doubt. You see, I always thought there would be something between growing up and growing old. A period of grace between acne and wrinkles. But there isn't. I'm not young anymore. I have nothing to call my own. No home, no family, no . . . children . . . God, how could I have children? I'm still just a child myself." I took another drink of wine. "How I hate a maudlin drunk. Anyway, I—what was that?"

The cry surrounded us, coming again and again, echoing on itself, cutting through the wind and penetrating the stone walls.

"That, Janna, is a banshee. Nothing to laugh at if you're in the open, but here we're safe."

There was another scream, and not the banshee. "The horses!" I said, and headed for the door.

Darla stopped me. "They're in no danger. Eduin's stable-man will see to them. It's not for nothing he sleeps in the stables. And in any event, there's a connecting passage, remember? No going outside."

"Sorry," I said. "I guess I forgot. That thing shook me."

"That's just what it intended."

"Intended? You can't tell me it knows we're in here."

"No, of course not. Quite likely it's just strayed down here."

"Down? You mean this is down from something?"

She laughed shortly. "My, yes. This is just the foothills of the Hellers. Banshees live high up, way beyond the snow line. Although some were kept as mantrailers once, I suppose none of them were ever domesticated. It was just a matter of turning them onto the scent or whoever and whatever you didn't like, and letting them kill it. Then when they got hungry again they'd come back to where they were used to being fed. Of course that's been illegal for years."

"I seem to recall reading an account about something like that." I hesitated. "Is there any way I could get a look at that thing? We have some descriptions of banshees at Base File, but nothing else. Not even a photograph." I had to use the Terran word there; no Darkovan one existed. But one would come into being, I suspected. Cameras were among the few things that the Comyn Council expressed an interest in having.

As I peered through the tiny attic window, I could make out the shape of the banshee through the snow. Banshees, as ugly beasts go, are not the ugliest. I have seen worse, far worse, some harmless and some not, on various planets. I have seen uglier, as I say, and as I told Darla. But not on Darkover.

"How I'd like to get a clear photograph of that," I said.

"How would you like to do better than a photograph?" Darla asked.

"What do you mean?"

"How would you like to have some samples from it?" As we closed the shutters and turned to go back to the lower floors, and warmth, the torchlight flamed her coppery hair to brilliance and lit an imp of mischief in her eyes.

"Are you crazy? Without any decent weapons it'd be suicide."

"Nonsense. We have hunted them for hundreds of years. In some parts of the mountains it is regarded as quite a sport. Besides, it looks to me as if that one's taken this up as its winter range. We'd have Zandru's own time getting past him to Thendara, so we might as well set out to do the job right. It would be a favor to our hosts. Not to mention that your job here was to gather specimens of local animal life, *ni var?*"

"Yes. But that, as you very well know, was to help determine which might be of Terran origin, if any. You can't tell me that ever came from Terra." I paused. "You're right about getting past it, though, I suppose. Janet Rhodes: zoologist, ecologist, banshee slayer. How will that look in my file, do you think? Well, what do we need? Besides a couple of high-powered blasters."

She grinned, and that imp was closer than ever to the surface. "Tomorrow I'll ask Eduin if he still keeps hounds."

By morning the wind had nearly stopped. When Darla had mentioned the possibility of hunting the banshee, Eduin had been enthusiastic. He raised no objection to the Free Amazon's part in the hunt, but I got the feeling he definitely thought that the *domna Terranan* would be better left out of it. Only by telling him that all Terran women were *Com'hi letzii* of a sort, and that I was contracted to do just this kind of work, did she convince him that I should go along. I wasn't sure whether I was pleased with her success or not.

Immediately after breakfast we went to look at his hounds. They were tall, thin beasts with rough shaggy hair, mostly white with reddish spots. Their muzzles were short and broad and their eyes were small and deep-set. They looked like the result of a three-way cross between a bull terrier, a Saint Bernard, and an Irish wolfhound. Eduin was saying something rapidly in Cahuenga, but his dialect was one I had trouble following.

"He says," Darla translated, "that he has no catch-dogs—Sharra terriers he means, most likely—but that since these dogs are open trailers, we should do all right. Open trailers bay on the track, so there is less danger of losing them. Dogs that don't bay can catch up to the banshee and get killed by it before the hunters find them, unless they have some catch-dogs to worry it and keep it busy. These dogs are fast enough to catch it, but too slow to get out of the way, if it turns. So we'll have to keep close. Incidentally, this is one of the nicest packs of deafhounds you're ever likely to see."

"Deaf hounds?"

"Yes. They're deliberately selected to be deaf, so that the banshee can't panic them with its scream."

"I see," I said. "And what keeps it from panicking us?"

"Ah," she said, *"there's* the sport!"

"Hmm. Well, I wouldn't want to spoil the fun . . . but, assuming the hounds corner this thing, and we catch up to it before it tears them apart. . . ."

"Yes?"

"What do we do with it then?"

She smiled mischievously. "We *could* ask it to stay around for mid-winter festival. But I suggest we try to kill it."

"With what?"

"Oh!" She laughed, then turned to say something to Eduin. Whatever she said must have struck him as funny, too, for he chuckled as he hurried off.

"I don't see what's so funny," I remarked sourly. "It's not going to politely step into a trap, and it would take one hell of a snare to hold it. It's a bit bigger than a rabbithorn, I noticed. I'm not used to hunting things that would just as soon hunt me.''

Eduin came back, carrying several long spears. He handed one to each of us, and used his own to demonstrate a particularly vicious twisting motion.

"You *Terranan* talk too much," Darla said. "Just stay with the party, right?"

"I'll stay so close you'll wonder which of us is you," I said.

I'd thought I was pretty fit, after months of scrambling over rocks setting snares, climbing cliffs to get birds' eggs and samples of plant life, riding horses where they could go, and walking where they couldn't.

After the first half-hour learning to manage snowshoes, I was sweating in the sub-zero cold. My legs, arms, and back all ached. I couldn't have said whether it was desire to uphold the Terran reputation that kept me going, or just the knowledge that if I stopped I'd probably freeze to death.

It got a little easier after a while, but I was worn out by then. The hounds had opened trail and Eduin and his men were hurrying to keep up with them. Eduin saw me falling behind and called to the men, but Darla said something and waved them on. She dropped back and took my arm.

"Come over here," she said, and led me to a sheltered place between two rocks that had somehow remained clear of snow. "Now sit." She gathered up loose bits of dry lichen and twigs and laid a fire.

"I'm sorry," I said.

"Not your fault, mine. Jaelle, my oath-mother, always said I was foolhardy. Too impetuous. And you should know her. Anyone *she* said was too impetuous—Evanda and Avarra! What an idiot I am to bring a *Terranan* . . . no, to bring any lowlander up here and expect them to keep pace with folk born and bred to it.''

"I've got the knack of these snowshoes now. I can keep up."

"No, you can't," she said, matter-of-factly. "Nor could the Hastur himself, if he came here unprepared. Get up and walk around a bit or you'll stiffen. I'll have a proper fire going in a little."

"What a fool Eduin must think me," I said, tromping obediently around in a circle. "After all the trouble we had convincing him I should go along . . ."

"You are not the first lowlander to learn that the Hellers have their name for a reason. Nor will you be the last. Eduin will think none the less of you for it, and it will give him more cause to brag about his mountains. They are, for the mountain folk, like the horses of Armida—fine strong beasts, beautiful, impossible to forget . . . and just a bit dangerous to the unwary! Besides, if he should take it otherwise, well, what is that to us? We are no men to play at *kihar* . . . honor-games." She stood our snowshoes end-down in the snow well away from the fire, and took a small metal pot and a package of dried herbs from her pack.

The fire was going nicely already, and I was beginning to get warm and comfortable. "Darla . . ."

"Hmm?" She looked up from the "mountain tea" she was brewing with melted snow.

"The way you speak about the mountains . . . are you Cahuenga?"

"I am *Com'hi letzii*. Darla n'ha Margali. That is all the lineage I need. But as you are *Terranan*, and therefore curious, yes, I was born not many miles from here. Mhari is my mother's daughter."

"Mhari? Eduin's Mhari? Why, she scarcely even spoke to you!"

"I dare say she does not approve of me."

"But you are sisters!"

"We have a common parent. But we are not, we have

never been, *bredini.*" She paused. "Forgive me if I offend you, Janna, but you and I, after such a little time together, are closer than she and I could ever be."

I was staring away to valleys and mountains misted blue with distance. I was not insulted. Yet I was Janet Rhodes of the Service, born on Meadow (but, as Darla had said, *Terranan* for all that). Darkovans were still, after all these months, a puzzle to me. Shunning a touch at one moment, they were exuberantly emotional the next; cold, withdrawn, remote as the Hellers themselves, then suddenly offering unexpected intimacies. I had no ready answer.

"Ah," she said after a moment, "I have said the wrong thing again. I wonder if any Darkovan will ever understand any *Terranan.*"

Her words were so close to my thoughts that it made me smile.

"If any do," I said, "it will be someone like you. You mountain people are more like us than the lowlanders, I think."

"Now *I* must wonder whether to be pleased or insulted," she said, but she was smiling too. "Janna, we are all of us sisters in the Guild House, but we feel . . . there is a saying: 'Too much pride, perhaps. Too many horses, maybe. But never too much love or too many sisters.' "

"We have no similar saying," I said.

"No, I suppose you don't." She turned away. "Are you rested now? I think we could catch the hunt after all." We could still hear the hounds some way off.

"We have no similar saying," I repeated, "but perhaps we should . . . *breda.*"

"Oh, *breda,* I am so glad!" She clasped my hands in hers. There was a curious intimacy in the gesture that I found somehow unsettling. "I have wanted to say it for so long. Now you will not have to leave after all." She released my hands and gave me a hug. Then she drew away. "What is the matter?"

"I'm sorry. I—that is, this doesn't change that. I still have to leave."

"But why? Have the *Terranan* no will of their own? Can you not choose to go or stay?"

"Sometimes, yes. But not always. I'll never forget you, Darla, or the time we've spent together. But I must go. It is my job."

She was quiet for a moment. Even the baying of the hounds had stilled.

"You could stay. Other *Terranan* have stayed."

"But don't you understand? To stay—I would have to give up everything. My rank, my job—Darla, it's all I have and I've worked so hard."

"For what, if not the right to choose?"

"Well, what if I asked you to choose like that? To come away with me."

"This is my home. My world. But you have no home. No family. You told me that. *Breda,*" she said softly, "how can you think of leaving? You belong here."

"No I don't. I don't belong any-damn-where. As you said yourself, I am a Terran."

"No you are not! You are Janna . . . Janet Rhodes," she replied, stumbling a little over the still unfamiliar sound of my name to get it right. "Yourself! Not 'a Terran.' So impersonal! As you might say, 'a book,' 'a stone.' "

"I *am* a Terran," I repeated stubbornly.

"Well, then, so you are *Terranan*. I am Darkovan. And we are both of us women, both people, and we both have *laran*."

"What? No!" She was guessing, she must be, I thought. *Deny it, deny it!*

"Janna . . ."

"No. Leave me alone. I do not have—I will not—I am no freak!"

"Certainly not. Nor am I." She hesitated. "I did not mention this before, because you so clearly did not want it mentioned. But, it is there. Janna, if you lived in a world where everyone but you was blind and deaf, would you stop your ears and bandage your eyes? And if you did, would it mean you did not have eyes and ears? When I became one of the *Com'hi letzii* I gave up every tie with the world and the past, save the binding of the Oath of Unbinding itself. But I did not, I could not, give up *laran*, any more than I could give up being *tallo*. Your *laran*, shielded and blocked as it is, is a gift too pure and strong to hide. You have only to open yourself to it, *breda*."

"No." All the carefully normal years, the words weighed so that they would not betray me . . . and here, after a few short months, she knew. "This is ridiculous," I said. "I don't know what you're talking about."

"Must trust always come so hard for you? You have been hurt so often you must hurt back. But we will not hurt you, *chiya*. I promise."

It was a promise that was broken before she made it. Why, why could she not leave me alone?

"None of us are alone, *chiya*."

"Get out of my mind, damn you!"

"I can't. Not while you are shouting like that. Every telepath this side of the Kadarin must have a headache by now."

I took a deep breath. "All right. All right. I'm sorry," I said. "You just don't understand."

"No, I don't," she said, "and neither do you. You speak the language very well, but you do not know what the words mean. You have. . . ."

The baying of the hounds sounded suddenly, frighteningly near, and so did another sound, like the breathing of some huge thing hard-pressed.

"Zandru take Eduin and his open trailers!" she exclaimed. "They've turned the hell-begotten beast back here!"

"Why didn't we hear them sooner?"

"They must have lost the trail. Been casting for it while the Zandru-damned beast circled around. Thanks be to Avarra they caught the scent before the banshee caught us! Get these things back into the rocks." She tossed a bundle at me. While she had talked, Darla had been working rapidly and efficiently, covering the fire with snow and stuffing everything back into our packs. I stood and stared, feeling worse than helpless.

"Go on!" she said, pushing me toward the rocks. "Get up there. Hurry! Unless you want to be a banshee's journey-bread." I went, and she followed closely behind me, stopping only to collect the snowshoes and spears on her way. She scrambled past me up the rocks, agile as a rabbithorn, then turned and pulled me up. All the while, the snuffling of the banshee and the baying of the hounds was getting louder.

We reached what seemed to me a rather doubtful safety, a high crevasse in the rocks, a slit like lips parted in a narrow grin, just as the banshee lumbered into the opening where we'd had our fire.

"You say you've seen worse?" Darla whispered.

The banshee swung its head from side to side, sensing the warmth of the dead fire, of the approaching hounds, and certainly of us. The head was naked, a skull covered in folds of wrinkled skin. The skin draped itself about the hooked beak, filled the hollows where eyes should be, and hung in unhealthy-looking bluish-scarlet layers along the neck. I knew that it was nearly deaf as well as blind, dependent on sensing heat and motion, but when it turned its head our way I held my breath and tried to sink down into the rocks. Even from where we were I could smell it, fouling the cold air.

"I lied," I whispered. "I was wrong. There isn't worse."

Then the hounds caught up to their quarry and the nightmare got worse, if that is possible. The pack was all around it, leaping and snarling, hanging from its beast's flesh like tumors, but it did not seem to feel them at all. It slashed with beak and talons, and two hounds were flung aside, bloody and dying.

I had the feeling I was about to be sick. Violently sick. The horror of the banshee was more than its odor, its scream . . . and suddenly I knew why it was so awful. The animal, nearly mindless, was at the same time a kind of telepath. A transmitter transmitting pure terror. The terror of insanity, uncontrolled paranoia. It screamed raw madness. The deafhounds, themselves telepathic to a degree, were responding to it as Terran dogs never would. It was driving them to a senseless fury that made them heave themselves against it again and again, careless of pain and death. I could feel Darla tremble beside me. She leaned over and vomited, dry retching heaves.

"Darla," I said, "don't. Shut it out." I had to grit my teeth between the words, but at least I could speak them. "Block it! It is only an animal. A stupid beast."

She looked directly at me, but I knew she didn't hear what I was saying. Her eyes were wide open, staring at nothing, green irises only a thin line around huge black pupils.

Her breath was coming in shuddering gasps and I could feel her heart pounding against her ribs. I didn't know what to do, but I did know that she couldn't go on like that. If the fear didn't kill her, she would go mad. I grabbed her shoulders and shook her. She was rigid in my hands. I slapped her, then again, harder, but I might as well have been striking a wooden doll. I could feel the growing chill of her flesh even through my gloves. Suddenly she stopped trembling. It was as if her body had given up the battle, leaving her alone in her mind. If she was breathing, it was very shallowly. I couldn't be certain. I stripped off a glove and felt for the pulse in her throat. The instant my hand touched her bare skin, the full force of her panic, the banshee-inspired madness, washed through me. I think I may have screamed. Then the . . . the blindness . . . came to my rescue. I pulled my hand away and was free. But Darla wasn't. I couldn't leave her to that. I was almost as afraid of what I would have to do as I was of the banshee itself. Quickly, before I had too much time to think about it, I pulled off the other glove and took her face between my hands. The fear was more bearable this time, perhaps because I had been expecting it.

"No," I said aloud. "Darla, listen. You have to hear me! None of this is real. This is something that does not exist. What is down there is only a beast, a stupid, foul, ugly beast."

I looked for some sign of awareness in her stare. At last it came and I remembered to breathe. Darla took a deep breath, then another, easier, and brought her hands up to cover mine. She closed her eyes for a moment, and I could feel her senses steadying. When she looked at me again, it was Darla, and it was as if none of the hell had ever been.

Down below us, dogs were still being killed, the banshee was still screaming, and it was still awful. But it was a normal horror, no nightmare. Eduin and his hunters had caught up with the banshee, and rushed to the aid of the hounds. Darla rolled away from me, then smiled a ghost of a smile and reached her hand down for mine, to help me stand.

"Thank you, *breda*," she said. "Now let's get down there and help kill that refugee from the Pit." She grabbed her spear and lowered herself down the rock. I didn't give myself time to think about that, either. I followed her. We were, after all, *bredini*.

About Barbara Armistead and "On the Trail"

Barbara Armistead says of herself that she was born in the vintage year 1929, edited her college magazine, "wrote the usual morbid poetry," then married, had four children and divorced in 1979. She credits her interest in writing to the fact that her "kids conned [her] into joining a Star Trek fan club." She has also acquired along the way six grandchildren. "Some days I'm two years older than Methuselah, some days I'm still sixteen." That, I think describes most of us who write for this anthology. After she had "come down from the ceiling" of the acceptance of her first professionally submitted story, Barbara reminded me that we had met at Worldcon in Los Angeles the summer of 1984, but correctly surmised that I had "met so many people, they wound up as an endless blur."

The main characters in this story, Rima and Lori, are, as most readers will remember, from Kindra's band in The Shattered Chain.

MZB

ON THE TRAIL

by Barbara M. Armistead

"Such a trip!" Rima tugged impatiently at a girth strap. "First, a cast shoe, then a broken pack saddle, a rainstorm like an inverted ocean, and now a washed-out trail! What next?"

Lori laughed, and carefully turned the stag pony in its path. She lined the pack animals up cautiously, and then mounted her own bay gelding.

"Don't fret, Rima. I know you're impatient, but traveling in the Hellers is always an uncertain thing."

" 'Tis not! It's as certain as death and winter storms; you can always expect trouble. Why Lisa ever picked such an out of the way place for a healing center, Avanda alone knows!"

"Peobably because they needed it more than some civilized place, wouldn't you guess?"

"Oh, Lori—I'm just grumbling. Let's try to find that trail you told me about. *This* one's no good anymore."

"It should be back about an hour's travel. I think I spotted it last night, just before the trail shelter."

Lori led the way down the sodden trail. The heavy rains after the spring thaw had turned the low spots into a morass, but Darkover's landscape is predominantly vertical and drains quickly. An occasional freshet leapt down the mountainside and tumbled in clamorous haste to the river below them. A few hopeful blossoms smiled in the grass and birds worked frantically to make nests for their families in the Hellers'

short-lived summer. They passed the trail shelter where they
had spent the night, and the stag ponies looked hopefully at
the feed bins. Lori chirped at them and passed resolutely on.
Rima brought up the end of their little caravan, her bulk
mounted on an immense gray mare.

The trail Lori sought was overgrown, and obviously un-
used. She pushed through the tangle of underbrush and pointed
proudly at a cairn piled carefully to one side.

"See—my father told me about that marker. I hope the rest
of the trail is still in passable shape."

"I hope so, too. I'm eager for a real bed and a real meal.
Trail rations are so—well, so bland, so all the same." Rima's
love of good food was evident in her bounteous contours, and
her ability to make a comfortable camp almost anywhere was
legendary. Lori, on the other hand, was lean and muscular, a
tomboy raised by her father on the traders' trails of the
Hellers. Discomfort was a relative thing for her; any shelter
would do, and Rima sometimes claimed that she never even
noticed what she ate.

The trail rose over a steep pass, and then dropped abruptly
to a narrow valley. They paused to rest the animals at a
sheltered spot near the crest of the trail, and ate a lunch of
meat rolls and dried fruit, washed down with icy water from a
spring. Snow fields stretched above them, and below them
was an awesome drop. The stream drifted away in misty
ribbons to join a merry cascade to the valley floor.

"Nice country," Rima shuddered. "Now I know why the
traders use the other trail."

"Banshee country up above, I bet. Let's go."

"Who made this trail, anyway? Any idea?"

"Sure. Bandits. Used to be a gang who lived in the valley,
and raided the traders and travelers regularly. The last of
them were killed off just a few years ago. There's not much
trade here anymore. These hill families have mostly died out.
Too much inbreeding—idiots, sickly kids, everything. And

famine. Used to see it when we were traveling, a lot. One valley—no crops, skinny kids begging scraps. Two valleys over, nut trees breaking down with crops, granaries overflowing. No communication. This country needs roads! Some way for people to circulate around a bit—'' She stopped abruptly, holding up her hand to signal to Rima. The trail was too narrow for Rima to move up and see what Lori had spotted, and she had to content herself with craning and peering over the trail edge.

''What's that?''

''Horses—and men. They're coming up the valley—looks like they're local. No packs. Too far to tell. Let's go on down.'' The trail descended in switchbacks; Rima watched the approaching group in a series of vignettes as they progressed. It became obvious that at least one rider in the other group was traveling under duress. He seemed to be bound to the saddle, and one of the others led his pony. They took a turn into a canyon which opened into the valley and disappeared from sight, apparently without spotting Lori and Rima.

''They didn't expect anyone on this trail, so they didn't look for anyone,'' Lori surmised. ''Looks like dirty work to me. Do we investigate or keep going?''

''Oh, dear—the goddess knows I want to keep going, But I suppose it's better to check up than leave possible trouble on the trail behind us. They *may* have seen us, and ducked out of sight until we passed. Any ideas?''

''I think we'll go on as if we hadn't seen them, just in case. See that grove of resin trees? Good place to pull off the trail. No one can tell from that canyon whether we stopped or kept going. I'll circle back on foot and see what I can find out. You can fix some supper and keep an eye on the animals.''

''Sounds good to me. Get along, horse; there's rest ahead.''

A short time later, Lori was perched in a feathery nut tree overlooking the canyon floor. She had reached her vantage point by elaborate and silent methods, but was now aware she could have approached with drums and cymbals like a Drytown lord, and not have been noticed. Three men lounged around a fire in front of a rude shelter of stone and thatch, and circulated a bottle, obviously not the first of the day. A trick of the wind blew their conversation to her in gusts and snatches.

"Stupid red-haired bastard! Fell into our hands like a ripe fruit—family'll pay well—he–he–he'll write the message soon's he sees how cold it gets here nights—just like Daddy used to do—" The rest disintegrated into raucous laughter. Lori slid down the tree and trotted swiftly toward the grove. Evening was approaching and she had the beginnings of a plan.

"They're kidnappers, apparently the offspring of the scum who used to operate hereabouts. Two of them look like twins, and the other might be their younger brother. None of them look very bright, but that one drools like a real moron. They're trying to follow in Daddy's footsteps, and they've caught some stupid local lordling with his pants down and are going to hold him for ransom."

"And we are going to—what? Go on to Ensendara like sensible people and tell someone in authority where to find them? Or behave like heroes in a ballad and rescue him, thus earning his undying gratitude and a skin full of holes?"

"If we go to Ensendara, the stupid man may be dead before anyone gets back here. They're going to try to freeze him into writing a ransom note. Guess they can't write themselves."

"And it's going to freeze, isn't it? Or close enough. Oh, hades, I hate things like this! I told you traveling in the Hellers was a sure way to find trouble."

"They're drunk, Rima. About three-bottle drunk, or I miss my guess. All we have to do is wait a bit, and when they drowse off, we snatch their lordling and leave. No fight, no fuss. They wouldn't hear an army of rotting cralmacs in an hour or so."

"Oh, all right. I guess we can't even leave a *man* to freeze to death."

"No, we can't. Hey, pass that soup over here. I'm hungry, too!"

Dusk was deepening into night when they approached the campsite in the canyon. They tethered the animals well back from the hut, and crept carefully to the shelter of some rocks near the clearing. A quick survey showed no guard on duty, and the smoldering remnants of the fire revealed no trace of the kidnappers.

"Now what?" whispered Rima.

"I think they're in the shelter—but where's their captive? Not in there nice and warm unless he's already agreed to write a note. Let's see—there are the ponies, in that shed behind—we'll need one for him to ride. I wonder if I can saddle one without a fuss."

"Be careful. I'll keep looking for him." Rima, despite her bulk, was as silent as a catman when she needed to be. As Lori slipped into the shed, she heard a snorting snore from the shelter.

"Drunk as lords. They're a fine bunch of kidnappers. Maybe they think no one will bother to follow them." She chose the largest pony, and swiftly saddled and bridled him, breathing a prayer that he was not one to object violently when first mounted. She led him carefully from the shelter and tethered him near the other horses. By the time she returned, Rima was waiting. Lori slid silently down beside her.

"It's getting cold fast, and I can't find your man anywhere. Did you get the pony?"

"Yes. I bet he's in the shelter. He was earlier, and they were probably too drunk to move him."

"That's the only place that's left. So how do we get him out?"

"I guess I go in and get him. Do you have the lantern?"

"Yes. Here—be careful. I'll be by the door."

Lori lifted the latch and eased the rickety door open enough to slide in. There was no fire in the tiny hearth; three heavily bundled figures snorted and snuffled in front of the door. In a back corner, there was a darker shadow. A gleam from Lori's lantern revealed a young man, bound and gagged, who had been stripped to his underwear. As Lori could feel the cold through her heavy trail clothes, she was sure he must be chilled clear through. She stepped carefully over the snoozing kidnappers and drew one of her knives to cut the bonds. At her touch the still figure toppled sideways. At first she thought he was dead, but a quick check revealed a pulse, weak but steady. She slashed the ropes, and lifted him carefully over her shoulder. She sheathed her knife and breathed a prayer of thanks that he was slight of build. Grasping the lantern, she turned carefully and started for the door. As she maneuvered around the bandits, she was suddenly grasped around the ankle.

"He–he–he–he—gotcha, you red-haired son of a bitch! How'd you get loose, anyway?" A sharp tug overbalanced Lori, who fell sideways, swinging the lantern as she went. The flame flared as oil slopped across the floor. "Hey, you ain't him! Wake up, Lugo! We got company."

Lori struggled under the weight of the helpless body, striving to reach her knife, to get her feet under, and to avoid the tiny flames which ran across the floor. The idiot was waking up, and the other form stirred to life, while her assailant held her ankle and yelled in drunken delight. He seemed not to notice the perilous fire in his glee at capturing an intruder. At last the kidnapee tumbled clear, and Lori grasped the knife at her waist. Wrenching her body in a circle, she slashed at the grasping hand at her ankle and was treated to a scream and a curse. The ankle was free. She drew her feet under her, and crouched to spring. The idiot rolled on the floor, spattering bits of flaming straw about as he yammered in confusion and fright.

The third brother was up at last, and groping desperately for his knife. The brother who had grabbed Lori was nursing his wounded hand, but when he saw a chance, lunged again at Lori. She leapt sideways, and he sprawled across the idiot, who began pummeling him vigorously.

"Rima! Rima! Give me a hand! This man's unconscious!" Lori slipped her second knife from its sheath at the back of her neck, and turned to face brother number three, who had at last drawn his knife. The litter of tumbling bodies and flickering firelight made a real knife fight impractical, but Lori knew too well that a slip or trip could be fatal, even when fighting drunks. The door sprang open under Rima's weight and the gust of fresh air fanned the flames to new life.

"Which one?" yelled Rima, surveying the mess on the floor.

"The one who's got no clothes on! Get him out—wrap him up—he's freezing!"

"Not too likely, in this mess," remarked Rima, but she grasped the nearly nude body by the quickest vantage points and started dragging him over the brothers who were trying to disentangle themselves on the floor. One of them made a desperate grab for him, and Rima planted a large foot on the hand, shifted her weight, and continued toward the door. Her victim's scream blended with a roar of rage from the third brother, as he charged across the floor at Lori. It would have been more effective if he had not tripped over a stray blanket and almost fallen headlong. His knife grazed Lori's tunic as he sailed past her. She sidestepped, turned, and brought the hilt of her knife sharply down between his shoulder blades. His momentum carried him a bit farther, but he caught himself before his face crashed into the wall. Intoxication had made him belligerent, but his coordination had suffered. As he turned, Lori brought her foot up in a fast snap kick and he doubled up, bellowing in rage and pain. Just then the idiot discovered his tunic was smoldering and rose up in a great muddle of blankets, brother and straw. Rima cuffed him swiftly and he went tumbling again, but his leg caught the back of Lori's ankle, knocking it sideways. She went down, but caught herself with one hand. Brother number three charged at her blindly, and she threw up her left hand in an instinctive guard. Her knife slashed across his chest and upper arm and he catapulted over her to a crash landing against the stone wall. The first brother started to crawl for the door, and Rima forestalled the movement by clipping him briskly alongside the head with a broken stool.

Lori regained her feet and hurdled the intervening mess to help Rima with the object of the rescue. He was showing signs of returning to life with a pugnaciousness that Rima squelched by wrapping him firmly in such blankets as she could snatch from the confusion. His indignant face soon glared at them from a grubby cocoon.

"You'd better do something about that fire, Lori," Rima suggested mildly. "Unless, of course, you want to roast these toads alive."

Lori sheathed her knives and scanned the tiny building. Spotting a bucket in the corner, she seized it and spattered its contents over the idiot and the floor, which showed the most signs of conflagration.

"Zandru take you for a misbegotten fool!" yelled one of the brothers, as an incredibly noxious odor filled the air. Choking and gasping, they all charged for the door, Rima dragging her swaddled charge behind her.

"You ninny! That was the slop bucket!"

"How was I to know? You wanted the fire out, didn't you? Well, it's out!"

"And so are we. I'm not going back in there. I'd rather freeze!"

"You're so right! But we've got to do something."

"I know. You tie up these bully boys and I'll build a good fire here where they were this afternoon, and hang a tarpaulin from those trees so it reflects the heat. With cloaks and things we should be all right till morning. Keep those worthless horse droppings down wind."

"Gladly. Especially *that* one!" Their victims seemed somewhat subdued; apparently their captors' speed and unusual choice of methods had bewildered them past any attempt to escape.

The next hour was busy. By the flickering light of the fire Lori and Rima bandaged, bundled, and tied. Their lordling had returned to querulous life and was busy expressing gratitude, shock at finding his rescuers were women, and irritation at the loss of his clothing, which apparently concerned him almost as much as his brush with death. Finally Lori silenced him by asking if he wished to go find his clothes among the slops, as she was perfectly prepared to let him. After that he sulked.

Rima finished her medical ministrations and began preparing grain tea. As she served a steaming cup to the rescuee, she asked, "And how do we address you, honored sir? I'd like to know more about this miserable mess and these equally miserable brigands."

Their acquisition turned a petulant face to the fire, and replied with a pomposity unsuited to his scruffy condition, "I am Dom Estoril Calavera, and my father is overlord of most of this valley. These—these unspeakable trash thought to demand ransom from him, and captured me as I was returning from a—um, er—a social evening in Ensendara. I stopped to answer a call of nature and they jumped on me. They must have been following me in the forest."

"I said they caught him with his pants down!" Lori crowed. "Spent a 'social evening' in some stew in town and went home half drunk. Never knew he was being followed."

"Why," inquired Rima mildly, "did you not write the

ransom note? Surely your father would have paid, or followed them in an attempt to rescue you!''

"Surely he would have, and then beat me soundly. But I
would have written the note, and gladly, except—''

"Except what?'' Rima prompted.

"Except that I cannot write! I am a gentleman, not a
cursed *Cristoforo* scribe!''

Lori collapsed in delighted laughter. When at last she
wiped her eyes, Rima rebuked her gently.

"For shame, Lori. Most of the 'gentlemen' of Darkover
are at the mercy of scribes and accountants who learned their
trade at Nevarsin, may the good monks be praised. Remember that the Renunciates *made* you learn to read and cipher,
so that no man could cheat you through your own ignorance.
Perhaps Lia can find some one of the Sisterhood who can
start a small school for those who would learn also.''

"With special classes in ransom note, perhaps.''

"No, I think kidnapping will go out of style when we get
these three to Ensendara. Now, do you keep the first watch,
or shall I? I refuse to let these pigs get all the sleep, and I
hope they have heads like rotting squash by morning!''

"You get some sleep, Rima. I'll watch, and I'm sorry this
wasn't as simple as I promised.''

"Lori, Lori—never since I met you has anything been as
simple as you hoped it would, and yet I keep on believing
you. So who's to blame? Call me in a couple of hours, little
one. And after *you* sleep, we will go to Ensendara. I shall be
very glad to get an honest meal.''

About P. Alexandra Riggs and "To Open a Door"

When she submitted this story to me, the author wrote, "This is my first attempt at writing. I have wanted to write all my adult life, but feared to expose my philosophy to rejection. Your work has made me less afraid to expose myself."

One of the things I always tell young writers is that to be a writer is a paradoxical state. A writer must remain very sensitive, keeping all her emotions close to the surface, or she will not be sufficiently aware to portray emotions faithfully. At the same time, the first experience of virtually every writer is rejection, so she must develop something like rhinoceros hide—able to cope with the inevitable rejections; otherwise criticism will destroy her. I have had to learn to take my own advice, and learn to ignore the criticisms of others while at the same time learning from the constructive criticism of editors and other knowledgeable people, while being able to dismiss from my mind the attacks of those who don't know what they're talking about.

Fortunately, perhaps, I did not need to expose P. Alexandra Riggs to that rejection at such an early stage. When I accepted the story she wrote that she was the mother of six adult children and the grandmother of three; that she had been a rape crisis *counselor, therapy group facilitator, crisis clinic and suicide hotline counselor and a retail store manager. It is a curious commentary on our society that she has been paid only for being a retail store manager. She lives on a small farm in Fallon, Nebraska.*

MZB

TO OPEN A DOOR

by P. Alexandra Riggs

The dreamer stirred. Her hand stroked the rough bed covering then stilled. Within her dream beauty swirled and sang.

"I love you, love you," he whispered into her auburn hair. *The words were like strong wine to her. The warmth of his breath on her cheek, the strength of his hand at her waist inflamed her senses.*

Laughing she pulled back to see him better.

"You are like a prisoner." He breathed heavily. *"She has no right to jail you."*

His hand moved to the small of her back pulling her to him. "Dance with me, dance and be free."

Then pivoting, he swung her into a stately spin. Her skirt whirled about her, the rich blue fabric swirling like a deep pool at her feet.

"Millim, time to rise."

At the sound of her mother's voice Millim woke, the music of the dance fading into nothingness.

The crude pallet she shared with her mother was still warm in the chill autumn morning. Millim snuggled under the fur cover, reluctant to start the day's drudgery.

"Come along, now. I've warm milk."

Her mother meant well, she knew, but Millim longed for hot bread and meat, not milk still warm from the beast.

And wine, she thought. *And beautiful gowns to whirl in.*

"Up with you, now." Her mother's voice was impatient. "We've beans to pick and cheese to make."

"Mother, don't you think of anything but work?"

Surprised at the sullen tone, Buartha stopped short at her task and looked at her daughter.

"Don't you yearn to be free from work, Mother? Do you never long for parties . . . long to dance?"

Buartha's face twisted in anguish. "Never!" She saw her daughter flinch. "Do not desire your own destruction, child." Buartha's voice held the certainty of ruin. "Wine, dance . . . men." Her tone sank into a litany of doom. "Men use . . . take . . . destroy."

Buartha stroked her daughter's hair. "I know that our life is hard, child." Auburn strands caught in the cuts and calluses of her hand. "But we are free. We submit to no man. Free . . . child. *We* live free."

"But *I'm* not free." Millim pushed her mother's hand away. "You call this freedom?" Her gesture encompassed the dingy hovel. "We slave . . . and still we live like animals." Millim stood and began to pull her clothes over her head. A long moment passed. "Mother I dream . . ." Her voice softened. "Such beautiful dreams. . . . Feasts, with meat roasted crisp; wine and the tables laden so as to break." Millim stared into a far distance. "Voices singing. . . ." She swayed gently. "Music, laughter, dancing . . . and gowns." Fingering her rough skirt, she looked up at her mother. "Gowns so full and rich—" she turned slowly with her arms spread wide—"they stand away from you as you turn." Abruptly dropping to the pallet, she buried her face in the fur and sobbed. "Mother how do I know this? How do I see such things?"

"You dream, child. That is all. You just dream." Within her heart Buartha was deeply troubled. *Oh gods . . . it is* laran," she thought. *Millim is growing to womanhood and the* laran *wakes*. Painful memories of her own awakening telepathy swept over Buartha. The most skillful of Darkovan telepaths, Leonie, Keeper of Arilinn Tower, had judged her gift modest, taught her control, then sent her back to her ambitious father.

Her father had greeted her with sneers and drunken fury at what he had seen as her deliberate failure to fulfill his ambitions. As she had always been a cherished child, she had not understood his anger, nor his drunken appraisal of her ripening shape.

"I did my best, Daddy." She had felt hollow inside from his rejection. "The *laran* . . . it wasn't strong, I . . . I just wasn't good."

"Good?" His breath had reeked of sour wine as he shook her viciously, then pushed her out into the street. "This is what you're good for now," he snarled as he scanned the street. He had sold her as a night's sport to a passing stranger, an equally drunk Comyn noblelord.

The stranger's projected lust had engulfed her; the pain as he took his pleasure had overwhelmed her. To protect her innermost self from violation worse than the ongoing violation of her body, she had blocked her *laran* completely until she felt it no more.

Filled with terror, she had fled from defilement, lust, and failure. Her reason paralyzed from shock, she had wandered for days, higher and higher into the Hellers until, at last, she had stumbled into this tiny hollow which she had then barricaded from the world. As time passed she had erased even the memory of *laran* and the easier, more elegant life she had led.

Now, after living more than sixteen years in total isolation with the child born of that terror, she remembered. Aloud she spoke brusquely. "This world is all there is for us, Millim, and the beans and cheese must be tended, else when snow covers the Hellers we will starve."

*   *   *

The triumphant scream of the banshee echoed against the rocks of the cliff and Togaim could hear answering cries through the Pass of Scarvel. It seemed as though every banshee in the Hellers was circling closer for a sure meal.

"Don't move, my Lady," he whispered to the Lady Snava. "Silence may help us escape the fate of the others."

He heard the soft jingle of her decorative chains as she sought to move farther into a small cleft in the solid bank. "Be silent." The pain of the gash in his side made his command sound a cry.

What a fool I was to take this duty, he thought. *Success would have meant promotion, but failure. . . .* He looked at the blood streaming down his belly. *And to die here without chance of honorable battle . . . to hide quivering like a rabbithorn trembling in its hole . . . what a fool's task."* Togaim spat in disgust. *"And for what? To deliver a spoiled wife to her even more spoiled master so that he might take his pleasure in the field.*

Death seemed certain. While the banshees gorged on the dead, Togaim thought they were fairly safe from the blind predators, but only if they did not move. The vile beasts depended on movement or warmth to find their prey. To move meant swift and sure death under the vicious talons and beaks of the huge birds. *If I could only reach my sword,* he thought.

It lay beyond his reach under the inert body of one of the pack animals. Togaim shuddered as the banshee ripped at the dead brute, gouging entrails and tearing antlers off in its eagerness to feed. "No hope with a feeding frenzy in progress." Togaim groaned aloud.

The nearest beast cocked its head to locate the source of the sound, then advanced toward him. Togaim pressed back against Lady Snava and prepared to die.

The sweet smell of blood gagged him as the curved beak ripped into the flesh of his chest. He fell full length backward on top of Lady Snava. The cleft crumbled inward under their combined weight. Falling dirt and stones rattled down, partially sealing them from the banshee. The rock fall seemed to have turned the cleft into a tiny cave.

A dimly lit edge just above their heads disappeared into the distance. The splash of water sounded faintly from beyond the far end of the ledge.

Togaim moaned and tried to lift his head. The movement caused him to gasp in pain. "Lady, can you see?"

"He tries . . . but can not reach us, sire." The jingling of her chains as she knelt to speak was the last thing Togaim remembered as he sank into unconsciousness.

"Those trails are too steep for a woman of my age, not to mention my size." Ramhara grumbled as she sat on a rock to remove a stone from her boot.

"Come on, Ramhara." Cara stood impatiently before the older woman. "We must reach the shelter before nightfall or risk our necks to the banshee. 'Tis fall, time of feeding frenzy."

The two women were similarly dressed in the loose breeches, heavy tunics and boots of the Free Amazon. Both carried long knives, just short of being swords. Otherwise a greater contrast could not be imagined. Ramhara was short and quite stocky. Her short gray hair still had a ginger cast to it as it curled softly from under the identifying white coif of a midwife and around her full cheeks. She appeared gentle and grandmotherly, only the confidence of her bearing warning that there might be more of sternness to her.

Cara was tall, lean, and sinewy. Her tightly curled hair hugged her head in crisp brown ringlets so short that at first glance she seemed to be a man. She was an *emmasca*, a woman who had found no peace in womanhood and so had undergone the illegal neutering operation. Her weathered face softened as she crinkled her eyes in amusement at her friend. "I told you to exercise for strength on the trip."

"And then my discomfort would have been months longer," retorted Ramhara with a laugh.

In the distance a screech sounded.

Ramhara stopped laughing to listen. "Banshee!" she cried. "They have something big."

Cara pulled her friend to her feet and started running back along the trail toward a stand of trees. "Hear how many there are." She gasped as she ran. "It must be the start of a frenzy. The sounds will attract every banshee around." She stopped at a huge umbrella-root tree, scrutinized the space beneath the gnarled roots, then started pulling at the leaves and debris collected there. "Help me enlarge this hole," she said.

"Can we make it hold both of us?" Ramhara began prying with a large limb at a crack between two roots.

Cara paused. "*Breda*—" she felt the casta word for sister soothe her as she spoke. "Where there is room for one we will make room for both."

Another screech sounded virtually on top of them.

"Hurry." Ramhara desperately pushed with the limb. "I have no desire to join their party." She threw her considerable weight against the limb. "Especially since I suspect that we would become the main course in this feast."

At last the roots came free. Both women crept into the den they had created behind the barrier of roots. The frenzy continued around them as the long day passed into night, and the women, safe within their cage of roots, prepared for sleep.

As night fell within the cavern of crumbled rock Togaim moaned weakly then sank deeper into his coma. Snava knew that without help he would die. She had stanched the flow of blood with her scarf, but that was all she could do without water to clean his terrible wounds. They would fester and poison him. Already he burned with fever.

Snava was faced with a dilemma. Were her hands not chained she might have been able to pull Togaim free from the rocks. Her chains, though decorative, effectively prevented her from moving him. Metal bracelets on her wrists with the attaching chain threaded through a firm loop at her waist made movement of one hand totally dependent on the other.

In Dry-Town tradition the length of chain denoted caste and standing. As first consort to Jolder, Lord of Shainsa, her chain was fashionably short. So short that she could reach only to her mouth with one hand before the other was drawn up to the loop at her waist. This put the ledge, with its chance for water, beyond her reach. She could not even pull herself farther away from the still prowling banshee.

Always she had been protected. Always servants had attended to her needs. Caged, coddled, and pampered she had never made a decision, never helped herself. Now she could not. Snava wept.

The dreamer turned restlessly in the dawning light, then cried aloud. "I'm trapped . . . I will die. Oh Gods, I'm afraid. . . ." She tore at the bars of her prison with desperate hands as the tears streamed down her cheeks. "Help me . . . please someone help me."

Cara grasped at Ramhara's flailing hands. "I'm here, Ramhara," she whispered. "You are safe, *breda*. The frenzy is done."

"Goddess," said Ramhara with a shiver. She stared at her ripped fingers and then at the broken tree roots. "I've not had nightmares like that for forty years or more. Not since I left the Tower." She ruefully grinned at her friend. "You'd think me an untried maiden with *laran* running wild."

"Was that what it was, *breda?*" Cara was still concerned.

"Yes. . . ." Ramhara seemed lost in thought. "Yes it was. Someone near is projecting too wildly to be a disciplined *leronics* . . . and too strongly to be left untrained."

Ramhara began to squeeze through the protective roots. "We must find her, Cara. . . . *Laran* that strong will drive her mad if left untrained."

Stooping, Cara crept from their cramped sanctuary. "I feel as though I'd spent the night in a cell." She laughed as she stretched. "Goddess, it's good to be alive." She nodded toward the pass rising above them. "Do you think your potential *leronis* is there?"

"Yes, I do." Ramhara shivered. "She seems to be trapped and frightened, perhaps that's why her projection was so strong."

Cara looked at her friend with horror. "The frenzy . . . Ramhara . . . she has been trapped by banshees."

The two Renunciates stared in revulsion at the carnage below. The banshees had left no body intact. The ground had run red with the blood of more than twenty animals. Cralmer guard, servant, beast of burden. All had died.

"Nothing survived that." Cara was pale.

"She lives, Cara." Ramhara started resolutely down to the massacre. "I feel her near."

They walked through a silence so absolute that it seemed even the song birds mourned the dead. Ramhara broke the heavy silence reluctantly. "I fear she has lost consciousness." She looked around uncertainly. "The images grow weaker."

"Look here, Ramhara." Cara began digging at a new rockfall. "See this?" She held a gilded tunic aloft. " 'Tis the style worn by Dry-Town guards."

"Listen. . . ."

Soft sobs were faintly audible. Kneeling to help Cara,

Ramhara uncovered a man's boot. They both intensified their efforts.

" 'Tis a guard." Cara gently removed a large stone from off of the young man's pelvis. "He's in bad shape, *breda.*"

Ramhara moved into the tiny cavern to help Cara pull the young guard free from the remaining rocks. Deeper in the cavern she saw a dark shape huddled against a ledge, sobbing. "I thirst. . . . I am so thirsty." Then she exclaimed, "Goddess . . . it's her. . . . Cara, she's chained."

Ramhara knelt to help the chained woman drink from her water jug. "You'll be all right," she soothed. "You're safe now." She shuddered as she glimpsed the woman's hands. The fingers were raw from attempts to climb the ledge. Finding no other injuries, Ramhara turned with dread to the wounded man. "Cara, I need more water."

Cara vaulted to the ledge, followed the splashing sound to its source, filled her jug with the cool water and brought it back to the midwife.

"My skill may not be enough for the size of your wounds, lad," Ramhara then said softly to her unconscious patient, as she cleansed the sores with the water Cara brought. "But you can not help babies into the world for more than forty years without learning something of the healer's art."

At last, Ramhara straightened up, hands pressed to the small of her back. "I can do no more here, *breda.*" Her face showed the strain of her long effort. "His wounds are clean now, but I fear the infection has taken a strong hold." She sat with her back to the ledge. "I brought so little medicine."

Her tired eyes fell on the chained woman, still huddled but no longer sobbing. She noticed now what she had failed to see before. "Ah, Lady . . ." she sighed. "You jewel your fetters. Is slavery then so sweet to you?"

Snava's voice was hoarse from weeping. "Decent women do not go forth otherwise. I am a decent woman. First consort of Lord Jolder."

"*Mestra.*" Cara's tone was patient. "We care not for your master's rank. Have *you* no name?"

"Snava." The answer was barely audible. "Lady Snava of Shainsa." She looked up at Cara. "That's mid sand desert. I was journeying to meet my master when . . ." Her throat constricted.

"Cara. . . ." Ramhara sounded puzzled. "She is not the one. She has no *laran.*"

Buartha shelled beans steadily in the early-morning light. *Soon time to milk and feed.* she thought. Luck had brought her the crippled *fuar-gabhar,* heavy with young, that first year. Even better luck had been the birth of twin kids, one a male, that spring. The mountain fur-goats ran wild in the Hellers but a broken leg had made this one easy to tame. *Yes indeed,* she thought as she poured beans into a large, crude basket. *A dam and a sire. . . . no need to leave our refuge . . . ever.*

She hefted the basket to judge its weight. *Should just about do us.* She set the basket down carefully. *It 'll have to, with the field stripped yesterday.* Prudently she set aside a small basket of beans. *Seed for next year,* she thought with satisfaction. *Year to year in my basket.* Shading her eyes she looked up at the huge red sun. "Time to milk," she grumbled. "The child can at least help with that. . . . Still sleeping, I warrant." Her tone became querulous. "She used to be so much help. . ." She shook her head. "Now just moons around . . . dreaming, she said yesterday . . . shirking, I call it."

She called aloud, "Millim. Come out here."

No sound broke the silence.

"Millim . . . it's time to milk."

Again no answer from the hut.

Still grumbling, Buartha pulled aside the rank goat-fur hanging that served as a door. The sticks and branches that formed the wall beside the pallet were broken and blood smeared. Millim lay senseless, her hands raw from tearing at the wall.

"Gods." Buartha ran to her daughter's side. "Millim . . . Millim, what's wrong? What happened?"

The young woman lay blue-lipped, not responding. Then she moaned softly. "I thirst . . . I am so thirsty." She licked her lips. "Water . . . please give me water."

"Wake up, Millim. . . ." Desperation cracked Buartha's voice. "Oh Gods, you can't be sick . . . I can't help you if you're sick." Frantically she looked around. "Water . . . you must have water."

Shaking, Buartha grabbed the mud-smeared basket of water to bring it to her daughter's mouth. It slipped from her trembling hand to fall, crushed on the dirt floor, with the water spreading into mud. *Millim must have water.* Mounting hysteria robbed Buartha's thoughts of reason.

Removing her tunic, Buartha ran from the hut to the small creek and threw it in. As she stooped to retrieve the wet garment and return to Millim, she stopped short. There in the mud was a bootprint. . . . A strange bootprint. Overwhelmed, Buartha sat in the mud and wept. In just one day both of her most dreaded fears had come true. An unknown illness had struck Millim and now a strange man had found the hollow.

"Oh Gods . . . Men have found us." Buartha shook with fear "Why now? Oh Gods, all is lost. . . . All is lost." Fearfully she looked around. *I can't leave Millim*, she decided, then looked hopelessly at the surrounding mountains. *And I can't carry her to safety.* Sobbing, Buartha threw herself face forward into the mud.

A strange voice broke into Buartha's grief. 'Excuse me. . . . Can I help?"

Startled, Buartha sprang to her feet, mud dripping down her face and from her bare breasts. Squinting through the mud, she could just make out someone tall and thin. Short brown ringlets topped a weathered face full of concern.

Buartha's chest tightened so that she couldn't draw a full breath. "Go away," she mouthed. . . . She had no air. . . . the words wouldn't come. . . .

She felt her heart beat loud in her chest. Then pain . . . ripping, tearing pain filled her world. She fell then, face into the mud.

"She wakes, *breda*."

Buartha opened her eyes and looked into the gentle face of an old woman.

"You are not seriously ill, *mestra*," The voice was reassuring. "It was the fear . . . you collapsed from fear."

Buartha saw that the round face was encircled by a white hood, the coif of a midwife.

"My name is Ramhara n'ha Silima." The soft voice continued its reassuring lull. "My friend and I were traveling from the Temora Guild House of Renunciates up to Nevarsin when we encountered a problem." Buartha felt soothed by the gentleness in the voice. "We mean you no harm, my child."

Funny to be called a child, Buartha thought . . . *Me with a child near grown*. Suddenly she gasped. "Millim! Oh Gods . . . What has happened to Millim?" She struggled upright. "My daughter?"

A firm hand pushed her back to the pallet. "She rests now, and so must you."

Reassured by the confident tone of the old midwife's voice, Buartha closed her eyes. As she drifted into sleep she thought she heard a strange jingling sound. *Surely those are chains I hear*, she thought. *Renunciates must have strange customs*. Then she fell into a deep, healing sleep.

Millim woke to a bright jingling sound. Her eyes flew open as she remembered. *People*, she thought. *There are people here*. Excited, she sat up and looked around.

"You feel better now?" The question came from a tall young man. No, it was a woman, Millim realized, but the build was masculine.

"Yes, thank you." Unexpectedly Millim felt shy.

"Ramhara still sleeps." The woman gestured to a large shape rolled up in a ball on the floor. "She labored to her limit yesterday. I can not make her understand that she is no longer young." Cara saw the curiosity in the girl's eyes. "I am Cara and a woman despite what you see." Her face became grave. "Unfortunately I had my looks changed before I understood that it was not being female that I hated."

Cara stood and crossed to another shape on the floor, this one unmoving. "I fear for his life." Cara stooped and felt the brow of what Millim saw was a young man. "His fever will not break."

Light streamed into the hut suddenly as the door hanging was thrust aside. Millim recognized the jingling sound that had awakened her as yet another woman entered the hut.

"You must not let him die." The woman's voice was imperious. "I command you to heal him. I need him to return me to my home."

"Unfortunately, *mestra*—" Cara spoke in even tones—"the Gods are not commanded by mortals. His fate lies with them not us."

"Oh . . . how lovely." Millim's involuntary gasp of amazement drew Snava's attention. "May . . . may I touch them?"

Snava saw that the girl's eyes were riveted on her jewel-studded chains. "You may approach," she said carelessly.

"Somehow *I* cannot admire instruments of imprisonment." Cara's voice broke in with grim amusement. "Tell her how you almost died from thirst because you allowed yourself to be so trussed."

"It was you." Millim's eyes widened with remembered horror. "I was with you. I was trapped too."

"*You* were not trapped." The gentle voice of the old

woman soothed Millim's beginning panic. "It was *laran*. You are gifted with powerful *laran*, my child."

Ramhara groaned as she heaved herself to her feet. "You see images," she continued after she had arranged her clothes. "You receive them from others when they are distressed or feel pain." She grimaced in wry memory as she looked at her torn hands. "Then you project them."

The midwife moved to check on her patients. First Buartha, then Togaim.

"If you do not learn control I fear for your sanity." Her skillful hands checked Togaim's bandages. "The talent to project clearly is extremely rare. You must go to Arilinn Tower. Leonie alone can channel *laran* so strong."

"She goes nowhere!" Buartha stood menacingly over the midwife. "Would you steal my child, old woman?"

Ramhara turned to look up at Buartha. "She is a child no longer, *mestra*," she said mildly. "Surely you can see that."

But Buartha was not listening. Ramhara's movement had brought Togaim into the angry woman's view. She stared with loathing at the unconscious man. "You have brought a man here." She hissed through her teeth, "A man to destroy my home." Like a mad woman she threw herself on the unprotected man and started to strangle him with all her strength. "He'll not live to despoil Millim," she raved. Her whole body began shaking with the passion of her efforts.

With difficulty Cara pulled her from Togaim's unresponsive body and held her still.

"Go to your mother, Millim." Ramhara's voice was troubled. "She fears for you."

Millim embraced her mother despite Cara's interference. "Mother," she soothed. "Don't fear so. There is no danger."

Ramhara examined her patient. Finding a steady pulse and shallow breathing, she knew that he would survive Buartha's attack. Survival from the banshee's attack was still in the hands of the Goddess.

"He lives, Cara."

Slowly the tension left Buartha. "I'll not assault him again," she said in a subdued voice. "Please release me." Her legs buckled under her weight. Cara and Millim carefully lowered her onto the pallet. "I've lost everything." The defeat in Buartha's voice was total. "Millim . . . our sanctuary . . . everything . . . gone."

"A sanctuary exists only when you can open its door, *mestra*." Ramhara's voice deepened with earnestness. "Otherwise it is a prison."

"But I sought to protect us." Buartha looked at her daughter with love. "I sought to spare her from evil."

"Your protection has turned her into your prisoner." The old midwife lowered her bulk to the floor. "I do not know why, *mestra*, but hate seems to turn us into the very thing that we hate." The old woman paused to collect her thoughts. "You hate men. Destroyers, you call them. Yet *you* destroy your child."

"Destroy her?" Buartha's tone was unbelieving.

"If she gets no training she will go mad." Ramhara continued in her uncompromising voice. "But beyond that, each person has an absolute right to choose to live their own fate."

The midwife shifted her weight. *"Mestra*, there is one life to a person and only one. You seek to live your daughter's life."

"But what will I do without her? How can I survive here alone?"

"There are alternatives to hiding away in secret." Ramhara seemed amused.

"Enslaved? In chains to a man's will?" Buartha stared in contempt at Snava.

Snava proudly lifted her head. "I choose to serve my master and by so choosing I live in peace with him. . . . He adorns me with jewels." Snava lifted the chains so that sunlight pooled in the gems. "I feast when he feasts, sleep where he sleeps, and live where he lives. He has nothing of value that I do not share." She looked around her with distaste. "I do not live like an animal."

Buartha looked at her home, all that she had so proudly made for their survival. She saw, for the first time, it seemed, the crudeness of her shelter. Poorly cured hides assaulted her nose; crooked and imperfectly woven baskets offended her eye; sour milk, turned brown from a mud-lined drinking basket, nauseated her. In shame she buried her face in her hands. "It's true, Millim." She spoke past muffling hands. "There are so many things you've never had. Gowns . . . real cups . . . not even bread."

"I seem to have thrived on muddy milk, mother." Millim's voice tinkled with laughter. "But, oh . . . I want to try other things." She pulled her mother's hands away from her face and looked deep into her eyes. "I . . . I want to visit the world of my dreams." Then she looked at the unconscious guard. "I want to learn of men . . . and life." Millim laughed delightedly. "Mother I will be able to dance."

Buartha looked past her daughter to the old midwife. "I did my best," she said. "My very best."

"Yes you did," Ramhara answered. "But sometimes, when we make a free choice, it turns out wrong. Freedom is not the same thing as wisdom."

Cara stood then and removed her tunic so that Buartha could see the terrible mutilation of her body. *"Breda,"* she said softly to Buartha, "I turned my hate against myself and freely chose deformity to womanly curves. I thought that my problems were due to my womanhood." She shrugged back into her tunic. "I was wrong." She then took Buartha's hand in her own. "I call you sister because you have mutilated your spirit as I have my body."

Ramhara spoke as she too reached to take Buartha's hand. "Learning self-love is not hard, *breda*. It can be done alone."

A gentle smile played around her old eyes. "But I needed help."

"You?" Buartha asked in disbelief.

"It took me my full half-year at Temora Guild House to erase my hate." She squeezed Buartha's hand encouragingly. "Where hate lives no love can grow, my child."

"Can you help me?" Buartha asked hopefully.

"We can." Cara and Ramhara spoke as one.

" 'Tis the reason our sisterhood exists." Cara said with a grin.

"Prepare yourself for the trail, Buartha." The old woman rose from the floor with difficulty. "Millim must go for training." Ramhara smiled openly now. "And so must you."

About Nina Boal and "The Meeting"

Nina Boal is a full-time student at present, studying to teach mathematics, has studied and worked in computer electronics and has taught retarded children. She is single and lives in Chicago with seven cats—one of her hobbies is raising and showing Siamese cats. Another, as one might guess from her story, is martial arts—in this case Japanese kendo *or stick-fencing. She has been published in* Fighting Women News, *a martial-arts fanzine, and in* Tales of the Free Amazons; *this story appeared in a somewhat different form in that publication.*

Nina says, "I have been intermittently involved in the feminist movement, and have never been convinced that there are biologically inborn 'male' or 'female' traits." Hence the world of Al Faa where "female" and "male" are reversed.

Although the main character of this story is a Free Amazon, it is actually a science-fiction story dealing with space travel.

MZB

THE MEETING

by Nina Boal

Mhari n'ha Linnell slowly walked up the mountain path. It was early spring and the sun was shining a brilliant red as it set—but a faint wind cut through the trees, hinting of winter past. Mhari drew her weather-ravaged cloak about her and tried to concentrate only on placing one foot in front of the other until she could reach her goal—a travel shelter where she might rest her body for the night.

Mhari was of the *Com'hi Letzii*, the Order of the Unbound, and she was a mercenary fighter by profession. Born Mhari Ridenow-Lanart, she had discovered early in childhood a talent for the sword. For a *comynara* it was an unwanted, unacceptable talent, misunderstood even by its bearer. The only one in her family who had ever understood or accepted her gift had been her younger brother, Rafael.

A longing cut through her as she thought once more of her brother. *Rafe, how I want to see you again; I think of you often!* She had not seen him for many years, ever since joining the *Com'hi Letzii*. *When Father disowned me, he forbade you to see me, but that can't stop me from having you constantly in my thoughts, or from praying for your safety!* The starstone she wore around her neck tingled as she sent the thoughts out. She remembered distant times, the joyful mock sword battles they had fought in childhood, when they had been in perfect rapport. . . .

She had to think about the present. Jobs had been scarce

recently. *Too many soldiers and not enough wars, these days*, she thought, trying to be philosophical. Defying custom, she traveled alone, rather than with a partner. She had sold her horse so now she had to travel by foot. *Just keep climbing*, she told herself. *Soon we'll be there. So tired. Tired? What does that mean?* Her fencing instructor used to say during weapons practice. *Nice, beautiful day; I really don't need to ride.* She suddenly felt pain, *Lira, my mare, my constant companion, forgive me. You now have a good home. I can no longer feed you or take care of you properly.* She thought of the farmer, his gentle wife and lively children, but she was barely comforted. She could only shrug her shoulders and think of the rest that would soon be hers at the travel-shelter.

Alone in the travel-shelter, a woman spread out her blanket and knelt upon it. She was dressed like no other woman on Darkover and, indeed, was a stranger to its shores and mountains. She was Akiira benNemma Amara, Lord of Imaza Province on Al Faa, The Land. She knew she was not on The Land but in a new land, far away and strange. This journey was the culmination of her training as a Light-Traveler. Through special techniques of meditation, she could will her body into its constituent molecules to travel through space on a beam of pure light.

Al Faa, Akiira thought. *The Land, my land which is my home which is unique.* But travel to other worlds was outlawed on Al Faa, outlawed since the Isolation many generations ago when Queen Tanaiyru Alfaya had reigned. The Queen had made a ruling that the unique culture of the nation of Ama, Deity of the Sun, and Her consort, Xeruo of the Moon, must be kept pure and uncorrupted by foreign influence.

The Order of the Light-Travelers recognizes no boundaries except those of the mind, had stated the Moon-priest Numio. Even though only a male and of peasant origins, Numio had been her teacher. *The Light-Travelers recognize no class, neither female nor male*—it was the doctrine Akiira struggled to accept. Even though she was a Lord and a Preserver of The Land, Akiira Amara was also an outlaw of an outlawed and secret order.

(A young man, hale and hearty, was on his way home from his sister's wedding feast. He stopped at the travel-shelter to rest. He was startled to see a slender young woman, dressed in leather boots, wide breeches, and a green tunic of finest wool bound by a darker green sash. She might have been a Free Amazon, he was thinking, but her flaming red hair was tied back into a long braid that almost reached her waist.

"Well, hello there!" exclaimed the young man, only to be further startled when the woman, in one sweeping motion, drew from a scabbard tied on her back a long curved sword. She held the sword over her head, using two hands.

"How dare you approach the body of Lord Akiira Amara!" she challenged. The man backed off and fled into the woods, deciding that yes, he *must* have had too much to drink at that feast. . . .)

Akiira knelt facing the sword and chanted the daily ritual that a warrior of The Land must repeat every day to preserve her relationship with her Companion who, like her, had a soul. Sheathing the sword, she took from her traveling sack delicacies from her own planet. She was about to light a cooking fire when another traveler came into the shelter. Unlike the young man, this traveler, being a woman, had more the appearance of a warrior. She watched the traveler take off a worn cloak and, without preparing supper, lie down to rest.

The warrior's hair, the same color as Akiira's own, was cut short. *On my own planet,* reflected Akiira, *only an outcast must cut her hair short.* Her own hair was tied back in the customary warrior's braid—never in her life had it been cut. The woman's weapon was much shorter than the swords of the Al Fai warriors and of Akiira herself, those so long that they were worn in long scabbards slung over the back. *I must remember that different planets have different customs.*

She wanted to make the acquaintance of this warrior. The techniques that allowed her to travel on a beam of light also allowed her to pick up strange languages within a short time. *"Z'par servu, domna,"* she addressed the other woman in Darkovan. "I am a traveler, not from your land, but from a planet far away."

The woman surveyed Akiira, sending out a telepathic field that encompassed Akiira's mind. She did not probe the other woman's mind; as a Light-Traveler, she was pledged not to use her powers for such a purpose.

"May I ask," replied the Darkovan warrior, "are you *Terranan?"* Akiira was puzzled. "From the planet Terra?" continued the Darkovan. "There are many *Terranan* on Darkover. I have even worked for a couple of them."

"No, not *Terranan,"* said Akiira. "I come from a planet simply called Al Faa, The Land. On Al Faa, there is a group dedicated to Light-Travel to other planets, and that is how I arrived here. That is also how I learned your language. My name is Akiira benNemma Amara, and on my planet I am Lord of Imaza Province. But here, I am only a stranger. If I may ask, warrior, may I know your name and family and to what service you are pledged?"

"My name is Mhari n'ha Linnell, *vai domna,* and I have no family save that of the *Com'hi Letzii.* I am a mercenary who hires her service out to those who pay for it."

A mercenary? Is she an outcast? Akiira wondered. On Al Faa, only an outcast, dismissed from her family and clan for some disgraceful act, would sell her services.

"No, *vai domna!"* exclaimed Mhari proudly. "I am not an outcast. I am a free citizen of Darkover and I make my living in a lawful way."

"Please forgive me, warrior," Akiira hastened to say. *Now I've done it,* she thought. *This is my weakness. I have diffi-*

culty interpreting social situations. But she read right into my mind.

"Let me explain," offered Mhari, "I was once of the Comyn, the ruling caste, born into the Lanart family. But I was born with a strange gift for the sword, which would have been welcome for one who could inherit our family estate. But of course I could not inherit."

"Do you have an older sister who is the heir?" queried Akiira.

"No, my younger brother, Rafael, is the heir."

"Your younger *brother* is the heir?" A sudden premonition of something highly irregular was beginning to form in Akiira's mind. "You see," she explained, "my mother, Lord Nemma Amara, gave birth to my five older brothers before she gave birth to me. Our clan was in a crisis because a boy cannot be lord of a province, only a girl."

Mhari's eyes were wide with wonder.

Akiira continued, "When my mother was near the end of her child-bearing years, she finally gave birth to me and the crisis was averted. Of course, we had the problem of finding suitable matings for my five brothers. But why were you passed over for your brother, of all people?"

Akiira could feel a gentle probing of her mind, and, seeing no harm, she lifted up the outer barriers.

"'I knew it!" shouted Mhari. "The roles are reversed! I *knew* it could happen! *Vai domna*, I know the answer!"

Akiira could only stare at Mhari. "Are you trying to tell me that your society is ruled by *men?*"

"Why yes," answered Mhari. "Men are the rulers. Women are only the child-bearers and beautiful objects of men's desires. Women cannot use a sword for the Comyn; they cannot even bear a sword. However, I was born for the sword. I left my family and clan and joined the Order of the Unbound; now I bear this knife." She indicated her weapon.

This is amazing, thought Akiira, *The Order of Light-Travelers kept warning me about alien cultures, but nothing prepared me for this!* She could not recall that the men on her planet had organized any Order of the Unbound. *They don't need to. They are quite content with their roles as caretakers, entertainers, and providers of seed for our children.* Then she remembered her teacher, Numio, and the other men of the Light-Travelers. *They are certainly not content with a man's role.* Maybe Darkover wasn't so different after all.

"So, to learn the sword, you had to leave your family?" Akiira asked.

"I . . . I was disinherited," Mhari replied, looking down. "My family severed all ties." She looked again at Akiira. "I don't regret what I did; I really had no choice. Most of us leave our families behind when we join the Unbound, but especially, I miss my brother Rafael. We used to practice fencing together when we were young, before I was forbidden to practice. But—" she sighed—"the world will go as it will, and not as I would like."

"You are a mercenary," stated Akiira. "May I hire you to escort me on a tour of your planet?"

"Oh yes! I will be at your service, *vai domna,*" said Mhari, brightening.

"You've taught me things about Darkover," said Akiira. "Now I will show you some things about Al Faa." She showed Mhari her Al Fai delicacies. "We will feast on these tonight."

"And tomorrow," declared Mhari, "I will give you a tour of my world."

Rafael Ridenow-Lanart was riding alone on a path toward Thendara. He had been visiting his father the night before, and he was returning to his duties as a Guardsman. Once more, he and Julian Lanart had quarreled over the same subject.

"Father," Rafael had asked during dinner, "when will you

forgive my sister, Mhari? When will you accept her back into the family?''

''Zandru's coldest hell will boil over,'' Julian Lanart had declared, ''before that happens! She is a disgrace, dressing like a man and selling her skills to the highest bidder!'' He had sneered. ''What sort of skills does she *really* sell, anyway?''

Rafael had lost his appetite. Linnell Ridenow-Lanart had lowered her face, blushing. ''Mother, say something to him!'' Rafael had pleaded.

''It is not in my place to interfere in my husband's decisions,'' Linnell had replied, keeping her eyes lowered.

My father never wanted a wife and daughter, reflected Rafael as he rode. *He wants slaves to wait upon his every need! That's what he thinks a woman's place should be. He should have been born in the Dry-Towns!*

He wondered where his sister was, what she was doing, *in what far hills do you now wander?* Like a protective brother he wondered, *Are you cold and hungry?* Mhari certainly didn't need his protection. In his service in the Guardsmen, he had heard tales of her exploits against the bandits that infested the Domains. *It's more the other way around. I fence in a practice hall against fellow Guardsmen. My sister fights real enemies.*

Suddenly, he had no time to think. A band of twenty mounted men came out from behind a clump of trees, surrounding him, grabbing his horse's reins. Their leader, a bleached-hair man spoke loudly to him, ''What a way to regain my *kihar!* This one will bring a good price in the markets at Ardcarran!''

Rafael looked at him in defiance. ''I will go to the next world and take several of you with me before that happens!'' he declared. He drew his sword and started slashing, immediately cutting down two of the men. Infuriated, the other men came up from behind, seizing his arms, disarming him. Al-

though he struggled wildly, the men held him as their leader
took a rope and bound him hand and foot. He was slung over
his horse like baggage on a pack-*chervine*, and tied, lying on
his stomach, so that escape was impossible.

He felt the leader's eyes appraising him as he hung on the
horse. "Allow me to introduce myself, *vai dom*," he offered
with false courtesy, "Omar of Tarsa, near Shainsa, *Z par
servu!* Yes, you'll be very valuable property!" Omar mounted
his horse and the band started off.

As Rafael felt his body pounded by every stride of the
horse, his mind reached wildly out, *Mhari! Mhari, my sister,
help me, come help me* . . .

Mhari walked along the road, escorting her employer, Lord
Akiira Amara. *How wide is the Universe to have societies
such as hers, where women are lords of estates? And yet she
is human, like the* Terranan *and ourselves. Maybe the Universe is not so big*.

She had sometimes gazed with amazement at the Terran
spaceships whenever her travels had taken her to Thendara.
But to be able to use mind-telepathy to travel across space on
a beam of pure light? What sort of *laran* was that?

"Telepathic abilities are a learned skill," stated Akiira.
"They are not hereditary—anyone can learn them. Even a
peasant boy could learn."

Mhari had always learned that *laran* was a trait of her
Comyn heritage; the Comyn were descended from the Gods.
If we could light-travel. . . . But then she remembered stories
about the Age of Chaos. *No, that would be too much for us to
handle*.

"*Vai domna*, why is light-travel forbidden on your planet?"
asked Mhari.

"Because our culture is unique, descended from Ama, the
Lord of Light, and it is felt it would be corrupted."

Mhari wondered, *we all seem to be descended from Gods*

and yet we so distrust each other. Perhaps the Gods are laughing at us.

As they walked on, Mhari wondered for a minute, *If I could go to her planet I wouldn't have to be a mercenary anymore. I could be her paxman—or is it paxwoman?*

She suddenly felt her knife tingling; it was sometimes a sensing device for her *laran*. She heard a voice in her mind, *Help me, my sister! Help me!*

Rafael, flashed in her consciousness. She saw a picture of him, bound helpless, taken captive by Dry-Towners, *just as they took Melora Aillard as Jalak's concubine and slave several years ago.*

Rafe, she sent back, *I'm here. Do not give up.*

"*Vai domna*," she addressed Akiira, "my brother is in trouble. I must go help him."

"I'll come with you." Akiira volunteered.

"It's not necessary. This involves my family; it doesn't involve you."

"I didn't spend years training with this," exclaimed Akiira, indicating her long sword, "so I would have to be protected like a weak helpless man!" *Besides*, Mhari read Akiira's next thought, *it will be a good adventure to tell the others back home.*

"Well, let's go!" shouted Mhari. "There's two of us and eighteen of them, so it *will* be a good adventure to talk about. That is, if we live to tell it!"

Mhari led Akiira behind some trees near a path. "They'll be riding here soon, "she explained. "We'll lie in ambush here. When they come, I'll try to free my brother, so then it will be three against eighteen; that will shorten the odds a bit." She heard Akiira whispering a ritual in her own language. *Avarra and Evanda!* she suddenly realized, *it's been five years, and I'm finally to see my brother in a situation like this!*

She saw them, the caravan of Dry-Towners, carrying their

captive. *Rafe, lie still!* she sent to him, *I have a companion to help me, you'll NEVER believe. We'll get you up and a sword in your hand. It will be just like our fencing practice of old. . . .*

Mhari, sister, I'm ready. She received his thought. She and Akiira waited behind the clump of trees.

"*Now!* Mhari cried, and they plunged into the band of Dry-Towners. Mhari's knife and Akiira's long curved sword slashed back and forth, cutting down one after another, over and over. Mhari's knife reached Rafael, cutting his bonds. She handed him a sword from a man she had killed, and they were three, fighting furiously. Then Mhari found herself facing the leader, as Akiira and Rafael were facing off with others.

"So Omar of Tarsa is facing one of you *menhiedrini*," spat the Dry-Towner, "and you are a Comyn sorceress, as well! Where I come from, a proper woman knows her place!"

"And where I come from," stated Mhari, "we do not keep people in chains!" Her rage began to rise as she felt her starstone begin to pulse. *How dare you lay your filthy hands on my brother!* She forced his mind to connect with hers. He was unable to move as she advanced, boring into him. *I'll be merciful,* she then decided, withdrawing her mind. She cut straight through his body with her knife, killing him instantly.

Seeing their leader dead, the few remaining men backed off and fled into the woods. Mhari and Rafael simply looked at each other, then embraced each other as kinsmen while Akiira watched.

"Rafe!" Mhari cried, her eyes moist. "It's been so long! I . . . I kept thinking that I would never see you again."

"Father forbade me to see you, but the Gods have willed otherwise," said Rafael, relieved. "You and your companion saved me." He looked at Akiira, "Please introduce me."

"This is Lord Akiira Amara, my employer," said Mhari, proudly. "She is a visitor from Al Faa, where the roles are the opposite from those on Darkover—you have to be a woman in order to be a Lord. She came to Darkover through the *laran* of Light Travel through space. She belongs to the Order of Light-Travelers."

Rafael bowed to Akiira. "You lend me grace." Akiira bowed in return. Mhari smiled at her brother's puzzlement, reading his thought. *So it's true, the roles can be different. They are not inborn.*

Akiira had read the thought, too. "In the Order of Light-Travelers, we recognize no roles. Just as Light is made up of constituent molecules," Akiira explained, "so are all people."

Akiira gazed into the sky. "I am going to have to return to my planet before I am missed. When it is found that I have Light-Traveled away from Al Faa, the penalty will be my death, and the disbanding of my clan." She laughed, almost bitterly. "My society does not believe in constituent molecules. They believe that we are different and unique. Why do I Light-Travel and endanger my entire clan? It's not logical but I sometimes feel the need to do illogical things." She reached into a pocket and took out two medallions that bore the symbol of parallel lines. She gave them to Mhari and Rafael. "This is the emblem of the Light-Travelers," she explained. "Two lines, side by side in equality. I hope they will make you remember me."

"Are you leaving us?" Mhari asked anxiously.

"I must," Akiira replied. She knelt on the ground. "Stay a little away," she admonished. "But you can watch. It takes a lot of concentration. Who knows, I may not land in the place from which I started, but in an entirely new time and place. I may never get home at all. We are still in the experimental stage." She smiled, "I want to give you my thanks. It is impossible to express how glad I was to be able to meet you."

"*Vai domna . . .*," Mhari began.

"Now I am going to start crying, like a man. . . ."

"Yes," said Rafael, "like a man." *Only a true man cries*, the thought came out.

"Perhaps we will all meet again someday," Akiira said. "Either I will return, or you will learn Light-Travel and will meet me somewhere else. *Adelandeyo!*"

Akiira Amara, Lord of Imaza Province on Al Faa, closed her eyes and began to focus her mind. Presently her body blended into a beam of pure light, and then she was gone.

Mhari looked at Rafael. "Did we dream this?" she asked.

Rafael was holding his medallion, gazing at the parallel lines. "I don't think so," he murmured. "In Thendara, I have had duty near the Terran spaceport and I have seen the off-worlders. Sometimes, I look toward the stars . . ."

"I've done the same thing whenever I've worked in Thendara!" exclaimed Mhari, "my brother, we think so much alike!"

"And if we didn't," said Rafael, "if you hadn't been able to get my message, if you hadn't had that talent that Father so despises, if you hadn't met your off-worlder friend—" he shivered—"I would have been merchandise in the markets at Ardcarran!"

"Rafe," offered Mhari, "no matter what our father has pronounced, we must stay in contact, we must keep in rapport."

Rafael nodded. "We must. Our father cannot keep a brother and sister apart."

Mhari took a small knife from her tunic. "*Bredu*, will you exchange with me?"

"*Breda*," began Rafael. He joined minds with her, *no matter where each of us goes, no matter how far apart we are, no matter what anyone says, we are* bredin. He brought out his small knife, and they exchanged.

"*Bredu*, where will you be going?" Mhari asked.

"To Thendara, Mhari, *Breda*, to rejoin the Guardsmen. And you?"

"Here and there, as usual, to look for work," Mhari replied.

"Why don't you come to Thendara with me?" Rafael invited. "There'll be work there. The spaceport is growing, and so are all the problems connected with it. There is always someone looking for protection."

"If nothing else, I can always get a job as a dishwasher," observed Mhari.

"At any rate, I need a good strong escort to accompany me on my way," said Rafael, "in case anyone else decides that I would make a good piece of property."

"Look!" Mhari noticed, "the Dry-Towners have left us a present." She pointed toward two horses who were still grazing, *Come here, pretty ones, we won't hurt you.* She mounted one of the horses and led the other one to Rafael. Soon both of them, brother and sister, were on their way to Thendara as the red sun continued shining in its noon brilliance.

About Diana L. Paxson and
"The Mother Quest"

Diana Paxson often says, when asked how she became a writer, that she "married into it." The fact is that she married my brother Don, and that after living among professional writers for many years, a buried creativity surfaced naturally. Diana has the distinction of being the only person who has appeared in every anthology I have published; but it's not nepotism, I just like her work very much. I suspect that I would enjoy her stories equally well if she lived at the far end of the country and I had never met her face to face; but I consider myself privileged to be her friend and sister— and to some degree her role model, as she herself has said.

At present she is teaching remedial reading while she completes the third novel in her fantasy series about Westria. She has also written a contemporary fantasy novel Brisingaman *(Freya's necklace) and a handful of excellent short stories of which this is the latest. She lives near me in Berkeley and has two sons, sixteen-year-old Ian, and Robin, eleven.*

MZB

THE MOTHER QUEST

by Diana L. Paxson

"Caitrin—are you in there? You have a visitor!"

Caitrin jumped, stared stupidly at the awl she held in her hand and carefully set it down on the leather pack harness she had brought to her room to repair. Stelle would scold her for pampering her grief this way.

"Caitrin?"

"Yes—I'm here." She fought to pull herself together. Her sisters in the Guild House were already worried about her— she must not give them greater cause. It was only that it had been so hard to concentrate since they told her about Donal. . . .

Caitrin closed her eyes, as if that could hide her last memory of him, silent tears running down his chubby four-year-old's cheeks as the door of his father's house closed between them. *My baby,* she thought, *I should never have let you go!*

"Well, are you coming down? It's a lady, with lots of fur on her cloak and copper clasps." Tani's voice squeaked with wonder. "She says you know her, but she wouldn't give her name."

Caitrin felt something constrict within her. "A Ridenow?" She could hardly speak the word.

"Could be—" Tani said cheerfully. "The man who escorted her here is wearing green and gold livery, and she has ginger hair."

Caitrin took a deep breath. "Tell her I'll be right down." She heard the girl's footsteps receding down the hall and thought it was just as well that Tani had brought her the message. Caitrin did not think she could face one of the older women of the house who knew what it was to lose a child; not now, when she had to confront a visitor who was one of her child's noble kin.

She peered into the tarnished mirror and tried to smooth her sandy curls. There was a grease stain on her shirt, she saw, and her loose trousers were ready for the rag bin. It was not the sort of outfit to be receiving Comyn ladies in. But what did it matter, after all?

Caitrin straightened, retied one of her sleeve-laces and opened the door. What mattered was that she had been pretty enough to attract Lord Edric Ridenow's attention on a Festival Night nine years ago, and drunk enough on the dancing and mountain beer to let him make love to her, and so Donal had been born.

And I did want a baby, she reminded herself with bitter clarity. *A little daughter that Stelle and I could raise.* But her child had been a son, and she had given him to be raised in his father's house four years ago, and now he was dead, so it hardly made any difference what her visitor thought of her.

Caitrin shivered as she went down the stairs, for the summer had been cool, and considered going back to her room for a shawl. But she did not have the energy, and she knew that in the visitor's parlor there would be a fire.

When Caitrin entered the parlor, her visitor was sitting beside the fire, working with great concentration on a piece of embroidery she had taken from her bag. Caitrin let the door close behind her, wondering, for Comyn lady though she might be, this was only a girl.

The latch clicked sharply and the girl jerked around, reminding Caitrin painfully of the way Tani's knock had startled *her*. Then she frowned. This child was obviously a Ridenow, but no one that she knew. . . .

"Domna?" Caitrin's tone asked the question.

The Comyn girl got to her feet with a sigh. "You don't remember me? Well, it *was* four years ago, and I suppose I've grown a great deal."

Caitrin took an involuntary step forward, her memory replaying her impressions of the only time she had been to the Ridenow's Thendara home. Once more she saw the paneled walls with their intricately woven hangings, the gaggle of nurses and maids clucking as they clustered around Donal, and casting disdainful looks at the tall Free Amazon who had brought him there. And—yes, there had been a girl of about ten, watching it all with wide gray eyes.

"Forgive me—" Caitrin said softly. "I do remember you now, but I never knew your name."

"I'm Kiera—" the girl said simply. "Lord Edric's oldest girl. When Donal came to live with us . . . You must understand that everyone was kind to him," she added in a rush, "but my father is so often away, and after her last baby died my mother's health became poor. There were plenty of people to take care of Donal, but no one to really care *about* him, except me. . . ." The gray eyes became more luminous suddenly, than Kiera took a quick little breath and blinked the tears away.

"And you came to offer me your sympathy?" With an effort Caitrin got out the words. "I thank you, Lady Kiera. I was—grateful—that anyone even troubled to notify me. I did not expect . . ." Caitrin swallowed and tried again. "How did it happen, my lady? They did not tell me. . . ."

Kiera had turned a little so that Caitrin could not see her face. She held out her long-fingered hands to the fire. "There have been many odd accidents among the Comyn recently—you may have heard . . ." she said almost apologetically. "Accidents, and assassinations." She bit off the words.

"Father sent me and Donal to Serrais for safety while he was off-planet, and while we were there someone came with a 'copter and captured Donal—" The words had come out in a rush and Kiera took a quick breath. "The Terrans picked up the 'copter on their sensors and sent fliers in pursuit. So the kidnappers turned toward the Hellers. They got caught in the cross-winds, we think, and they went down."

Caitrin shuddered, wondering what it must have been like for Donal, first to be seized by strange, brutal men, and then the swift fall and perhaps flames . . . "My poor little one—" she whispered blindly. "What a dreadful way to die . . ."

"But that's why I came—" said Kiera in a strained voice. "I don't think he died. Even though he is only my half-brother, we were very close, *Mestra* Caitrin. When something happened to him, I always knew. And several times since the accident I have sensed him. Father is still away, and my mother—everyone—says it's only my grief deceiving me. But why would I *imagine* Donal in a great forest, with furry people around? Mestra, I think that Donal is still alive!"

"And you believe this Comyn girl?" The way Stelle said it was not quite a question.

Caitrin sighed and settled her head more comfortably on Stelle's well-padded shoulder. Blue Liriel shone through the window, and she could see that the other woman's round face wore a small, quizzical smile.

"Why should Lady Kiera lie to me? It cannot have been easy for her to come to the Guild House, raised as she has been. If she has *laran* she could have sensed Donal—and she's old enough to have developed it by now, isn't she?" Caitrin let the question hang in the air. After training as a Darkovan healer, Stelle had studied nursing with the Terrans. She would know.

There was a moment of silence and then Stelle began to

stroke her hair. "Yes . . . it's possible. But it's such a long chance—Caitrin, I don't want you to be hurt again!"

"Again!" Caitrin pushed herself up on her forearms and stared down at the dim blur of Stelle's face. "Did you think it has stopped hurting, ever since I heard? Oh—how can I expect you to understand? You didn't carry Donal, or bear the pain of bringing him into the world!" She gasped as Stelle's strong hands closed on her arms.

"How can you say that to me?"

Caitrin tensed to pull free, but after a long moment Stelle let her go.

"*Breda*, I'm sorry," Stelle said softly. "But even if *you* don't remember, *I* know how I held you while you labored, feeling every muscle in your body strain against me until I thought I was in labor too. And I remember how afraid I was when it went on, and on, and there was nothing I could do!"

The last words were wrenched out of her, and Caitrin bent, finding Stelle's face in the darkness, kissing her until she was calm again. "And it was just after Donal was born that you volunteered for training with the Terrans," she whispered. "I thought you were unhappy because I was so involved with the baby, and you didn't want to see!"

"I hated every hour I was away from you," Stelle said fiercely, "and every one of Donal's smiles I wasn't there to see. But the Terrans had knowledge that I could use to save others from so much needless pain. I thought that if you wanted to bear another child, there would be something I could do!"

"Then you do understand," exclaimed Caitrin. "That's what it is like for me now! When I thought Donal was dead I felt so helpless, but now, if there is even a *chance* he is alive I have to find him!"

"And if you don't? Or if you find his bones?"

Caitrin shook her head violently. "At least I will have done *something!* At least I will have *tried!*"

"Well, do you think you can *try* not to rain all over me and lie down so that we can figure out what to do now?" Stelle's voice wavered, but there was pleasure in it, and Caitrin found herself weeping and giggling weakly at the same time. She tried to stop, hiccoughed, and snuggled into Stelle's arms.

"I'm going to hire a guide in Carthon—"

"Stop there—" said Stelle. "You said *I*. Are you by some chance intending to go on this banshee chase alone?"

"*Breda*, Donal is probably with the Trailmen. . . ."

"Yes . . ." Stelle's voice was slow, amused.

"To get to the Trailmen's country you have to cross the Hellers." Caitrin pounded the pillow in exasperation. "I was born in the Kilghard Hills and I've run pack trains through some rough country, but this trip won't be easy even for me!"

"I'm glad you know that," said Stelle equably. "From what Kyla n'ha Rainéach told me, you would be foolish if you thought otherwise."

"Kyla!" Caitrin had only met the famous Amazon guide once. She remembered a wiry young woman with hair like a moonless night and stubborn eyes, but Kyla was a legend in the Thendara Guild House. She had taken a party which included not only a Terran doctor but Regis Hastur himself over the Hellers to the Trailmen and back again.

She whistled. "When did you get to talk to *her*?"

"She was Dr. Allison's freemate for three years. She lived with him here in Thendara when I was working at the TEMS hospital. I was the only other Amazon around, so naturally she talked to me." Stelle paused and took Caitrin's hand, and when she spoke again her voice held no teasing.

"She told me quite a lot, Caitrin—about the Trailmen, and about the road. I may not be hill-hardened as you are, but I'm strong, and I swear to you by Avarra's midnight robe that I will endure whatever I must to help you find your child. Anyway, I'm certainly not going to tell you anything unless you take me along!"

Stelle's arms went around Caitrin and Caitrin held her tight, at once clinging and clung to. She could feel the other woman's heart beating heavily beneath her own—for a moment she even fancied they were beating together. *All right,* she thought then, *we'll do it together, as we have done all the important things. . . .*

"Now that's decided, just exactly when are we leaving, and what shall I prepare?" said Stelle, as if Caitrin had spoken aloud.

Caitrin laughed. "Kiera has the money to outfit us. We'll travel fast and light to Carthon and then buy the mountain gear we'll need."

"Kiera . . ." said Stelle slowly. "I wish I had met her. Do you trust her, Caitrin? Will she go through with it, or is this just Comyn temperament?"

"I trust her—I like her better than her father—" Caitrin broke off as Stelle began to laugh. "She's like a young tree just budding . . . slender but already strong."

"Should I be jealous?" Stelle murmured against her hair.

"It's not like that." Caitrin frowned, trying to understand, herself, what she wanted to say. "She's—if I had borne Edric a daughter, Kiera is just what I always imagined she would have been." Caitrin sighed. She had wanted a daughter so desperately, but she would not risk bearing another male child that the rule of the Renunciates would force her to give away.

"And besides," she went on, "you know that I've never really loved anyone but you."

Stelle kissed her then, and Caitrin began to touch her in all the sacred places, for there would be no time for this once their journey began. They moved together with the certainty of long loving, and afterward they slept, as they had for the past eleven years, breast soft against breast and thigh curving over thigh.

*   *   *

"It's hard to believe that we came over that without wings!" Stelle said, a little breathlessly.

Caitrin's quick glance confirmed that Kiera and the guide were still picking their way down the slope. Then she turned to smile at Stelle. Her freemate was staring at the mountains behind them, and Caitrin let her own gaze travel up, and up again, to the great ridge of the Hellers whose edge cut the sky, at this altitude as deeply violet as the *morada* flower, like the serrated blade of a Dry-Towner's knife. But it was a blade forged of shining ice that curved down to the deeper notch of the pass they called Dammerung.

Yet just now Caitrin found the mountains less impressive than the woman who was wondering at them. Those Terran exercises Stelle did so religiously must be worth something after all, for although the older woman had lost some of her comfortable plumpness, she had not slowed them down.

And Kiera was just as much of a wonder—Caitrin ran a finger beneath the shoulder-strap of her pack to ease it and began to step carefully downward again. The air was warmer here, and Kiera had taken off her knitted cap. Her gingery hair looked redder in the sunlight. Caitrin watched her moving ahead, thinking she had the precise grace of a young chervine, and wondered if *she* had been possessed of so much energy at the age of fourteen. Certainly she had not expected it of a gently reared daughter of the Comyn—but then Kiera had spent most of her time roaming the hills around Serrais until a year ago.

And that leaves only me, she thought glumly, remembering how her bones had ached in the mountain cold. But it was not the physical hardship that weighed on her, she knew. The worst of the climbing was over. She should have been walking as lightly as the others now. But she looked over the undulating sea of foliage that flowed down from the conjunction of the Hellers and the glimmer on the horizon that was the Wall Around the World, and she felt cold.

If he is still alive, my child is down there somewhere . . .
Looking at such an immensity of forest it seemed to her as
impossible to find one small boy in its vastness as to locate a
jewel lost in the Shainsa sands. She looked back at Kiera. *She
says that she is still sharing dreams with Donal*, Caitrin told
herself. *I have to believe her, or I might as well have let the
wind take me off that ledge just below the pass. . . .*

The trail ahead was partly blocked by a fallen tree, and
rocks had piled up behind it till it was almost level there. The
hill-trader they had hired in Carthon to guide them stopped
and waited until she reached him.

"There lies your way, Mestra Caitrin—" He gestured
northward. "The treaty I have with the Mountain-Root People has guarded us so far, but when we break camp in the
morning I must go westward to their Nest near the Ice-River
Falls." He paused, and seams carved in his face by a lifetime
spent out in all weathers deepened as he frowned.

"You are sure that the little one you seek is not in the
west?" He turned to look in that direction. "They are good
folk, by the falls. They would receive you kindly if you came
with me."

Kiera shook her head. "It is to the north that I have sensed
him, Master Coram, and it is there we must go."

"Then I am sorry indeed, for they do not like strangers
there." He turned back to Caitrin. "And then there is another
thing, and you must forgive me for saying it, Mestra—"

Caitrin held up her hand, wanting to spare him, for she had
learned to respect his uncomplaining endurance, and he had
the gentle courtesy of those who spend much time alone with
the great hills.

"You think that they will shut us out of their 'cities'
because we are females, and alone?" she said. Even Kyla
n'ha Raineach had pretended to be under Jason Allison's
protection at the City of the Hundred Trees, and she must

have been already half in love with him to have strained her Renunciate's oath so far.

Coram answered with a deprecating shake of his head. Caitrin sighed, wondering if she had underestimated that difficulty. With the Hellers and the Forest to get through, the customs of the Trailmen had seemed the least of their problems.

"The women of the Forest have nothing to fear from us," Stelle said stoutly. "Surely they will understand we only want our child!"

Master Coram had no answer to that—none of them did—but anxiety nagged at Caitrin like the pain of the blister she had got from her stiff mountain boots as they continued down the trail.

"Caitrin, you had better let me look at your foot again—" The gentleness in Stelle's tone was deceptive.

Caitrin sighed. "It's all right, really. I wish you wouldn't fuss so." But she stuck out her foot obediently as Stelle squatted down.

"Then you shouldn't have brought a nurse along!" returned Stelle, unlacing the high boot.

Caitrin leaned back, trying to see through the canopy of branches to the sky. The light of their little fire flickered red on tree trunks and leaves. It was a very little fire, for though the Trailmen had learned to use it a generation ago, they still feared open flames. But at least the air was warmer here. The damp winds from the distant sea carried a gentler climate to the forests before they swept over the Hellers and, rising, exchanged the rest of their moisture for the mountains' chill before they howled across the high desert of the Dry-Town lands.

"Ouch!" Caitrin sat up suddenly as Stelle dabbed something stinging and antiseptic over the raw place.

"This will only hurt for a moment," said Stelle calmly, tearing off a length of gauze.

"It's all the fault of these Carthon boots—men's boots—I

should have known better . . ." Caitrin said bitterly. She had been about to replace her old trail boots when she heard about Donal. They had left Thendara in too much of a hurry to have new boots made, so they had bought men's boots in Carthon, thinking there would be no one to be shocked in the hills. Caitrin had forgotten the subtle differences in shape and proportion between a man's foot and a woman's, but it might have made no difference. She had never before worked in boots that were not specially made.

"You really ought to soak your foot in hot water," said Stelle. "But this should do. Remember to keep it clean and dry."

"I think it's wonderful that you know so much about healing—our own ways and the Terrans' too," said Kiera from the other side of the fire. "My father has traveled, and understands there is value in both, but my mother—" She stopped. "So many people think anyone from off-planet is some kind of monster. . . ."

Stelle grinned. "The Trailmen probably think of *us* that way."

"That's what my Uncle Lerrys said," answered Kiera.

Caitrin watched her. The fitful light changed her face from that of a child to a grown woman and back again. *I should never have let her come*, thought Caitrin. But Kiera had been as stubborn as Stelle. She shuddered to think what Edric would do if she lost one of his legitimate children trying to save his *nedestro* child, even though that other was a son. Comyn blood was too valuable to risk.

But that was precisely why she had to let Kiera come with them. Not only did the girl know what Lerrys Ridenow had said of his own adventures in this country, including a few words of the Trailmen's tongue, but it was her rapport with Donal that would lead them to him.

"And even you—the Renunciates—" Kiera used the proper term to show she meant no disrespect—"my nurse used to say terrible things about you all, but when you brought Donal to our house you did not seem strange. But I did not understand, then, how you could bear to give up your child.'' She added, ''Why did you decide to become Free Amazons? Is it because you can only live together this way?''

Caitrin turned her face away to hide the quick sting of tears. *Do you understand, child?* she asked silently. *I don't, not anymore.* Stelle gave her arm a quick squeeze of comfort and then began to tell Kiera how she had wanted to be a healer and how Caitrin had wanted to work as a guide, free of the responsibilities of husband and family. They had met each other in the Guild House, and then they had had that reason, too.

Kiera is almost old enough to take the oath of a Renunciate, or to marry, thought Caitrin. *Would I have chosen this path if I had known the price I must pay?* she wondered then, *Even for my freedom—even for Stelle?*

Caitrin stared up at the platform of woven wood, barely able to see it through the thick leaves. It swayed and trembled as if something were moving up there. Faintly she heard voices like the twittering of birds. She moved a little closer to one of the huge trunks that supported it, wincing as her weight came down on her left foot. She knew she should get Stelle to check it again. But later. When they had Donal back again.

It had taken them a week to find this place, following Kiera's instinct and the rough map Stelle had copied from the Terran archives.

She let out her breath in a long sigh. ''Kiera—'' she spoke softly, ''Are you quite sure that Donal is here?''

The Comyn girl reached into the breast of her tunic and pulled the blue crystal out of its silk bag. She looked into it, shook her head a little as if to clear it, then looked again.

''Yes . . .'' she said slowly. ''It's very strong. He's upset—

they want him to eat something and he thinks it's nasty. He's crying—now they've smeared it on his lips and he is licking them—oh! It tastes good!'' She laughed, and Caitrin laughed too.

As if startled by the sound, Kiera took a quick breath, blinked, then slipped the starstone back into its bag.

"All right," said Stelle practically, "what do we do now?"

The logs just overhead quivered, and Caitrin glimpsed luminous red eyes through the leaves. "Kiera—I see one of them up there— Can you greet him? Tell him we're friends. Perhaps there is someone here who speaks *casta*."

Kiera nodded, cleared her throat, and trilled a phrase. It sounded pretty, and apparently it was accurate, for the eyes disappeared and in a few moments one of the Trailmen swung down through the branches, coming to rest a few feet over their heads.

Caitrin stared at him, reminding herself that his child-sized body, furred like a beast's with pale hair, held an intelligence which, if different from her own, must still be respected. She had to believe that, if she had any hope of getting him to return her son.

"People of the Land-Beyond-the-Mountains—we do not often see your kind here—" He spoke very softly, and Caitrin strained to hear. She moved closer, and without visible effort he pulled himself higher into the tree. "You are females, I think? We have enough females here—" His *casta* was slow, but comprehensible.

"Honored One, we do not come to add to the number of your people, but to take someone away," Caitrin said carefully. "There is a child of the Big People among you—my child. I have come to take him home."

The Trailman uttered a high trilling phrase, and was answered, more elaborately, from above.

"The woman of the Old One lost a baby, and she has taken

the Big Child as her own. He is woman's business until he is grown.''

''Then let me talk to the women!'' cried Caitrin. As she darted toward the tree pain stabbed her foot suddenly as if something had broken there, but she scarcely noticed. A knotted vine hung down the trunk. As the Trailman scurried upward she jumped for it and began to clamber after him.

She had only gotten six feet when she saw the edge of the platform suddenly flowering with furry faces. She paused, staring up at them, and something hurtled through the leaves.

''Sisters!'' she cried, stretching out her hand, and then her arm went numb as she was struck by the first stone.

Pain lanced through Caitrin's leg at every running step, echoing her mind's agony. *Donal! Donal!* Every yard she put between herself and the Trailwomen took her farther from him, too.

Stelle, laboring through the undergrowth ahead of her, tripped on a vine and went down. Caitrin scrambled after her and pulled her to her feet again. For a moment they stood, breathing hoarsely, but they heard no patter of footfalls, no creak of branches or rustle of leaves. Kiera stopped, turned, and came back to them, sniffing at the air like a hunted rabbithorn.

''There's no one near . . .'' she said after a moment had passed.

Caitrin nodded and took an incautious step forward, stumbled as the pain burned along her nerves again and, swearing, grabbed for the support of the nearest branch.

''What is it?'' asked Stelle. ''Did you turn your ankle?''

Mute, Caitrin shook her head, started to walk away from her and bit her lip as her weight came down on the foot again.

Stelle's eyes narrowed. ''It's that blister, isn't it? Sit down—'' She pointed to a fallen log. ''Yes, now—Kiera will tell us if there's danger.''

Caitrin's nerves twitched with the need to keep running—out of the Forest or back to the Trail City and her child. But her muscles would not obey her, or perhaps it was the authority that Stelle had put on, as a priestess her veil, that constrained her. Kiera came softly across the fallen leaves and stood watching with wide, frightened eyes.

It was that look that defeated Caitrin. Suddenly dizzied, she let Stelle take her elbow and force her down.

"Will she be all right?" Kiera asked softly as Stelle pulled off the coarse stocking.

"It's dirty—infected again, I suspect, but I'll have to clean it to see. I'll need a lot of water, and a fire."

"You can't build a fire here!" exclaimed Kiera. The tree trunks around them were furred with dry lichens and dead leaves carpeted the ground.

"We must find a pool or a stream." said Stelle. "We passed a rivulet a little ways back—if we follow it we may find a spring."

Sick with pain and despair, Caitrin let Stelle half-carry her through the gathering dusk under the trees back to the watercourse and along upstream. It was almost full dark when the canopy of branches above them thinned suddenly and for the first time in a week they saw Liriel and Kyrddis sailing across the sky. Later that night Marmallor would rise as well, but by that time the first two moons would be down. At this time of year, Idriel did not appear until dawn.

Caitrin gazed wistfully at that gentle light, wishing she was back in Thendara, watching them from her window in the Guild House there. From next to her came a long sigh.

"Look—" said Kiera softly. "Oh, Caitrin! It's beautiful!"

Caitrin blinked, for she had the sudden, confused impression that the stars had fallen to the ground. Then she realized that she was looking at the reflection of the two moons in the pool, fragmented by the ripples caused by water falling from the rocks above in a shimmer of crystal drops like those of

Avarra's necklace. And it was not only the light of the moons—the air was alive with glowflies, amber and amethyst and rose, blinking in and out of existence as they hovered above the water or darted among the surrounding trees.

She took a deep breath of cool, moist air, feeling the peace of the place soothe her spirit as the air cooled her skin. With a sigh she sank down on the mossy bank, admiring the swift efficiency of Stelle's movements as she began to build a fire. Kiera dug into the pack for their big kettle. She straightened, took a step toward the water's edge, then stopped.

"There's something here—someone is watching us . . ." She peered into the shadows. Caitrin sat up quickly and scanned the woods, but nothing was moving there except the glowflies. The Forest was dark, impenetrable. Even the air seemed to still.

"Hurry up, child," said Stelle. "I'll have the fire going in a moment."

"Yes." After a moment's hesitation, Kiera bent to the dark water and let it flow into the kettle. Something flickered in Caitrin's peripheral vision and her foot throbbed as she jerked around to stare into the trees. Suddenly the night's beauty made her afraid.

She shivered. *I should never have let Stelle and Kiera follow me here . . .* Then Kiera brought the water back up the bank and Stelle suspended the kettle from a tripod she had improvised over the fire.

"Good—" said Stelle. "Now, let's see—" Gently she lifted Caitrin's foot so that the firelight shone on it, dipped a cloth into the warming water and began to cleanse it.

And from somewhere far too near came a shrill twittering. The shadowed trees dislimned . . . they were moving, they were furry bodies, pale in the gloom, rushing in to surround them with the firelight flaring ruby in their eyes.

Trailmen! No—Trailwomen, and now there was nowhere

they could run. Caitrin pushed herself to her feet and wrenched free her long knife.

"*Feo!*" Fire . . . Caitrin caught that word even garbled by the twittering.

"What is it?" said Stelle angrily. "Are they upset because we lit a fire here? I thought they used it too. . . ."

"No," whispered Kiera. She stood with her eyes shut and her hands over her ears. "Not anger—awe . . ."

Caitrin grabbed her arm. "The Ridenow Gift—use it girl! Are they afraid? Will they attack us now?"

Kiera was trembling. The Ridenows were said to have the Gift of empathy with nonhumans, but Kiera would never before have had to use it.

"I'm getting images . . ." she whispered. "I see processions coming here, making offerings to the pool of woodland flowers. This is a sacred place, where only the women go. . . . They're confused. They would kill a male who came here, but we are females, and we found it alone, and Stelle . . . was doing the healing ritual . . . with water and fire. . . ."

Caitrin turned to look at the Trailwomen, still holding to Kiera's arm. Waves of pain washed through her from her foot, but she could not let it master her now. She let go of Kiera and balanced carefully.

"Show them your starstone!"

Trembling, Kiera obeyed. Uncovered, the matrix crystal caught the blue light of the moon as if it had been chipped from its radiance. Then Kiera cupped it in her palm and it glowed with its own swirling fire.

The Trailwomen twittered and backed away. Kiera's fingers closed around the stone and she took a quick breath.

"It's stronger now—" she said. "They've heard of starstones. They think I'm one of the *chieri*—"

And they were not so far wrong, thought Caitrin, remembering the legends about the Comyn. "Can you send your thoughts to them?" she whispered. "Try! Tell them we can defend ourselves, but we mean them no harm."

Kiera frowned, concentrating. "They want to know why we came."

"We came for healing—" Stelle was on her feet beside them now.

Caitrin hobbled forward and mimed cradling an infant in her arms. "We came for my child!"

As if in answer, the circle gave way before her. The Trailwomen were looking at the waterfall. Caitrin followed their gaze and realized that there was a cavern behind it, and in that darkness something stirred.

The Trailwomen began a slow, crooning song. Something came down the path from the waterfall, something that glowed.

Caitrin stared, feeling the hairs rise on her scalp and arms. And gradually her straining vision showed her a Trailwoman, moving with the careful dignity of age, resplendent in a cloak woven with the feathers of birds. The light came from the firepot she cradled in her arms.

"Fire—" whispered Kiera. "She is the Keeper of the holy fire. They use it, but they fear it still, and keep it here, near the water with the oldest woman of the tribe as its guardian."

The priestess moved slowly down the pathway and came to a halt at the edge of the circle of light cast by their own fire. She lifted a hand, and the singing abruptly stilled. A staccato burst of speech with a question in it broke the silence that followed.

"Tell her that we're priestesses of fire, too, and we want our child," said Caitrin. Kiera nodded and concentrated on her crystal. For a moment Caitrin's gaze was caught by its swirling fires, then, dizzied, she looked away. She wanted to shout at those alien faces, to threaten to set the woods ablaze if they did not return her son—but this place forbade such sacrilege. She stepped toward the old priestess and held out her arms.

"Old Mother—" she cried, "which of you would not grieve if your child were held captive far away? Give me my boy, I beg you—give me my child!"

There was another burst of twittering, then all was still. After a moment Kiera touched her arm. "They say that the boy must choose. . . ."

Caitrin rolled over on her side and opened her eyes. The last time she had allowed herself to do so she had seen only the formless gray of the hour just before dawn, but now the rosy light of sunrise was replacing it. To the north, the first rays of the red sun struck fire from the snow-fields of the Wall Around the World. Mauve Idriel glowed just above the horizon, and in the Forest, birds were tuning up for their morning song.

Dawn . . . she thought, watching the brightening sky. *They will be bringing Donal soon.* She sat up, careful of her bandaged foot, though Stelle's treatment seemed to have helped it already. Stelle and Kiera were still huddled close beside her, deep in exhausted slumber still. But she had not been able to do more than doze, despite her weariness. Certainly she could not sleep now.

A rosy sheen was hiding the darkness of the pool. The rising sun coppered the tops of the trees, then its first rays slanted down across the ferns that filled the area between the Forest and the pool and the vines with their little tight-curled white flowers.

She could see now that there was a pathway through the ferns. Two pale shapes sat beside it—their guards. Caitrin wondered if her own movement had awakened them, but as they got to their feet they turned toward the shadows beneath the trees, and stood still, listening. Caitrin held her breath until the pulse pounded in her ears, but she could hear nothing but the soft voice of the waterfall.

For a moment Caitrin considered getting up to join them, leaving her companions sleeping by the pool, but they had suffered together through all the trials of this quest—Stelle and Kiera had a right to share its ending.

She reached out and found Stelle's shoulder, shook her gently. Stelle mumbled sleepily and Caitrin shook her again.

"Be quiet and wake up, Stelle—I think they're coming now."

She leaned toward Kiera, but the girl's eyes were already open. Silently the three women got to their feet and stood waiting, watching the dark gate of the Forest and the lengthening rays of the sun. And finally they saw movement, more pale shapes that formed from the darkness—Trailwomen with necklaces of dried berries and the feathers of birds, and the smaller figures of their young.

And then Caitrin saw something pale as the others, but smooth, and she heard the faint scuffling of someone trying to walk quietly over fallen leaves. As the group emerged fully from the Forest the red sun struck gleams of copper from Donal's fair hair.

The Trailwomen stood still, letting him continue on. One of them was twisting her long fingers and the others patted her. *It must be the female who adopted Donal*, thought Caitrin. *She must love him too . . .*

For a moment the boy did not seem to notice he had left his companions behind. Then abruptly he realized that he was alone, and focused on the three humans standing by the shore. Caitrin took a deep breath and clenched her fists. Her arms ached with the desire to reach for him, her legs with the need to run to him. But the Old Woman's meaning had been clear—Donal himself must make the decisive move.

And so she held herself still. *Soon*—she thought, *I only have to wait a moment longer now.*

And then Donal's sweet laughter broke the silence.

"Kiera!" he cried, "Kiera—you've come for me!" And he ran into his sister's arms.

Caitrin yanked the pack strap taut and jammed shut the

clasp. One more to tighten and the pack would be ready—all their gear would be ready, thank Avarra, for it was high time they got moving again. They had been three days journeying already, and they still had the Hellers to cross. The weather was holding so far, but who knew how long that would last, and it would be harder returning with the child . . .

She heard Donal's clear voice and Stelle's calm answer. He was telling her something about the boy who had been his friend in the Nest. Caitrin felt her eyes stinging again and blinked rapidly.

It was not Donal's fault. As soon as she could detach him, Kiera had explained that it was Caitrin who had come for him and thrust him into her arms. But although Donal allowed her to hug and kiss him, there was no warmth in his response. It was as if he had tried to erase all memory of her when she left him with his father.

And what difference would it make in the end? Caitrin asked herself bitterly. Either way, she was going to have to part with him once more, and surely it was better for him to feel the pain of it only one time. *It should be enough that I have rescued him*, she told herself sternly. *Perhaps he will be able to forgive me when he is a man.*

Which was all quite sensible, but not much help when her throat tightened and her eyes burned with hot tears.

She reached for the second strap and began to pull on it.

"Can I help you with that?"

Caitrin looked up. Kiera was standing a few feet away, as if she were afraid to come nearer without being asked. *Have I showed my pain so obviously?* Caitrin wondered. She managed a smile.

"Just put your foot on the strap while I thread it through the clasp."

They finished strapping the pack and Kiera leaned it against a tree. Caitrin straightened, rubbing her leg. Her foot was healing nicely, but she still tended to favor it, and her leg muscles took the strain. Donal had picked up a stick and was carefully stripping off the bark to make a walking staff.

"In four or five years he can go climbing on his own," said Kiera, watching him. "But Father will probably send him to the Cadet Guards. The men will take over his training completely then."

Caitrin gave her a bleak look, wondering how that was supposed to comfort her. "I understand," she said. "Until then you will continue to watch over him?"

"Oh, of course—" said Kiera, flushing. "But you don't understand. What I meant was that then he won't need me anymore."

Just as now he doesn't need me . . . thought Caitrin, looking at the ground.

"And then I want to come back to you."

Caitrin lifted her head and stared at Kiera, trying to read the message in those wide gray eyes. Ragged and dirty as she was after a month on the trail, she seemed much older than the delicate child who had come to the Thendara Guild House, and in an odd way, more beautiful.

Caitrin looked at her, and thought, *You have stolen Donal's love, and mine, too.*

"I want to come to the Guild House; I'll be of age then—" Kiera blurted, blushing again. "Will you be my oath-mother, Caitrin? Or, if they allow it, you and Stelle together?"

Caitrin felt the tears rolling down her cheeks and did not try to check them. Unable to speak, she held out her arms. Kiera came into them, and for a moment Caitrin could only hold her tight. Then she lifted her head, and across the clearing she met Stelle's wise smile.

About Elisabeth Waters and
"Child of the Heart"

After accepting both this story and Diana Paxson's "The Mother Quest" I realized that they were both on the same theme . . . an Amazon who has given up her child, and must come to terms with that painful choice. Jamilla, in Elisabeth's story, arrives at a different conclusion from that of Diana's protagonist Caitrin; but, I think, an equally valid adaptation.

This is one of the things which has been strongly criticized in the concept of the Free Amazons; the idea that no woman may live in a Guild House with a son over five years old. I am aware of all the arguments on both sides; at the time I created that restriction (it is dealt with at length in Thendara House) *I was in touch with some feminist communes which were coming apart because some resident women could not allow these "baby men" (no I'm not making this up) to invade "women's space" and were willing to break up their homes over it. Nobody ever said that all Amazons (or all feminists) were perfect, or even rational. Show me a society which is!*

Elisabeth Waters makes her home in Berkeley, and lives in my household with two other women, a grown boy, a dog, and two cats. We sometimes call it a Guild House, sometimes a "pagan convent."

The grown boy, my son Patrick, causes very little conflict in this household of females (even the cats and dog are female) and Patrick, 20, occasionally comes in handy to take out the garbage—a line stolen from a delightful parody play entitled Free Amazons of Ghor, *by Randall Garrett and Vicki Ann Heydron—Mrs. Garrett—The basic premise of* Free Amazons of Ghor *is that John Norman and I should collaborate on a DAW best-seller; the ensuing ructions are hilarious, not to say hysterical.*

Lisa works part-time as my secretary and accountant, and has made several stabs at the family trade of writing, appearing first in the anthology The Keeper's Price, *for which she wrote the title story. She has also sold a story to the Andre Norton/Robert Adams anthology,* Magic in Ithkar, *which we hailed as her first sale "outside the family" and is working (not very hard) at a novel. She also works part-time for a computer company, and helped me to choose a word processor so user-friendly that it could be accurately described as cuddly.*

MZB

CHILD OF THE HEART

by Elisabeth Waters

Jamilla n'ha Gabriella lay in her bed feeling barely alive. She didn't have the energy to get up; in fact, she felt that she might never move again. Her mind told her that it was after sunrise and she should have gotten up when she woke up an hour ago, but the body simply refused to obey.

Keitha had explained to her that this was a perfectly normal feeling—they called it depression, and Jamilla could certainly see why. It was a consequence of the changes in her body from giving birth, and in Jamilla's case it was made worse by the fact that her baby had been a boy and she had given him to his father and his wife to raise. But Edrik had been born a month ago, surely she should be feeling better by now!

Booted footsteps came down the hall, and her oath-sister Perdita came rapidly into the room. "Jamilla, for Evanda's sake, get up! You know you'll feel better once you're up and moving—I can't understand why you lie in bed and brood for an hour every morning! And if you pull this on the trail tomorrow, I'll dump you out of your bedroll into the coldest stream I can find!"

Jamilla dragged herself out of bed and reached for her clothes, feeling the tears start to her eyes. Thinking rationally, she knew that Perdita loved her; they had done guide work together ever since the end of Jamilla's house-bound time. But at the moment she felt herself to be a horrible person and that everyone hated her and that everyone was right to hate her.

As she was lacing up her tunic Perdita came over and patted her consolingly on the shoulder. "I'm sorry, Jamilla. I know you miss Edrik, but lying around thinking about it doesn't help. Why don't you go see him this morning—we don't have to leave until afternoon."

Jamilla tied the laces and reached for her belt. "I'm not going to see him, Perdita. It's better for him not to know me—that way he won't miss me."

"I'm not sure it works that way." Perdita shrugged. "But it's your business." She turned to the door. "I'll go start getting the supplies together. Be sure you eat a proper breakfast before you join me."

They got the supplies packed, ate dinner at the Guild House, and then went to pick up their charge—a nine-year-old boy going to study at Nevarsin. His father was a goldsmith and a friend of Perdita's, who took leave of his son with a long series of exhortations on proper conduct, ending with ". . . and don't give them any trouble, Coryn."

"Why should I, Father?" Coryn said with an air of wide-eyed innocence that positively screamed 'trouble!' "Aren't they my aunts?"

Jamilla raised an inquiring eyebrow at Perdita, who gave her an "I'll explain later" look, and they headed out of the city.

The road was wide enough near Thendara for them to ride abreast, and Jamilla tried to engage Coryn in conversation. "Are you excited about going to Nevarsin?"

"No."

"You've traveled before?"

"No."

He seemed very constrained by something. "Are you nervous about the trip? It's really not all that bad."

"If it's not all that bad, why did my mother die on it?" Coryn snapped.

"Your mother?" Jamilla was startled.

"Mara n'ha Kindra," Perdita explained. "She died in a rock fall about five years ago. I knew her slightly; she was usually at Armida."

"If you knew her even slightly, that's more than I ever did," Coryn said bitterly. "She obviously didn't care to know me." Apparently this rankled, for he went on, "Father may think Renunciates are noble and wonderful, but I think she was a bitch. No doubt it would have been different if I'd been a girl, but since I was a boy I got thrown out like a whore's mistake! Your precious oath says that you're all mothers, sisters, and daughters to each other, but Zandru help any son of yours, for no one else will!"

He kicked his chervine and rode a bit ahead of them, while Perdita kept a wary eye on him. Jamilla continued to lead the pack animals, but she felt stunned and shocked. The cynicism and bitterness would have been dismaying in anyone; in a child of nine, they were appalling.

Coryn stayed ahead of them until they reached the first fork, when he fell back to ride behind Perdita while Jamilla and the pack animals brought up the rear, but he didn't utter a word for the rest of the day.

Unfortunately, that silence didn't extend to his sleep. Jamilla was having trouble sleeping, and when she finally did manage to doze off, she dreamed that her baby was crying for her. She tried to go to him, but she couldn't move, and the crying went on and on and on until she thought she would scream. And she was awake and the crying was still there. She crawled, shivering, over to Coryn's bedroll, and discovered that he was the source of the noise. He was sound asleep, and he was whimpering—the forlorn sound of an abandoned, hopeless child. Jamilla shook him gently, and he started up, banging his head into her jaw.

"Nightmare?" she asked sympathetically.

He looked sullenly at his lap and pressed his lips tightly together.

"Want to talk about it?"

"Why should I want to talk to you? You don't care about anything. You're just an Amazon. Do what you please. Take off when things get inconvenient—I'm not going to trust *you* for anything!" He lay down with his back to her, and Jamilla returned to her bedroll and tried to stop shivering.

Was her son crying for her, she wondered, and would he feel, when he grew older, that she had abandoned him because she didn't want him? Would he understand that she was doing what she really believed to be best for him, regardless of what it cost her? And *was* what she was doing the best thing to do?

She didn't hear Coryn cry again that night, but she wondered if he lay awake for the rest of it.

He was silent the next day, but started crying again in his sleep that night. Jamilla quietly moved her bedroll close to his, and very softly, being careful not to wake him, sang a lullaby. Apparently enough of it got through, for he stopped crying and slept peacefully. He gave her a strange look when he woke in the morning and found her near him, but he didn't say anything. And that night, when they made camp, he put his bedroll near hers—not as close as they had been in the morning, but much closer than the other side of the fire where he had started.

Over the next couple of days he became slowly more approachable; he began to ask questions about the route they were taking and the strange plants along the trail and why did the stars look so much brighter than they did in the city. It was the day before they were due to reach Nevarsin when they passed a gully littered with the remains of many rockfalls. At the moment the road was clear, but there was still enough of the mountain hanging overhead to make it plain that this could change at any time. Coryn looked very nervous as they rode through that section, and he carefully waited until they were out of it before asking, with studied casualness, "Is that where my mother died?"

"I believe so," Perdita replied, "but it's usually quite safe; I've been through there dozens of times. Anyway we're through it now."

"Right." Coryn said. "All through it." But Jamilla noticed that he shivered for quite a while afterward.

That night he put his bedroll so close to hers it was almost touching, and she wasn't surprised when the crying started. This time it escalated rapidly into sobs, followed by a scream of "Mother!"

Perdita, several feet away, woke up at that, but Jamilla, already gathering Coryn into her arms, shook her head, and Perdita lay down again.

"Mother, mother, don't leave me!" Coryn cried, still mostly asleep, but clinging desperately to Jamilla.

"It's all right, chiyu," Jamilla murmured soothingly. "I'm here, I've got you, it's all right." She repeated the reassurances until the tight clutch relaxed and Coryn drifted back to sleep, then she tucked him, bedroll and all, carefully in beside her.

When she woke the next morning he was sitting beside her, watching her. "I had a funny dream last night," he announced. "I dreamed I was looking for my mother under all those rocks, and then there was this old woman—really old, older than anyone I've ever seen—and she said that all Renunciates were my mother because they were all sisters and daughters of the same mother—so does this mean that you're my mother?"

Jamilla smiled as she hugged him. "Yes, Coryn, that's what it means. That's what the Oath is about—it's not intended to cut us off from our families, it's supposed to make us all part of a bigger family.''

And Edrik is still part of my family, she realized, even if he is a boy and can't live with me—Edrik is still my child. When she returned to Thendara she would see him, even if it was more painful for them both than a clean break. They would both come to terms with that, painful or not.

Coryn hugged her good-bye at the entrance to Nevarsin Monastery, and hugged Perdita too, ''because if Jamilla's my mother, you're my aunt.'' Then Jamilla and Perdita started on the trip back to Thendara—and their other son and nephew.

About Deborah Wheeler and "Midwife"

Deborah Wheeler's first professional sale was to my anthology Sword and Sorceress, *which she followed up with an even better story for* Sword and Sorceress II. *Naturally I asked her for a story for this anthology, and she came up with "Midwife," which is not what one would expect of a story with that title . . . 'nuff said.*

Deborah is a youngish woman with a four-year-old daughter; she started writing stories (mostly about animals) in her teens, without professional success, then put her writing ambitions on hold "in favor of more socially 'serious' matters such as health care." She "got side-tracked into psychology for a while" and did a master's degree at Portland College; then was an instructor in physiology and bacteriology at her chiropractic college and was Dean of the school when her daughter Sarah was just an infant. The result, she says, was "total burnout" and she felt lucky to quit before it left too many scars on either of them. She is a Black Belt in Kung Fu, and actively supports martial-arts training for women. Currently she is volunteer-teaching a program of infant swim at the local Y.

MZB

MIDWIFE

by Deborah Wheeler

The nest was empty except for a large dark egg. The second piece of good luck was that the entrance to the banshee's lair was partially blocked by snow and debris, which meant that it could not return without giving Gavriela ample warning. Unfortunately, it also meant that she was trapped in a small, smelly place until she could dig herself out.

Gavriela n'ha Alys sat back on her heels and considered her situation. She had not cried since her oath-taking, and she did not cry now. She should have waited at Nevarsin for her Renunciate escort, who had been delayed by bad weather. Gavi had thought only of her own driving restlessness and the quickening snowfalls; she would *not* spend another winter snowed-in, no matter how precious the medical records she was copying. Her replacement, a smiling, self-sufficient sister from Temora, had already settled in; there was nothing between Gavi and the trail to Thendara but a stupid rule about not traveling alone, so she had seized the opportunity. Then she had realized she was being tracked, and had imagined bandits, or worse. In her fear she had become lost in the heights.

Gavi ran sweating hands over her trail-stained trousers. Surely she could afford to rest a little, trusting that the avalanche which had driven her to this shelter had also destroyed, or at very least delayed, her pursuers. She could not face them, or outrun them, even if she managed to find her pack animal. Her fighting skills were barely adequate; her escort would have been a competent woman with a sharp blade and ready fists. But she was alone. . . .

All the smiths in Zandru's forge can't mend that broken egg, Gavi told herself sternly. *And speaking of eggs. . . .*

She went over to the brown oval, breathing through her mouth to avoid the stench of banshee living habits. It lay a little distance from the central pile of bone and offal. In the half-light she could detect a regular pattern of bumps and splotches on its surface. The egg was as ugly and smelly as its parent.

Her eyes lit on a large bone which appeared free from shreds of putrid meat. She identified it as the scapula of a *chervine*. She picked it up, reassured by its smooth dry texture, and turned back to the plug of snow and gravel. The bone spared her mittens from being shredded when she would need them later. Still, digging was hard work, and as her body heat soared, Gavi had to shed her outer layers of clothing.

Once or twice she thought she heard a sound from behind her, and turned, fearful that the banshee might have returned through another opening. She could not understand why the parent was absent—didn't banshees incubate their eggs? Even in the partial light, she could see that the lair had no other entrance. She had cleared a space almost large enough to crawl through when the egg began rocking violently. A curved beak, glistening wet, emerged from a jagged slit.

Gavi's first impulse was to launch herself through the narrow aperture, regardless of damage to skin or clothing, but caution stayed her. What if the hatchling displayed the legendary speed and appetite of an adult banshee? It might seize her before she could draw her knife. Or, worse yet, what if it caught her midway through the opening?

Cr-rack! Fragments of shell splintered the rude floor. Behind the beak came a bony head, poking vaguely at the hole which was still too small for passage. The creature made a soft burbling noise.

Gavi gave a short, nervous laugh. "You stupid bird! Get your nose back inside so you can peck your way out."

As if in response to her words, the egg began gyrating violently, and the cries escalated to shivering moans. The movements became so agitated that Gavi feared it might topple itself and split its skull on the rocks. She forgot the birthings she had witnessed, mute and miserable, in her childhood village. Her Guild Mothers had wanted her to train as a midwife or animal-healer, but she would have none of it. She had retorted that she had seen enough innocents die and had changed enough breech-clouts to last a lifetime. She had fled to the Thendara Guild House to escape that cycle of pain and incompetence. She had not added that she had *felt* each dying mind call to her.

Now the struggling banshee chick had got itself coiled around her guts in the same way. She could sense its desperation as if it were her own, could *feel* its fading strength as it battered its soft head against the unyielding shell.

"Idiot, not like that." Gavi put the *chervine* scapula down and stepped closer to the egg. She drew her short knife and thrust it into the shell, using the blade as a lever to widen the opening. The chick quieted as soon as she touched its prison. It was still wet with amniotic fluid, but not as odorous as she had expected.

As soon as she had cleared an opening for the head, the thrashing began again, forcing her to step back lest the thing knock her from her feet. Soon the rest of the supple neck emerged from the splitting shell, then a rounded body on two thick legs. Except for the scaled hide on its feet, the chick was covered with wet down and looked very much like a huge drenched fowl. Even in the gloom, Gavi could see that it had no eyes. She stepped back, her heart pounding. Of course, it hunted by sound and detection of body warmth. Its head swung back and forth as if sniffing the air. Any moment now it would sense her and strike. . . .

The banshee chick took an unsteady step and began a wavering croon. *Think, stupid!* Gavi shrilled at herself. *What do newborns need? Food, of course! And if you don't give it anything else, it'll eat you!*

The small pack which she usually carried had not been lost along with her baggage animal. Gavi lifted the flap and took out a packet of dried meat. Fighting to control her trembling, she held out a strip. The chick continued its piteous cry, rocking back and forth on taloned feet. She approached closer, dangling the food under its nose. Suddenly the bird crouched, belly low to the floor, and opened its mouth.

"Look, stupid," Gavi said as she dropped the jerky into the chick's gaping beak. "Here it is. Who would have thought you'd need hand-feeding, a big ugly brute like you?" The parent banshee would be doing the feeding under normal circumstances.

The banshee chick swallowed the meat strip in a single gulp and resumed its begging posture. Gavi shook her head and fed it another, and another. She was no longer trembling, but now concerned about her food supply. If it was satisfied with everything she had, it might not attack her, but what would she eat before she could reach help? And if her meager hoard was not enough, it might decide she would make a fine dessert.

The chick gobbled all of the meat plus some dried fruit and porridge meal, then closed its beak with a resounding snap. Still keeping its visibly bulging belly to the ground, it sidled up to her. Gavi told herself that this could not be an attack stance, and forced herself to stand still. The chick's down was beginning to dry and to fluff out around its head and neck as it rubbed against her boots and thighs. She found herself tempted to touch the soft feathers.

Evanda and Avarra, it thinks I'm its mother! Repulsive as

it might be to her human eyes, she supposed the gangling thing must be appealing to an adult of its own species.

"No! I may have helped get you out of that Zandru-cursed shell, but I won't be a nursemaid to you, or anything else!"

But it was clearly no use. She had fed it, and spoken to it, and now it brushed against her legs in a fumbling caress, anchored to her body warmth. Banshees had a reputation of being as stupid as they were deadly, and sheer instinct had imprinted her upon this one's brain as its sole source of food and love.

"I suppose that's one small grace," she said, moving toward the lair's opening. "If you think I'm your mother, you won't try to eat me. There's just a little more to clear away here. No, don't butt me with your head, you silly bird. You'll start a slide and bury us both! Get *back!*" As the chick lunged past her, she grabbed it with both hands around its thick neck. The down looked fluffy, but was covered with a sticky film. As soon as she touched it, the bird ceased struggling and took up its loving croon.

"Shut up. Just don't get in my way, and we'll both be free. I can be on my way to Thendara, where any reasonable woman would want to be for the winter, and you can be somewhere else, as high and as far away from me as you can get. Understand?" The banshee chick rubbed its head against her hip and intensified its hum of devotion.

Gavi pulled herself through the hole, noticing with some exasperation that she had made it amply large for the chick. While it wriggled and flapped through the opening, she got to her feet and looked around. There was no sign of her *chervine* on the new snow, but neither could she see any trace of her followers. The red sun had dipped well toward the horizon.

She pulled on the last of the clothes she had shed during her dig. She still had some time before dark, and should waste none of it. With nightfall would come deathly cold and hunting banshees, if she should still be above the tree-line.

She oriented herself as best she could by the position of the sun and slope of the mountainside, and began to climb down. The chick flopped after her, wailing in distress.

"Oh, stop it. I'm not your mother. It's no good pretending that I'm a heartless brute for abandoning you. You belong here, and I don't. Get busy hunting something else. Shoo!" She made fending motions with her hands, and the infant halted, swinging its head from side to side in puzzlement. In the full light of day, it was even uglier than she had realized.

"I don't have time for this, I've got to be going. No, don't start that racket again, I can't take you with me. Poor thing, I know the light makes you sleepy—so go find some place to curl up, and let me be about my business." Finally, seeing the chick resume its belly-down posture of adoration, she screamed, "Get out of here, you disgusting thing!" with such feeling that the creature, whimpering mournfully to itself, retreated to the mouth of its lair.

She passed the tree-line before dark, cold and scratched from a tumble on loose rock. One ankle throbbed ominously, her elbow was bruised and swollen, and her mittens were torn, but on the whole she had come off lightly. She was able to force down a portion of her food and find a sheltered spot beneath the branches of an evergreen grove. She made a bed of the dry fallen needles and buried herself in them for warmth.

Gavriela awoke chilled on one side. A rather large and soft lump had planted itself along the length of her legs. She wrinkled her nose as a distinctive odor reached her, and opened her eyes.

The banshee chick, now noticeably larger than the day before, butted its head against her, warbling contentment. Gavi felt her guts rebel at the smell and hissed, "You stupid bird, what are you doing here? No, you're not allowed to follow me. Oof! Idiot, get off my foot! You belong up there,

above the tree-line, and you're supposed to be nocturnal."
She got to her feet and surveyed the fawning monster.

"You seem to have done well enough without me. All that
gore on your chest must be leftovers from dinner last night.
Ugh! Your table manners could be improved. No, I won't let
you near me until I've cleaned you up a bit. Hold still!" The
pine needles were absorbent and would make the thing smell
better.

She discarded the last handful of soiled leaves and pushed
the chick away. "Now go, do you hear me? I don't want
you! Scat!" The chick sidled a few steps away, the heat-
sensing eye spots on its skull shining in the wan sunlight. Its
croon degenerated into a mournful sob.

Gavi could not suppress a smile. "You do make the most
ridiculous noises, but that makes no difference. Off you go."
She turned on her heel and proceeded down the slope.

She knew the bird was following her, keeping hidden in
the shadowed shelter of the rocks. Banshees were torpid by
day, and the direct sunlight must make any activity difficult.
If only the thing would give up and go back where it belonged! she fumed, wondering if she had created a perverted,
daytime, human-loving monstrosity.

Before long she found the trail of wild mountain *chervines*,
and knew that it would lead to a source of water. Upon
examining the prints, she detected the impressions of shod
hooves. If Evanda's own luck were with her, her pack animal
had survived, and she stood a chance of recovering her food
and gear. She quickened her pace along the trail.

Gavi stumbled into the camp without warning. Just a turn
off the main path, and suddenly she was practically in the lap
of a strange man, hastily rising from a cook-fire. It was too
late to rectify her error. She had been so preoccupied with
escape from the banshee and finding her lost pack animal,
that she had forgotten the men who had shadowed her the day

before. She knew she could not hold her own against multiple experienced attackers. Against one, maybe . . . Her small knife felt steady and solid in her hand.

The man before her, wiping his hands on his homespun breeches, was clearly no bandit and he seemed to be alone. Gavi let the tip of her knife drop, but did not relax her fighting stance. Her eyes lit upon her *chervine*, tied to a branch on the far side of the fire, partially unloaded. Her precious warm clothing and blankets lay scattered irreverently in the dust.

"That's my animal and my pack."

The herdsman's face reddened in a twisted grin, showing badly decayed teeth. "Ho-oh-oh!" he exclaimed in a thick provincial accent. "Finder keeps all, that's the law of the hills. You be stranger, p'raps you not know the law. Who be your man?"

"I am a free woman, I answer to no man."

"Naw! But yet, I have hear of such. Lordless wenches you be. A bedding and a beating will soon lesson you, ho-oh-oh! Unless you relish them in the reverse order." He guffawed, much impressed by his own humor.

Gavi pressed her lips together in revulsion. And she had thought the banshee chick ugly! It was only a natural creature, bound by instinct. It meant her no personal harm and knew no better, whereas the man before her, sniggering as he approached, had at least the outward seeming of rationality, yet was incapable of decency or honor. She thrust out her knife so she could be sure he saw it.

"I warn you, I am prepared to defend myself."

He halted, but his unpleasant expression did not change. "What, with that little pinsticker?" He chuckled, looking down at his expanse of fat-cushioned gut. "Naw, wouldn't do more than scratch. Might be good for pickin' teeth afterward."

Gavi fought to keep from trembling, realizing the weakness of her position. One part of her mind kept arguing, *He's*

*trying to bully you into defeat, don't listen to him! A Free
Amazon never gives up, haven't you learned anything? What
would your Guild sisters say to that? You can still aim for a
vital target. His fat won't protect his throat or eyes. You can
use his own weight against him!* But her psychological de-
fenses had been breached, and she knew he could see the
despair in her eyes.

The same fury which had driven her from her father's
house to the gates of the Thendara Guild House boiled up in
Gavriela's heart. *No!* she stormed. *I will not be cowed like
some dumb beast! I know I've little skill as a fighter, but if I
cannot stop him any other way, it's my corpse he'll have to
rut on. May Avarra have mercy on my soul!*

She took a step backwards, considering flight and discard-
ing the idea. She was weakened from her night of exposure,
and to be caught from behind would sacrifice any fighting
advantage she might have. She tightened her grip on her
small knife and took a deep breath. There was still a slim
chance she could stun him enough to escape.

The herdsman made a quick movement, closing the distance between them by half. Gavi knew that she could not
have outrun him, even panic-fueled. She prepared for the
shock of his attack when suddenly the air shattered with a
horrendous ululating cry. It stunned her, freezing her heart
and almost causing her to drop her knife. Again came the
shriek, so close she could not determine its direction.

The effect upon the man was equally astounding. Color
evaporated from his face, leaving him ashen white, and he
began to tremble violently. "Banshee," he whispered. "Ach,
'tis doom for sure, to hear a banshee under the bloody sun."

" 'Tis doom for sure to lay a finger on me or mine!" Gavi
cried. "Did you think I meant to defend myself with this
small knife alone? Get you gone before I summon the demon
to swallow you up!"

For a moment she feared that his native shrewdness would

give him pause, but his wits had fled along with his ruddy complexion. He vanished down the trail, leaving the remains of his own camp behind. Gavi did not stop shaking until he was well out of sight.

The wailing came another time, softer and more defined in direction. She could see the chick above her now, moving down with unexpected grace. The *chervine* gave a hoarse whicker, its eyes rolling in fright, and pulled at its tether. Gavi petted it soothingly.

"No, stop, you dumb bird! You'll scare the wits out of my baggage, and then I'll be right back where I started. All right, I'll come up to you. Just stay there!"

The chick seemed to have grown since the morning, its feathers smoother and less fluffy. Its hunting wail died into a croon of ecstasy as she approached it.

Relief swept away terror as Gavi bent to the banshee, her arms going automatically around it. It was long minutes before she could sob, "Oh, you ridiculous, disgusting bird, you saved me! I was dumb enough to travel without an escort, and you volunteered to be mine."

She sat back on her heels. "What am I to do with you now? I can't stay here, even if I wanted to, not with winter coming on. No, stop butting me with your beak, those teeth are sharp! Listen, idiot—oh, who's the idiot? Me for breaking a rule meant to protect me, or you for thinking I'm your mother?"

The banshee, still humming in delight, snaked its neck along the side of her thigh. She stroked it hesitantly, feeling the oiled smoothness of the feathers overlying its baby down. "You truly can't come with me," she said in a soft voice. "You shouldn't even be awake now, it's unhealthy for you. And you've got to go back to the heights where you belong, just as I've got to return to Thendara." She realized that part of her had grown attached to the infant, ugly though it might be. She had helped birth it, had fed it, cared for it, spoken to it as a companion . . . and now she must let it go. She must make it return to its natural environment. But how? Scolding had not deterred it, although she owed her life to that failure.

Gavi took the hideous head in her hands, carefully avoiding the sensitive eyespots. She fumbled in her heart for the words that would make parting as much an act of love as following.

"You must go your own way, my friend, as I must go mine. Not because you are ugly in my sight, or because there is no bond between us. But rather because your life must be up there, where you can flourish. You are a child of the Gods, no less than I, and they have made us different. Return to your own place with my blessing. *Adelandeyo*. Go in peace."

The banshee chick huddled still and warm by her side, its croon thrumming like a heartbeat. Gavi could see no flicker of response or of comprehension. Why had she expected it would understand? Banshees were so stupid as to be practically brainless, she had always been told. It was the victim's own fear that enabled them to survive.

The chick dropped its beak with its wicked hook and razor serrations, caressing her thigh with the polished outer surface. Then it heaved itself to its feet and departed upward with surprising speed. Gavi watched until it was out of sight, then rubbed her hands and clothing with scented leaves before approaching the *chervine* again.

As she shook out and repacked her clothing and sleeproll, Gavriela thought, *It couldn't have understood me, but it did. Maybe I spoke to it in the same way it reached me from its shell. If I can midwife a banshee, I can learn to love anything. The Guild Mothers were right, I ought to be using my gifts, but not for watching babies die . . . for helping them live. But they'll never believe the birthing that taught me that lesson!*

The *chervine* butted her with its soft nose as she led it down the slopes toward Thendara and home.

About Maureen Shannon and "Recruits"

"Recruits" derives—according to the author—from the story "There Is Always an Alternative" by Pat Mathews (see "Girls Will Be Girls"). Maureen says, "I found myself musing on the kind of woman who would want to join, and I couldn't believe that all would be so bitterly intense. Surely some petitioners would just be misfits for one reason or another; hence 'Recruits.'

This is a jolly story, a pleasant change from the usual Free Amazon story, which suggests, "behind every Free Amazon lies a story, usually a tragedy" —justified, of course, because in a society like Darkover, whenever a woman chooses to opt out of her life it is a serious business, not to say grim. Nevertheless, without minimizing the seriousness of a woman's painful choices, it's nice to take a rest from the unrelieved tragedy of some of these choices.

Maureen Shannon is an instructor at Kankakee Community College, where she teaches creative writing, freshman composition, and vo-tech communications (whatever that is). She is the mother of two daughters, seventeen and twenty, and the grandmother of two boys. She lives in the country (Clifton, Illinois) with three dogs, six cats, and one horse.

MZB

RECRUITS

by Maureen Shannon

"It's a lovely house," gushed Esarilda, "and in such an excellent location!"

Nearly everyone else would have looked at the dumpy female next to me as if she had lost her wits. The building we were staring at had been a lot of things, including a brothel and a mercenaries' barracks, but one thing it had never been was lovely. Standing three stories tall and three rooms wide, the shabby blackstone faced, nearly windowless, onto the narrow lane in which we stood. A large empty lot to our right held the charred remains of a warehouse and was filled with the smelly, unsightly refuse of several dozen years. To our left a sleazy alehouse shared the high west wall of our house. Across the street was another tavern flanked by a few small shops. At the end of the dead-end lane, a large, spreading building housed a combination flophouse, tavern, and brothel.

But I agreed. It was a lovely house and a lovely location, for the house belonged to us and represented the first expansion of The Sisterhood of the Sword, whose first house had been established only a few short years ago in Thendara. And already that house was so filled to overflowing with newly pledged Sisters that crowding had become a major concern for us. Then, a man whose sister had given up prostitution to become one of us, died and left us this property in Caer Donn. So Esarilda and I had come to inspect it, to see what needed to be done and to prepare for whatever recruits came our way. But I couldn't help worrying about my ability to run a sisterhouse even though I had lived in the Thendara Guild House since I was five. Would I find anyone to join us? In Thendara only word of mouth brought us our new members, for we were pledged by law not to seek new members actively. How would anyone ever know that we were here ready to receive recruits? If we did get any, would I be able to manage so that we all lived harmoniously together?

"Let's go in," demanded Esarilda. She was shivering in the chill, late-winter wind. I took the huge brass key from its chain about my neck and unlocked the massive, copper-plated door. But it took both of us to shove it open enough for us to slip through. And the door must have been masculine for it protested with a harsh screech as we pushed it in.

The center room was a small stronghold, built that way, no doubt, when the building housed mercenaries. Only one door broke the solidarity of the massive wooden walls and slits in the ceiling gave defenders above the ability to pour boiling water on invaders. It appeared to me that a few staunch swordswomen could hold off an army from this room.

This door led into a second hall with a stairway leading upward and doors set into each wall. We poked and pried our way through every room, Esarilda uttering delighted cries at each new discovery. For her everything appeared to be an asset, from the huge, old-fashioned kitchen to the numerous small bedrooms on the second and third floors. I tried to share her optimism, tried to tune in vicariously to the zest with which my companion, twenty years older than I chronologically but ever younger emotionally, faced the world.

"Come here and look," she called. "Come see what's in the back, Maellen."

I followed her through the back door of the kitchen into a narrow passageway that led, Esarilda had already discovered, to a small dairy and thence into a stone barn of decent size. Both buildings were a mess, the former occupants having cleaned nothing. Harnesses and tools rotted in huge, composted piles of manure while large crocks, which had once held milk and cheeses, lay so scattered about that it was impossible to note immediately whether any were still whole.

"Quick, quick, Maellen. Out here! Just see what else we have."

Feeling somewhat like the tail of the donkey—always trailing behind—I went out of the barn into the long, narrow garden of the house. Esarilda's latest treasure was three scrawny trees whose bare branches still held a few withered fruit. Esarilda, hopping about like a bushjumper, her short hair frizzed about her head like that creature's bluish flagtail, had disappeared into a small building set within the end wall. Now she came out, wiping spider webs from her face, which was wreathed in smiles. "Come see, Maellen," she called again. "What a find! This is a poultry house and guess what? There is even a fowl sitting on a nest full of eggs!" From the tones of her voice, you would have thought she had discovered wealth beyond compare. She urged me to enter and view the little brown hen with my own eyes.

"No, no," I said, pausing in the doorway and eyeing the years-long accumulation of webs and dust and dead insects. "I can see her quite clearly from here. She looks indeed to be a treasure. But come away now, Esarilda. It's near noon and I am getting hungry. Perhaps the alehouse next door serves food."

With the alacrity of a child, Esarilda trotted off across the garden to the back door. I felt a little guilty about using the lure of food on her, knowing it was something that she could never resist. But there was a lot to do yet if we were to sleep tonight in our new sisterhouse. So much for just two women. How soon, I wondered, before we could find others to join us.

We reconnoitered for a moment or two outside the door of the alehouse whose enchanting sign proclaimed that this was

The Roaring Rabbithorn. An odd name, indeed, but as soon as I met mine host, I was charmed by the perspicacity of the namer. The main clientele appeared to be tradespeople from the various small shops, including some women, so my companion and I entered and found a small table next to the wall where we had a good view of the front door and could, if we found ourselves attacked, make a quick exit through the passageways leading out to the privy at the end of the alehouse garden. My host himself came bustling up to take our order. "And what will it be, *domnas*?" he asked, his deep bass voice booming from an exterior that was as round and jovial appearing as a woodsbear. "The speciality today is tripe stew and my wife's made an excellent fruit pastry. Will you have that? I assure you," he went on, giving us no time to answer, "it's the best thing on the menu today. Not the only thing, oh, my, no. My Carla's too good a cook for that. But the very best. So, will it be stew and pastry?"

Barely giving us enough time to shake our heads, he was off with a bound like that of a startled rabbithorn. Esarilda clapped her hands with glee. "Now there," she affirmed, "is a nice man."

My mother once told me that everyone who joined our sisterhood had a tragedy in her past. I knew this was true of Esarilda, though I had never heard the particulars, my mother refusing to gossip and myself reluctant to disturb her present cheerful outlook with questions about the miseries of the past. Men had surely mistreated her, as with most of us, yet she could still find redeeming qualities in some of those she met. But I had no time to marvel anew at my friend's character for the host's wife had issued from her domain to direct the placing of our food. She was as tall, thin and calm as he was short, round and boisterous. Once the bowls and plates had been set before us, she waved him off to another table and, drawing out a bench, seated herself at the table with us, giving us a questioning look as she said, "May I join you?"

"We'd love it," Esarilda told her, through a bite of stew. "Hmmm, this is the best tripe stew I have ever had. You are a wonderful cook." She underlined her sincerity by scooping another large bite into her mouth.

Our hostess dipped her head in as grateful an acknowledgment as any noblewoman's. She gestured for me to begin eating. "I am Carla and you are the new owners of the house next door," she began. "You are members of the Sisters of the Sword. It is not just that I recognize the earring in your ear or your red tunics, though I've a cousin in Thendara Guild House who has been to see me a time or two dressed as you are. No, it's that brass key about your neck, *domna* which I've seen many a time when old Larren was here for lunch. He told me last winter, when he was so poorly, what he intended to do with his property—indeed, there's hardly a soul in Caer Donn he didn't tell, so proud he was of 'my sister, the swordswoman'! I've been waiting for you to arrive."

I put down my spoon. Her words and face were calm and I was hard put to tell whether she was welcoming or hostile.

"Did you perchance see the sign over the door as you entered?"

"Yes?" I was polite, yet reserved, but not so Esarilda. "So clever, Carla, really a delight. Who painted it?"

"My daughter Shaya. And she is why I have been waiting for you to arrive. She's a good girl, Shaya is, and a decent cook if she puts her mind to it. But there's the rub. 'Tis seldom she wants to put her mind to it. Painting pictures like that jolly drawing of her father on the alehouse sign or carving little statues like those on the mantle," she waved toward several dozen wooden statues, all with the same whimsical quality of the painting. "I've found good marriages for my other girls so that now there's only the two little ones and Shaya left. But what man wants a wife who's always dreaming? Shaya's a bit frail, I doubt you'll make a swordswoman of her, but my cousin tells me that there are other duties in a Guild House.''

"But, Carla," I protested, "members of the Sisterhood must come of their own free will."

"Oh, it's her will to join you, but I am just breaking the ice for her. She's a bit shy, my Shaya. She's above stairs. Will you go up when you have eaten?"

I nodded, still reluctant. Those who pledge to us must be sure in their determination because of the opposition they will meet. Too many men—and women also—feel that our Sisterhood is unnatural, unseemly, a danger to the relationships of men and women throughout the Hundred Kingdoms. As domineering as this woman appeared, I feared that her daughter was being thrust upon us for some devious purpose of her own, perhaps that of a spy.

Esarilda was first up the stairs, bouncing up the steep steps as if she had not just consumed enough food for three big men. "Hello there!" I heard her say. "Your mother says you want to join the Sisterhood." I was a step behind so my first impression of Shaya was the melodic quality of her voice as she answered Esarilda in bell-like tones.

"Yes. It has been my greatest dream since first Cousin Callie returned to tell us of the Sisterhood. Please do say that I might try."

My heart sank when I saw her. Frail she most definitely was, and crippled besides; a childhood illness had left her with one leg shorter than the other. She was as short as Esarilda but twice as slender with a mass of brown hair that haloed her too-thin face with its huge, dreamy eyes. How could she defend herself? This woman could never take up a sword and face down a man.

"But, Maellen, really, neither can I," remonstrated Esarilda and I was sunk with shame to realize I had spoken aloud.

Shaya spoke in her little, soft voice. "Cousin Calli says that not all sisters are cut out for fighting. Some hire out their services as guides or outfitters and others stay within in the Guild House and do the sewing, cooking, cleaning and so on. I am a very good seamstress and my mother has taught me much of her cooking skill. Truly I can be an asset to the Sisterhood if you will only let me try. I paint also,'' she added modestly, ''and many people say that my paintings are good. I could paint a sign on the front of the house that would let people know that this is the Sisterhouse. And I sing and play so that I could entertain the sisters in the evenings.'' Her words came in a rush and when they ended, she sat staring at me with those wide, sad eyes. I was not sure that Shaya was the kind of woman the Sisterhood was looking for; most of my mother's recruits in Thendara were adults who had lived rough, hard lives. Yet, our rule was to allow any woman who wished to belong to take the pledge for one year. After that, if she liked the life, she could pledge for three years and finally become a lifetime member as Esarilda and I were.

"Very well,'' I decided. "If you wish to join us on a year's probation, you may.''

"May I come today?'' Shaya struggled to her feet, propping herself with a beautifully carved crutch. She makes beauty out of necessity, I thought. She and Esarilda will do well together.

"The house is a mess,'' I warned her. "There is no clean place to lay our heads tonight and I doubt anyone has cooked a meal in that kitchen for years.''

Shaya laughed with delight. "Then already there is something that I can do. I shall help cook and clean that we might eat and sleep well tonight.''

She was as good as her word for between the three of us we scoured out a room on the second floor for each of us and spread clean linen brought from Thendara on the beds. Although we had no time to tackle the kitchen before supper, Carla knocked at the garden door at eventide with a tray full of luscious food. Her usual sober face was wreathed with smiles as she watched Shaya tuck into her food with an enthusiasm that was more typical of Esarilda. "Good," Carla praised. "Already you have done good for her. Never ate she that well at home." She left, promising over all our protests, that she would be back on the morrow to clean the kitchen. "Let my other girls help their father without me for once," she ordered. "It will do them good."

It was just past noon on the following day when the four of us were startled by a resounding bell. We jumped, our hearts pounding, and looked at one another. Then Shaya began to laugh. "It's the doorbell," she chortled. "I remember hearing that sound when the mercenaries lived here. Oh, my, the way we acted, you would have thought that it was Zandru coming for us from his darkest hells!"

Befitting my position as housemother, I went to answer the summons but I was glad that the other three trailed along behind me. I put hand to my sword, for which I was acclaimed somewhat of a master. Would I already need to defend our house?

Carla had to come and help me wrest the stubborn door open. I looked down the seven steep steps to the street where stood a girl, a dog, and a donkey with the ugliest bird I had ever seen perched on its back. The decrepit-seeming donkey had a patchy coat and a skimpy mane with just the faintest wisp of a tail. Moreover, its belly was swollen so huge with pregnancy that it appeared that any moment it might be airborne. The huge Rouser hound stood taller and broader than the donkey. After looking us all over, he yawned, revealing formidable fangs and than sank to the ground and began licking his massive paws. The bird cawed, lifting its bedraggled crest and staring up at me with glittering dark eyes sunk deep in its naked, ugly head.

"I have come to join the Swordswomen," said the new-comer. "Do you have a stable for my friends?"

She was as extraordinary as her animals. There was no

mistaking her pregnancy; like the donkey, she was so huge one expected to see her float off in the brisk wind. At some time she had hacked off her hair so that now it curled all about her head in one-inch ringlets of a pale, pinkish-yellow shade. Her eyes were gray-green and slanted either side of an up-turned, freckled nose.

"Well? Are you going to keep me standing about here in this cold and damp or do I come in?"

A little aghast, for this newest petitioner seemed even more unsuitable than the first, I directed her to the gate at the back of the garden, going back through the house to unlock for her. Carla had taken herself off to The Roaring Rabbithorn, chuckling to herself while Esarilda and Shaya had scurried upstairs to clean another room for our latest recruit.

I led the girl to the stable, apologizing for its derelict state. "No problem, no problem," said the girl. Although her movements were clumsy, impeded as she was by her huge belly, nevertheless, they were knowledgeable. "I've a little grain left for Casilda"—she patted the donkey as she guided her into the stall to which she had added some old straw— "but Fang has had the last of the meat I had with me. You'll have to get more for his supper." The Rouser hound seemed to know she was talking of him because he rubbed his broad head against her shoulder. His mistress gave him a quick pat before turning her attention to the bird.

"Come, come, my precious," the girl crooned to the bird as she lifted her to a makeshift perch, checking her jesses to make sure her legs were not chafed. "Seefar is not really mine," she was explaining. "Not like Cassilda and Fang who have been mine since I was a child. I found her as I was coming this way. There had been a battle and she had been wounded and left for dead, I think. So I brought her along. I couldn't let her spy for the wrong man, now could I? No, of course, I couldn't." A little dazed, I suggested that we go in and see to her comfort, now that her companions had been cared for. When the dog started to follow, I suggested she leave it in the stable but she said she couldn't do that until the creature felt comfortable in its new home. So while I warmed porridge for our newest petitioner, I fed the hound on scraps from lunch. They were both eating as if they hadn't had a good meal in weeks when Esarilda and Shaya joined us. It was Esarilda's friendly manner that drew forth the information I had been too reserved to ask.

"Kadi," she answered when Esarilda asked her name. "My uncle styles himself a king in the Kilghard hills where I have been fostered since I was a babe in arms. He planned for me to marry his youngest son for my mother was a *nedestro* daughter of a Serrais lord and he wished that *laran* for his grandchildren. I've only a little of it myself, not all enough to qualify me for the towers, although I was at Neskaya Tower for a while to learn how to control my gift."

She saw the awe in Shaya's face and hurried to reassure her. "Really, it's very little. Just enough *laran* for me to work with animals and nothing more. Really. Please don't dislike me."

Shaya's giggle rang out like tiny bells. "As if I could! I think it's wonderful no matter how the townspeople mutter about the *Hali'imyn*. But, don't worry. People are always treating me as if I'm strange because I can paint animals as if they were alive. It shan't make the slightest difference to me. You may even sleep in my room with me tonight if you wish." Having been raised with her fourteen brothers and sisters, Shaya had been in ecstasy at the thought of a room of her own but she gladly relinquished the privilege to offer comfort to the newcomer.

"Perhaps I'd better not," said Kadi. "My baby could come at any time." It was the first she had spoken of her pregnancy. Glad to have the subject in the open, Esarilda caught the girl's hand in her own, smiling all over her round face.

"When's the little darling due?" I grimaced slightly at her gushing tone. I knew that Esarilda had borne a number of children herself, though none lived that I knew of. You would have thought that babies would no longer be a novelty. Having lived in the Guild House for most of my life, I had seen any number of babies come and go. If they were girls, they would be allowed to stay and be raised as one of us. But if they were boys, they could remain only until they were five. Finding foster homes for them, and witnessing the agonizing separations of mothers and sons, had strengthened my resolve never to have children. Small chance, really, since I planned never to take a man for a lover. I dropped my musings with a thud when I heard Kadi's answer.

"Any time now if my reckoning is true. I was really praying to Avarra that I could get here in time. You see, I conceived last spring. There were four moons and you know they always say what you do under the four moons should be neither remembered nor regretted. Well, I don't regret that night." She sighed deeply and closed her eyes, a look of dreamy contentment on her face. Opening her eyes, she saw our startled faces and blushed. Climsily, she patted her tummy. "And this is something that has to be remembered."

"Who's the baby's father?" asked Esarilda, passing Kadi some bread and cheese. I shook my head. I would never have dared ask something so personal. If I did, the other person was sure to be offended. I guessed it must be Esarilda's sincere caring that made others accept the most personal questions.

"He was a technician at Neskaya, one who had been kind to me when I first went there. He is dead now, dead in the same battle that wounded my poor bird. So many are dead now, including my uncle, and the cousin he would have forced me to marry, had I not claimed that my baby was many-fathered. Had he known that the baby's father was a son of a Ridenow lord, he would never have thrown me out but would have begun scheming to claim more power through my child. Well, it's done now. I've had a long journey to get here. I was on my way to Thendara when I met some Swordswomen who had been in the battle and they told me to come here. So I did." She leaned forward to lift her legs upon a bench and then eased back in her chair. Her smile of contentment was as warming as the fire in the stove. "How good it is to come home. I have wanted to belong to the Sisterhood since first I heard of it during my stay in Neskaya Tower. A life without a man to order one about, to say "do this" or "do that" and make decisions for me as if I had no more brain nor will than a half-witted child. How good it will be."

I exchanged glances with Esarilda. Did we have a rebel on our hands? There were plenty of rules for living in the Sisterhouse. Sometimes it seemed to me that we were hedged in by all those rules that made our existence possible without daily battles with guardsmen and others who resented our freedom from masculine control.

Esarilda gave her head a tiny shake, her frizzing hair flying up and then settling back into place. She reached forward and took Kadi's hand. "Come, child, it's your bedtime now."

She helped our newest recruit to her feet and had turned to lead her to the stairs when suddenly Kadi bent over and clutched her belly, a startled expression on her face. She gave a small yelp. "I think, maybe, that the baby is coming tonight."

Later, when we had her in her bed, she gave me a wan smile. "If I'm lucky, before much longer, you'll have another new candidate for Swordswoman."

I hated to upset her so I decided to say nothing about her having to give up a son. Time enough to tell her later, I thought, but, as usual, Esarilda rushed in. "What shall you do if it's a boy?"

Kadi was concentrating on her breathing and didn't answer

for a moment. After the spasm had passed, she gasped, "I shall send word to Darril's father. There are so few males left alive in his house since the years of battles that Darril's father will welcome a *nedestro* grandson."

"Won't you mind giving up your baby?" Shaya asked curiously. She was sitting to Kadi's side, the Rouser hound stretched out at her feet.

Kadi shook her head, clutching Shaya's hand tightly as she breathed rapidly through her mouth. When that contraction had passed, she answered Shaya. "No, because I didn't really choose to have a baby now. If Darril was still alive, it might have been different. But I don't think so; I doubt he would have wanted to leave the Tower and I have been planning to be a Sister of the Sword for several years now. I think I will make a good swordswoman."

Then she had no time for more conversation. Esarilda had been midwife at Thendara House for several years and she claimed that she had never seen a birthing proceed so quickly and seemingly effortlessly. The training that Kadi had received in Neskaya Tower helped her control her pain and the weeks she had spent traveling had rendered her body strong and healthy. By late afternoon, Kadi delivered not one but two red-haired sons. They were small but vigorous and their lusty cries delighted Esarilda no end. "Most of my children never drew breath," she said wistfully, "but these little lordlings will cry all night if they're not satisfied. Hush, hush, my sweeting."

The pealing of the bell gave me a good excuse for leaving the too hot, too loud, too emotional room. I didn't even mind that Shaya and Esarilda stayed behind, cooing over the twins while their tired but triumphant mother looked on.

Two women stood at the top of the steps, their faces indistinct in the wavering light of my torch. "Is this the house of the Sisterhood of the Sword? Yes? Then we seek sanctuary."

Feeling harrassed because so much was happening so fast, I bade them enter the hall. Here there was more light and I could see them more clearly. One of them was a heavy-set woman, strong and healthy, with a commanding air. It was she who took one last look down the street and then put her shoulder to the door. The door I had struggled with all day slid smoothly shut. "Well," I thought, more or less coherently, "at least I can find a job for this recruit. She can be door-keeper." Then I shook my head, realizing that I was getting silly.

"I am Mhari and this is Clea and we have come to pledge to the Sisterhood of the Sword. This is the right place, isn't it?" Without waiting for my answer, she continued, "Where is the housemother?"

"I am the housemother. And I will take your pledges but I warn you that we of the Sisterhood take such an oath seriously." I drew myself up. A worrier I might be, but as a staunch advocate of our principles, I could be unmovable. "We require that you understand what is involved in becoming one of us."

For the first time, the smaller woman spoke. "We know we have much to learn but we do understand some of what the Sisterhood stands for. The wife of one of the guardsmen at Castle Hawkridge ran off to join the Swordswomen. She had borne three children in three years and said she was tired of being a brood mare. Alaric went after her, to knock some sense in her and bring her back, but she had joined the Sisterhood and refused to return. He hung around for a while and learned what he could about them. Finally, he gave up and came back but all that winter he griped about their organization. What we heard, we believed in." Her voice was a little shrill when she had finished as if she were afraid that she could not convince me and they would be turned away.

Mhari put her arm around Clea protectively and kissed her

cheek. Defiantly, she looked at me. "My husband took Clea for his *barrranga* but it is I who love her. We have heard that the Swordswomen can be lovers of women without being thought vile and unnatural by the other sisters."

"Well, yes, that is so. But it is scarcely a good enough reason to join the Sisterhood."

"Oh, it is not the only reason," Mhari spoke firmly. "I was given in marriage by my father who cared not that I pleaded against being forced to accept my husband. He was much older than I and had already buried two wives. But I did my duty and gave him four sons. He was such a lecher; he had at least a dozen bastards scattered about the countryside. Then he forced Clea's father to give her to him—really, to *sell* her. And he turned my sons against me as well."

Now it was Clea's turn to reassure Mhari. She murmured a few soothing words and patted the other woman's hand. Mhari smiled sweetly at her and looked again at me. "My husband was ever a fool and chose the loser's side in battle. Now he and my sons are dead and Castle Hawkridge has been given to one of the lords who follows the Hastur king. We would have been part of his prize, to do with as he wished. So, Clea and I packed our belongings, took the riding horses that were ours, and left."

"At first," Clea told me, "we were afraid that we would have to make our way through the country where the battles are being fought to go to Thendara. But last winter our lord, who does business here in Caer Donn, heard about old Larren's will. So we came here and have waited until you arrived. We only heard this morning that you had come. So here we are. Please say that we may stay." Then she gasped and drew back against Mhari. Mhari looked over my shoulder and then shoved Clea behind her, drawing a long-bladed knife and holding it low as if she knew how to use it. I whirled around. Kadi's Rouser hound stood in the doorway behind me.

"It's all right," I said, relieved. "Fang belongs to one of the sisterhood."

Then Shaya limped into view. "Oh, Maellen, Kadi is worried. She has been waked from her sleep by her link with her donkey. The beast is having trouble delivering and Kadi wants to go and help her but Esarilda forbids her to leave her bed. I thought perhaps my mother could help. She has been midwife to all my sisters and sisters-in-law. Maybe a donkey isn't much different." She was so worried that she paid no attention to our newest recruits.

"That is a job for me," said Clea. "My father was a blacksmith who also practiced healcraft and horse-midwifing. A donkey is not different from a horse. I am sure I can help."

"You go back and reassure Kadi," I told Shaya, "and I will take our new sisters to the stable." On the way there, I explained to them that Kadi had just borne twins and could not leave her bed. "I'm sure she is fretting," I added. "She and her animals are *laran*-linked."

The Rouser hound went with us and lay by the donkey's head. I had had little to do with animals and therefore could not help marveling at the comfort the dumb creatures seemed to give one another. Clea knew exactly how to help the donkey deliver and soon I was amazed to see the new-born struggle to its wobbly legs. Awkward though it was, it had soon found its way to its mother's side and then Clea was guiding its head to the life-giving warmth of the donkey's milk. When it had drunk its fill, Mhari picked the creature up and started to walk to the door.

"Where are you going?" I demanded.

"Why, to take this little one up to its mistress. She'll never rest well until she sees that it is safely here."

The Rouser hound bounded ahead of her and I followed, shaking my head. A dog in a birthing room had been strange enough, but a donkey?

When Kadi saw Mhari enter, with the donkey's spindly baby legs dangling and his ridiculous, too long-eared head swiveling as it peered around, she sat up in bed and reached out her arms. "Oh, how kind of you to bring her to me," she cried. As she stroked the donkey's soft baby fur, she smiled at Mhari who had put her arm around Clea. Both of them grinned back but it was Mhari who said, "Well, what are sisters for?"

Esarilda and Shaya, each holding a twin, had come to stand by the bed and admire the donkey. The room was alive with the good will generated by the four of them.

I shook my head, grinning from ear to ear myself. It was certainly the oddest—but the most delightful—bunch of recruits ever to come a housemother's way.

We were off to a good start.

About Mercedes Lackey and
"A Different Kind of Courage"

One of the main points made (and made again) about the Free Amazons is the point that all women are not suited to earn their livelihood as mercenary soldiers or mountain guides. From the beginning these have been the most popular and visible Free Amazons; but there are many others, and perhaps the second most popular plot about Free Amazons is the story about the woman who establishes herself in a more traditional role, as healer.

Mercedes (Misty) Lackey lives in Oklahoma, and her main occupation is "computer programmer," but she lists writing among her hobbies, along with needlework and sewing; she had had several stories published published in the small semi-pro fantasy magazines (in these days of diminishing markets, that would count as publishing credit) and is a musician, having had several songs published in small folk-singing journals. She also tapes opera performances for us when they aren't broadcast in the Bay Area. She calls her taste in music catholic, ranging from folk to opera; calls herself a "reformed chocoholic and inveterate Cokaholic" (knowing her, one is certain she refers to soda pop rather than illegal chemicals), and "would like to become good enough at writing to support (herself) without having to punch a timeclock." Wouldn't we all!

MZB

A DIFFERENT KIND
OF COURAGE

by Mercedes Lackey

Rafi rubbed at the scars on her hand surreptitiously as she sat on her saddle in the tiny, ill-kept traveler's shelter, hoping neither of the other two Guild Sisters with her would notice the movement. Caro, tall, lean and lantern-jawed, moved quickly and efficiently around the walls, stuffing moss into the cracks that the wind continually whistled through. Lirella, smaller than her freemate and much more muscular, had brought armloads of firewood inside and was preparing a hot meal. Both of them had made it very plain to Rafi that her efforts at helping them had only hindered their work.

The scars ached, as they always did when her hands were cold, and Rafi was afraid that if the two older women noticed her stealthy massaging, they'd regard it as one more sign of weakness.

Her hope was in vain; Caro's gray eyes, so quick to detect any movement around her, fixed on Rafi's hands. Caro's long face showed no expression that Rafi could read, but then Rafi had only known the older woman for six months. Rafi froze, and Caro's eyes flickered briefly to her face before looking away again. The glance had been neutral, noncommittal—but Rafi wilted anyway.

Neither Caro nor her freemate Lirella had wanted Rafi along on this trip, but there hadn't been a great deal of choice for any of them. ''Our orders from Thendara House are to deliver this package directly into the hands of the Keeper at

Caer Donn,'' Guildmother Dorylis had said. "And yes, yes, I know the Domains will have nothing to do with Aldaran—officially. Like us, the Towers do not always pay any more than lip service to the 'official' policy. That is why they rely on us to run errands like this one for them. The Sisterhood knows nothing of what is in that package, nor do we care, and the Keeper at Elhalyn knows that. There is some danger attached to the carrying of it, which is why Thendara has asked that I pick our two best mercenaries to convey it—but there is a problem there. Neither of you are Comynara, nor are you familiar with the protocols surrounding a Keeper. I frankly doubt that you'd be let anywhere near her. Rafi, on the other hand—''

Rafiella had blushed as red as the unruly hair on her head.

"I know, I know. She had Keeper training at Neskaya,'' Caro had replied, combing her graying brown hair with impatient fingers. "She would be admitted with no questions asked.''

But Rafi had heard the words Caro had not spoken. *'Keeper training—which she failed at, as she fails at everything she tries.'*

Rafi had tried not to show she'd heard the thought.

The result was that the three of them were sharing the dubious shelter of a poorly maintained waystation deep in the Hellers in the dead of winter. Lirella had made no secret of the fact that she felt Rafi's presence was holding their pace to a crawl, and was the direct cause of their having to settle for this place instead of the shelter of the Guild Hall at Caer Donn they'd hoped to reach this night. Caro had been more circumspect, but Rafi could still feel her disapproval.

"I—is there anything I can do?'' she asked in a small voice.

Lirella gave an undisguised snort. Caro's blond partner never made any attempt to disguise what she felt. Rafi had been no help at all in the unsaddling and tethering of the *chervines*—she was afraid of them—could barely control her own when riding, and her fear had communicated itself to the animals, making them jump and shy. She'd barely pulled her own weight in getting their gear under cover. Granted, she had managed to light a fire using her starstone when neither of the other two could coax anything out of the damp tinder that was all that was available. But she wasn't any better at cooking or setting up camp than she was with the *chervines*.

"Patience, *bredhyina*," Caro said in an undertone. "She's only recently out of seclusion. And when, in a Tower or lady's bower, would she have learned anything of rough camping?"

"It's not just that—" the other woman replied softly. "It's that she's such a—a—wet rag!"

Caro stifled a smile with the back of her hand. "Wet rag" was indeed an apt description of their newest, youngest Sister. Lirella had tried, without much success, to teach her both armed and unarmed combat, but the girl had not only shown no aptitude for what was the mainstay commodity at the tiny Guild House at Helmscrag, but had displayed a level of incompetence that Caro wouldn't have believed if she hadn't seen it with her own eyes. It wasn't that she hadn't *tried*— she'd fallen all over herself (quite literally) trying. Lirella finally refused to teach her any more after she'd nearly broken an ankle attempting a simple lunge. And as for the Training Sessions—!

She'd run out of the first one she'd attended sobbing hysterically. Caro was convinced she still cried after each one, but at least now she did it in private. During the Session, she would sit, hands clenched in her lap or constantly rubbing at the scars that crossed them, pale as Lady Death herself. She spoke only when directly questioned, and then in so soft a voice one could hardly hear her. A wet rag indeed!

Nevertheless, she was no less Caro's Sister. "I can think of one thing that would be helpful—" she began.

"Yes?" The girl all but tripped over her own feet, jumping up.

"The only wood here is wet and half rotten. If we're to get any heat in here tonight—well, there must be some deadfall around here. If you'd take the axe and try to find some—"

Rafi took the proffered axe and hurried out into the snow—but not quickly enough to miss Lirella's weary, "Aren't you afraid she'll cut off her own foot with that?" Tears stung her eyes, and away from the critical observance of the freemates, she let them fall.

Lirella was right—she very well might cut off her own foot. She'd come close enough to doing just that with the wooden practice knife at least a dozen times. The knife she wore now was only for show—she had no intention of ever drawing it. If she did, she'd be more a danger to herself and her Sisters than to any attacker. Why had she ever taken Oath?

Don't be any stupider than you have to be—she told herself sadly. *You know why you took Oath.*

That terrible day, that horrible day when the *leroni* at Neskaya had sent her back to her father, saying she hadn't the "strength" to bear further training as a Keeper, and hadn't the nerves for further work in a Tower. She'd tried—oh merciful Avarra, how she'd tried—but the pain, the burns every time she touched someone, every time someone touched her—the limits of her endurance had been reached, and quickly. The shame she'd felt at being unable to bear what little Keitha, a mere child, had taken without a whimper, had made her wish she'd died in threshold as so many had.

Her father had stared at her when she stood before him; his eyes hard and appraising. For as long as she could remember, he'd called her "the useless mouth to feed." She hadn't the prettiness that had made it easy to find husbands for her sisters, she wasn't capable of handling the staff of the castle when her mother died. He'd been openly relieved when

Neskaya had asked for permission to train her as a Keeper. And now she was back, useless to Neskaya, as she'd been useless to him.

"Zandru's Hells, you're a dough-faced little thing," he'd said finally, with disgust. "All that time at the Tower, and your looks still haven't improved. And what I'd do with you, if it hadn't been for Lord Dougal, I have no idea. However, the old lecher's lady has gone to her rest, and he wants alliance with our house badly. You're no prize, but you're marriageable, and that's all he wants. He's got no heirs, so see that you give him one quickly. He'll be here within a tennight; we'll hold the *di catenas* ceremony as soon as he arrives."

Rafi had stood frozen in shock and dismay. She'd all but fainted on the spot. All she could see in her mind was the image of her mother, wrung out with child after child, finally dying trying to deliver her last. Her father's voice, sharp with impatience, had finally brought her to herself. She'd curtseyed clumsily, made some kind of appropriately grateful comment and left his presence with the uncertain tread of one gone blind.

No one bothered to keep watch on her—no one would ever have expected her to run away. She'd always been so completely obedient, succeeding in that if in nothing else. So no one had stopped her or even questioned her when she left the castle, made her way down to the village, and found the tiny Renunciate Guild House there. She'd known of nowhere else that she'd be safe, for even in her sheltered life she'd heard of Dougal, and the way his wives kept dying, attempting to give him the heir he so desperately desired. To wed him was to receive a death sentence.

She'd not thought beyond taking shelter with them; she'd never had much to do with Free Amazons before. She'd heard tales, of course, some flattering, most not; and had tended to dismiss most of them as midsummer moonshine.

The one thing she had been certain of was that no woman or girl who had taken her Oath need ever fear a man's overruling again.

The little world beyond the Guild House doors had taken her completely by surprise. There, it seemed, women were free to be as strong, as clever, as self-sufficient as any man. They were free to order their own lives completely, subject only to the few rules of the Guild. Rafi had been dazzled—she'd never dreamed that such a thing could have existed. She found something else within those walls as well. The Sisters of the Guild *cared* for one another.

She stopped, leaning against a tree, too blinded by tears to continue pretending to hunt for wood. She'd had such hopes that here, at last, she'd find something she could do *right* for a change. She'd wanted to *belong,* to find her place in that camaraderie. After seeing the care, and yes, the love these women had for one another, she knew there was nothing else in the world she wanted more. But she'd failed in the Guild, just as she'd failed everywhere else.

She couldn't have guessed, of course, that the sole trade of the women at Helmscrag Guild House was the sale of their abilities as fighters, guards, and guides. Of the eleven women at the tiny Guild House, only the Guild Mother herself never undertook such missions. Unfortunately for Rafi, her woeful lack of physical abilities was as great as her lack of beauty. As a child, she'd always been last chosen in games—in fact her presence on a side guaranteed an automatic handicap—and last as a dancing partner. Learning even to defend herself had been an insurmountable task.

Lirella had decided to give an extra spur to her by being more than usually hard with her. All that had brought was painful bruises and plentiful tears.

Try as she would to keep herself shielded, her *laran* had made the thoughts of her fellow Renunciates painfully clear to her. Lirella considered her to be a sniveling coward. Caro simply thought she was abysmally stupid. Guild Mother was convinced that the root of her difficulties lay in too much self-pity, and that she needed to be bullied out of it. The rest shared those opinions to a great or lesser extent. The overall consensus was that she was completely undependable and a regrettable waste of time. Even her appearance was a faint embarrassment to them. Her clothing always had the look of having been slept in, and no matter how carefully it was cut, her hair never failed to look like an untidy hay-rick. She hardly gave the desired impression of the self-sufficient and self-reliant Renunciate.

Perhaps her father had been right to label her as useless. Certainly her Sisters were sure that she was. And that had hurt worse than anything else that had happened to her.

So once again she found herself the unwanted tag-along, the handicap on the team. The feeling of being left out was made more intense by the special relationship between Caro and Lirella. It was rather ironic that the only thing that had pleased the Guild Sisters (and slightly softened Caro's own attitude toward Rafi) had been her reaction to that relationship. Rafi simply hadn't been the least upset by it, and that had surprised all of them—they'd expected her to react with hysterics when she learned of it. But her only reaction had been a wistful envy.

It must have been thinking of the freemates that brought a shrill of alarm from her *laran.* She was taken out of her morass of tears with a shock. Something—something was very wrong at the camp!

She clutched her starstone and tried to will far-vision, then cried out in pain as for a moment she saw through Caro's eyes, and felt the sword-strike Caro was taking in her own flesh.

Guild Mother had warned them of danger—and she had been right. The danger had been greater than any of them guessed.

Rafi floundered through the snow back toward the little shelter, but she had come farther than she had thought. By the time she reached the camp, the fight was over.

Four dead men lay in the gathering dusk; Lirella was down, unconscious. Caro was bent over her, trying to rouse her while holding an ugly wound in her own thigh in an effort to stop the bleeding.

Even as Rafi came into sight of them, Caro collapsed over the body of her freemate.

Rafi did not even pause to think; perhaps it was the absence of critical eyes on her, but she moved surely and without hesitation. Her first action was to tightly bind the worst of the wounds hoping to slow or stop the bleeding; her second to check the women for damage not immediately visible. Although she'd had little training in the use of her *laran* for healing, she had learned to monitor, and she used that skill now.

Caro was in deep shock, and suffering from heavy blood-loss; Lirella was in a worse condition. She'd taken a blow to the head that had broken the skull. Rafi did what little she could to ease the pressure she could sense building there, but Lirella needed better and more expert care, and quickly.

Rafi knew she'd be unable to move the women into the shelter alone; either of them outweighed her, and they'd be dead weight. She stood frozen in indecision, but the urgent need to get them out of the snow and into shelter goaded her on. She thought hard for a moment—then remembered the *chervines*, still hobbled in their lean-to behind the shelter. She did not dare let her fear of the animals come to the surface. She brought the one they used as a pack animal around to the front of the shelter and harnessed him, moving slowly and carefully, both to keep from startling him and to avoid making mistakes that would have to be undone. He snorted at the scent of the fresh blood, but to her relief did no more than that. Tethering him next to Lirella, she ran into the shelter and brought one of the blankets from her bedroll outside. She used her knife to make a hole in each of the top two corners, and fastened ropes as securely as she could. She spread it out on the snow, and rolled Lirella onto it as carefully as she was able, then tied the ropes to either side of the *chervine*'s harness. She took his bridle, trying to project calm at him, and led him slowly into the shelter, dragging Lirella on the blanket. When Lirella was safely inside, and bundled into her own bedroll, Rafi repeated the procedure with Caro.

It was long after dark now—she discovered to her immense relief that Caro had lied about the state of the wood. She soon had the fire built up to a respectable enough blaze so that she was able to administer what little aid she could to her Sisters without fear of them taking a worse chilling than they already had. She stripped them of their bloody, torn garments, cutting them away where she had to, all the time working slowly and thinking out each step at a time. Then she rebandaged their wounds, this time with proper bandages and medication, and rolled them back into their now-combined bedrolls. She knew they needed to be kept warm, and this way they would have the combined comfort of each other's body heat and presence.

But she knew very well that both of them needed more help than she could give them. She didn't dare leave them alone—even assuming she could control one of the *chervines* well enough to ride in search of aid, she had no idea in which direction the nearest help lay. She sat in an agony of indecision, absently rubbing the scars on her hands, trying to think of an answer, when the very feel of one of those scars gave her the answer she needed.

Distance was no barrier to *laran*, particularly not in the Overworld. And there was a Tower nearby, and within it trained Healers, and all the help she needed.

She had no one to monitor her; though it would be dangerous, she'd have to do without. If it had only been her own life at stake she'd never have dared—but it wasn't. Caro and Lirella's lives hung on whether or not they received expert care, and soon. She had no choice. No matter how they felt about her, she was bound by her Oath and by the way she had come to like and admire them to give them whatever help lay in her power.

She bundled herself into what blankets she thought she could spare, made sure the fire would not burn out in her "absence," and checked once again on her patients. When she was satisfied that she'd done everything she could, she settled herself as comfortably as she was able, and forced herself to begin.

This had been one aspect of the training she'd done well at; one by one, she erased all outward sensations from her mind, concentrating only on the starstone in her hand. For one brief moment, her fear returned, and held her back, (*I could die out there . . .*) but she mastered it, although it remained in the background, and fell deep into the depths of the stone.

Then she was *out,* and staring down at her own body.

I am a dough-faced little thing, she thought, looking at the untidy child-woman in the heap of blankets, her face tear-streaked, her hair sticking out every which way. At least she was better ordered in the form she wore when *out*—no more attractive; in fact, rather sexless and slender to the point of emaciation, but at least not so—messy.

But this was no time for thinking of herself. Quickly she let her mind move her into the Overworld, the overlight taking the place of the solid world she was leaving behind. Now she stood on a gray, endless plain; she cast about her for the Tower, whose manifestation she knew *must* be here—

And it was. Shining with a light of its own, it called her with the solid familiarity of the one at Neskaya, and she hurried toward it, calling out with her mind and heart, and hoping someone within it would hear her.

A figure suddenly flickered into existence between her and

her goal, and from the aura of power she wore, Rafi knew
that this must be the Keeper. Her face tended to shift and
change within the veils she wore, but the feeling of contained
and controlled power was constant and unmistakable.

"Child—" the Keeper said within her mind. "You disturb
our work. What possible reason can you have for doing so?"

Rafi did not bother with explanations, but simply opened
her mind to her and spread it all out for the Keeper's examination. The telepath exclaimed in sharp surprise, and Rafi felt
her add a bit of her strength to Rafi's own, steadying her and
supporting her as Rafi felt herself begin to fade.

"I will send help, little Amazon. It will come as soon as
may be—but you must keep them alive until it arrives. Thus,
must you do, and so—" Like birds returning to the nest, her
instructions settled in Rafi's mind; Rafi knew that if her
strength held she'd have no difficulty in following them.
And, she willed fiercely, her strength *would* hold, for however long it took—

"Now, child, you are unmonitored, and to remain would
be dangerous. Hold fast, and remember that help is coming."
she gave Rafi a kind of mental shove—

Blue fire sprang up all around her for one instant, and she
was curled, half-frozen and cramped, in her blankets by the
fire. She was exhausted, and she ached all over—it would be
so good just to lie here, and let the cold take her. It would be
so easy to slip into sleep; already the cold seemed less. She
was so very tired. . . .

Caro moaned, and the sound woke her to her duty, acted
like a goad. She disentangled herself from her blankets,
moving slowly because of muscles gone stiff, and went to
check on her Sisters.

No sooner did she touch the older woman's hand, than the
Keeper's instructions fluttered to the surface of her mind. For
one moment she shrank into herself in fear—for to do as
she'd been told would open her to more pain than she'd ever

borne before—but Caro moaned again, and though the fear remained, she knew she could not bear to allow her Sisters to suffer any longer. She tried to summon what little courage she possessed, bolstered that little courage with the words of her Oath, and went to work.

Carefully she eased into rapport with Lirella. The Keeper's instructions had been very clear and, as long as she worked slowly, were easy to follow. The pressure of the fracture had to be relieved, and the clot that was forming broken up. The rest could be left until more expert help arrived. When she'd done all she could for Lirella, she turned to Caro, and forced the bleeding that soaked her bandages to slow and stop.

All the while, she couldn't help but be conscious of the deep and vital bond between the two women. It was something she'd been aware of for far longer than anyone in the Guild House had guessed—no one with even a touch of *laran* could have missed it—and the extent of their affection never failed to amaze her. She'd never seen anything like it; certainly her father had never shown any such love for any woman, and emotional bonds were forbidden to those being Keeper-trained. Even now, she was conscious of a twinge of envy. She would have given a great deal to have someone care for her the way these two cared for each other. The presence of that bond spurred her on when nothing else could. It would be unthinkable to let something like that die when it was within her power to save it.

It was hard, bitter work. It took every last dreg of energy she had left—and she'd had none to spare after that unmonitored trip into the Overworld. Time after time her fear and the pain she shared with her Sisters drove her out of rapport with them. Each time that happened, she knew she could never force herself to finish what she'd begun. And yet, when the tears of pain stopped, one look at Caro's twisted face or Lirella's gray, pinched one was enough to send her back into rapport again.

When at last she was finished, colder than she'd ever been before and throbbing with weariness, her work still was not complete. The Keeper's instructions had included the fact that both women would need fluids to replace the blood they'd lost, and quickly. So Rafi crawled to the fire, unable to raise enough strength to walk, and set pans of snow to melt there, then carefully spooned the tea and broth she made down their throats. When dawn came, both women were out of immediate danger, and Rafi heard the sound of hoofbeats just outside.

The shelter was suddenly filled to bursting with people; Rafi crawled out of their way into a darkened corner and collapsed into her blankets.

"Zandru's Hells!" swore one young man, whose fiery hair proclaimed him unmistakably Comyn. "How in the name of all that's holy did anyone untrained keep these two alive so long?"

No one bothered to answer his question, which was purely rhetorical anyway. Though their energy made them seem to be many more, there were in fact only four of them. There were two Healers, one of them the young man, the other a gray-haired woman, serene and confident. With them were two girls, a little older than Rafi, to act as monitors; both of them were petite and very attractive, and seemed to be related. It seemed as though the four of them were long accustomed to acting as a team. Rafi learned from their bantering that they had set out immediately as soon as the Keeper had awakened them, and it had taken them all night to reach this shelter. They seemed amazingly fresh and energetic to Rafi, but all four were experienced travelers and had long ago learned the secret of dozing in the saddle.

Rafi watched them from her corner; they seemed to drift in and out of focus constantly, now appearing as ordinary mortals, then seeming to be half transparent, and showing sparkling nets of energy within themselves. She had lost her hold on the passage of time, and it seemed to her that it was only moments before the *leroni* had both Lirella and Caro sitting up and beginning to speak groggily.

Oddly enough, it was Lirella who thought of her first.

"Rafi—" she muttered, trying to think despite a blinding headache. "We sent her out to get wood—"

"Keighvin, Keeper said there was a third, the one who called us! Where did she go?" the girl who had monitored him exclaimed.

Keighvin's eyes were drawn irresistibly to a huddled bundle in the corner. He rose and in two long strides was peering down at it. A dead-white face looked up at his, seemingly composed of little more than skin stretched over a skull and eyes.

Rafi stared at the young Healer, trying to read his thoughts. All that she cared about now was that Caro and Lirella were in safe hands; she was far past caring about herself. It was the work of a moment to learn from his mind that all was well with them; with relief, she sighed, and let go—and the shelter and its occupants began to fade away.

"Zandru's Hells!" Keighvin exclaimed again. "Somebody help me!"

"She did all that by herself?" Caro asked incredulously. All three of the Renunciates were sitting bundled in fur robes by the newly mended fire. The *leroni* had brought everything they'd thought might be needful, and it was just as well that they had. Neither Healer had wished to move the wounded women for at least a day, and as for Rafi—she was in no better shape than her two Sisters.

"All that, and more," the second Healer, Gabriela, replied. "I doubt I would have thought of using the *chervine* to drag you into shelter. I certainly wouldn't have had the courage to go out into the Overworld for help without being monitored."

Rafi was finally warm again, and was in a drowsy state of

half-awareness where it didn't seem to matter that people were talking about her as if she weren't there. In fact, the conversation was rather interesting.

"And I don't know about you, *mestra*," Keighvin said, cradling a mug of hot tea in both hands, "but to be brutally frank, I don't think I'd have exhausted my resources the way she did for anybody. I'll have you two know that it was touch-and-go for a few moments whether we could keep her from slipping away altogether. She came very close to killing herself by sheer exhaustion in order to save the two of you—she damn near worships both of you, you know. Takes her Renunciate Oath completely literally, we all saw that in her mind. And I'd still like to know how someone with no Healer training managed to keep both of you alive long enough for us to get here."

"That just doesn't sound like the Rafi I know." Lirella seemed baffled.

"I'd say you know her a lot less well than you thought," Keighvin replied with a lifted eyebrow.

"We have a saying in the mountains—" the monitor Caitlin said diffidently. " 'A child lives what he learns.' From what I could see, it seems to me that your Rafi has been told she's useless at every turn. When you're told you're a failure, you tend to become one. And I mean no harm, *mestra*, but she's not exactly suited for the life of a mercenary. Without intending to, you set her one more task she was doomed to fail at."

"That clumsiness, for instance." Keighvin sipped his tea thoughtfully. "It's not something she can help. There's something wrong between *here*—" he tapped his forehead "—and *here*." He held out a hand. "If you had *laran* I could show you. I'm surprised Neskaya never told her; it might have saved her a lot of needless grief."

"Can it be mended?" Caro wanted to know.

He shook his head regretfully. "Perhaps in the days of my grandfather's grandfather, but not now. We lose more skills every year. It isn't anything incapacitating, in any case. All she needs to do is remember never to move without thinking.''

"Which is something a fighter can't afford.'' Lirella reminded him.

"Who told you she *had* to become a fighter?'' he said. "My sister is with the Guild at Elhalyn, and she couldn't fight her way out of a henhouse. She's a Healer, as I am, and a midwife. My father refuses to acknowledge her existence, but we who follow the Healer's path are a bit more pragmatic; I happen to think she does more good where she is than wearing herself out as a brood mare. She's given me a lot of respect for the Guild, by the way. Why don't you send this child there? Rima is constantly sending me letters complaining that she needs an apprentice desperately. From the way she tended you, Rafi surely has the talent for it.''

To her own amazement, Rafi heard herself saying quietly, "Please—I'd like that.''

Six pairs of eyes turned to meet hers; five with astonishment, one with amusement.

"So, the rabbithorn finds a voice.'' Keighvin filled another mug with tea, poured in a generous dollop of honey, and brought it to her. "It's not an easy avocation, you know,'' he said, sitting on his heels beside her. "You spend yourself constantly, often in behalf of people who are ungrateful afterward, and you seldom get to sleep a full, uninterrupted night. You'll see things that will break your heart, sometimes. That will be even more true for you than it is for me, because *you'll* be seeing the battered children, the abused wives, and you won't be able to do anything about their condition except treat the hurts and hope that your own example will show them they needn't live with abuse unless they want to. You'll need strength of spirit the way your two Sisters here need strength of body.''

"Yes, but—'' she said, a little timidly ''—you said I have the talent—and—I did things *right*—you said so!''

"In very deed, you did," Gabriela said warmly. "And there's your answer, *mestra*." She looked full at Caro. "Again, it wasn't your fault, but the way to give this girl confidence is not to try to bully her into fighting back, but to give her something she can *succeed* in. She's no coward, not when it comes to risking herself to save others. She just has a different kind of courage than either of you are used to seeing."

Rafi looked at the scars on the hand that held the mug. "I—I am a coward," she said. "I can't bear pain. That's why they sent me away from Neskaya."

"Poo." The fourth member of the party came into the conversation for the first time. "I can't take much pain either. That's why they made me a monitor. Some of us just have less tolerance than others. That certainly doesn't make you a coward. You had enough bravery to run away from your father, didn't you? I'm pretty sure I wouldn't have dared do that. And you were brave enough last night to do what you knew had to be done, no matter what it cost you. That's a whole lot braver than I am."

"So speaks Gwenna, who dug out the three of us with her bare hands when we were half-buried by an avalanche last year," Keighvin said to Rafi in an undertone.

Rafi stared at the young woman in wide-eyed astonishment. If someone who had done *that* said that *she* was brave—well, perhaps, just perhaps—

"So, what is your verdict? I know what Rima's answer will be if you offer to send her this young Sister of yours. I have worked often enough with Renunciates to know that the craft of the Healer is as honored as the craft of the fighter. I've met Rima; she's a good teacher. When she's through with Rafi, you probably won't recognize her, and she'll be a Renunciate any Guild Hall would be proud of. What is your answer?" Gabriela asked Caro.

"First and foremost, we have to complete our mission—"

Caro replied thoughtfully, as she looked at Rafi with new eyes. "I can't speak for the Guild Mother, but—"

"But?"

"I think, once she hears what we have to say—it *must* be yes."

The *leroni* looked terribly satisfied with themselves—Keighvin grinned at Rafi broadly.

As for Rafi, she sipped her tea in silence, her eyes gone thoughtful and shining, as she contemplated a future that had suddenly become brighter than her wildest dreams—and deep within her, something grew a little stronger.

Confidence, and a different kind of courage.

About "Knives"

One of my first concepts of the Free Amazons was as an honorable alternative for women who do not fit into their society's regular models. This would also mean a refuge for women who have tried to fit in but have encountered the injustices in a society of men: battered wives, and another tragedy all too commonplace in a society where women are in the power of men, the sexually abused or exploited child. Marna, in this story, travels from the first step in escaping such a life-style (simply getting away) to a level of understanding and even forgiveness.

MZB

KNIVES

by Marion Zimmer Bradley

Marna shivered on the cold steps as she heard the bell jangle somewhere inside the house—this strange house which she had never expected to approach. The sign, she knew, said that this was the Guild House of the Comhi-Letzii; but Marna could spell out only a few letters. Her stepfather had told her mother that there was no point in teaching a woman to read more than enough to spell out a public placard, or sign her name to a marriage contract. Her own father had had a governess for her, insisting that she should share her brother's lessons. She swallowed hard, the pain like a knife at her throat, remembering her father. He would have protected her, when even her mother would not. No, she told herself, she would not cry, she must not cry.

She wondered which one of them would open the door; maybe the tall one she had seen at Heathvine, riding astride like a man, her little bag of midwife's supplies on the saddle behind her. *I could have spoken to her at Heathvine*, Marna thought. But then she had been too frightened, too intimidated. Her stepfather would surely have killed her if he had suspected. . . . She winced, as if she could feel his hard hands on her, the knife again, sharp at her throat. He had forbidden her to speak to the Amazon midwife, and emphasized the threat with heavy pinches which had left her upper arm bruised and blue.

She looked around apprehensively, as if Ruyvil of Heathvine

might come around the corner at any moment. Oh, why didn't they open the door? If he found her here, he would surely kill her this time!

The door opened, and a woman stood in the doorway, scowling. She was tall and wore some sort of loose dark garments and for a moment Marna did not recognize the midwife who had come to Heathvine. But the woman on the threshold recognized the girl.

"Is your mother ill again, Domna Marna?"

"Mother is well." Marna felt her throat close again in a sob. *Oh, yes, she's well, so well that she can't risk losing that handsome young stranger she calls husband. She'd rather think her eldest daughter a liar and a slut.* "And the baby, too."

"Then how may I serve you, mistress?"

Marna blurted out, "I want to come in. I want to—to join you. To stay here as one of you."

The woman lifted her eyebrows. "I think you are too young for that." Then she noticed the way Marna was looking around her, glancing back at the open plaza, the main street running up toward it, as if an assassin's knife sought her. What was the girl afraid of? "We need not stand and talk on the doorstep. Come in," she said.

Marna heard the great bronze hasp close with a shiver of relief that ran all down through her. Now she remembered the midwife's name. "Mestra Reva—"

"We do not accept young women here; you should go to Neskaya or Arilinn for that."

Neskaya was four days' ride away; Arilinn was away on the other side of the Kilghard Hills. She had never been to either place; the Amazon might as well have told her to go to the Wall Around the World! She swallowed hard and said hopelessly, "I do not know the way."

And she had no horse, and any traveler she might ask to take her there would be as bad as Dom Ruyvil, or worse. . . .

"How old are you?" the woman asked.

"I shall be fourteen at midwinter."

Reva n'ha Melora sighed, taking in the girl's twisting hands; fine hands which were not worn with work; the good stuff of her gown and shawl and shoes. "We are not allowed to accept the oath of any woman before she is full fifteen years old. You must go home, my dear, and come back when you are grown up. It is not an easy life here, believe me; you will work very much harder than in your mother's kitchen or weaving-rooms, and you have obviously been brought up to luxury; you would not have that here. No, dear, you had better go home, even if your mother is harsh with you."

Marna's voice stuck in her throat. She whispered, "I—I *cannot* go home. Please, please don't make me go."

"We do not harbor runaways." Marna saw Reva's eyes flash like blue lightning. "Why can't you go home? No, look at me, child. What are you afraid of? Why did you come here?"

Marna knew she must tell, even if this harsh old woman did not believe her. Well, she could be no worse off; her mother had not believed her, either. "My stepfather—he—" She could not make herself say the words. "My mother did not believe me. She said I was trying to make trouble for her marriage—" She swallowed again; she would *not* cry before the woman, she would not!

"So," said Reva at last, frowning again at the girl. Yes, she had seen, at Heathvine, how Dorilys of Heathvine doted on her handsome young husband; Dom Ruyvil had feathered his nest well, marrying the rich widow of Heathvine. But Reva had seen, too, that the swaggering young man cared little for his wife.

Marna blinked fiercely, trying to hold back tears. "It began while my mother was carrying little Rafi—Mother wouldn't believe me when I told her!" she sobbed. "I *didn't* want to," she said, through the sobs. "I didn't, I really didn't. I was so afraid—he—he threatened me with a knife, then said he would tell Mother I had tried to entice him—but I never played the harlot, I didn't—'' She looked down at the tiled floor, trying not to cry. She thought she felt a gentle touch on her hair, but when she looked up, Domna Reva was striding around the room angrily.

"If what you tell me is true, Marna—''

"I swear it, by the blessed Cassilda!''

"Listen to me, Marna,'' the woman said. "This is the only circumstance under which we may shelter a girl not yet fifteen: when her natural parent or guardian has abused her trust. But we must be very sure, for the laws forbid us to take in ordinary runaways. Has he made you pregnant?''

Marna felt crimson flooding her face; she had never been so ashamed in her life. "He said—he said he had not, he had done—done something to prevent it, but I don't know—I wouldn't know how to tell—''

Mestra Reva said something obscene, stamping her foot; Marna flinched.

"Not you, child. I cursed the laws which say that a man is so wholly master in his own house that his wife and women-folk are no more protected than his horses and dogs. Such a man should be hung at the crossroads with his *cuyones* stuffed in his mouth! Well, stay then,'' she said with a sigh. "It may make trouble, but that is why we are here. You walked all the way from Heathvine?''

"N—no,'' she stammered. "He came to market—he is drinking in the tavern, and I slipped away, telling him I wanted to buy some ribbons—he even gave me a few coppers—and I ran. Mother had made me come, she wanted me to choose some laces for her, and when I begged her not to send me with Ruyvil, she slapped me and said she was sick of my lies—'' Marna looked down again at the floor. Ruyvil had boasted, on the ride in, that on the way back they could find the shelter of a travel-hut, and this time, he promised, she would like it and she would not need to be threatened with a knife . . . That was why she had taken this desperate step, she could not bear it, not again.

Reva saw her trembling hands, the shame in her face, and did not question any further. It was obvious that the girl was telling the truth and that she was frightened. "Well, you may as well stay and have some supper. Hang your cloak in the hall." She led her along into a big stone-floored kitchen where four women were sitting at a round wooden table.

"Go and sit there, beside Gwennis, Marna," said Reva, pointing. "She is the youngest of us here, Ysabet's daughter." Gwennis was a girl of twelve or thirteen; Ysabet a dumpy, muscular-looking woman in her forties. Beside her was a tall, scrawny woman, scarred like a soldier; she was introduced as Camilla n'ha Mhari. The last was a small gray-haired woman they called Mother Dio.

"This is Marna n'ha Dorilys," said Reva. "She is too young to take the oath here, but she will be here as foster-daughter, since her natural guardians have abused their trust; she may cut her hair and promise to live by our rule and take oath when she is fifteen." She dipped Marna a ladleful of soup from the kettle over the fire. Mother Dio, at the head of the table, cut Marna a chunk of the coarse bread and asked if she would have butter or honey. The soup was good, but Marna was too tired to eat, and too shy to answer any of the questions the girl Gwennis asked her. After supper they called her to the head of the table, and the old woman cut off her hair to the nape of the neck.

"Marna n'ha Dorilys," she said, "you are one of us, though not yet oath-bound. From this day forth, our laws forbid you to appeal to any man for house or heritage; and you must learn to appeal to none for protection, and to defend yourself. You must work as we do, and claim no privilege for noble birth; and you must promise to be a sister to every other Renunciate of the Guild, from whatever house she may come, and shelter her and care for her in good times or bad. Do you promise to live by our laws, Marna?''

"I do."

"Will you learn to defend yourself and call on no other for protection?''

"I will."

Mother Dio kissed her on the cheek. ''Then you are welcome among us, and when you are old enough, you may take the Renunciate's oath.''

Marna's neck felt cold and exposed, immodest; she looked at her long russet hair on the floor and wanted to cry. Ruyvil had played with her hair and fondled the nape of her neck; now no man would ever say again that she had lured him with her beauty! She looked at their coarse mannish garments, the long knives in their belts, and shivered. They all looked so strong. How could she ever learn to protect herself with a knife like that?

"Come, Marna," said Gwennis, taking her hand. "I am so glad you have come, there is no one here that I can talk to—I am so glad to have a sister my own age! The girls in the village are not allowed to talk with me, because they say my breeches and short hair are immodest. They call me mannish, a she-male, as if I would teach them some wickedness— you'll be my friend, won't you? I mean, you *have* to be my sister, it's the law of the Guild House, but will you be my friend, too?''

Marna smiled stiffly. Gwennis was not like any other girl she had ever known, and Marna's mother would not have approved of her either, but she had always obeyed her mother's rules, and much good it had done her! "Yes, I'll be your friend.''

"Take her upstairs, Gwennis, and show her the house," said Reva. "Tomorrow we can find her some clothes—your old tunic and breeches will fit her, Ysabet. And tomorrow, Camilla, you can show her something of knife-play and self-protection before you are on your way back to Thendara.''

"You must go to the magistrate for a report, Reva," Camilla said, "for you have been at Heathvine and you know her family. You can tell them how likely it is that Ruyvil had abused this girl as she said. I met with that fellow Ruyvil when he was still a homeless nobody; I can well imagine he might use his own step-daughter foully."

Later that night, before she was tucked into a trundle bed in Gwennis's room, Reva came in and asked Marna a number of questions. When Reva made her take off her shift, she remembered nasty things she had heard of the Guild House, but the woman only examined her briefly and said, "I think you were lucky; you are probably not pregnant. Dio will brew you a drink tomorrow and if your courses are only delayed by shock and fear, we shall know it soon. But I can testify you have been badly treated; a man who takes a willing girl does not leave *that* kind of mark. This is so I can swear to the magistrate that you have been raped, and were not, as your mother said, just playing the harlot. Then we may lawfully shelter you. Go to sleep, child, and don't worry." And Marna fell asleep like a baby.

The Guild House of Aderes was not a large one; only four women lived regularly in the house, although sometimes traveling Amazons like Camilla stayed there for a few days or a season. Reva, the midwife, provided most of their cash income; otherwise they lived by selling the fine kerchiefs they wove from the wool of their animals. Marna, who had been taught to do fine embroidery, encouraged them to decorate the kerchiefs with pretty patterns. They also had an herb garden and sold medicines, and when their cows were fresh they took butter to market. It was a hard life, as Reva had said: they spent most of their days in weaving or working in their garden. For days, Marna trembled at every knock on the door, fearing Dom Ruyvil had come to drag her away, but soon she grew calm. She enjoyed her new life. Some of the things she learned were a delight; she was taught to read, and soon could write a good hand. She did not like cooking and scrubbing floors, but every woman in the house had to take turns at the heavy work, as they did with the shearing, spinning, and weaving of the wool. The old emmasca, Camilla, who had been a mercenary soldier and lived in Thendara Guild House, gave Marna a few lessons in knife-play and unarmed combat, but Marna was not very skilled at it; she was timid and clumsy, and the more Camilla yelled at her, the more helpless she felt.

When she was older, they told her, they would send her to Thendara Guild House for the regular half-year of re-training. Meanwhile she must learn their ways. Mostly they kept her in the house and garden, but one day Gwennis was sick, and they sent her to the market with butter. She had been there several times with Mother Dio or Ysabet, and knew the basic rules of Amazon behavior in public: to speak to no man except on business, not to talk to the village girls, who might be punished for associating with her. Marna thought this was foolish. The girls should know that there was a better life than slaving as drudges for their parents until some man bought them like animals! But the law was the law, and in order to exist at all, the Amazons had been forced to make compromises. One was that they might not recruit any woman who did not seek them out of her free will. Marna suspected that a little discreet recruiting was done anyway, but while she was still too young for the oath, she must obey their rules meticulously.

So she walked along, her eyes bent strictly on business; she went to the dairy-woman's market stall and gave the woman her butter. Mother Dio had told her they needed honey; she had packets of herb dyes in her pocket, and she should try to barter for it. Marna spent a pleasant hour in the market, and finally started back to the Guild House, the crock of honey wrapped in a burlap sack; she had traded it for some madder dye.

It was beginning to grow dark. As she passed the tavern, a young man unhitching his horse from the rail, so drunk that even at this distance Marna could smell the stale reek of wine, called to her, "What about it, girl, want to spend the night with me? Hey—don't be so damned unfriendly!" He turned and staggered toward her. "Aaah—one of those bitches trying to wear a sword like a man!" He caught heavily at her arm. "What you want to spend your life with those women for? Why don't you want to be a real woman, huh?" He fumbled at her.

Marna, shaking, pulled herself free and fled, clutching at the crock of honey. The man yelled drunkenly, "Aaah, go on, who the hell wants one of you bitches anyhow!"

Her heart beating, racing, her mouth dry, Marna tried to compose herself. Was there something about her, that she looked like that kind of girl? Dom Ruyvil had accused her of leading him on, too, even when she cried and tried to stop him. What did she do that made men act that way? She put her hand on her knife hilt. If the man had really tried to hold her, could she have drawn her knife, tried to frighten him away with it? Could she have found the courage to strike?

Half blinded by tears, she did not see where she was going until she ran into a tall, heavy man on the cobbled street. She murmured a well-bred apology, then felt her arm seized in a heavy grip, and heard a hated voice.

"So, little Marna! You lying slut, you've made a fine mess of my life—Dori came near to sending me away! Running and whining to those filthy bitches, and now you're one of them!"

She struggled to free herself of the heavy grip.

"You! Ruyvil!"

"You will say stepfather, or dom, when you speak to me," he snarled.

"I won't!" she cried. "You're not my father and I owe you nothing—not respect, not obedience, nothing!"

He slapped her, hard. "No more of that! You're coming home where you belong. Look at you—brazen as you please in boots and breeches, your hair cut off, showing your—" He used a filthy word. "Come on, you—I've got a horse, and I'm going to take you home to your mother, and by Zandru's toenails, if you tell her any more tales, I'll break every bone in your body!"

She faced him, shaking, but braced by what the women had told her; she must learn to defend herself and appeal to none for protection. "Everything I said to mother and the magistrate was true—"

"Ah, you wanted it, you dirty little slut, you can't tell me you weren't making eyes at every stable-boy and armsman—"

"I *do* tell you that!" she retorted. "You can lie all you want to my mother, but you know perfectly well what the truth is—"

"You can't speak to me like that!" His heavy hand knocked her sprawling to the ground; she lay there in terror, watching his knife come out of its sheath. . . . With some last resource of strength she scrambled to her feet, grabbed up the miraculously unbroken honey-crock, and run like a *chervine*, dodging into an alley; no skirts to hamper her this time! She pounded in panic on the door of the Guild House; but by the time Gwennis opened the door, her breathing had quieted. No, she must not tell. They had made it so clear she must learn to defend herself.

And I couldn't defend myself, she thought in despair. *I couldn't get my knife out of its sheath at all, I never thought of it, I ran like a rabbithorn! I should have killed Ruyvil, thrust my knife into his guts! But I was afraid. . . .*

Did he really think I led him on? Is there something about me that makes men think that? That other man, the drunken one at the tavern, he thought so, too. . . .

"You're out of breath," Gwennis said. "What's the matter, Marna, have you been running?"

"Yes—it was late, and dark, and cold, I ran to warm myself," Marna said, and was angry at herself for lying. But Gwennis, she knew, had been trained to defend herself. How she would despise Marna if she knew what a weakling she was!

Marna stayed in the house after that, as much as she could, and every time she went out of doors, it seemed to her that Dom Ruyvil must be lurking around every corner. But as time went by, she grew less afraid and at last she was willing to go to the market again. In three months, she would be fifteen and could take the oath lawfully; and then she would be safe. At this season there was a good harvest of herbs, and the women of the Guild House shared a stall with the dairy-woman who sometimes sold their butter. Marna spread out the little packets of herbs meticulously, proud of the delicate lettering she had done on the front of each packet—she wrote the clearest hand in the house, now, and designed all their embroideries. As she finished, she looked up to hear a familiar voice.

"Is your golden-flower well dried? If it is, I will have two packets—Marna!" the woman said with a gasp, and Marna stared into her mother's face.

"Marna! So this is where you went! Oh, Marna, how could you? Oh, my little girl—where is your pretty hair? What have they done to you, those awful women! Marna, won't you even kiss your mother in greeting?"

Marna wanted to cry. She wanted to shout, *Yes, it was Dom Ruyvil who abused me, but it was you who let him do it, you who wouldn't believe your own daughter* . . . but before her mother's weeping face she could not stand and refuse her. She hugged her mother, thinking, *Now I am taller than she is, I am bigger than she is—she could never learn to defend herself.*

"Oh, you look so grown up and so—so stern and awful!"

Dorilys of Heathvine said, "Have they made you swear to all kinds of evil things, my poor baby? Oh, blessed Cassilda, I will never forgive myself—"

Marna kept her voice hard. "So you believe me at last?"

"Oh, Marna—" Her mother spread out her hands. "What could I do? He said he would take his son and leave me—and I was alone in the world, your brother is in Thendara now as a cadet, I am alone with the babies—and if Ruyvil is angry with me, what shall I do? A woman has no choice but to live with her husband—and if I had made complaint to a magistrate, he would have beaten me or worse—"

"It's all right, Mother, I understand," said Marna, with a choking pain in her throat. She did *not* understand. She would never understand. If she had a daughter, if a man had treated her daughter that way, she certainly would not have continued to love the man, to share his bed! She would have called the magistrates, had Ruyvil thrown into the middle of the street! But her mother had not even had the strength or the good sense to run away.

"Marna—oh, my little girl, won't you come home? I promise you—you can have one of the maids to sleep in your chamber—he will never bother you again, I promise you! I miss you so, there is no one I can talk to, no one I care about—"

"No, mother," said Marna gently, but without pity. "I will never live under your roof again. I will come and see you sometime when Dom Ruyvil is away from home, if you will send me word; or you can come and visit me at the Guild House."

"The Guild House? What could I possibly—Ruyvil would be very angry with me if I spoke to such women!"

"Oh, Mother," Marna said impatiently, "they are women just like you, except that they do not let men beat and abuse them! They are honest women who live by weaving and selling herbs!"

"Hmmph! What evil things have they taught you? What man will marry you now?"

"None, I hope!" Marna said crossly. "Believe what you like, Mother, I would not change my life for yours! And if you think I live an evil life in the Guild House, why, get up the courage of a goose and come and visit us and see for yourself how I spend my days!"

When her mother had gone weeping away Marna ran after her—she had forgotten the packets of golden-flower; yes, she must take it, she looked pale. No, forget the money, she had picked and dried it herself, it was a gift . . . and as she began packing up the wares in the booth, for the sun was going down, she felt better. Yes, in spite of her anger, she loved her mother, was glad to see that she was alive and well.

Unless that bastard Dom Ruyvil kills her some day, beating her, or keeping her bearing children until she dies of it!

Well, there was nothing she could do. She said, "Where is Ysabet with the pack animal, Gwennis? We should load it, to be home before dark. There is not much to load, we have sold all the embroideries and all the kerchiefs but three."

"The embroidered ones sell better," Gwennis said. "You were right, Marna. Who was that woman you were talking to?"

"My mother," said Marna, and said no more.

Gwennis, full of questions, stopped at the look on Marna's face; she said only, "Here, help me untie this bridle-rope, we will have everything ready for Ysabet when she comes—Zandru spit fire!" she swore, as the rope twisted on the edge of the booth, something caught, and the packets of herbs and the kerchiefs came cascading down, with crocks of butter. The girls scrambled to pick them up, but one crock of butter had split and slimed the kerchiefs and the cobbles in front of the stall.

"Well, I will go and borrow a mop, and clean it," said Gwennis heavily, looking around the half-deserted market;

most of the stalls were empty now and the shadows were falling, red and thick, across the marketplace. "Rinda at the tavern will lend me a mop, I bandaged her ankle when she sprained it."

"Don't leave me alone," Marna begged, "it's so dark, wait till Ysabet comes with the horse!"

"But someone could slip and fall and break their neck!" said Gwennis, shocked. "Don't be such a coward, Marna! You must learn to be alone."

Gwennis went, and Marna, shivering, packed up the herbs. Then a rough hand seized her, and a voice she feared and hated growled, "So here's where you've been hiding, eh? Filthy slut, I'll teach you to talk like that to your mother. She told me she'd seen you here. You're coming home with me now, and no nonsense about it! Feel this?" Marna felt a knife-edge at her throat. Ruyvil pressed hard; she felt the skin break, and blood trickle down.

"Now will you behave?"

In deadly fear, Marna nodded and the knife moved away from her throat. Ruyvil's hands were rough on her. He said, "Now you come on, without any more fuss. Make a laughing-stock of me, will you, telling tales so your mother can't get decent maids to stay, and complaining to a magistrate about me? I tell you, Marna, I'll teach you a lesson if it's the last thing I do! You're coming home where you belong, and people are going to see that I can rule my family and my womenfolk and no damned magistrates butting in! Fine thing, when a man can't handle his own affairs without the government on his back! It's not as if you were any real kin to me, as if I'd done you any harm!" He gave her wrist a vicious twist. "Give me your hands!" She saw a length of rope in them: he would tie her, drag her home—

She wrenched away, screaming. He jerked at her, flung her down. "Marna, I'll kill you for that!" he rasped. She grabbed at her knife, clumsily, in deadly terror. Oh, he would kill her,

with that knife—but better that than be dragged home knowing he could do his worst—but suddenly he had her knife,
too, and she cursed her clumsiness.

"You let her alone!" came a scream behind them, and
Gwennis swung the heavy mop-handle; Ruyvil's mouth burst
open with blood. Swearing, he ran at Gwennis with his
sword, and Marna, grabbing up her blade, hardly knowing
what she did, thrust herself between them; her Amazon knife,
not quite a sword, was braced right against Ruyvil's belly.

"Make one move," she said, astonished at how loud and
firm her voice sounded in the deserted market, "and I'll run
this right through you, *step*father!"

He howled in rage. "Put that thing down! What the hell—?"

Gwennis had scrambled to her feet, recovered her own
knife. She came and took Ruyvil's sword, saying, "I ought
to cut his throat. But we have trouble enough here. I'll tie his
hands and he can get loose later—who's to say if the magistrate would believe us? Here, Marna, you tie him, you can
make a better knot than I can. He won't get *that* loose before
we're safe in the Guild House. And if he wants to tell how
two girls under fifteen bested him, well, let him talk and be a
laughing-stock!"

Ysabet came with the pack-animal and looked at the furious, cursing Ruyvil, his hands tied behind him. She said,
"Listen to me, Dom Ruyvil, your stepdaughter, whom you
have abused, is being sent to Neskaya Guild House; do you
want a public examination by *leronis* so that everyone in the
countryside knows she told the truth?"

He calmed at last and said sheepishly, "No. I will swear—"

"Your oath is not worth a piece of fresh horse dung," said
Ysabet, "but if you do not molest us further we will leave
you alone, though I would willingly make you incapable of
molesting any woman again." She gestured with the knife
and Ruyvil flinched and howled, begging, pleading, weeping.
Marna wondered why she had ever been afraid of him.

As they went homeward in the dusk, Gwennis said—Ysabet had walked a little ahead with the horse—"If your stepfather was following you, lying in wait for you, why didn't you tell us?"

"I was ashamed," Marna muttered. "So much was said about learning to defend myself, not asking any other for protection—"

"Yet you must protect your sisters, and they must protect you," Gwennis chided gently, an arm around Marna's waist. "That is what the oath is all about, that we swear to care for one another—would you not have protected your mother? You found courage to draw your knife when he menaced *me*—"

Marna began to weep. She could not protect her mother from Ruyvil; her mother did not want protection, would not appeal even to her sisters. Worse, her mother had thought so much of Ruyvil that she would not protect her own daughter. For the first time since she had come to the Amazon house she wept and wept, sobbing even after they were inside the Guild House. Gwennis was alarmed at her crying and sent for Reva, who gave her wine, and finally slapped her.

"I can live with what Ruyvil did to me," Marna said, hiccoughing, tears still streaming from her eyes, "and I can defend myself against any man now. But what I cannot bear, is that my mother would not protect me, that she would even let her daughter be misused, rather than lose the man she loved . . . that she did not love *me* enough to quarrel with him . . ." She cried and cried, clinging to Reva, while the older woman, kinder now, held and comforted her.

"But that is what the Amazon oath is all about," Gwennis repeated. "Any of us will protect you, as your mother should have done; as women must always protect each other. I can't make your mother care for you as she should have done— what's done is done and there's no mending it. But you have an oath-mother now, and many sisters. And you were strong to defend *me*, if not yourself!"

"You didn't deserve it," Marna sniffed. "I mean, *you* hadn't done *anything*. I couldn't let him hurt you!"

Gwennis's arms were around her. "But *you* hadn't done anything either, and *you* didn't deserve it, either," she said fiercely, "and if that old wicked man made you think you did, then that's worse than what he did to you in the first place!" She kissed Marna on the cheek. "I'll miss you, sister, if they send you to Thendara for training," she said, "but you'll come back, when you've learned how to defend yourself and how to live with everything you have to live with, *breda*." Shyly, she took her knife from its sheath. She said, "You defended me when you wouldn't defend yourself. Will you exchange knives with me, Marna?"

After a wide-eyed moment, Marna drew her own knife, and solemnly, they put their knives, each into the other's sheath, then embraced. Marna said, almost crying again, "I do not want to go away! I love you all, and you have been so good to me—"

"But you have sisters everywhere," Reva said gently. "Soon you will take the oath; and then you will be one with us."

Marna put her hand on Gwennis's knife in her sheath. Yes, her sister's knife had been drawn in her defense; now she could draw it in her own. One woman had failed her, but, looking around at her sisters, she knew that no one of them would ever fail her. With amazement, she realized that Dom Ruyvil had not destroyed her; he had driven her into a new life, a real life. What she thought was the end of the world had brought her here.

He had set her free.

About Jane Bigelow and "Tactics"

Jane Bigelow lives in Denver, with her husband and "Alphonse the alley cat." One wonders why so many science fiction people have cats, as opposed to only occasional dogs or—say—hamsters. She has had non-fiction published in several local newspapers in Boulder and the Denver area, but "gave up on journalism after a series of bounced paychecks, failed newspapers, and editors who could as easily hire a veteran journalist from Chicago or New York for very little money more than I was asking—Denver is a popular place to live." She has also had poetry published, in Fine Arts Discovery *and elsewhere, and currently works as a cataloger for the Jefferson County Public Libraries, a job which allows her unlimited access to new books and a four-day week. "Tactics" is her first fiction sale.*

Although the characters in "Tactics" are not, strictly speaking, Free Amazons, they are independent women in the spirit of the Amazons.

MZB

TACTICS

by Jane M. H. Bigelow

Bronwyn sighed a little as she looked at her husband across the room. To be sure, a man must take care of the defense of his family, any man, and much more so if that man is a lord. Very true. But need he talk sword and shield techniques, battle plans and strategies for hours when he had only just arrived home?

I will be a proper lady of your hall, Donal, she thought. *But this evening is one more stone in the wall we are building between us.*

He looked up at that. Some thoughts clearly got through the barriers they had learned to erect. He made some laughing remark to the men of his command, and came over to her.

"Lady wife, I am aware that all this bores you to tears, but if you want a roof over your head, you will let me work on its defense without constantly interrupting my thoughts." His voice was low, but throughout the hall there was a kind of stir, a mental babble, as the more telepathically sensitive determinedly put their thoughts elsewhere.

"It was not my intention," she murmured against her own rising anger.

"Still no more shielding than a twelve-year-old? Bronwyn, you are the mother of three—"

"And soon to be the mother of four," she cut in. Then, raising her voice a little, she continued, "My lord, I am weary." She turned toward the rest of the hall. "My lords, my ladies, I fear that I must retire early. That need not cut short anyone else's evening. Isolde will see to your comfort in my absence." A tall, auburn-haired woman rose from her seat near a branch of candles and bowed slightly.

In her room, Bronwyn allowed herself the luxury of lighting the fire in one swift blaze of anger instead of the pedestrian fuss with flint and steel that her teachers had said was better, unless one really needed to light a fire with *laran*. . . .

There was a light step behind her and an exaggeratedly quavering voice proclaimed, "Child, child, what is this? Where was the need? It is wrong to chain a dragon to cook your dinner!"

Bronwyn turned slowly—one does not whirl at eight months gone—and then laughed, half against her will. Her younger cousin Danilys stood, bent, supported by an imaginary cane. For a second, extreme old age sat heavily upon her; then she, too, laughed. Casting off the glamour, she came over to the fire and stood looking down at Bronwyn. "How I wish I could do that whenever I wanted to! Was Donal boring on again about fighting, Bron?"

"Blessed Cassilde, yes! On and on. Oh, Danilys, why am I still fool enough to wish that he'd talk to *me* now and then? He used to, you know. We used to be so open to each other. Then the fighting broke out again, and he wasn't even here for Liriel's birth. When he did come back, it seemed as if his mind was as sore as his body, nor was I in much better case. Not that I really had too much to complain of, physically," she added. "I'm really quite good at having babies. Only unfortunately they're the wrong sex."

"This one, too?" Danilys asked sympathetically.

"I refused to be monitored this time. Don't look so shocked! If I knew this one was a girl too, I couldn't help being angry. That's too dangerous to this baby—I've got plenty of *laran*, but Father pulled me out of Neskaya Tower to marry me off before I'd learned much control, you know that!''

"Yes, I know." Danilys looked subdued for a moment. Then—"Well, *breda*, we shall have to make Liriel a tiny sword instead of a baby-doll, and teach her tactics instead of needlework. No, maybe we'd better teach her needlework too. Then she can stitch people back together after she defeats them, and make herself the fanciest sword-belt ever seen!''

"Oh, yes!" Bronwyn said and laughed. "All embroidered with little pink flowers, so that no one will say she's not a lady.''

Danilys kilted up her skirts and began a wild pantomime of thrust and parry. Her lanky, raw-boned body was suddenly graceful as she darted about the room to portray both fighters. Just as she leaped nimbly over a small stool, Donal entered the room.

Quiet fell immediately. He bowed stiffly to both women and then, turning to Bronwyn, said, "My dear, if you are going to leave the hall on pretext of tiredness, it would be well not to make so much noise that I must come up here to assure myself that we have not been attacked by bandits.''

"One hundred feet up a tower?" Danilys asked. "Anyway, I'm the one making all the noise. Yell at me.''

"I am not yelling." He was getting close to it, though, thought Bronwyn. This much ill-temper was unlike him. Puzzled and a little worried, she reached out to his mind and was shocked to feel him barricade himself completely. Never, even in that worse quarrel when he had raged at her for the third girl child, had he closed himself to her as if she were not even kin. He glared at her—*do his enemies see that look in battle?* she wondered—and flung out of the room, slamming that door, too.

Bronwyn stood, still bewildered, as Danilys came over and put an arm around her. "Help me get ready for bed, will you?" she asked. "I believe I truly am tired.''

Even Danilys knew that something major had happened. That was obvious from her carefully averted gaze as she helped with the now-cumbersome process of changing into night clothes. Trying to ease the tension humming in the room, Bronwyn summoned a laugh as Danilys unlaced her low felt boots. "Oh, how happy I'll be to do that for myself again!"

"I'll be glad, too." Was that coldness in Danilys's voice? Was anyone at all normal this evening? Bronwyn wondered.

"Danilys?" she asked.

"I'm not mad at *you*, Bronwyn. I'd like to tell your precious Donal what I think of him, though! He knows better than this! Why do you take it, anyway? Yell back at him. It's fun."

"Not for me, *breda*. I hate fighting, I always have."

The comfort of the wide, fur-covered bed made it easy to stop worrying. Bronwyn sighed with pleasure as she settled in, and was soon asleep.

Danilys watched her for a little, making certain that she was really sleeping, then made her way to the door by the dim light of the night candle. On her way back to her own room, she worked off some of her pent-up energy by shadow-fencing with her reflection in the hall's polished stone. Her skirts hampered her, though, and she dared not kilt them up here in the more public parts of the castle. As it was, she startled a guard considerably.

In her room, she sat half-dreaming as the bathtub filled with water from the hypocaust. Maybe she could join the Renunciates. . . . Was it really true you had to cast off all family ties? The Free Amazons she'd seen on the road near Cuillincrest seemed to know how to take care of themselves perfectly well, but it sounded lonely. Ah, but she could learn so many things! And she would be free to travel. She had seen them working as guides for ladies, and aside from the danger of being stuck with a whimpery lady for a while, it looked like the perfect life. Best of all, she would be spared being married off to some insensitive clod. Given her almost total lack of either useful *laran* or dowry, he'd probably be some widower in need of a new wife to manage his house and the children whose births had killed the first wife.

That led to where her thoughts of the Renunciates always led, to Bronwyn. How could she leave her cousin, who seemed likely to go on bearing two babies every three years for a long time to come? Danilys reflected that Bronwyn should at least accept the marriage for the political arrangement that it was, and stop fretting. So Donal had stopped being romantic; well, most men did, from what she'd seen. She'd never had the opportunity to find out whether the rare freemate marriages between women worked out any better. Bronwyn had always been a terrible romantic, in any case, as well as having far more *laran* than most women outside a Tower. That's where she'd really have been better off. The only child of the lord of a domain, however, was not to be wasted on a Tower.

With a jolt, Danilys abandoned her thoughts to find herself staring at a stone-cold tub of bathwater. After a cold and hasty wash, she leaped into bed to lie in a small curled lump.

Perhaps because she was cold, she slept lightly. Just before dawn, she awoke abruptly with an overpowering sense of something being wrong. She could hear nothing unusual, but the feeling was too strong to ignore. If it was only some unremembered nightmare, she would simply have to apologize most humbly.

Quickly, she rose and fastened her old wool robe about her. Finding her slippers took appallingly long, it seemed. Then she was off down the halls, hurrying to Donal's room.

It was just bad luck that he was not alone, and therefore less inclined than ever to pay heed to his wife's hoyden of a cousin. She was still inventing new threats of what she would do if he refused to send a messenger around to the sentries, when there was an outcry at the west gate, and the alarm bell was rung frantically.

"And half the men home on furlough!" Donal groaned. He leaped out of bed, dressing as he ran to the stairs. Shortly, Danilys heard him shouting orders, trying to get all the likely approaches reinforced.

Danilys turned to the pretty girl who'd shared his bed that night. She still looked half-asleep.

"Do you know where Isolde sleeps?" Danilys asked. The girl nodded. "Good. Then go to her, please, and tell her to prepare hot food for the men, and organize some of the women to tend the wounded. I will be with her presently, but I must go to Lady Brownyn first."

Bronwyn was already awake. "We're being attacked?" she asked as Danilys came in.

"I'm afraid so. Donal's already out on the walls. How are you feeling?"

"Oh, I'll do. Help me get dressed and I'll go down to the hall. I can at least help direct things." She overrode Danilys's attempted protest. "*Chiya*, I know you have my welfare at heart, but if I sit up here doing nothing, I'll go mad. Do you think I can shut it out, what's going on down there?"

"No. No, of course not. Here, for goodness sake, I'll help!" Danilys got Bronwyn into her clothes, then sped back to her own room and scrambled into her own.

Getting the servants organized took little effort; most of them had plenty of experience with medical care and food distribution. Even so, the first of the wounded arrived before the preparations were finished.

They were few at first, and had suffered mostly minor wounds. A man would laugh, and curse his own clumsiness, and be eased over the pain by a girl's joke and a mug of hot wine.

Then there were more wounded, and worse wounds, and the healer who had already come to the castle to help birth

Bronwyn's baby was busy instead trying to stop internal bleeding or steady a man's heartbeat. Danilys was never sure how long Bronwyn had been standing still, her hand to her side, before she saw her.

"Bronwyn?" No answer. "Bron, please, *breda*, is it the baby?"

"What? No, no—Donal's wounded, here. He won't leave the walls! He's got to, he will if I have to go out and drag him off." Her eyes lost focus again, and Danilys guessed that she was arguing with Donal.

That guess was confirmed when he limped into the hall a few moments later. He was scowling. "Damn it, Bron, why do you think I learned to block you out? Do you want to kill all of us, including the baby? How can I possibly fight and argue with you at the same time? If I wasn't so damn tired you couldn't do this!" He sat down heavily as Danilys pushed a chair up behind him, striking the backs of his knees.

"You, too?" he moaned.

"That's a bad wound, Donal, by the way you're standing. Let someone dress it—yes, I know it'll take time. That's why you're going to give me your armor and sword and let me go convince the men you're still out there, tough old bird that you are, directing things." She pulled off his helm while he sat gaping at her, but the mail tunic was another matter. He sat with his arms clasped firmly at his sides, going whiter than ever with the effort.

"Donal! Please, what good is it going to do if you stagger back out there and faint? Without you to give orders, or someone they think is you, it'll all fall apart. Get your wound seen to, get some food. I know you haven't eaten all day. Let me stand in for you just that long. It's a siege, not an open battle. I'll be in very little more danger than if I stay here and risk getting run down by some servants with a soup cauldron."

"Danilys, are you out of your mind? Do you think this is a children's game of snow-forts? Because you've never learned to be a lady, you think you can be a war leader instead?" Donal bellowed.

The healer intervened. "Sir, just let me bind your wounds. That will be needful in any case. I don't even have to monitor you to tell that."

For a moment, Donal hardly seemed to hear. Bronwyn could tell his thoughts were elsewhere, probably out in the battle, though his old habit of always shielding his thoughts kept her from knowing for certain.

Then he sighed, and his eyes focused again. "I wish you had *laran*, Danilys. Then I could guide you from here. As it is, I don't see how—"

"Donal, you can tell me what to do *now*. You've said yourself this keep's a defending army's dream. As for children's games, well, I was *good* at snow-forts. I could make people do what I said, too!"

That was true, Bronwyn remembered. She had a clear memory of Danilys, her outgrown dress ripped at the hem, leading Bronwyn herself and a horde of other slightly bewildered children to victory by scrambling up the rabbithorn's mountainside trail to the back of a snow-fort. *And I detested playing war!* she recalled.

"I hope you're right, Bron," Donal said wearily. "My wounds have stiffened too much while I sat here. At least the armor should fit her. Listen well and learn fast, Danilys. We were winning when I had to leave, but those fools are pulling it all to pieces, fighting over who's to give orders. No bright ideas of your own, mind! And stay back out of arrow range!"

Danilys nodded, her eyes glowing. "Yes, I promise. Here, let me help with the tunic."

She was alarmed to see how much help he needed in getting it off, and signaled the healer, Margolys, to come back quickly. As Margolys worked, Danilys listened and concentrated harder than she had since she was thirteen and being tested for any vestige of trainable *laran*. Then she took her cousin's armor and sword and left by a small side door.

In Donal's room, she seized a pair of his trousers. Her hand shook a little as she struggled into the tunic. *Please, Evanda and Avarra! Let me carry this off. Let me be able to use the glamour just once to cast an illusion on command! I can handle the rest of it. I've listened to Donal enough over the years to know his tactics, but I need a glamour!*

With joyful amazement, she felt it come. The world looked distant, now, and everything seemed slightly slowed down.

She rushed downstairs again and out to the battle. Sure enough, each chief of every minor clan that owed Donal service had his own ideas of how best to fight the battle. Bellowing to make herself heard over the battle and the rising wind, Danilys strode forward.

Bronwyn had watched the door close as Donal leaned against her shoulder. *At least Danilys will know her way around out there*, she thought. *When we two first came to Cuillincrest, I thought I would never persuade her that it was most improper for my cousin to climb battlements and chatter with guards.*

The healer spoke, concern in her voice. "Will you let me monitor you, *vai dom*? There is more pain and weakness in you than this cut accounts for."

He frowned and shifted position slightly, trying to feel any one pain among all the bruises and muscle-aches. It wouldn't be the first time he'd taken a wound and not known it until someone else had told him. Too good a barrier, one healer had told him. He shifted again, willing himself to relax, to let the healer monitor him more fully.

Suddenly Margolys grabbed for more bandages. "Quick, help me get him flat!" she ordered Bronwyn. Hurriedly,

Bronwyn threw down her cloak and helped shift him to it. She had felt the sick, cold qualm as a gash high on his right leg re-opened.

"Don't try to stay in rapport, *vai domna*," the healer cautioned. "You and that baby can't spare the energy."

No doubt Margolys was right. Merciful Avarra, how her back ached! *And yet*, she thought, *what I am most tired of is waiting and worrying and never being able to really do anything for anyone, even my daughters. There seem to be fewer wounded coming in, but is that good or bad? Donal never meant her to be out there this long . . .*

Feeling that she must do something, she looked around. There were more bandages not far away, and they would be needed; fetching them ought to be within her capacity. She levered herself up and went for them.

When she got back, she was appalled to see Donal bleeding even more heavily, and Margolys blue-white with the effort to keep him alive.

Never mind what it costs me, Bronwyn resolved. *I am not just going to stand here and watch him die!*

She flung herself into rapport, avoiding Margolys's cell-deep efforts to force the bleeding to stop. Even in her desperation, she knew that she could be of no use there; that took years of training. *But his will*, she thought. *If I can strengthen his will to fight—it was always so strong, surely it won't fail now*.

It was like stepping onto a wide, flat plain, where all the colors were curiously wrong. In the far distance she could see him clearly "Donal!" she cried. "Donal, wait!"

There was only a wordless feeling of anger and regret at so much undone, and a terrible loneliness. Then he knew her, and his mind reached out in a frantic embrace. *Not yet!* both of them cried out. She struggled to keep them both aware and fighting, fighting his death and fatigue. There was a brilliant flash of light, and she sat staring bewildered at the healer.

Margolys looked at her closely, saying, "Forgive me, *domna*. You could not save him, and you could have lost yourself. I have seen it happen." She waited until she saw understanding in Bronwyn's eyes, then quickly continued, "*Domna*, you must not wail for him! Remember, everyone thinks he's leading the battle!"

Bronwyn nodded, and huddled her shawl around her as she tried to think what to do next. Then she realized that someone else was going to have to deal with the problem. She was going to be extremely busy, herself . . . "Come to me as soon as you can leave the wounded, Margolys," Bronwyn said, and made her way to her rooms.

Outside, Danilys cursed as the storm broke. Heavy wet drops slashed down freezing as they hit. At her order, the archers hastily unstrung bows to protect the precious bowstrings. No one could aim in that veering wind, anyway.

The attack seemed less fierce. Was it possible that the weather would come to their aid? Peering futilely into the storm, Danilys cursed again, and made for the north wall. The attackers would have the wind at their backs there.

Halfway, she was met by a messenger. "They're bringing up siege ladders!" he gasped.

"Where in Zandru's Hells did they get those? No, never mind, I know you don't know. Tell Dhuglar to send his pikemen over there, maybe they can push the ladders off if the bandits get that far. Damn this weather!" Hastening to get to the wall herself, she skidded on a patch of sleet and almost fell.

Then she grinned. She wasn't the only one who could slip and fall! "Bring Dom Cerdic to me, fast," she ordered the messenger who'd been following her.

She was still in luck; the messenger found him nearby. The head of Donal's personal guard, Danilys thought, was probably the likeliest to follow even the oddest orders.

"Cerdic, can you spare ten men to haul our biggest kettles of water out to that north wall?"

"Water, *vai dom*?"

"Yes, water. Pour it on the walls, the ground—with the storm, it'll make everything too slick for them to keep themselves upright, let alone a siege ladder."

Cerdic stared, chuckled. "Right!" he yelled, and then was gone, still laughing.

Soon, scummy water joined fresh on the north wall. "Slowly—let it freeze!" Danilys yelled; but the water that failed to freeze flowed down to turn the already-wet ground below into a bog. Faced with ice and mud, unable to protect themselves from the spears being hurled from above, the bandits broke and fled.

Margolys had quickly turned the wounded over to her assistants among the folk of the castle. She reached Bronwyn as she was struggling to undo her outer robe, tears blurring her sight. Gratefully, Bronwyn let the healer take over.

This one was harder than her other labors. The sounds of battle kept her from working with Margolys to time her breathing and her efforts. Her battle and theirs seemed to merge, and merciful Avarra! she was so tired. "Just a little more, *domna*, just a little. Now, sweetheart, now! He's almost here." Margolys never lied. Once more then.

Bronwyn's son's first cries were nearly drowned out by cries of victory from the keep's battlements.

Downstairs, the men were trampling back into the hall. Victory yells and armor-rattling mingled with demands for food and the rattle of pans.

Danilys hung back a little, nerving herself to take off her helm and with it her disguise. She had felt the glamour leave her when the bandits fled and she became aware of her own weariness.

For the first time in several hours, she wondered where

Donal was. At first, she had fretted that his messenger would come when she could not easily retire and be replaced; then the fighting had demanded all her attention.

Now she was truly worried, particularly when the hall grew quiet. Was Donal dead? Emerging a little from an alcove, she saw Margolys standing on the dais, a small bundle raised triumphantly. The bundle gave a good lood squall. "We have won our battle, too!" the healer cried. "Behold Lord Donal's son!"

Yet another burst of cheering echoed through the hall, and Danilys staggered as one of her neighbors thumped her heartily on the back and mumbled something even Donal would have thought faintly obscene.

The helm felt smothering, but she left it on. She must have time to think. The crowd was pushing her toward the dais; what in the name of all the gods and goddesses was she going to say when she got there?

Margolys met her on the bottom step of the dais. As she leaned forward to take the baby, Danilys whispered, "Donal?" and Margolys whispered back, "Dead, *vai domna*."

Personal mourning will have to wait, Danilys thought as she forced herself to mount the dais. When the men knew what she'd done, it was going to make the battle look quiet.

Well, boldness had carried the day before. Perhaps it would now. Danilys handed her young cousin back to Margolys and removed the helm. "Here's bitter news after the sweet," she called out. "Lord Donal is dead!"

The hall went completely quiet for a moment, then filled with the roar of angry male voices, still hoarse from battle, asking each other what in the Nine Hells this girl thought she was doing, why she had tricked them, and what they were going to do about it.

Getting them to be quiet again looked impossible. Her first two tries were failures. She felt close to panic. She simply had to get control somehow.

"I don't care!" one man's shout echoed over the rest. "I don't know what's going on here, but it smells damn funny, and I'm headed back home! We don't know how Lord Donal died, or when!"

"Don't be an idiot!" someone else yelled. "You want to die in the storm, or run into the bandits? You want to draw them back here to see who's left to fight? I've had enough of your stupid notions!"

"Yes! Think! All of you!" Danilys yelled into the moment of relative quiet that followed. "You all know there must be a leader in battle. One voice must command, or the host scatters, and its enemies pick off the men one by one. I took the lead for a few moments only, I thought, to let them see to his wounds. I followed his orders, in all that I did. When no more messengers came from him, I had to go on! And we won!

"My cousin is dead, yes. But will you kill the rest of his family with him? His wife, his heir, the babe just born? Do not leave us now! Give us a few days, only that, to decide how to go on from here. Then listen, and decide whether to honor your old loyalties, or forge new ones." She paused for breath, watching them.

They were far from convinced, but they were tired and willing to let it rest for a little while. The same man as before, though, shook his head quickly and shouted, "Led by who? You? A woman can't hold a keep!"

"This woman has just done it, friend!" she shot back, "and you were among the first to hop to obey! Now—for the love of all the gods and goddesses, let us all get fed and cleansed and cared for." She signaled to Isolde, and the housekeeper set her serving girls moving among the men with bowls of good, thick stew, chunks of nut-bread and pitchers of heather-beer. Soon all seemed inclined to worry about tomorrow, tomorrow . . .

Danilys drew Cerdic and the chiefs of the two largest clans

aside and explained to them that she must talk to Bronwyn before they could decide exactly what was to be done. They were to send word at once if there was any real trouble from the men, though, and not to worry about disturbing her!

Cerdic regarded her gravely. "No need to worry, *vai domna*," he said. "They'd be fools to leave anybody who can lead a battle that well first try—and I'll tell 'em so!"

Danilys murmured something suitably modest, but not shy, and went upstairs to Bronwyn. She lay curled upon her side, smiling in her sleep, and Danilys hesitated to wake her. Perhaps it could wait. . . .

But Bronwyn was too strong a telepath to lie sleeping for long with someone in the room thinking so intensely. She stared at Danilys in confusion for a moment, and then smiled. "You did manage! I knew we'd won, but I fell asleep before I could find out about you. Oh, Dani, I don't think I could have stood to lose you, too!"

Danilys came quickly to the bed and tried to hug Bronwyn. "Dani, your armor!" she protested.

"Sorry, I hadn't thought." Danily struggled out of Donal's chainmail and then hugged her. "How are you, *breda*? Do you feel able to talk?"

"Oh, yes, I feel perfectly rested now, just a little . . . light-headed."

"Well, I won't stay long. Margolys will chase me out if I try. I do need to know if I have your consent to continue commanding the men—if they'll let me—at least until we decide about the future."

"Yes, of course, I'll tell our own captains tomorrow." Neither one wanted to try to look very far into the future just then. As they sat silently, Margolys came in and shooed Danilys off to her own room and the enormous meal Isolde had sent up. She stayed awake just long enough to devour it.

Whether by the mercy of some god, or because winter was indeed coming on fast, the next few days were quiet. Donal,

Lord Rockraven, was buried. His lady wept a little more than custom required, but showed more sense than some who knew her had expected.

The arrival of a messenger three days after the funeral startled everyone. The winter might be mild this year so far, but no winter was a good time to travel.

When the man had been fed, Lady Bronwyn received him in the keep's smaller hall, declaring to Danilys that she refused to freeze in the great hall for anyone less than the King himself.

The messenger, therefore, saw a weary-looking woman awaiting him in a room whose faded tapestries barely managed to keep out most of the cold drafts that seemed to plague every place that he had stayed on this journey. There were only two guards present, and another woman stood in the paxman's place behind the lady.

Danilys frowned fiercely at him. What was the fellow grinning at? Bronwyn frowned also, able to tell that the messenger was sure they would be very glad to hear his master's gracious offer. Would they, indeed?

The man continued smiling as he presented the wax-covered packet he had carried so far. "The Lord Serrais bids me give you his condolences on your loss, *vai domna*, and prays that he may aid you in your troubles."

After slitting the packet open with the small eating knife that hung at her belt, Lady Bronwyn took her time in reading it. She sat very still for a moment, then forced a smile.

"Tell the Lord Serrais that, much as I appreciate the honor of the message, it is much too soon for me to consider such things. And now, you must be weary. Dhuglas—" She motioned to one of the guards. "Show our guest to his quarters, and see that he has all he needs."

Danilys needed no telepathic ability to tell that Bronwyn did not want to discuss the message in the hall, where anyone could hear what was said. An amazing number of people seemed suddenly to need advice on common winter problems, and it was some hours before Danilys and Bronwyn could escape to Bronwyn's rooms.

There, Danilys perched on the wide southern windowsill and looked inquiringly at her cousin. Bronwyn made a disgusted face.

"A marriage proposal! It must have been sent as soon as the news reached Serrais, and at that, the messenger must have killed horses getting here. Dani, what am I going to do? I don't want to marry again, and even if I did, how could I?"

"We'll have to think of something to fend them all off, Bron," replied Danilys. "Serrais is crass beyond belief to have written so soon, but others will follow after a more polite interval."

"Oh, well, we've got it solved, then! Shall I go study at Neskaya, bringing my four children with me? 'Pardon me, I'm applying for training of my *laran*—yes, I know I'm about fifteen years over age. Yes, I do have a few encumbrances; this is Liriel, this Linnell, the redhead is Annilys, and here is the heir to Cuillincrest, Donal-Rafael. The lands of Cuillincrest? Oh, I couldn't quite decide what to do about that.' Or maybe we could put about a rumor that I've been horribly disfigured by a fever, not that I think that would stop most of them! It's just the lands they want!" Bronwyn turned and stared into the fire, her shoulders shaking.

Danilys jumped down off the windowsill and ran to her. "Bronwyn, don't! I'm sorry if I sounded stupid. I was trying to think how to work up to telling you an idea I had back there, when I could tell what the message was. *Breda*?" She touched Bronwyn's shoulder hesitantly.

Bronwyn turned to face her. "I'm sorry myself, Dani. You didn't deserve that. What's your idea?"

She doesn't sound very hopeful, Danilys thought. *Still, I've gotten used to winning over skeptics, lately. . . .*

"Bronwyn, the only way to get rid of these unwanted

suitors is for you to be already married. No, let me finish! It isn't done very much anymore, but you know that women may still take each other in freemate marriage. It's been done before, to protect a woman from just such unwanted attentions. I—I wouldn't really bind you, you know. As soon as Donal-Rafael's old enough to manage on his own, or if you change your mind about remarriage, we could dissolve it easily enough.'' She stopped, wishing passionately that she could read the thoughts behind Bronwyn's blank face.

Then Bronwyn smiled, the first real smile in weeks. "Bind me? Oh, Dani, you're the loser in this! I ought to argue with you, but I can't make myself do it!'' Laughing and crying, they embraced each other.

"There'll be gossip, you know,'' Bronwyn pointed out when they had regained control.

"I do know. We know the truth; some will believe it's to protect Donal-Rafael's heritage; and for the rest—well, 'They say. What say they? Let them be saying'!'' Danilys grinned, and swept the hair out of her eyes.

Brownyn strolled over to her sewing box. "You know, Dani, I think I shall have to make an embroidered sword belt after all. It can be a wedding gift!''

"Oh, yes, please,'' Danilys laughed. "Only not *pink* flowers. I hate pink!''

About Joan Marie Verba and "This One Time"

Here we have another story not about "Amazons" as such, but a heroic tale enlarging on the "Legend of Lady Bruna"—the childhood of the famous Darkovan heroine. For those who are disturbed by minor inconsistencies between Joan's Bruna and mine, I suggest comparing the Racine play El Cid *with the Sophia Loren movie of that name—or compare either with the original Spanish* Cantar del mio Cid. *Legends grow and become enlarged—that's why they're legends.*

Joan Marie Verba is a charming young woman whom I met first at a convention in Minneapolis, Minnesota—whose climate is very like that of Darkover. She entered each of the three Starstone *short story contests for Darkover fiction, and had stories printed in* Starstone; *but this is her first professional appearance. She has written a science fiction novel and is writing a second—which is what I recommend to all young writers while they collect rejection slips on the first.*

MZB

THIS ONE TIME

by Joan Marie Verba

Allira Elhalyn-Alton stood in the doorway of her home, watching the riders pass through the gate. It had been only a few hours since the messenger had come. To her husband, Dominic-Lewis, it was the word he'd been waiting for. Baldric Kadarin's raids were taking a large toll—those not killed outright died a slower death, starved or malnourished, for Baldric took food as well as lives. The previous year's growing season had been poor; this one's did not look more promising. Lord Alton had assembled guardsmen under his command at Armida and sent out scouts to bring back word when Baldric again came across the Kilghard Hills. At last, the message came. Leaving a few of the younger men behind, Domenic now rode out, determined that this raid would be Baldric's last.

"Why must *we* always stay behind?" remarked Allira's eldest, who stood beside her. Allira gave a resigned shrug in answer as she turned to go inside. She always felt she should have named this daughter Echo, not Bruna. Even before Bruna developed *laran*, it seemed she was able speak Allira's mind before Allira spoke it herself.

"Lady Alton?" said a voice behind her as she stepped onto the threshold.

"Yes?" she answered, turning back.

Cathal di Asturien stood in front of her, a step down so she could look at him directly. "Lord Alton gave orders to keep a man on watch at all times," he said, "and lock the gates. I would not plan on going out riding until he returns."

Allira nodded. "I doubt, though, if you will have anything to deal with, except boredom. Baldric is too far away to do much harm to us."

"Baldric is not the only bandit in the hills, lady," Cathal replied

"We've not been bothered by bandits in a long while."

"Nonetheless, lady . . ."

Allira waved his objection aside. "I know, I know, your orders."

"Yes, lady," Cathal said, bowing and descending the stairs.

"I should've cut my hair and put on Kennard's or Gwynn's clothes," Bruna muttered behind Allira, when Cathal was out of earshot.

"Your father allowed us to learn to handle a sword so we could defend ourselves if need be. I doubt if following him is what he had in mind," Allira replied in an ironic undertone.

Bruna crossed her arms and nodded toward the retreating line of riders. "If I were a man, *I'd* be heir to Alton and *would* be riding with them."

"And if I were a man, I'd be on the throne in Thendara!" snapped Allira, more forcefully than she had intended. She sighed, reaching out with her arm and hugging Bruna to her side. *Bruna, little Echo, why must you always remind me of my own frustrations?* Allira sighed, kissed her daughter, and released her. Bruna said nothing, but turned and went into the house.

Allira sat on the couch in front of the hearth, wrapping a blanket around herself and staring into the fire. As a bride, she had come here in the evenings to be by herself; as the years passed, she grew to regard this spot as her own personal sanctuary, where she could think undisturbed after the family and servants were asleep.

What was to become of Bruna? Allira, too, chafed at feminine restrictions, but she loved her family, and she had enjoyed the work she did in the Tower before she married. Bruna seemed to take little interest in either home or *laran*. Yet these were the only choices available. Domenic was unlikely to tolerate a grown unmarried daughter in the house much longer. Bruna would have to choose the Tower, as Allira had done at her age. What else was there . . .?

Allira awakened as a door slammed. Tossing the blanket aside and smoothing her wrinkled dress, she went out of the hall to the entryway to investigate.

". . . all the men you can! Hurry," finished Cathal as he clapped the other guardsman on the shoulder. The man, his back to Allira, nodded and left quickly.

"What is it?" asked Allira calmly.

"Men coming down from the heights, Lady Alton," Cathal said urgently. "I told Lorenze to wake the servants and gather the men. The women and children will have to get to somewhere safe."

"Bandits?"

"I don't know, lady, but it's best to be safe. They aren't coming by the road, and they seem to be taking some pains to avoid being seen, though they're doing a clumsy job of it."

"We have a cellar with a strong lock on the inside," Allira volunteered. "It's next to the kitchen. I'll get the children."

Not waiting for an acknowledgment, Allira ran upstairs, jerked open the first door, and went to the nurse's bed, shaking her awake. "Charlena, wake up all the children and get them downstairs to the herb room—now. There are men coming this way. I'll get the baby."

Charlena stared wide-eyed for a moment, then nodded, getting out of bed and fumbled on a robe.

The door banged against the bedroom wall as Allira entered, waking Linnea. She was where Allira had left her, in a crib by the bed. Startled by the noise, Linnea screamed loudly until Allira picked her up. As usual in the morning, Linnea was wet, so Allira wrapped the oilcloth around Linnea's waist and set her on the bed. Allira grabbed her hard leather jacket and pants, slipping on the pants under her petticoats and tying them. She fastened the jacket over her clothes, then took her sword from the cabinet and buckled it on. Linnea watched her idly, sucking her thumb. *Good thing she's weaned*, Allira thought. She picked Linnea up, oilcloth and all, grabbed a handful of diapers, and headed for the hallway.

"Here, Charlena, take the baby." She handed over Linnea and the diapers, and led the way down to the cellar, followed by a band of sleepy youngsters.

"Mommy, where are we going?"

"What's going on, Mom?"

"Why are you wearing your sword, Mother?"

Allira ignored the questions, heading for the cellar. Bruna strode up, dressed as if for sword practice. She met Allira's eyes for an instant, nodding.

Stopping at the cellar entrance, Allira looked at the servants and their families, already assembling. She spotted the old steward among them. "Eduin?"

The man stepped forward, brushing a stray hair from his face with a gnarled hand. "Yes, my lady?"

"Get everyone into the cellar. Bolt the door and don't come out until someone brings word that it's safe."

"Aren't you coming, my lady?"

"No." Before Allira could add another word, she found herself rocking on her heels, as Kindra and some of the other children pushed against her, clinging to her skirts.

"I don't want to go down there, Mommy, I want to stay here with you," Kindra said; her brothers and sisters echoed agreement.

Allira disengaged herself gently. "I know you want to stay with Mommy, but you have to go with Charlena and Eduin. You mind them, now!"

Eduin reached down and picked Kindra up. "How'd you like old Eduin to tell you about the time he outsmarted an old banshee?" he said, carrying her down the stairs.

"You never met an old banshee," Kindra said skeptically.

"Oh yes I did," said Eduin, turning and winking at Allira as he disappeared, every child in the household in tow.

As the last of the crowd went down the steps, Cathal came around the corner. He started when he saw Allira and Bruna armed and dressed, but continued toward them. "You ought to go down there, too, Lady Alton, Lady Bruna."

"How many men do you have, Cathal?"

"Nine, Lady Alton, Lord Alton took almost everyone who could handle a sword."

"How many are heading this way?"

"About a dozen, I'd say. Hard to tell in the dark, lady."

"With Bruna and me, you'll have eleven, which should even the odds somewhat."

"Yes. lady. But—have you ever killed a man, lady?"

"No. Have you?"

Cathal bit his lip. "I've been in the Guards ten years now, lady," he said simply.

"I've had thirty-six years of training, in case of rape or ambush. I've never had to use what I've learned, but I'm at least as skilled as some of the men you have with you." She turned to Eduin, who had come back up the stairs and was standing by the doorway. "Get inside and lock the door. We'll come for you as soon as we can."

"Yes, my lady," Eduin said, as he retreated down the steps. The door swung shut, and Allira heard the thud of a bolt being placed.

"What will Lord Alton say if you're killed, lady?" Cathal pleaded.

"What would he say if the raiders killed all of you for lack of numbers and then decided to burn the house down around the rest of us?" Allira answered, entering the hall. There were seven men clustered around the fireplace. They turned and stared in shock at Allira and Bruna standing at the other end of the hall. Before anyone could say a word, a man burst through the entrance nearest the front of the house.

"They answered my challenge by throwing stones at me! They're scaling the wall now. I've bolted the first door, but there are other ways of getting in."

The men turned to Cathal. "If they've made it that far, we'd better let them come to us," he said.

"What about the ladies?" someone blurted out.

"The ladies will take care of themselves," Bruna said caustically.

Allira caught Bruna's eye and smiled. Bruna's sword was unsheathed and ready. She hadn't bothered with petticoats, as Allira had done, but wore only a leather jacket, leggings, and the sword. Though the outfit couldn't stop a strong thrust or a direct down-stroke with a heavy longsword, it did provide protection against a casual slash or a glancing cut. Allira fervently hoped the girl wouldn't forget her footwork. . . .

A great bang echoed through the house. The windows rattled with the vibration.

"The doors should hold against anything they might have," volunteered Allira.

"Yes, but they'll try the windows next," said Cathal, as the sound was repeated.

A shattering crash was heard. "Seems as if they've already discovered the windows," Bruna observed, gripping her sword and turning it toward the sound, off in another room.

Yells could be heard outside. The shattering continued, but the pounding at the door stopped.

"Bolt the hall doors!" Cathal ordered. Everyone rushed to the nearest door to slam and secure it. "That will give us a little time, at least," Cathal continued.

"What good is that?" asked Bruna.

"If it's food or money they want, they may just loot the house and leave us alone," said Allira.

"Aye, Lady Bruna, it's always better to avoid a fight if it can be helped. Never lost a man yet in a battle that never started."

Everyone was silent while footsteps could be heard tramping through other rooms in the house. Allira breathed deeply, trying to control her apprehension. A sensitive telepath, she was picking up the tension from the men in the room, ranging from normal fear to near panic. Domenic had told her this was usual for people anticipating a fight, and that he often picked up these feelings himself. Knowing this, though, was proving to be of little comfort to Allira. She was feeling ill, but she shook it off. For one time, even if it was only this one time, she was not going to be pushed aside, protected. She was going to be responsible for her own safety, fully aware of the dangers and consequences.

The seconds dragged on. Allira began to itch in hard-to-reach places. She heard floorboards creak as the footsteps came closer to the hall.

The door beside Allira split suddenly under an axe blow, flying open with a bang. Allira stepped clear as a man stood at the threshold, pointed a sword at her, and said, "There's the sorceress!"

Allira turned, swept her sword left and found herself engaged with another of the invaders. She quickly assumed an attack position as the man hacked savagely at her. She parried the blow easily and tapped the man lightly on the shoulder, as she did every day to her opponents in sword practice. Surprised to find Allira defending herself so effectively, the man paused for an instant. Embarrassed and startled at using practice techniques against someone who might really kill her, Allira also hesitated—long enough for the man to recover and slice at her ferociously. Allira, bringing all her skill to bear, blocked him at every move. Just as she was beginning to see weakness in his defense, she felt something brush her jacket. Looking down briefly, she saw to her horror that there was a sword against her, held by still another man. Allira jumped back; she intended to note as she did so, whether or not the blade had blood on it, but she slipped on something and fell to the floor.

Not looking down, but keeping an eye on the intruders as others stepped in to defend against them, she scrambled to her feet again, planting herself on a firm, dry spot. All the men and Bruna were not occupied; Allira chose the first person fighting more than one man and split the opposition. Her body, she was pleased to notice, moved instinctively, correctly, leaving her mind free to plan future moves. Slowly, she and her new opponent moved away from the main body, both battling aggressively. Time was lost to her until she found an opening for a *balestra* and used it, making a swift thrust through the heart. Seconds after the man hit the floor, two guardsmen rushed up, hovering over the body.

"He's dead, lady," one of them said, needlessly.

Allira looked from the dead man to her sword and back again. Then she turned, slowly, surveying the room and counting heads. Seven were standing, all of them recognizable as the original force guarding the hall. Bruna was among them.

"Are you hurt, Mother?" she called from across the room.

"No," Allira answered, looking down at her clothes. There was blood all over them, as well as on the sword. She walked to the center of the room, trying to avoid the pool that had formed on the floor. As she skirted the periphery, she looked down at the men lying there. She'd tended wounded men before, both at the Tower and at Armida, but she had never seen anything like this. She swallowed hard, fighting off nausea.

"Here, Mother," Bruna said, handing her a long rag. Allira wiped her hands and forehead, then cleaned the blade and sheathed it.

"Lady Alton?" Cathal called, getting her attention.

"Yes?" Allira answered, turning toward him.

"Could you take care of Caradoc here? He's hurt."

Allira walked over and looked at the youth, barely sixteen. He moaned softly as she examined him as gently as possible. Determining that he was not beyond aid, she began to rise to get her medical kit, only to find Bruna tapping her arm with it. Allira nodded, accepting it, and knelt again to attend the youth. When she finished with him she turned to the other men. So absorbed was she with her task that she did not notice that no one had spoken to her until she was binding the arm of the last wounded man.

"Lady Alton?" the man asked weakly. He was one of the invaders, not much older than Cathal; what was left of his shirt was faded and threadbare.

Allira nodded. "Yes," she acknowledged kindly, continuing the bandaging.

"You are—not as Baldric described you," he observed.

"Oh?" Allira inquired curiously.

"He said you were an evil sorceress, sending demons to blight the land with the power of your starstone."

Allira put a hand lightly on the man's forehead. It was hot to the touch. She ripped a clean rag free from the bandages and dipped it in a bowl of water nearby, wringing it out. "A matrix is a telepathic amplifier, nothing more," she said softly as she worked. "At the Tower I learned to use telepathy, not to conjure demons." She placed the cloth gently on the man's head.

Cathal stepped up behind Allira, looking down sharply at the stranger. "If you ask me, it is Baldric who is the demon, raiding our lands, robbing us of food, killing our people."

The man looked up at Cathal. "No, Baldric is a good man. He brought us food. My children, my wife . . . starving until Baldric came. He killed only when necessary . . . only when they refused to share. . . ."

"He was refused because there *is* no food to spare, man! We're starving too!"

"But we have no food left! Our stores are gone . . . our crops . . . hardly out of the ground . . . game is scarce. Baldric said the Lady Alton. . . ." The man turned his head away and blinked wearily. The cloth slipped off; Allira caught it and replaced it.

"Watch what you say about Lady Alton!" Cathal warned.

Allira sighed. "Baldric has long had a grudge against the Altons. He was driven out of the Guards in disgrace for wounding an officer. You have been used, my friend."

The man shook his head slightly and closed his eyes. Allira stood up stiffly. Cathal caught her arm, helping her to her feet.

"You look very pale, lady," he said. When Allira did not reply, he added, "Perhaps you should rest now, lady."

Allira stretched; a sharp pain rippled across her left side. Placing a hand over her ribs and breathing shallowly, she felt the pain ease.

"What's wrong, Mother?" Bruna said, striding up beside Allira and taking her other arm.

"I don't know, I didn't notice any pain there before . . ."

"Where, Mother?"

"Left side," she said, looking across the hall. "What happened to all the blood?"

"We cleaned it up while you were tending the men. The dead we carried behind the stables. Cathal set some of the others to digging graves for them."

Allira shook her head sadly. "Poor men."

"They would've killed you, lady," Cathal said.

"I know," Allira said softly. "Bruna," she continued, "tell Eduin to come out now. Move the men you can into the guardroom. If they can't be moved that far, bring in some of the cots and get them off the floor, at least." Allira sagged weakly. Cathal and Bruna helped her to the couch.

"Just have to rest," she said, lying on her right side and closing her eyes.

Allira heard voices. Without opening her eyes, she lay still, deciding she must have slept. The surface she was on was rough; she must still be on the couch. Feeling too tired to open her eyes for the moment, she listened to the voices.

"That was well done, contacting me by matrix, Bruna," said a familiar voice. "Are you sure you're not hurt?"

"Unscathed, Father," answered Bruna.

"Many of my men do not do as well in their first fight," said Domenic. "Perhaps you should have been a man, too?"

Silence followed. Allira attempted to open her eyes, and found it took more effort than she had anticipated. All that happened at first was a slight flutter of the eyelids. Concentrating more, she was able to open them wide enough to get a view of her immediate surroundings.

Coming slowly into focus in front of her, standing at a right angle to her field of vision, was Gabriel. He was leaning forward, his hands on his knees. With typical eleven-year-old brashness, he blurted out, "Mother, you look *awful!*"

Allira tried to laugh, but all that came out was a weak snort, followed by a pain in her side. She closed her eyes and winced, trying to control her breathing.

"Here, dearest, drink this." Allira tried to raise her head, failed, and felt someone lift her head for her. Someone slipped a pillow under her head.

"We had to take several stitches in your side, but it could be worse—your ribes seem to have stopped the blade from going farther," said Domenic reassuringly. "You'll have a scar, though."

Allira managed a weak smile. "The babies?"

"All the children are fine. Charlena took the younger ones upstairs by another way and told them Mommy was sleeping. The other ones are here, though—as you no doubt have noticed."

Allira looked away from Domenic and saw her children's faces clustered around the couch, looking at her anxiously.

"Baldric?"

"We got him," Domenic said. "The poor beggars following him were more starved than our men. Wasn't much of a fight."

"What now?"

Domenic shrugged and knelt next to the couch. "I don't know, Allira. We divided what little food we had, and sent the survivors home. We have little more than they do, and when that runs out. . . ." His voice trailed off.

Allira tried to raise her arm in order to clasp his hand, but managed only to wiggle her fingers. Domenic saw the gesture, took her hand himself, raised it gently and pressed it to his lips.

"The important thing, for now, is that you're safe, dearest," Domenic said, replacing Allira's hand gently at her side. Stroking her hair, he added, "You did very well, they say."

"Bruna," Allira began, weakly.

"She did well, too."

"As well as a man, Father?" teased Bruna, who was standing, looking over the back of the couch.

"Yes," Domenic agreed, reluctantly. For a moment, his face looked strange; Allira wondered if he was having a flash of the foresight that sometimes came to the Altons. At last, he sighed, and said, "You will always do well, daughter." He stood up, facing her.

Bruna smiled. "I intend to, Father," she said confidently.

Allira looked from husband to daughter. Somehow comforted by the expressions she saw there, the feelings that she sensed, she drifted into a peaceful sleep.

About Margaret Carter and "Her Own Blood"

A request for biographical data from Margaret Carter after accepting her story brought a reply on amusing stationery bearing the legend "Here's to Pure Theory—May it Never Be Useful to Anyone." I'll drink to that.

Margaret Carter is working on a Ph.D. in English; her dissertation was on "Fiend, Spectre or Delusion; Narrative Doubt in the Supernatural in Gothic Fiction." She also edited a classic collection, Demon Lovers and Strange Seductions, *(Fawcett, 1972) and her paper on C.S. Lewis has been accepted by the Kent State University anthology,* Lewis as Critic.

She says her early writing was "inspired by Dracula *and her main ambition is to write a novel of supernatural horror." She is a Navy wife, submitted a list of her past addresses that looks like the Travel Guide to America, and has four sons, ranging in age from two to seventeen.*

"Her Own Blood" is not technically "about" Free Amazons, but suggests new parameters for women trying to make a place for themselves in a male-dominated society, and that's what the Free Amazons are all about anyway.

MZB

HER OWN BLOOD

by Margaret L. Carter

Her head dull with pain, Gwennis uneasily scanned the crowd of servants and freeholders crowded into Dom Elric Serrais's judgment hall. She still had no clear notion of why her mother Alanna had so abruptly decided to bring her here this morning. The pair of them had no petition or demand for justice to place before the minor Ridenow lord they served. Unless Alanna planned to complain to the *vai dom* of her husband's beating of Gwennis. That guess seemed far-fetched, for even a herdsman held that much right over his offspring.

Besides, this beating was only the latest and worst of hundreds. As Gwennis had been milking the family's one dairy beast this morning, a sudden pain had ripped into the back of her neck. She had glimpsed the stable cat pouncing on a rodent amid the straw. But knowing that her choking agony in fact belonged to the tiny, squirming creature had not kept her from doubling over with a scream, as (it seemed) her own neck was snapped. The walls of the lean-to stable spinning around her, she was dimly aware of the milk-pail spilling on the earth and her father descending upon her. Through the new pain of fists hammering her head and face, she heard the roar of the familiar abuse: "Feather-brained six-fathered brat! Do you think milk comes out of the ground like water?"

After her father had gone about his work, Gwennis had shown the new bruises to her mother, whose only comment was, "It's getting worse. He'll kill you someday." The words were spoken with matter-of-fact flatness, for the incident was too common to waste emotion on.

Gwennis sometimes wondered why she hadn't already become the witling her father thought her. These seizures, with the invariable consequence, had been plaguing her for two years, since she was thirteen. Her first experience had centered on the birth of her youngest brother. While Alanna breathed and strained under the midwife's hands, with hardly a moan, Gwennis had lain doubled up in her loft bed, shrieking with every renewed wave of rendering pressure. Her father, Piedro, never affectionate even before that night, had cuffed her for the noise and thrown her out of the house. She soon realized that she could feel the pain of any suffering creature, human or animal, within a distance of a few score feet. The only saving points of this curse were its limited range and the fact that it was confined to creatures complex enough to be aware of pain. She did not have to share the death of every fly or flea. And in sheer self-protection she had learned (when given time to collect her wits) to grope toward the center of the agony and mentally damp down the pain. Nevertheless the attacks were so frequent that at least once or twice every tenday she was chastised for breaking crockery or pulling up a vegetable instead of a weed in her disorientation. She'd found, too, that she could no longer bring herself to eat meat, a quirk that, along with the fits, made her mother and sisters call her sickly and "vaporish." As for Piedro, he accused her of shirking and (incomprehensibly) "putting on airs"—as if fainting at the most disastrous moments were something to be proud of!

As the morning wore on, Gwennis soon wearied of straining to hear the details of her neighbors' grievances over the low burr of conversation pervading the hall. She and Alanna stood in a corner waiting their turn, sipping from the waterskin they'd brought and nibbling a few dried fruits. This was the closest Gwennis had ever seen Dom Elric, a tall, spare man whose bronze hair had faded almost entirely to gray. She knew nothing of him beyond common talk, and he was said to be just and generous enough. Married four times, he was now a widower with only one surviving child, a boy less than five years old. The boy, rumor said, suffered some strange illness likely to kill him long before adulthood. Dom Elric's was a small estate, and he was unlikely to find a fifth family willing to give him a daughter for a bride. His heir presumptive was an *emmasca* cousin, and Dom Elric's household was managed by his widowed, childless sister. Gwennis had never seen the *vai domna* but had heard that after her husband's early death the lady had refused her brother's order to remarry and instead chosen some undefined but scandalous way of life.

By noon the hall was empty except for Dom Elric's house servants and a few stragglers gathering up their children and possessions. Alanna drew Gwennis with her to bow before the lord's high seat. "*Vai Dom*, I have a boon to ask of you in private."

He frowned, though not forbiddingly. "I cannot call your name to mind, *mestra*."

"I am Alanna, wife of Piedro, your chief herdsman. The need concerns my eldest daughter here."

Gwennis, still muzzy with headache, wondered how her mother could think of appealing to the overlord about Piedro's harshness. Any man's power over his own children—short of murder—was beyond interference. Gwennis felt Dom Elric's pale gray eyes upon her, as if he could strip off the front of her skull and stare into her brain. With a momentary shiver, she thought perhaps he could. Didn't all the Hastur kin have sorcerous powers?

After a moment's thought, he said, "Very well. I will speak to you in the coridom's office."

Minutes later, an obviously disapproving steward escorted mother and daughter to a small, plain room furnished chiefly

by a desk and a pair of low couches. Dom Elric took a seat
and motioned the two of them to do the same. "You needn't
stand, in private. Now what is this important matter of yours?
It had better be enough to justify this nonsense."

"I only sought to spare you embarrassment, *vai dom*,"
said Alanna. Gwennis was astonished at the sly insolence,
quite unusual in her mother. "This is my daughter, Gwennis.
She was festival-got, on Midwinter fifteen years past. That
night I lay with several men, including my betrothed. Only
one of them could have given her *this*." She clutched a lock
of Gwennis's flame-colored hair.

Gwennis stood in shock, marveling at her own naïveté. All
this time she'd thought Piedro's favorite epithet, "six-fathered,"
a mere random insult. No wonder her father—no, foster-
father—loathed the sight of her. And almost as great a marvel
as her own parentage was the thought that her drudge of a
mother, with lined face and dishwater hair, could once have
been fair enough to tempt a nobleman. For that matter, who
could imagine this grave lord reveling so frivolously?

He was speaking again: "What is your petition, *mestra*? If
you want me to acknowledge her, the time to bring up that
matter was fifteen years ago."

Alanna gazed blankly at him. "I never thought of that,
vai dom."

The statement was simple truth, Gwennis realized. All the
woman wanted was to get rid of her daughter in a way that
would ease her own conscience. Alanna continued, "She has
the vapors, she's too sickly for outdoor work. My man beats
her, and I'm afraid for her very life. I ask you to give her
some position in the Great House where she can work without
fear. She's not strong, but she's neat-handed and not as
simple-minded as she looks."

Gwennis cringed at the harsh description. Who would venture to buy a dairy beast or *chervine* with such specifications?

After one of the meditative pauses seemingly characteristic

of him, Dom Elric called the coridom, waiting just outside the door, and ordered, "Ask Domna Calinda to come here."

A moment later a middle-aged woman, as tall as her brother, entered the room. Gwennis was surprised to see that her auburn hair was cropped short like a boy's, though her dress was like any lady's. "Calinda," said Dom Elric, "have you use for a new maidservant?"

After a sharp glance at him, the lady's eyes raked Gwennis up and down. "Can you sew, girl?"

Alanna answered for her, "Not fancy stitches, of course, but she's good hand at plain sewing."

Domna Calinda turned to her brother. "We could put her to mending the linen."

"Very well," said Dom Elric. "You'll stay here, child. Go with Domna Calinda, and she'll instruct you in your duties."

Gwennis's mother gave her a stiff embrace. "I'll bring your clothes tomorrow. Work hard, and don't give the *vai domna* any trouble." She was gone before Gwennis quite realized what was happening.

The lady said with a sound that just missed being a snort, "Come along, girl, don't stand there gaping."

If Gwennis' new life as a servant in the Great House was a lonely one, she did not fully realize that fact. She had been lonely at home, too. Even before her infirmity had come over her, being the eldest as well as the object of Piedro's sullen dislike had set her apart from the younger children. And in the last couple of years, her sisters had drawn farther away, out of resentment at her lesser ability to work and half from a superstitious fear of her "queerness." The only real affection she shared was with her baby brother, who was more like a pet than a friend. Nor did Alanna, constantly overworked, have time or inclination to bestow special care on her "different" daughter. As for material conditions,

Gwennis found her bed in the maidservants' dormitory luxurious after a lifetime of sharing the loft in a two-room hut with four sisters. Food, too, was more plentiful and varied in the Great House. The work came easily enough to her deft fingers. Best of all, she need not fear beatings; physical and even verbal abuse were things not tolerated under Domna Calinda's rule. In fact, for the first eight days of her new employment Gwennis had no "fits" at all.

On these summer mornings, after the sun melted off the light layer of overnight snow, the maids often sat at their mending in the castle courtyard under the fruit trees. On one such morning the other two girls assigned to this task told Gwennis something of the lord's family.

After a cautious glance toward the inner door, Hilary, a slightly built blonde, said, "Well, Gwen, you've been here almost a tenday. What do you think of Domna Calinda?"

The idea of passing judgment on the lady of the house rather daunted Gwennis. Her only thought on the subject so far was gratitude that the lord's sister, though forbidding and sharp-voiced, was never cruel. She murmured, "The *vai domna* hasn't been anything but kind to me."

"Of course, but haven't you wondered about her hair and her—well—that mannish way she has?"

Naturally Gwennis wondered, but she was far too timid to speak aloud so bluntly. "I've never seen a lady's hair cut that way," she ventured, keeping her eyes on the bedsheet she was hemming.

Hilary smiled with satisfaction at the chance to regale a newcomer with gossip already known to the rest of the staff. "I daresay you've never even heard of the Free Amazons."

Startled into looking up, Gwennis retorted, "I'm not all that ignorant. But I don't know anything about them. Women who live like men—is *that* what—?"

Hilary nodded. "Domna Calinda is one of them. After her husband died so young, she wouldn't marry again—spurned the man Dom Elric promised her to. They say he was furious when she ran away to join the Amazons.''

The other servant, Ysabet, a few years older, added, ''The *vai dom* almost drove her from his door when she came back, after his last wife died in childbed. I was here—there was a terrible scene.''

''But he let her stay?'' said Gwennis, curious in spite of herself.

Hilary shrugged. ''He had to. He couldn't take care of a new baby without a woman. Besides, she'd learned a scribe's work among the Amazons.''

''She only came back for the sake of little Lerrys,'' Ysabet said. ''I don't think she'd put up with it otherwise.''

''Put up with—?'' said Gwennis.

''The *vai dom* never has forgiven her for being an Amazon, and he doesn't let her forget she's a scandal to the family. I expect she'll stay only as long as the poor child lives.''

''Which won't be long.'' Hilary sighed.

Gwennis had only glimpsed the boy as he played in the court on fine mornings under his nurse's eye. ''What ails him?''

''Why, don't you know?'' said Hilary, dropping her voice out of deference to the melancholy subject. ''He has some illness of the blood. With every tiny cut his life is like to bleed away. He's almost died more than once already.'' As the door opened, she glanced round and picked up her neglected work.

Lerry's nurse Mhari emerged from the house, leading the young lord by the hand. He was small for his age, not much taller than Gwennis's brother, but otherwise no casual observer would have guessed him to be sickly. The truth was immediately obvious, though, from the nurse's anxious fluttering as he freed his hand from hers and began hopping on one foot from one paving-stone to the next.

Mhari seated herself on a bench near the three girls. "If only he could understand he has to be careful," she said. "But it's so important not to make him afraid of everything." She continued turning to watch his every move while at the same time making conversation about the upcoming Midsummer festival. Her constant twitter of parenthetical warnings to the boy belied her wish "not to make him afraid." Gwennis, finding the woman's anxiety contagious, caught herself covertly following Lerrys from the corner of her eye.

Tired of his hopping game, he clambered up on one of the stone benches against the wall, trying to reach a low cluster of blackfruit. "Lerrys, come down this minute!" said Mhari, a sharp tone replacing her patter of routine directions. Like any normal child, he gave her a sidelong glance, assessing her seriousness, and crept an inch or two higher. "Lerrys, I told you to get down!" She stood up and moved toward him.

Seeing the coveted fruit still out of reach, Lerrys drew one knee up onto the lower ledge of the wall. "No—stop!" He turned to grin at his nurse, and one foot slipped. As he tried in vain to clutch the rough surface of the wall with both hands, Mhari's arms reached out for him just too late. Twisting as if to brace himself, he fell face down on the flagstones.

Pain exploded in Gwennis's head at the same moment that the child's wailing pierced through her. He cried less from pain than fear—if too young to understand caution, he was not too young to remember the results of past injuries—but the hurt, too, was real. Pressing her hands against her temples, Gwennis mentally groped for the source of the agony and squeezed, as if choking it out of existence. She felt the pain as a ball of clay within her fists, and she compressed it into a tiny pebble, then into nothingness. Somehow blood was part of the pain, which could not be stopped until she forced the blood back to its wellspring and dammed its flow. When at the last the red flood of pain was diminished to a trickle, she became aware enough of her own whimpering to make herself stop.

Meanwhile, some small part of her saw Mhari snatch up the child, heard the nurse cry, "Get Domna Calinda—hurry!" Lerrys had cut his lip and bumped his nose, and blood streamed from both injuries. Trivial to an ordinary boy, they obviously were not so to him. In a moment the lady of the house rushed in and stared, astonished, as the bleeding slowed of its own accord.

When her seizure passed, Gwennis felt Domna Calinda's eyes on her. "You," the lady whispered.

Now, thought Gwennis miserably, she knows my sickness, and she'll send me away. "Forgive me, *vai domna*—only a second of faintness—it won't happen again."

The lady seemed to pay no attention to her words. "How long have you had this *laran*, girl?"

"I don't know what you mean, my lady—*laran* is only for the Hastur kin."

Domna Calinda leaned toward her and said in a harsh whisper, "And what do you call yourself, with that hair? Do you suppose I can't guess why my brother took such a sudden interest in a herdsman's daughter?"

In the confusion no one else seemed to have noticed this interchange. Domna Calinda took the sobbing boy from Mhari and pulled up the legs of his leather breeches. "Avarra grant he has no bruises this time. You'd better take him upstairs to rest." She accompanied the boy and his nurse inside without another glance at Gwennis, who picked up her sewing and tried to act as if her behavior had only been panic at the sight of blood.

In her narrow dormitory bed that night, Gwennis was roused from sleep by a hand on her shoulder. Starting up, she saw Mhari, wrapped in a worn bedgown, haloed by the light of an oil lamp she carried. "Get up! The *vai dom* wants you in Master Lerrys's chamber."

Scrambling into a tunic and skirt, thrusting her feet into clogs, Gwennis muttered in half-awake bewilderment, "But I don't even know where that is."

Mhari pulled her along the dark corridors into a part of the castle new to her, the lord's own quarters. Through the girl's mind ran the thought that Dom Elric had been told of her defect and was about to dismiss her. Only later did she recognize the absurdity of the notion that the lord would discharge a servant in person, or at midnight. Mhari drew Gwennis into Lerrys's bedroom without knocking. Domna Calinda and Dom Elric were both there, the latter still fully dressed; it must not be so late at night, after all.

"Come here, girl," ordered the lady, when Gwennis paused at the door.

Approaching the bed, she saw Lerrys, pale, in a groggy half-sleep. Somewhere in the background she felt a dull throb of pain. Dom Elric said, "My sister tells me you have a *laran* that can ease my son."

"She—she said so, *vai dom*. But I know nothing of sorcery."

"Well, you must try." Turning down the covers, he pulled up the boy's nightgown to show a deep purple blotch on one knee. "When he hurts himself, he often bleeds under the skin for hours. Can you stop this bleeding as you did the other?"

Gwennis almost physically staggered under this demand. Never before had she tried to control her curse under calm reflection. What he wanted of her was to reach out to the pain instead of fleeing it. She wasn't sure she could nerve herself to that ordeal. All she said was, "I don't know, *vai dom*. I have never tried."

"Do your best, then." He sighed.

She felt Domna Calinda's eyes boring into her. She turned away from that stare and focused on Lerrys' bruised leg. Almost at once the room, the bed, and the outline of the child's body faded away. She saw only the dark lump of pain. This hurt, unlike the initial injury, was not overwhelmingly intense. She could easily free herself and retreat from it. But instead she had to advance upon it, immerse herself. With a long, ragged breath she mentally moved closer, until she saw the hurt as a sluggishly spiraling current in a stagnant pool. It threatened to draw her in, drag her under, drown her. She barely stopped herself from pulling back.

Now she, too, was bodiless, only a hovering spark of awareness. Skimming the surface of the murky water, she saw the source of the pain and blood as a gap in the muck on the pond's bottom, from which burbled a stream of foul-smelling ooze. She realized that she could fight her fear of being engulfed only by diving in voluntarily. She plunged to the deepest center of the pool and blocked the outlet with her own being—what she visualized as a point of light containing herself. Though the poison nearly choked her, she concentrated on pouring out light to neutralize it. In a moment the flow stopped, and the rhythmic beat of the pain slowed and then vanished.

She'd won! In a burst of joy she soared upward. Instead of finding herself back in her body, she discovered she was floating above Lerrys's bed. She saw the child, Mhari, Dom Elric, Domna Calinda, and herself, slumped in a chair; she noticed that her own eyes were glazed in trance, and the nurse was supporting her shoulders as if she could not hold herself up.

Domna Calinda was saying, "Look, she has done it! I've never seen such strength in someone so young—and without even a matrix."

Dom Elric gripped Gwennis's shoulder. She was jerked back into her body, blind with dizziness, the room whirling around her. Through a buzzing in her ears she heard him saying, "Child, you have done me a great service. Thanks to you, no matter how often this happens, my poor lad will have a chance of living as long as the Gods allow—even if he cannot survive to manhood. You are my *nedestro* daughter—''

The lady interrupted, ''This is no time to speak of such things. Can't you see the condition she's in?''

He shrugged her off. ''I must say it. Child—Gwennis— you are my daughter, and I will acknowledge you as such. I'll see to it that you are married well, and your son will be my heir.''

Domna Calinda half-lifted Gwennis to her feet. ''Enough of this. Come, girl, you must rest.''

Gwennis obediently took a step away from the bed. At once the buzzing in her head swelled to a roar, and grayness closed in.

When consciousness returned, she felt immediately that the sheets against her skin were not the coarse cloth of a servant's bed. Reluctant to open her eyes, for fear the dizziness was lurking in wait, she lay still and listened for a few seconds. Someone sitting next to the bed shifted position, rustling skirts. Gwennis knew before she looked that Domna Calinda was there. Opening her eyes, the girl found that she was in a small but well-furnished room, faded tapestries on the walls, curtains around the bed, and a down-stuffed quilt over the sheets. The lady, staring at her, held a cup of something hot.

''Can you sit up?'' she said. ''You must drink and eat.''

Gwennis automatically obeyed her mistress. The room lurched and her stomach with it. She turned her head away from the offered cup.

''You must,'' the lady repeated. ''The exercise of *laran* always drains the body.''

Accepting the steaming bark tea with a grimace, the girl was surprised to find that after the first sip its warmth was soothing. After drinking half the cup she felt no nausea as she faced the next offering, a bowl of nut porridge heavily laced with honey. ''Is it really *laran*, my lady?''

"It is, and very strong," she replied tartly. "Would there be all this fuss otherwise?"

Gwennis was beginning to understand why she was lying in a private chamber, waited on by the lady of the house, but she was still not bold enough to question further. By the time Domna Calinda left, ordering her to sleep, she remembered Dom Elric's promise—to acknowledge her and make her son his heir. If she ever had a son—the whole situation seemed dreamlike. Before this day she'd only half believed herself Dom Elric's daughter. Now she had found, or been found by, her own kind, people of her own blood. A place would be made for her; she would belong. Her "illness" was, strangely, incomprehensibly, no longer a curse but a gift. So why wasn't she happier? Perhaps she would be after becoming accustomed to the idea, after it became real to her.

For a while she slept. It was a couple of hours later (as she found) that she was again shaken out of sleep. Dom Elric and Domna Calinda both stood over her. "Get up, child," he said. "Lerrys is bleeding internally again—we need you."

As Gwennis sat up, again the whole room seemed to rock, worse this time. She felt that any moment it might start spinning fast enough to tear itself from the house and whirl away through the night.

Domna Calinda said, "You need not come, girl. Elric, she cannot be expected to function again so soon."

"Stop interfering," he snapped. "I told you already, we have no choice."

More alarmed by being the subject of a quarrel than by the sickening disorientation, Gwennis clutched the bedpost and tried to stand up. "I will come—" The whirling sensation intensified. She felt herself thrown forcibly out of her body. At once her sight and hearing became dazzlingly clear, while all other physical sensations were mercifully blotted out. Suspended somewhere near the ceiling, she looked down on

Dom Elric and Domna Calinda wrangling over her own limp form.

"You see?" said the lady. "At this rate you'll kill her, at no benefit to your son. I'm no *leronis*, but I know well enough what threshold sickness can do. And they say the stronger the *laran*, the greater the hazard."

"Her strength is what Lerrys needs right now," said Dom Elric. "And I'll risk anything for him."

"Including the life of this child who's too ignorant even to know what you're asking of her? And if she dies, what becomes of your last hope for an heir?"

"That need wouldn't exist if you had any decent sense of family loyalty. If you'd done your duty and remarried—"

"I did my 'duty' once at your behest—married a man I hardly knew and got a stillborn child that almost killed me in the birthing. When Lorill's death set me free, I counted it a second chance from the hand of the Goddess."

"And threw it away on those Amazons. Unnatural bitches— ought to be outlawed, teaching women to put selfish wants ahead of the needs of your own blood and clan."

At some point during this conversation, Gwennis saw herself lifted onto the bed and felt her consciousness sink down into her body. Yet it still seemed that she could hear the two voices as they trailed along the corridors and watch their progress through walls somehow melted into transparency.

"Selfish?" Domna Calinda retorted. "Is it selfish for a woman to seek what all men have by birthright, the choice of their own destiny?"

"What choice? Do you think I took four wives for the sheer pleasure of it? But I know the importance of getting an heir of my own blood, even if you don't."

"Then you are a fool, brother. And that girl will be sacrificed to your folly, as I almost was. Poor wretch, she'll probably think it a great honor, marrying to give you a grandson!"

Gwennis's strangely extended sight followed them to Lerrys's chamber, where Mhari wept at the bedside. Gwennis felt the child's hurt as a distant, dull red pulsation. It seemed that she stretched out phantom tendrils and stroked the injured limb until the red faded to cool clarity.

Then she was back in the curtained bed, firmly lodged in her body as random waves of sensation washed over her. Longing to escape once more into that discorporate condition, she could not find the way. Trapped, she cried out soundlessly, for how long she could not tell. Finally a hand grasped hers.

When her head cleared, it was still dark. Domna Calinda, silhouetted by a single candle, sat by the bed again.

"I—I think I called you, my lady."

Domna Calinda nodded. "I heard you, though my own *laran* is quite unexceptional."

"I'm sorry to be such trouble."

"Trouble?" the lady snorted. "My brother thinks you are a gift straight from the Lord of Light."

"How is the little boy?"

"Well, for this time at least."

Keeping her eyes lowered, Gwennis forced herself to speak her new misgivings. "*Vai domna*, I—I'm not sure I want to marry a nobleman, or—or whatever the *vai dom* is thinking of."

Domna Calinda's sharp glance convinced Gwennis that the lady knew Gwennis had overheard the earlier quarrel. "And what would you do instead, my girl?"

"I heard you speak of the Free Amazons—that they give women a choice of their own destiny."

"Would you go to the Renunciates, then?"

"I don't know," said Gwennis. "To be a warrior—and turn away from men forever—" Though, Gwennis thought, her experience of men so far left her with no great eagerness to know them better.

The lady said with a thin smile, "Do I look to you like a swordswoman? We follow any honorable trade. Our whole creed holds that all women are different, just as all men. You, for instance, might be destined for the healer's craft."

This idea struck Gwennis as a revelation; she had never seen herself as capable of any distinctive skill. "Do you think I could?"

"Perhaps—who knows? It takes more than *laran* alone. As for turning from men, that is a misunderstanding, too. Many Renunciates join in freemate marriages. We only vow not to become the property of men or bear children for pride of house or clan."

Gwennis thought for a moment of how Dom Elric, though he doubtless meant kindly enough, wanted her only for the benefits of her newly revealed *laran*. No more than her foster-father did he take an interest in Gwennis, herself. Here was some chance to learn what that self really was. "Yes—I would like to go to them."

"If that is your true wish, I can put you on the road to the Guild House at Serrais. Can you face a day's walk alone? You must leave before dawn, without an escort or even a riding beast, if you hope to escape Elric's notice. He'll be enraged as it is when he finds you've gone."

Gwennis recognized the cautionary remarks as a first test of her resolve, her readiness for independence from ordinary protections for female "weakness." (She caught a flash of an unspoken doubt: "This girl acts like a rabbithorn in a banshee's claws. The Guild House is no refuge for incompetence.") "I'll do what I must, my lady. But—but Lerrys. If I leave now—"

"Then he will be no worse than before you came. I am not the keeper of your conscience, Gwennis, but doubtless you don't know how dangerous an untrained telepath can be. Later you may be in a condition to help him more."

For the first time the lady had called her by her given

name. Gwennis threw back the sheets and stood up. This time there was no dizziness. "Then I *will* go to the Guild House. And I'll come back, if Dom Elric will have me, to help my half-brother—after I have found my own way."

About Susan Holtzer and "The Camel's Nose"

One of the major peculiarities of Darkovan culture is a distinct technophobia; which has led not-too-intelligent readers to deduce that I am personally either a technophobe or a libertarian. Nothing could be further from the truth; I owe my continued existence, as well as the lives of at least two of my children, to technology, and I consider libertarianism (in practice, if not in theory) a vicious kind of social Darwinism, "survival of the richest." (Please don't bother to write and try to convince me how wrong I am; I have been known to return political tracts to the Post Office endorsed "obscene mail; return to sender.")

Why, then, did I make Darkover technophobic and anti-government? Well, it seemed a good idea at the time; Darkover is at most a thought-experiment (Gedankenexperiment, in the language of philosophy). Societies can be "tested to destruction" and at least on paper and in fiction, Darkovan culture works. Susan Holtzer has taken Darkovan technophobia and, with a little hair-splitting, created an amusing story of an entering wedge for technology.

Susan says that she has written "every conceivable kind of non-fiction, including three futile years in middle management trying to convince a muddle of middle-managers that there is no such word as tutee.'' *(One who receives the attentions of a tutor? If there isn't, obviously there ought to be; a gap in the language invites neologisms and solecisms.)* She calls herself a ''60s political burnout who finds more reality in science fiction than in contemporary America.'' *(Nevertheless she is a fan of the Green Bay Packers and would rather give up her right arm than her Apple. Okay, so she's left-handed, but you can't get much more contemporary than that.)*

And without much more contemplation of the nature of reality in science fiction or contemporary America, let us contemplate Susan's attempt to intro-duce (limited) technology to Darkover.

MZB

THE CAMEL'S NOSE

by Susan Holtzer

Elinda leaned closer to the aircar engine, her face only inches from the spinning rotors. Use all your senses, Sam had said. Well, her eyes told her nothing, and her nose discerned only the normal smell of superheated fuel. She cocked her head, listening.

"Well?" the man behind her snapped impatiently.

"I think . . ." She hesitated. "The timing mechanism isn't firing properly."

"Aye, but why?"

"That would be the microprocessor, wouldn't it?"

"Would it?"

"All right, yes it would," Elinda said angrily. "Diagnosis: replace microprocessor."

"Dammit!" His anger made her wince. "Listen!" He yanked her forward until her nose nearly touched the engine. "Can't you *hear*, girl? That low-pitched, burring sound—that's metal on metal."

She concentrated, shutting out the other sounds of the Spaceport around her. After a moment she sighed. "Of course. And the microprocessor is off because it's trying to compensate for the motion of the rod." She pointed. "That one."

"Right!" Sam McCann's freckled face beamed at her. "You'll make an engineer yet, for all you're a girl and a barbarian." She took his words for the compliment they meant, knowing that to the stocky Terran, a barbarian was anyone who didn't love and understand machines. It was a word he applied equally to men and women, Darkovans and Terrans.

"Come on," he said, slamming the cover over the offending engine. "Let's go drown the taste of oil in a glass of good Terran beer. My treat."

As they trudged across the expanse of concrete, he looked at her quizzically. "You're a queer sort of Darkovan, you know."

"I certainly do know." Elinda laughed. "When my father got really angry at me, he'd say I even came out of the womb backward."

"Still," Sam persisted, "you're the only Darkovan, man *or* woman, who's chosen to learn our engineering. Oh sure, there's a batch of you Free Amazons training in our medical department, but you're the only one even remotely interested in anything mechanical. What I can't figure out," he said seriously, "is how you even got to know you *were* interested."

"My brother," Elinda answered. "When I was seven years old, he came home with a little model of a helicopter he'd bought in the Trade City. It was just a toy, a curiosity; after a few days he gave it to me." She paused, remembering.

"Then one day I saw a real helicopter pass overhead, and I couldn't understand why it flew and mine didn't. So I took the model apart and put it back together, trying to figure it out. After that, I took the water pump apart to see how *it* worked. That's when my father beat me for the first time."

She didn't add, that's also when I decided to take oath as a Renunciate. Someone said once that every Free Amazon had a story, and every story was a tragedy. Well, hers was probably less tragic than most. She cast around for a change of subject, and her eye caught a flicker of movement.

"What in the world is that?"

"Where?" They had left the concrete Spaceport area to cut

through the courtyard of the Transient Barracks. Sam followed her pointing finger. "You mean the kid on the bicycle?"

"Bicycle?" Elinda had received a full sleep-course of the Terran language at the start of her training, but this was a word she could not recall.

"It's a kid's toy, to ride around on."

"I want to see it." She trotted across the court and stood for a moment, watching a boy ride in swift circles on the strange device. It moved too fast for her to see the mechanism clearly.

"Can you ask him to stop?" she asked Sam, who shrugged good-humoredly and waved to the boy.

"Do you mind if the lady examines your bike?"

"No, sir." The boy halted in front of them and dismounted with a flourish. "It's a Himal'ya racing bike. See? Fifteen speeds, hydraulic brakes and a Filene derailleur. I'll need that kind of power on Castel—that's where we're going."

Elinda knelt on the ground beside the bicycle, oblivious to dignity or the rough pavement, and examined the vehicle. "I see," she said, more to herself than the others. "All operated from these cables. Drive chain, gear ratio, brakes. . . ." She looked up at the boy. "How fast does it go?"

"Flat out, nearly 50," he stated proudly.

"Fifty kph?" Elinda stood and met Sam's amused look with an expression of excitement.

"Sam, I want to talk to Cholayna. Come with me? Thank you very much," she told the startled boy. "Come, Sam." Man and boy shrugged and grinned at each other, and Sam allowed himself to be dragged toward the Terran HQ.

"You want *what*?" Cholayna Ares leaned forward across her desk and stared at the girl seated before her.

"Bicycles. They're two-wheeled, foot-propelled mechanical devices to ride on." Elinda grabbed a pen from the desk and started to scribble a sketch. Cholayna, choking back laughter, held up a hand.

"Never mind. I know what bicycles are. But what on earth do you want one for?"

"Not one, several. For the Guild House. Don't you see how marvelous they'd be?"

"Why don't you enlighten me," Cholayna said dryly.

"Just think!" Elinda bubbled, heedless of the other woman's tone. "They're fast, they're quiet, they're clean. They don't need to be saddled, or fed, or curried, or stabled. And they'd never get sick, or tired, or colicky." She threw out words like sparks from a pinwheel. "Oh, they can't replace horses, of course, not for long trips, but they'd be a gift from the Goddess for the endless small errands we're always running. And some of the streets in the center of Thendara are so cramped you can hardly get two horses past each other, while the bicycle doesn't take up nearly as much space."

Bicycles! Cholayna Ares, head of Terran Intelligence on Darkover, the second highest ranking Terran on the planet, considered the girl, and her request, with thoughtful care. Behind that innocent moon-face, she knew, Elinda n'ha Mardra had probably the finest mind they'd found among Darkovans. Perhaps, Cholayna thought, the finest mind *on* Darkover. Elinda's intelligence tested off the scale, her creativity index was higher than Cholayna's own, and even her mechanical dexterity tested in the 95th percentile (thank the Gods she was one of the rare Darkovans who was naturally right-handed).

But bicycles! The child was still only seventeen, after all.

"It's the preparation time that's the problem with horses," Elinda continued. "I've seen Marisela waste minutes and minutes, trying to decide if it's quicker to walk than to take time to saddle a horse."

"Have you discussed this with other members of your Guild?" Cholayna asked curiously.

Elinda shook her head. "I just saw the bicycle this afternoon."

"Do you think they'll share your enthusiasm?"

"Whyever not? Free Amazons aren't afraid of new things. If something works better, we use it." Cholayna heard the girl's unconscious arrogance, and wondered. She leaned back in her chair, thinking.

Our biggest problem here is the Darkovans' resistance to machinery. They not only refuse to use it, they refuse even to let it be used outside the Terran Zone. But the ban refers to *powered* devices. As far as she could remember, the treaty made no mention of bicycles. She sputtered with inward laughter—who on earth would even have thought of them?

Bicycles, now. Non-threatening, non-proscribed mechanical devices. Filling the streets of Thendara, accustoming even the most conservative Darkovans to the presence of machinery.

"The camel's nose," she murmured.

"I beg your pardon?" Elinda asked.

"An Alphan folk tale," Cholayna responded. "About a large, smelly desert animal which tricked its way into a tent by begging for shelter in tiny increments."

"I see." Elinda nodded, and Cholayna realized with some surprise that she did.

"Bicycles." Cholayna laughed. "Will half a dozen do?"

"What'll the Old Man—sorry, what'll the Coordinator say?" Sam asked dubiously.

"Russ Montray? Not a thing. Haven't you heard? His transfer's come through; he's leaving as soon as the new Legate is appointed. Right now, he's so happy he'll say yes to anything." She turned to Elinda. "Give me a week."

The bicycles Cholayna delivered were an adaptation rather than a copy of the Himal'ya racing design. Elinda had asked for heavily treaded, puncture-proof balloon tires beneath a tough magnesium alloy frame, and a compromise five-speed gear system. It would not have the pure speed of the boy's racer, but it would stand up better to Thendara's rough cobblestone streets. She had also added a carrying basket over the rear wheel, and lowered the horizontal support bar so that skirts, if the Amazons chose to wear them, would not hike up indecently.

She demonstrated them to her Guild Sisters with a breathless enthusiasm that, to her dismay, went largely unshared. Few of the women agreed even to try the strange devices, and after one or two trips into the City, they too firmly refused. After several tendays, Elinda had to admit that her wonderful vehicles were not an unalloyed success.

"I'm going to the market for new boots this morning," Torayza said one morning at breakfast. "Does anyone want to come with me?"

"I'll ride with you," Elinda volunteered. "I'm meeting Sam there."

"Thanks, but I'll walk," Torayza said firmly. "I'm in no mood for abuse, jeers, thrown rocks and threats."

"Just ignore them." Elinda shrugged. "Why let those *cralmacs* bother you?"

"We can't ignore them, and you shouldn't either," Fellina asserted. "Honestly, Eli, you're making us all objects of ridicule." There were murmurs of agreement around the table.

"It's true." Rafaella glared at Elinda. "At the next House Meeting, I intend to ask Mother Lauria to forbid them."

"I have no right to make such an order," Mother Lauria responded. "This is not an oath-matter, nor have I that kind of authority over free women. No one is required to use them."

"No one but Elinda does anymore," Rafaella declared angrily. "Still, humiliation to one of us brings humiliation on all."

"So long as Elinda comports herself properly and causes no trouble, we have no right to object."

"Well, there *will* be trouble," Rafaella persisted. "People are already demanding that Council ban them from the City."

Elinda stared at her plate unhappily. She had been so sure their delight in the new vehicles would match her own. And now even her own use of the bicycle was in jeopardy.

"I was so sure they'd be delighted," she told Sam mournfully when she caught up with him in the market square.

"You're just ahead of your time, that's all." He turned his bicycle. "Come on, I'll race you to the Spaceport."

Together they sped through the narrow streets, laughing. The jeers and catcalls of passersby, which Elinda had always ignored, were now a challenge; defiantly, she increased her speed. Sam, bent low over his handlebars, swept by her triumphantly as they reached a corner and he headed past her into the turn.

She heard the shouts as she made her own turn, but by the time she looked up it was too late. She saw Sam in a tangle of horses and men and spinning wheels, saw the flatbed dray canted at a steep angle against the building to her right, its load of lumber spilling across the road before her.

She wrenched desperately at the handlebars, struggling for balance as the bicycle slewed wildly. Then at last she regained control, shooting past an open-mouthed workman and up onto the dray, rocketing at an impossible angle across the tilted surface and then down again with a jarring thump onto the street beyond and then she was finally clear and coasting to a stop.

"Sam!" She leaped off the bicycle and scrambled over the pile of lumber. "Are you hurt?"

He was on the ground, half under and half on top of his bicycle, one leg entangled in the chain. Around him, a knot of enraged workmen shouted curses and threats in furious counterpoint. Sam shook his head groggily and tried to stand, but the bicycle twisted and slipped, yanking him onto his back. The workmen stopped their shouting to roar with laughter.

"Zandru's hells!" Elinda swore in Darkovan. "Would you laugh at a man's injury?"

"I'm all right," Sam said with a weak smile, understanding her tone rather than her words. He disentangled himself at last from the recalcitrant bicycle and got painfully to his feet, massaging his shoulder.

"And what of my men?" A beefy, dark-haired man moved forward to confront Elinda, contemptuously ignoring Sam. "Should they be uncomplaining targets of attack by misbegotten *Terrannen* machines making every street a hazard?"

"Anyone may have an accident, dom Kennet, even on horseback." She spoke mildly, determined to avoid trouble. Kennet, of all the worst luck. She recognized him with dismay as a local builder who was the loudest and most hostile of Thendara's anti-Terran voices. "He's raised xenophobia to the status of an art form," Cholayna said of him once.

"A horse would not careen arrogantly through the streets expecting everyone to get out of his way, nor plow unseeing into a group of innocent men. A horse would not turn traitor to his nature," he glared at her Amazon leathers, "nor to his own kind by consorting with his enemies." This time his glare fastened on Sam, who shrugged helplessly and sketched a half-bow.

"Elinda, what the hell is he saying?"

"You don't want to know," she said grimly in Terran. Then, switching to Darkovan: "You have my apologies, dom Kennet. More I cannot do."

"But Council can." This time Kennet spoke with savage satisfaction. "After this incident I believe they will agree to forbid these indecent, unnatural machines from Thendara's streets. Or will you argue that your obscene device is better than a horse?" The men behind him sniggered at his sarcasm.

"Under some circumstances, yes it is," Elinda replied, her face flushed with anger.

"Under some circumstances," Kennet spoke the words slowly, milking them for effect, and the men whooped with derisive laughter. "Perhaps you'd care to defend that statement?" Elinda's hand went to her knife in reflex reaction, but Kennet grinned and shook his head. "Oh, not with steel, *mestra*. But . . . a race, perhaps? Your obscene machine against my steed here?" His grin widened.

"What now?" Sam asked nervously.

"He's just challenged me to a race—bicycle against horse," Elinda told him in Terran.

"A sucker bet, on that bike of yours. Forget it, lass. Let's just apologize and get out of here."

"I can't, Sam. And anyway . . ." She looked around thoughtfully at the smirking men, the huge drayhorse, the dray itself leaning drunkenly against the building.

"Elinda, don't be daft. That bicycle of yours can't outrun a horse."

"Look at her," Kennet said loudly. "She must get permission from her *Terranan* master even to deal with an affair of honor."

"His honor too is at stake," Elinda replied in Darkovan, then switched once more to Terran. "Sam, can I use some heavy equipment at the Spaceport to set up a track?"

"Yeah, I guess so. Sure." He threw up his hands. "But you'll get creamed, girl."

"Maybe not." And to Kennet: "I said under certain conditions. Will you race me under my conditions?"

"Under any conditions you care to name, *mestra*." His eyes glittered. "And the stakes?"

"If I win, you *and your men* will ride only bicycles, rather than horses, for any travel less than half the length of the City, for a period of four tendays. And there will be no more talk of banning them from the City."

"And just supposing you lose?"

"You get the bicycles. All of them. We will no longer

have them to ride in the City, and you will have a wealth of metal to melt down for your own use.''

''Done! Where and when?''

''Five days from today. The edge of the Terran Zone, behind the Spaceport.''

''*Su serva, mestra.*'' He bowed ironically. ''Please be sure the machines are there, so that I may take them away at once to be melted.''

''Oh, they will be there, *vai dom,* for you and your men to ride off on. Come on, Sam,'' she switched to Terran. ''Let's get to work.''

''You bet *what?*'' he demanded as they walked their battered bicycles toward the Spaceport. ''Elinda, what are you going to tell Cholayna? You can't be giving away Terran property.''

''But that's the point, isn't it? To get Darkovans accustomed to machines?''

''Lass, lass, you don't think you're going to *win?*'' Sam groaned. ''That's not a Himal'ya racer you've got there; it's a big, slow piece of transportation.''

''I'm going to win anyway,'' she insisted. ''And you're going to help. Listen.'' She spoke rapidly as they walked, and after a few moment Sam's expression changed. He was grinning broadly as they passed the Spaceport gates.

Kennet arrived promptly on race-morning, surrounded by a boisterous entourage and riding not the heavy drayhorse but a fine racing steed. Looking at the sleek animal, Elinda felt her confidence evaporating.

''Oh, Sam! That's a Syrtis racehorse.''

''Yes, and I'll wager he's just made a bad mistake.'' Sam's voice was soothing. ''That animal's accustomed to perfect conditions—nice smooth track, experienced race-rider, everything just so. Your bicycle alone might spook him, never mind the track itself.''

''Maybe you're right.'' Elinda looked at the wide oval and tried to regain her optimism. ''I wish some of my sisters were here.''

''As well they should be,'' he muttered angrily.

''They did not wish to see me humiliated, Rafaella said.''

''Well, at least one of them changed her mind.''

Elinda followed Sam's gaze to the dark skin and black Terran uniform of Cholayna Areas. Beside her was another figure, clad in Amazon leather.

''Mother Lauria. Bless her, she must feel a responsibility to be present. Oh Sam, I've got to win.'' She embraced the older Renunciate. ''Thank you for coming. With you here, I can't lose.''

''You would win even without me, I think, *chiya*, although I am glad I could be here for you.'' She smiled gently. ''I for one have every confidence in that mind of yours.'' Her tone spoke of quarrels within the Guild, and Elinda felt a spasm of guilt.

''Mother, I would not want to be the occasion of dissension among my sisters.''

''Nor shall you be,'' Mother Lauria answered firmly. ''They will see that you would not bring shame to the Guild.''

''Come on, Elinda,'' Sam said, interrupting. ''They're getting ready.''

Elinda moved to the flags that marked the starting point, shaken with sudden recognition of the responsibility she had so casually accepted. The race abruptly ceased to be a game.

Kennet, astride his horse, stared aloofly over her head. A tall, middle-aged man in the rough garb of a *cristoforo* stepped forward and held up his hand.

''I am Father Domiel, *mestra*.'' He bowed to Elinda. ''I have been asked to certify the race. Have you objection?''

''None in the world,'' Elinda answered with real relief. ''You understand the challenge was 'under any conditions.' ''

''Yes.'' The man nodded, and Elinda caught a glint of red

in the graying hair. "I will examine the site now, if you please."

"Of course." Elinda stepped with him onto the track and Kennet, still on horseback, followed behind, looking around negligently. But as he reached the surface of the track he yanked back on the reins and stood in his stirrups.

"Zandru's hells! What sort of trick is this?"

"Trick, dom Kennet?" Elinda shrugged. "These are the conditions I specify. Father Domiel? " She stood still while the men looked at the track she and Sam had created.

It was nearer round than oval, circling for a distance of nearly 300 meters. The actual riding surface, six meters across, was nearly smooth, with just enough grit to provide traction for Elinda's tires. A broad white line separated the surface into inner and outer lanes.

And the whole riding surface was canted at an angle of 30 degrees to horizontal.

"My conditions," Elinda stated. "Three times around the track, start and finish at the flag, participants not to cross the center line. Right of decision to Father Damiel."

"This is absurd," Kennet sputtered. "How can anyone race on a surface tilted like a . . . a landslide? The risk to the horse is unacceptable."

"Is dom Kennet then stating that there *are* conditions under which the bicycle performs better than the horse?" Elinda asked coolly. "If so, he is conceding the terms of the wager."

"No!" Kennet raged. "I do not believe your misbegotten device can ride on such a surface either."

"That is what we are here to find out. Father Domiel?"

"The conditions are not the same for each participant," the man answered. "The inside track is shorter than the outside."

"I yield the inside to dom Kennet," Elinda said immediately. She preferred the outside in any case—if the horse lost its footing and fell, she must not be underneath.

"Then there are no objections," Father Domiel's expression was bland, but he looked at Elinda with eyes narrowed in calculation, and she thought for an instant she saw his lip quiver. Quickly, to forestall further argument, Elinda moved to the starting point.

Straddling her bicycle, she stood at the highest point of the track, wheels pointed almost straight down. This, she knew, would be the trickiest bit—if she skidded and fell, or lost control for an instant, she would slide downward across the center line and immediately forfeit.

Kennet, his face suffused with fury, gathered the reins in both hands, while behind him his men shouted ribald encouragement.

"Shut up, you fools!" he shouted at them as the horse slipped on the track and tried to back up, seeking level ground. Forcing himself to calm, he patted the animal's neck and urged it downward to the inner lane. But when he turned it sideways to the slope the horse rebelled, skittering in discomfort.

"Take your positions, please." Father Domiel held the flag high; as it dropped, Elinda leaned her weight forward and shot down the slope. Desperately cautious, she turned the handle bars upward, felt the wheels skid, applied her rear brake to slow her descent, and then she was parallel to the slope, the white dividing line to her right, moving forward along the track. She bent forward, feeling the wind whistle past her ears as her speed increased and she rocketed into the turn, clinging at an impossible angle to the slanting surface of the track.

Only after the second turn, as she neared completion of her first circuit, did she dare look up, seeking her competitor. What she saw brought on such a spasm of laughter that she nearly lost her balance.

Kennet had not yet reached the first turn. He was keeping his horse on the track through sheer force of will, but nothing he could do would make the animal accept this unnatural surface. The horse, ears laid back in protest, was moving in short, staccato bursts, every now and then jerking his head downward in a vain search for the horizontal.

She swooped past them and into her second circuit, knowing Kennet would not give up easily. As she rounded the far turn again, she saw him dig spurred heels viciously into the animal's sides. The horse lurched forward, staggering against the slope. Kennet, encouraged, used his spurs once more. The horse, goaded beyond endurance, whinnied loudly and tried to rear; then both downhill feet skidded on the slick surface and he fell, rolling toward the center of the track as Kennet desperately leapt clear.

Elinda pressed forward for her third and last circuit of the track, gleefully watching man and horse scrabbling on the dusty ground, each trying to flee the other.

She passed Father Domiel's flag for the third time to triumphant whoops from Sam and Cholayna. Even Mother Lauria, she noted, was waving her arms and laughing aloud. She drove her bicycle upward and off the track and wobbled to a stop before her friends, suddenly exhausted almost beyond endurance.

"Are you all right, *chiya*?" Mother Lauria supported Elinda as Sam took hold of the bicycle.

"I'm fine. I think." Elinda giggled with reaction.

"You realize what you've done," Cholyana said severely.

"What?" Elinda asked, suddenly fearful.

"You've gone and lost all your bicycles." Cholyana laughed and pointed at the furious faces of Kennet's men. "Now we're going to have to produce another dozen of the things, and how the hell am I going to explain *that* budget item to the new Legate?"

About Patricia Shaw-Mathews and "Girls Will Be Girls"

Pat Mathews had been a science fiction fan since age ten, a Darkover fan since 1963 (she does not tell us how long elapsed between the two), and an active fan since 1975. She has written a number of Darkover stories (appearing first in The Keeper's Price *with the landmark Free Amazon story "There is Always an Alternative") and has appeared in* Sword of Chaos *and in the anthology* Greyhaven. *Her first stories were printed under the name Patricia Mathews; now, to avoid confusion with the romance writer Patricia Matthews, author of* Love's Tender Fury *and many other such novels, Pat calls herself Patricia Shaw-Mathews. She also wrote an intelligent study of C.L. Moore in Tom Staicar's anthology* The Feminine Eye.*

She is married, and has two daughters, two cats, a dog, and a guinea pig; in the intervals of caring for these, she is a bookkeeper and is studying to be an accountant. She also admits to having originated the joke about the tax form for aliens: 1040-ET.

MZB

GIRLS WILL BE GIRLS

by Patricia Shaw-Mathews

"Your childhood has put chains on you," Guild Mother Julienne of Port Chicago told the newly made Free Amazons, and Dalise n'ha Dionie let out a snorting laugh.

"Not me," she whispered explosively to the carrot-top on her left.

"Well, they tried," Catlyn n'ha Dorilys conceded with a giggle.

Ariane n'ha Linnet leaned back with a smug grin. "My people knew better," she said, and leaned back a little farther. Her chair toppled backwards, spilling her into the laps of two of her new oath-sisters. The whole room rocked with laughter. Guild Mother Julienne tried to skewer Ariane, Catlyn, and Dalise with one cold eye, to no avail.

It was not an auspicious beginning.

Catlyn was short and slender, with carrot-colored hair and violet eyes. She had tried on the sloppy, floppy costume she was issued, spent five minutes trying to believe that she would actually be expected to wear the thing, gave it up, and set about correcting the obvious flaws in its design. She looked, the Guild Mother reluctantly decided, almost dashing.

Dalise had made hers more comfortable by rolling up the pants legs and trying to tie the coattails around her impressive waist. She was a large, sleepy-seeming young woman with an abundance of dark hair and no-colored eyes. Ariane, her inseparable companion, hadn't bothered to tamper with her uniform, but looked back at the Guild Mother with all the blank good looks of a Terran advertising poster, her superbly muscled body impeccable in Guild House-issue clothing. Why did the Guild Mother feel like a hunter with a banshee by the tail?

With uncharacteristic reticence, Dalise waited until she was a room's length away from the Guild Mother and the meeting before exploding, "Six months behind walls! I joined the Guild to get away from that!"

"From the trap into the cookpot," Catlyn said in deep disgust. "Well, children, how do you like our new governess?"

"You didn't notice the tree outside our room," Ariane said irrelevantly. "That six-month rule was made for those who don't know how to behave. You heard her say so. Well, obviously, we do. Officially, of course, she can't take any cognizance of that, so—what she doesn't know won't hurt any of us."

Dalise chortled. "Yeah!"

For quite some time, Ariane, Catlyn, and Dalise took their turns in kitchen and stable, learned to read and write and use weapons, and followed the rules of the house. They could not be called model Renunciates. There was, thank Avarra, only one of those in Port Chicago's Guild House, the sorely misnamed Allega n'ha Felicitas, who was also the Guild House faultfinder. Lines of battle were early drawn.

Guild Mother Julienne had to reluctantly acquit her three newcomers of pinning the nickname "Allergica" on their hapless sister; only one of her women who was studying Terran medicine would even know the term. But when Allergica—Allega! came bursting into the Guild Mother's office in tears, and giving off a very bad odor, there were only three immediate suspects for whatever prank had caused this. Unfortunately, the victim knew it too.

"You have to get rid of those three troublemakers," she demanded through her tears.

One did not demand that a Guild Mother do anything. Mother Julienne looked calm, a feat accomplished with long practice. "What did they do?" she asked, folding her hands.

"They stuffed the bottom of my bed with stable sweepings!" Allega raged.

Guild Mother Julienne kept her mouth extremely still and tight. When she could trust herself to speak, she said, "If I could prove that, I would nail their hides to the wall. But neither of them has had stable duty over a tenday, and a housebound Renunciate would be very conspicuous carrying a bucketful of stable sweepings through Port Chicago House. Bring me proof, my child, and I will be glad to act."

"You'll get it," Allega promised, and stormed out.

Shortly afterward, at martial arts practice, the instructor called on Allegra to demonstrate the art of stand-up wrestling. Allegra's eyes gleamed under her close-cropped hair. "One of you come up here so I can demonstrate. You! Gorgeous!"

Ariane didn't bother to ask who Gorgeous might be, but immediately stood up and strolled into the ring. Allegra began with a simple but effective hold—and found herself flat on her back on the floor of the ring, her neatly combed hair all in disarray. Ariane smiled. "Brothers," she said succintly, and went back to her seat.

That night, in the third-floor attic room they shared, Ariane dressed in her finest Amazon costume and pulled a small sack of copper coins out of her personal-effects box. "I think it's time for a celebration, don't you?' she asked.

Dalise grinned. "I get an allowance, too," she said with triumph. "That way I'll stay away."

Catlyn, whose finest was by now a thing of glory, tucked a cloth flower into her curly red hair while Dalise spread butter liberally on the window casement. It opened without a squeak.

Ariane, the athlete, was out first; then Dalise, whose every

step on a branch was a nerve-wracking venture; then Catlyn.
The two smaller girls helped haul Dalise over the wall; then
they went to explore Port Chicago.

They roamed through the flea market, bought food at
stalls, giggled as they passed through the red-light district,
and finally ended at the Terran Enclave, watching strange
lights and vehicles. While they were staring at a spaceship,
they heard someone say, in badly accented Darkovan, "Hi!
Want to see the ship?"

They turned around to see a pair of young men in strange
uniforms, smiling at them. The Guild Mother's constant warnings against dealing with strange men or accepting invitations
did flash briefly through Dalise's mind; it never touched
Ariane's or Catlyn's. Ariane put out a hand. "Ariane n'ha
Linnet," she said.

"Dave Mittelstadt, Chuck Baker, Linda Sanchez, and Bob
Johnson," the first young man said, extending his introduction to the two others coming out of the ship, all dressed in
identical costume.

"Where's a good place to go drinking?" Chuck Baker
asked.

"We're first-year Survey Service trainees," Linda Sanchez
explained, as Dalise, who knew every place to eat and drink
in any place she visited, led them to the White Cralmac.

Three beers and an incredible amount of munchies later,
Dalise said, "What does Survey do?"

"Explore new worlds," said Linda Sanchez. "Seek out
new civilizations. Go where no man has gone before. And
that reminds me. Dalise?"

"The shack in the alley, behind the garbage pile," Dalise
said. "Survey sounds like fun. Wish I were a Terran."

Bob Johnson nudged her. "Keep this under your hat, honey,
but the grapevine said the C.O. is thinking about it. Opening
up the Service to indigenous personnel. The trouble is, most
planetbound cultures are also culturebound. Reminds me . . ."

He finished his beer and ordered another. "Why can't anybody on these Godforsaken frontier worlds make a decent pizza?"

Linda Sanchez came back from the little house behind the White Cralmac and settled down to emptying a full mug and a full plate. "Lose a little weight, and I think you might give it a try. Chuck, why don't you mention these three to the skipper and see what happens?"

"How do we know they'll be around?" Chuck Baker asked.

Catlyn and Ariane looked at each other. "We'll be around," they assured the Terrans.

The seven of them, arm in arm, reeled down the street, singing, "My mother was the Keeper of the Arilinn Tower . . ." just as Allega, who was posted to milking duty that morning, came out of the barn with two full pails. The Amazon knew her duty.

"Ariane! Catlyn! Dalise! Report to the Guild Mother immediately and give her a full account of this disgraceful behavior! Do you realize the effect your disgraceful conduct has—"

"That's twice," Catlyn said, with interest. "Don't you think she should find some new words?"

"Hasn't the good reputation we have so carefully built up over the centuries, *any* meaning to you? Scandalously drunk! Consorting with strange men!"

"We didn't get a chance to do any consorting," Ariane contradicted her indifferently.

"With Terrans! Aliens!"

The four Survey trainees would have stood up to a man, but decided to a cadet that retreat was the better part of valor, with Allegra screaming the walls down in a language they could not possibly command as well as she did. "Bye, girls," Dave Mittelstadt said, and fled.

*　　*　　*

Guild Mother Julienne was not amused. Behind closed doors, she said, "The six-month rule was made for a reason. Women who do not live under the protection of their families must learn to conduct themselves with extreme discretion and do absolutely nothing that could possibly reflect upon the reputation of the Guild. Otherwise, people would get the wrong idea about us, and it would make trouble for everyone. We have nothing against an evening's outing in the company of each other—*when* you have learned how to behave properly! But Renunciates do not allow themselves to become intoxicated in public; they do not initiate conversations in public places with strange men, or allow themselves to be picked up; and they do not disgrace our world by behaving like women of the streets in front of Terrans! Do you understand?"

Ariane closed her mouth, as it had hung open throughout the lecture. "I certainly do, Guild Mother!"

Julienne nodded. "Very well. You have behaved as children. You will be treated as children. You will be confined to your room for the next forty days, except for lessons, duty, and meals. You may go now."

This time they waited until they were in their room before exploding. "But we didn't do anything wrong!" Dalise raged.

"Certainly we did," said Catlyn, doodling a hanging woman on her wall with the pen she used for her literacy homework. "We broke the six-months rule. And we got caught."

"Allergica is a blot on the face of the Guild," Ariane said languidly.

"Not a blot, a turd," Catlyn said fervently. "Do you realize she keeps trying to put my *hair* on report?"

"That's because hers isn't as pretty as yours," Dalise answered. Suddenly they looked at each other and grinned.

Their door was not locked, and Guild honor forbade a guard. Catlyn, the smallest and sneakiest, opened it in the middle of the night and quietly went to the junkroom in search of a razor with which to accomplish their revenge. "I couldn't find one," she apologized. "But I found something to keep us from getting too bored."

"Where are you going to get paper?" Dalise asked practically.

Catlyn shrugged. Ariane glanced around the room. "It's a very dull room," she suggested. "It could use a little decoration."

So the entire Guild House was amazed at the good grace with which its three delinquents were taking their confinement. They worked hard at their lessons, did their various duties diligently; the plan to shave Allegra's head went by the way for a while, and they hummed with contentment.

A tenday after they had been discovered in the dawn, the Guild Mother summoned them. She seemed as happy with them as she was ever likely to be. "The Terran Coordinator at Port Chicago has spoken to me about opening the Survey Service to Darkovan women. *If* we can demonstrate to him that we can behave ourselves properly among the worlds, as well as demonstrate our ability to learn the work. I understand we have you to thank for the idea, so something good has come of this episode after all."

The three looked at each other, overjoyed. Then the Guild Mother said, "The first experimental call will consist of Allegra n'ha Felicitas, Bruna n'ha Callista—"

"Not Bookworn Bruna!" Dalise exploded.

"Dalise n'ha Dionie!" Guild Mother Julienne snapped. "If you cannot learn to control your impulsiveness and your temper, you will have no chance to as much as speak to the Survey Commander! Terrans make much of literacy. I have chosen those who are apt in it, and who will be certain not to disgrace us by an impulsive act."

"The Terrans I saw didn't seem to be much concerned about grace and disgrace," Ariane said, leaning back in her chair. "They were having a good time, just as we were."

She leaned back too far; her chair fell over. Hopefully, she added, "I didn't do that even once when I was with them."

Guild Mother Julienne decided it was hopeless. "Well, I did think you would want to know," she said, and dismissed them again.

They returned to their room, now decorated with a spring scene and a pair of picnickers, with a raging bull behind them and a little boy skinny-dipping in one corner. Allegra had been tossed by the bull into another corner, and lay in a most undignified position. Thoughtfully, Catlyn sketched out a spaceship with a background of stars and moons.

The mural was finished shortly before their confinement was up. Ariane counted out her few remaining coppers. "Well, this does call for a celebration," she conceded. "And we won't be caught this time, with Allergic out picking faults among the Terrans."

Dalise grabbed her finest embroidered shirt. "Well, let's go!" she whooped.

Once again they climbed down the tree and over the wall, and headed for the spaceport district with the faint hope of running into their Terrans, or even others. On the way to the spaceport district was the red-light district, and as they passed the House of Red Lanterns, a pimp lounging outside called out, "Looking for work, girls? I can get you some." Cackling, he followed up his comments with remarks about their appearance. His girls, hanging out the window, laughed appreciatively.

Ariane looked at Dalise. She came at him from the left, Dalise from the right, and knocked him to the ground. The pimp tried to pull a knife, and did try out a wildly imaginative variety of curses on them, beginning with aspersions on their sexuality. The girls shouted nasty names and made noise, but never left their windows. Ariane drew back a fist and crashed it into the pimp's jaw, decking him. Catlyn, meanwhile, had taken a small pot of red paint and was

decorating the walls of the brothel with a bold slogan: AMA-
ZONS RULE! Then they ran.

They were still laughing as they circled the spacefield and
rounded one of the Terran right-angled corners. A middle-
aged Terran male was coming around the same corner, and
ran directly into Dalise, knocking them both down.

The Terran stood up. "I beg your pardon, *mestra*," he said
stiffly, in formal Darkovan.

Dalise rubbed her head. "I'm sorry. I should have looked
where you were going. Hey! If you're Terran, maybe you
know Linda Sanchez, Bob Johnson, Dave Mittelstadt, and
Chuck Baker," she said, pronouncing the strange names very
carefully. "They're in Survey. One of them was going to tell
his C.O. about us."

The Terran looked at them in bemusement. Catlyn suddenly looked down and saw the red paint all over her hands
and giggled. "Just a little work of art," she explained.

Ariane put out a hand and in the pure, liquid, formal
Darkovan of the highest nobility said, "You honor our house,
sir—?"

"Randolph Lawrence, *mestra*. Is there another organization similar to the Renunciates of Port Chicago, that I have
not had the honor of knowing?"

"We are from the Guild House in Port Chicago," Ariane
answered, "Have you the honor of knowing our friends?"

Randolph Lawrence took a black square device from his
pocket, touched it, and watched a series of characters of the
Terran alphabet crawl across the screen. . . . In thought, he
asked, "Do you know mestra Allegra n'ha Felicitas and mestra
Bruna n'ha Callista?"

"The bookworm and Allergica," Dalise answered. "Better
than I'd like."

"They're our sisters in the Guild."

"Stepsisters. Wicked ones."

Randolph, smiling, offered his arm to Ariane. "Young

ladies, I think I would very much like to talk with your Guild Mother. Do you think you could arrange it?''

Then a shrill screech split the night. ''There they are!'' cried an outraged pimp. Behind him came two men in the black and green uniform of the City Guard, and a grim-faced Guild Mother Julienne.

''I think it's *been* arranged,'' Catlyn said thoughtfully.

Guild Mother Julienne held her hands together tightly, as if to keep from slapping her three delinquents silly. ''I'm afraid this means the end of your career in the Guild,'' she said, very calmly, ''unless you can demonstrate a desire and ability to keep discipline.''

''Excuse me, *mestra*, just what have they been guilty of?'' the Terran asked.

Guild Mother Julienne set her lips. ''I'm afraid this is an internal matter, sir. Not even the Terran Coordinator has any jurisdiction over Guild discipline. *Or* its lack.''

''My whorehouse!'' the pimp screamed. ''They painted my whorehouse all over with Amazon slogans and you dykes are going to pay for this!''

The Terran Coordinator started to laugh. ''Suppose they simply clean it up? Under the supervision of their Guild sisters, of course. I'm sure a couple of my students could be released from their classes long enough for that. And then, *mestra*, I'd like to talk to you about the possibility of recruiting these three young ladies for the Survey Service. They've certainly demonstrated an ability to get along with Terran personnel!''

A short time later, at the Sign of the White Cralmac, Randolph Lawrence was saying, ''We were about to cancel the project and give up the idea of recruiting Darkovan women for the Survey Service, when these three came along. You see, *mestra*, in Survey, you have to work with all races and cultures, many different sets of customs, and many different sorts of manners. You have to be able to get along with people of different mores readily, and I'm afraid the students you sent me were entirely too culturebound.''

The three had heard the term before; Guild Mother Julienne had to ask. The Terran Coordinator answered, ''Rigid, overcontrolled, unable to tolerate the slightest breach of their homeworld's decorum. There wasn't the slightest chance of them surviving basic training, I'm sorry to say. Now, these three—''

''These three are completely unable to keep discipline,'' the Guild mother interrupted, a little sadly.

The Terran Coordinator smiled reminiscently. ''Military discipline?'' he asked gently.

The Guild Mother grinned broadly for the first time since Ariane, Catlyn, and Dalise had joined them. ''I think, once they finish their basic training with us, it would be an excellent idea! But only if I can have your oaths to keep discipline until your six months are up!''

With complete seriousness, Ariane said, ''You have my oath, Guild Mother.'' After all, it would only be for a few months, and *the Coordinator* hadn't asked her for such an oath. She began wondering what pranks one could play aboard a starship.

About Susan Shwartz and
"Growing Pains"

Susan Shwartz made her first appearance in The Keeper's Price *and has since appeared in* Analog *science fiction magazine and many anthologies, including two which she herself edited,* Hecate's Cauldron *(DAW, 1982) and* Habitats *(DAW, 1984).*

"Growing Pains," might be said to be written in contrary motion to another story in the anthology—Pat Mathews's "Girls Will Be Girls." It repeats the theme in Thendara House *that misfits in their own society may be as maladapted to the Guild House as they were to the society from which they came. The stories make a similar point, but are as different as their authors.*

Susan Shwartz lives in New York City, is single, and works in advertising and media.

MZB

GROWING PAINS

by Susan Shwartz

"Be silent, Catriona, or we will have you removed," Mother Rayna ordered.

Though the Music Room was cold, Catriona n'ha Mhari wasn't trembling from the damp chill but from rage. She leapt to her feet. The other Renunciates in her training group huddled together, most of them already in tears. The armsmistress had called Doria a coward. The cook had berated Pavella for laziness. And she, she had been called a nibnose whose tongue hinged in the middle and clattered at both ends, just for asking questions.

"Spoiled baby, sit down and be quiet until we bid you stand!"

Catriona was tired of being housebound, more tired still of Training Sessions, and worst of all, of being talked at when she wished to learn, or told she wasn't listening, or wasn't thinking just because she didn't see things their way, she thought resentfully.

Rage made her vision blur, and she had to gulp till she could keep her voice from shaking. "I have had enough of this! I've had enough of you too! I think you enjoy playing games with us, games we can't win. If Sheera brushes her hair, she's vain; if she doesn't, she's a slut. If I ask questions, I'm impertinent, but if I obey, I'm simply doing it to please. Do you really think we have to endure this to be free? I've heard kinder words from Dry-Town Traders!"

The older women shouted, appalled, at that last statement, which Catriona perfectly well knew was outrageous. But it served them right, she thought. Holding up one roughened hand, she shook back her collar-length red hair and shouted too. "Enough! I'm leaving here, and you can chew on that!"

Mother Lauria, one of the oldest women in the Thendara Guild House, long retired and much loved, looked up with eyes filmed with age.

"Where will you go, *chiya*?" she asked. Her voice was so gentle Catriona feared she would cry. Then her resolve would melt, she would promise to try again, and she could be molded into a proper little Amazon just the way other Darkovan girls were trained to be wives.

"To the *Terranan!*" she spat. "And if I see you all over a blade's edge, it will be soon enough."

Some people learn only by doing. But, child, be careful of what you wish for. You may get it. Lauria's lips did not move, and no one else seemed to hear her words; Catriona realized that the strange, untrained part of her mind had lifted them from the old woman's thoughts. *Laran*, again. As a child, *laran* made her sickly, vulnerable to accusations of spying. As she grew older, she realized it was only another way of talking, of knowing things—and she dreamed of learning more about it at Neskaya, which had the reputation of taking in those *laran*-gifted who were not true Comyn. But when she went there, the *leroni* would not even speak to her. Times had turned dangerous, with the rise and fall of the Forbidden Tower.

What had that left her? She wasn't Comyn; marriage to a man sharing her peculiar gifts was beyond her reach, even if she'd wished to marry. Marriage to one of the head-blind would have been like coupling with a cralmac; unthinkable. So Catriona had thought out her options and come to the Guild House, hoping to learn skills that would make her independent of the whim of guardian, Tower, Hastur, or anything else. Renunciates learned what they would, went where they would—even among the Terrans. Catriona had had a foster brother, half-Terran and wholly abandoned till her family had taken him in and fed him. Lucky Ann'dra. When he turned fourteen, he had gone to the spaceport and traded in his worn tartans for Terran black, his knife for the forbidden blaster of the Terran Empire. Now he spoke with Darkovans and Terrans alike, perhaps even to the rare, exotic nonhumans that glided along the narrow streets of the Trade City.

Ann'dra had promised to help her find work among the *Terranan*. When she had mentioned that to the other women, they had flung the oath at her . . . *appeal to no man for protection as of right*. It wasn't protection; Ann'dra wanted to even the scales, but they didn't see that.

She was out of the Music Room, her feet pounding too rapidly for dignity on the wide-boarded stairs into the front hall. She slipped and all but crashed headlong upstairs into the heavy, dark wood doors. Knowing how absurd falling upstairs made anyone look gave her the strength to hurl the doors wide and make a dramatic exit. The crash as the doors slammed shut rattled shutters on half the houses on the street.

Light rain drifted down from the foggy, violet sky of twilight, cooling her face. Tiny moons shone green in the sky, and the last embers of the Bloody Sun's sullen light smoldered from the Guild House's translucent windowpanels and the puddles in the street.

Now what? she thought.

She backed up, trying to see the tower of Terran Headquarters. Though the squat, overhanging roofs of this quarter of Thendara blocked out much of the sky, finally she saw its stark, arrogant height. All she had to do was keep it in sight. Once she reached whatever passed for gates among the *Terranan*, she would give her name and her foster brother's. He would be *paged* (that was the proper word), and he would

come to help her find proper, honorable work that would let
her talk to Terrans, tour the great ships, perhaps even see the
worlds from which they came. Already she had learned some
Terran, not just the curse words she and her friends had
giggled over, but important phrases like *medical technology,
computers, trade restrictions*, and *colonials*. Thank the Goddess she learned so rapidly!

The lights turned strange as she neared the Terran zone.
For one thing, there were more of them, and they were an
oppressive yellow, nothing like the comfortable gloom of the
Guild House. Beneath the sharp light, men (and a few women)
in the sleek black leathers of spaceforce, scandalous blasters
holstered at their hips, cast impossibly long shadows and
stared insolently at her, a stranger, thin for her age, and—this
far away from her normal haunts—unsure.

The first woman she approached for directions took pity on
her. "If you're looking for the *checkpoint*," she said in
disastrous *cahuenga*, "It's that way."

The guard eyed her suspiciously until he made up his mind
that she was actually a girl. Then, for a brief moment, he
became alarmingly friendly. His indulgence, coupled with
complete skepticism in the face of her explanation, left her
tongue-tied. She stiffened with indignation as his eyes raked
her thin body up and down. Did he really think she was
pregnant and trying to trick Ann'dra into claiming the child?
She blinked back angry tears, reminding herself that if she
chose to see herself as he saw her, she was truly in chains.
Patiently, persistently, she repeated her story until finally she
convinced the man at least to *call* Ann'dra.

And wasn't it just Zandru's luck that he was away on
assignment? She pulled her hand free of the guard's not-all-
that-fatherly patting, and wandered off. *Andrew* (as they called
him here) was expected back within the tenday. Sure.

What in the name of the Seven Hells was she going to do
till then?

No wonder the Renunciates had called her a hothead. She had flounced out of the Guild House with no savings, few plans . . . oh, did she ever have a lot to learn! Perhaps the women in the Music Room had been trying to protect her from the consequences of her rashness. Maybe they were right when they'd said she had no brains under that red hair, just fire and smoke. She ought to have planned better. She would have to now.

She drew in a deep breath and regretted it. Her stomach promptly gurgled, reminding her that she had skipped dinner, intending to fill up on the cider and fried cakes that were usually spread out after Training Sessions. She stuck a hand into her pockets with no real hope. She had very little money, and she'd need to save what she had for lodgings until she could find work. What skills could she offer? Some strength, more talent for learning languages, experience with a knife, with horses and *chervines*—if worst came to worst, she could wash dishes. The Guild House had seen to all of that, she thought, and felt what she knew was going to be the first of lifelong pangs about her broken oath.

She rubbed at her ear thoughtfully, and then smiled. Her earring, the type each Renunciate wore, had been a gift of an oath-sister. It was copper, and would bring a tidy sum if she pawned it. The idea hurt. So did her conviction that she was no longer entitled to wear the earring. She would make herself pawn it, and once she had lawful employment, she would redeem it, she promised herself, though she'd probably never wear it again.

In the streets around the Terran Zone, she found a dealer too poor to be choosey, but too close to Terran Security to be a thief. He had a clever face and chestnut hair, cropped short in imitation of *Terranan* styles, and he spoke Darkovan with an accent that made Catriona suspect it was not his birth-tongue. Nor did he haggle as a normally larcenous, conventional merchant would. *Well, if you're stealing horses, steal thoroughbreds*, she thought, gleefully pocketing coins after five minutes of bargaining. Then she saw how he looked at her hair, how his glance slid down to her neck. She stopped herself from raising a hand to touch the thin copper chain she had worn ever since her abortive trip to Neskaya. *This much we cannot deny you*, the *leronis* had said. Hanging from the chain was a tiny leather pouch, and in it, though she could not use it . . .

Once she had overheard Domna Keitha and another one of the Sisterhood discussing the *Terranans'* unhealthy curiosity about *laran*. She had flushed, knowing that she wore one of the matrix crystals: a toy, perhaps, useless since she had no training in its use, not even the half-knowledge gossip sometimes carried. That conversation had stopped the instant she came into earshot. She sensed that people disliked talking about *laran*—or Comyn—at all, and especially around her: red-haired, tense, given to strange fancies. At least, bless Evanda and Avarra, she no longer got falling-down-dizzy after a wild dream or before she bled.

This merchant seemed too curious about that chain. He raised one thin eyebrow, reached out a forefinger too soft to be honest, and pointed, almost touching the pouch concealed in her tunic.

Lights in the mean shop blurred into redness, she felt sweat drip down her ribs, heard the crackle of flames, and then . . . *one man was tall, his hair as fair as a Dry-Towner's where it was not gray. The other man was slighter, his hair the red of Comyn, though much shot through with white. They stood beside truesisters, twins, and flames exploded around them, drew closer and closer. At first they sought some escape, then drew together, gazing into a great blue crystal in which appeared the face of a darker woman, warning . . . and then the flames swept over them*. They were gone . . .

Stunned by the warning, the regret, yes, and a strange

triumph she felt, Catriona swayed and raised a hand to her forehead.

"So?" murmured the pawnbroker. "Another of the Forbidden Tower?"

Catriona couldn't see both his hands above the counter, and she disliked the look in his eyes. She shook her head and left quickly.

As she walked, she damned her weakness. Clearly she had burst right into something that looked very dangerous. *Let's see if I can vanish*, she decided. She made three quick turns, and glanced behind her, taking pains to make it appear casual. No one appeared to follow her. She walked past merchants' stalls and narrow shopfronts. As she pulled her collar up over her neck against the dampness, she heard the old muttering behind her, "*Tallo*," linked with more sinister words, hisses about fire, forbidden powers, a tower burnt . . . Clearly, she should cover her hair.

She stopped at a clothing stall, hunted in the bins that practically lay out in the middle of the street until she found a second-hand cap, and prepared to bargain.

To her amazement, she was told that they could not dream of taking money, of giving her such an unworthy cap . . . sweet Avarra, they actually wanted to give her the marl-fur cap displayed on the wall? A cap that fine would make her conspicuous. Finally, she made them compromise on her accepting a cap of thick, warm wool trimmed with less ostentatious rabbithorn pelts. After covering up her red hair, Catriona headed for a foodstall.

Caution made her think before simply walking into the first one. That one looked too costly. If Ann'dra were to be gone for a tenday, she'd need to watch her money. Besides, she thought with a gurgle of wry humor, with her hair covered, she would have to pay for food or board. A second foodstall looked dirty, and she didn't want to risk tainted food. The next one looked half-filled and quite clean, though shabby, so she walked in. The sausages cooking in back smelled wonderful, but she ordered porridge and hot milk with honey to stir into it, foods she knew were nourishing and cheap.

By the time she started her second mug of the sweetened milk, her hunger and excitement had abated enough for her to think of other things. Like her broken oath. Like her temper, which made her say hateful things to her sisters. At least her oath-mother had been away. They would tell Devra, and she would be so disappointed!

Catriona sniffled into her mug, then wiped her nose defiantly. *Don't start getting homesick*, she told herself. *You can't go back there*. Like all scoldings, this one did little to raise her spirits. Goddess, how she was going to miss the future she had thrown away. *Well, girl, you'll just have to be oath-mother and sisters to yourself, now, won't you?*

She promised herself that she'd find friends among the *Terranan*. That didn't encourage her much either. Someone had spilled water on the table and not wiped it up. She could see lights reflected in the water, and her strained, pale face. The water rippled, and she realized with horror that she was crying again.

Think of something beside your wretched self, Catri! She looked around. At the table past the family with the two small boys, sat a tall man, who sat hunched over, talking to a woman whose conservative dress didn't quite match her striking features. They looked familiar to Catriona, though there was a look of recent, almost unendurable sorrow that hurt to see. The woman leaned forward, moved her mug of cider with great deliberation, and met her companion's eyes. "I told you, speak *cahuenga*." Both the glance and the words drew Catriona's attention.

"I said that I still think meeting out in the open is foolish."

"Fools don't survive a lifetime spent in the game," the woman snapped. "Where's the best place to hide a needle? Among other needles. Where do you hide a Darkovan? Among other Darkovans. In the Terran Zone I'd be an oddity, the spy who went over the wall and—'' she grinned mirthlessly— ''came in from the cold. Or, as the case may be, ran away from the fire.''

''Don't torture yourself, Mags,'' said her companion and laid a hand over hers. She pulled it free automatically. ''All right, so you say you knew something was about to happen to them. Not that I believe that, but let's assume, just for the sake of argument, that it's true. If you'd gone to them, you'd just have burned along with the rest. . . .''

The woman's hand balled into a fist and her mouth tightened. Wait . . . the vision of the crystal, of the tall man and the lord, staring into the crystal, and in it, the face of the woman called Mags . . . that was no proper name.

Catriona made herself small in her chair. *You do not see me*, she thought at the room. For an instant, lights flashed and her sense of balance faltered, and she knew that they did not.

''What are you going to do now?'' the man asked. ''This new Legate's worse than Montray for spinelessness. The man won't intervene even of Comyn weren't involved. Can that Guild of yours hide you?''

''You leave my sisters out of this!'' The woman spoke quietly. Her dark eyes flashed. ''I can't inflict myself on them now. The political situation's bad enough that fanatics are likely to attack any—'' She used a Terran word that Catriona knew meant wild horses, but also outsiders, nonconformists. (What *was* a maverick?)

''Well, Magda, I suppose you know what that leaves you?''

The woman's head dropped as if all her energy and defiance had gone out of her. ''I know. Leave Darkover. Go to Alpha and maybe teach the next generation of Intelligence officers. And do you know what I'm going to teach them first? I'm going to teach them not to love the people they work with.''

Exile . . . a living death, away from my world, my memories, my loved ones . . . no, their ashes. The woman's anguish kindled Catriona's wild talent and made her flinch.

"I'll live through it, I suppose," she said.

"I want your word you'll be on the next ship out of here."

She looked up as the man rose. "Do you want an oath, too? My Service one—or the Guild's?"

He half-bowed. "Your word is good enough for me, Margali—as always," he said, and left, moving swiftly. Catriona knew that he would blend with the crowd outside. Hide a needle among other needles, as the woman Margali had said. Then the other things she had said added up. Catriona realized that she had eavesdropped on the fabulous Margali n'ha Ysabet, about whom older Renunciates told many stories—that she was part of the Forbidden Tower, or Comyn, or *Terranan*, or dead, or all of them at once. Catriona had never gotten all the stories squared away.

"Come out, little spy." Margali's voice brushed Catriona's ears like a cold gust from the Hellers. It was impossible to disobey, so Catriona walked over to join the older woman.

"You overheard us, and I don't mean with your ears," she said. "No, imbecile, don't pull off your cap. I know what color your hair must be." She stared at Catriona. "Did the Guild House send you to find me? Goddess, they take 'em young these days. You don't look old enough to have sworn the Oath more than three months ago."

Catriona flushed and hated herself for it.

"If that's true, what in all of Zandru's freezing hells are you doing out of the Guild House?"

"I ran away," Catriona admitted. Margali looked at her as would one of the House Mothers, waiting for the rest of the story. "They were always criticizing me for overhearing, when it was my *laran*. They said they wanted me to ask questions, but when I did, they would tell me to shut up. What's that but learning to obey their rules, and how's that different from obeying some man? So I stomped out of a Training Session. And now I'm forsworn. . . ." She finished up with a dismal little sniff.

Amazingly, Margali almost smiled. "You *are* a wet mess, aren't you? It's like you escaped an avalanche, just to stumble onto a nest of banshees. You've listened into something that could cost you. . . ." She broke off and laid a hand on the younger woman's arm. "I should have barriered. But not to worry, at least about the Guild. When I was housebound, some man—I think his name was Shann Macsomething, but you'd have to ask Keitha—tried to get his wife back. He brought hired swords and attacked the place. One man surrendered, but I was so blind angry, I killed him anyhow. Damned near got myself thrown out for it. Tell me, *chiya*, are you over your tantrum now? Could you go back now, beg pardon—and mean it?"

If the girl drops out of sight, they'll forget her; one less innocent at risk. Catriona was past surprise at reading Margali so clearly.

"They wouldn't take me," Catriona said. "But my foster brother works among the *Terranan*, and I thought I'd go to him. Not to support me," she said in scorn at the idea, "but he said I could learn to do a job like his."

Margali's mind touched hers, seized on a visualization of Ann'dra, and then released. "I've met him. He'd do as he promised. But wouldn't you rather enter the Service without leaving such a mess behind you?"

Catriona had to nod. The Guild's blessing meant a great deal to her. Margali hesitated, as if weighing risks. Then, clearly, she came to a decision.

"Then come on. I'll take you back myself. Except for the embarrassment, I don't think it'll be too bad. And to tell you the truth, child, I rather think you've earned the embarrassment."

Catriona followed Margali out the door. She ought to be

ashamed to spy on the woman, then inflict her childish problems on her when she ran in danger of her life! But a deeper, surer instinct told her that Margali too was eager, desperately eager, to return to the Guild House . . . *see Keitha and Lauria and all the others who remember my Shaya before I go into exile, maybe forever.*

They were halfway home, back down the wet, narrow streets, which filled now with a sort of glistening fog, when Margali stopped. "Hear that?"

When Catriona managed not to ask, "No, what?" Margali awarded her a tiny, approving nod. She stiffened, trying to listen with all her senses for the rustle of garments or the pad of soft-shod feet, or to see the shifts in the mist that put Margali on the alert.

"For once, I'd be glad to see the City Guard," Margali whispered. "Yes, I know, *appeal to no man . . .* but it's their job. I've no wish to get spitted here by a gang of fanatics determined to stamp out the last of the Forbidden Tower. And I'll be damned if I get you killed along with me. I think we'd better change plans, girl. If they come at us, if I shout, you run!"

Did she want to get herself killed? Catriona thought. Margali was trying to help her; she couldn't allow that to happen. "I won't go!" she blurted, despite Margali's frown. "I am not 'child!' I am Catriona n'ha Mhari, and even if I did walk out on my sisters back at the House, I won't abandon you."

Margali shook her head. "So they still train them up right," she commented. "I notice, however, that you ran out unarmed. Let's see how good you are with this." She produced a bootknife and handed it to the girl. "We'll keep on moving, but at the slightest sign, you guard my back, and I'll guard yours."

Catriona forced herself to walk sedately down the street, closer and closer to the Guild House. The place between her shoulderblades where a thrown knife might hit quivered. Now she could see the carved doors she had slammed only a few hours ago. Suddenly, Catriona's awareness twinged, and she pushed Margali aside, then heard the clatter of a knife striking a nearby wall.

"Come on out, you bastards," Margali shouted, sounding almost relieved to be done with stalking and skulking. But there were six of them, and they looked determined.

"Get to the door and ring the bell," Margali told her and drew her long-knife. As the intelligence officer faced the men, Catriona dashed forward and rang the bell used by women seeking refuge, then ran back to help Margali. Inside, she could hear footsteps, hear the armsmistress shouting for weapons, and she remembered her vow, "If I see you over the blade's edge, it will be soon enough."

Soon enough: and that's what it was. Catriona was never happier to see the grim faces of the armsmistress and her sisters. Margali hooked a foot behind one man's knee and sent him spinning, then pounced, bending over him for the kill.

Vengeance. Catriona caught Margali's thought. *It's mine, but if I take it here, I put all my sisters in jeopardy.*

"Put up your rotten little sword," she hissed. "There's been enough blood shed." She spat on the ground and looked over to where the other Renunciates were subduing the rest of the men. She gestured contemptuously. "Now, get the hell out of here!"

Women surrounded Margali and Catriona, urging them up the steps and into the hall. Catriona listened as Margali explained. Suddenly, Lauria, guided by Keitha, was in the hall and Margali started sobbing in her arms, clinging to the frailer, smaller woman like a girl who has just sworn her oath. Finally, she looked up.

"I couldn't save Jaelle, but at least—this young one: do you remember her?"

Catriona pulled off her cap. Without the earring, her ear

felt bare in the light. "I sold it," she admitted. "I wanted to buy food and lodging till I got work from the *Terranans* . . . I only wanted to talk to them, to learn what they have to teach, and . . . oh never mind, I'm *sorry*. And then I met Margali, and . . ."

Wordlessly, the old woman embraced Catriona. Her cheek was wet.

"Catriona heard them attack before I did. And I think she probably made the difference between my caring whether I lived or died," Margali spoke up. "Tell me, Keitha, does she remind you of anyone you've ever met?"

"Her temper's as hot as yours," Keitha observed. "Or Jaelle's."

"That's what I think too. And I think she's just made this whole planet too hot for her. When I get on tonight's ship, I think she'd better come with me. I'll finish her training, and she'll get her wish. Maybe she'll even get tired of talking to people—and start listening instead. If that ever happens, we'll have one good worker—and a sister to be proud of." (*And you can start, my girl, by learning some control over that* laran *of yours—and your temper, too!*)

A number of armed, prosperous-looking Renunciates escorted their sisters to the checkpoint and left them there in the safety of *Terranan* guards and yellow lights. Margali and Catriona headed for the Field. Catriona gasped as the sidewalk jolted beneath her feet, and clung to a railing as it inclined steeply, taking them to the ship's docking port.

Inside the ship, she tried not to flinch at the barrage of questions, of examinations, or as a medic injected her with a box of needles that buzzed and stung. Her arm felt hot and swollen after that, and her head ached numbly.

"You need the drugs to get through Jump," Margali explained, but Catriona felt too woozy to ask what "jump" was.

"Want to go lie down?" Margali asked.

It would be interesting to investigate their cabin, and the idea of a soft, quiet bed was infinitely appealing. Nevertheless, Catriona shook her head, regretted doing so, and headed for a viewport. She wasn't a baby, and she wasn't going to be sick.

But as the ship lifted into the violet sky, unsettling her nerves and taking her away from Darkover, Catriona's eyes filled. She was suddenly, shockingly afraid. *What have I done?* she asked herself.

She remembered old Lauria's words. "Be careful what you want; you may get it."

Then she looked out the viewport at the innumerable, blazing stars—and she knew that she had.

About Jaida ń ha Sandra and "The Oath of the Free Amazons: Terra, Techno Period"

Jaida, whose name was originally Kim, has been a member of my household and my foster daughter since her seventeenth year. She was the first to make a legal name change to the Amazon version of her name, probably due to a family conflict whether in college she should use the name of her biological father, her stepfather, or her mother's maiden name. Sensibly, she said "a plague on all their houses" and became simply Jaida, daughter of Sandra.

At an "Amazon workshop" held here in Berkeley a few years ago, Jaida presented a "modern" or "Terran" version of the Oath, which became in my mind the foundation for the Bridge Society and was used as background for the most recent Darkover novel City of Sorcery.

Jaida, with red hair and green eyes, looks very much like a Darkovan and could pass for Romilly in Hawkmistress. *She is a graduate of UC Berkeley and is at present doing graduate work in linguistics in Australia.*

MZB

THE OATH OF THE FREE AMAZONS: TERRA, TECHNO PERIOD

by Jaida ńha Sandra

From this day forth I renounce the right to marry save as a freemate. No man shall own me and I will dwell in no man's house as his mistress. *Nor shall I hold or keep any man against his will.*

I swear that I am prepared to defend myself if I am attacked by force, and that I shall turn to no man for protection.

From this day forth I swear I shall never again be known by the name of any man, be he father, guardian, lover, or husband, but simply and solely as the daughter of my mother.

From this day forth I swear I will give myself to no man save in my own time and season and of my own free will, at my own desire; I will never earn my bread as the object of any man's lust; *neither will I use my sexuality to manipulate or trap any human being.*

From this day forth I swear I will bear no child to any man save for my own pleasure and at my own time and choice; I will bear no child to any man for house or heritage, clan or inheritance, pride or posterity, I swear that I alone will determine rearing and fosterage of any child I bear, without regard to any man's place, position or pride, *yet responsibly considering the love and need for fatherhood that a man may have.*

From this day forth I renounce allegiance to any family, household, incorporation, or church which exacts unquestioning obedience from its members and take oath that where

303

my conscience dictates, I will strive to change those laws which threaten or harm too great a number of living beings.

I shall appeal to no man as of right, for protection, support or succor: but shall owe allegiance only to my oath-mother, *to my proven friends*, and to my employer for the season of my employment.

Free Amazons shall be to me, each and every one, as my mother, my sister, or my daughter, born of one blood with me, and no woman who seeks my help with sincerity shall appeal to me in vain.

From this moment, I swear to obey only the laws of my conscience and the Spirit, and any lawful command of my oath-mother, my true teachers, and my elected leader for the season of my employment. I shall allow no man to pass judgment upon me or determine the path which my life takes. And just as I will be ever vigilant in renouncing all attempts to control me or take power from me, so also will I seek always to be straightforward and honorable in my dealings with all other beings. If I prove false to my oath, then I shall submit myself to the teachers in my life, for such discipline as they shall choose; and if I fail, then may every woman's hand turn against me, and may I be brave in the ultimate judgment and mercy of the Goddess.